Stephen Clegg was born in Stockport in 1947. In 2008 he retired, having run his own businesses for many years. He is now happily married with children and grandchildren.

In 2012 his first novel 'Marias Papers' was released and his second followed in 2013. Both books were nominated for prestigious awards, and his second, 'The Matthew Chance Legacy' became a finalist in The People's Book Prize 2013/14.

This book is dedicated to my son Iain Stephen Clegg and my daughter Nicola Jane Drake – the two delightful people who led me into the world of story-telling I find myself now.

Stephen F. Clegg

THE EMERGENCE OF MALATERRE

AUSTIN MACAULEY
PUBLISHERS LTD.

ISBN 978 184963 825 8

www.austinmacauley.com

First Published (2014)
Austin Macauley Publishers Ltd.
25 Canada Square
Canary Wharf
London
E14 5LB

Printed and bound in Great Britain

Acknowledgments

A huge thank you to my beautiful daughter Nicola Drake, my loyal friends and test readers Jayne Miles, Jean Dickens, Lorraine Middleton, Michele Norton, and Ted Wylie. Also to my loving wife Jay, who supports me so magnificently in all aspects of my writing.

Preface

Naomi regained consciousness and tried to open her eyes, but the blindfold was so tight that she couldn't see a thing. Her ankles were tied, her wrists were bound behind her back, and she was gagged.

She could tell that she was on a bare concrete floor, and she knew that she was somewhere very large and hollow because the slightest sounds echoed around the room. She also picked up a distinctive smell. She coughed, listened, and then coughed again, but drew no response. She made a loud "Hmming" sound but that, too, was fruitless.

She had no idea what time it was, or even what day it was.

The last thing that she remembered was being spun around – dragged to an old jeep with a hand clamped over her mouth, and then something being jabbed into the side of her neck.

Now, she was hungry, bound, shoeless, and lying on her right-hand side. She adjusted her position, sat up, and banged the back of her head against something hard. She cursed, drew her knees up, rocked forwards, and then attempted to stand. She got halfway up, but her ascent was halted and she dropped back to the floor and banged the base of her spine.

She rubbed it and then fiddled about behind her back until she found a length of rope tied to her wrist bindings. It was linked to a metal 'H' frame girder which she presumed to be a roof support. The linking rope felt approximately twenty-five millimetres thick, was soft, and greasy. She'd felt rope like that before, but couldn't recall where.

She adjusted the position of her hands and established that the girder was rusting; that was a bonus.

Out of the blue she heard something. She remained still and listened. It was the distinctive 'chug' of a boat engine. She'd heard numerous throughout her life, and she knew that she was listening to a canal boat. That was encouraging too, because the sound may have been coming from the Rochdale canal.

She waited until silence had descended, and then wasted no time. She began to abrade the rope against the base of the rusty stanchion.

Fifty metres away, sitting in the gloom of the huge deserted silo, her captor watched in silence through a pair of night-vision binoculars…

Chapter 1

Monday 12th June 2006. The Historic Research Department, Walmsfield Borough Council, Lancashire

At 8:55am Helen Milner walked into the Historic Research Department and looked around.

"Morning Naomi – it's a bit smaller than I remembered," she said.

Naomi Wilkes, the Head of the department said, "Welcome to the fold, and welcome to my tiny world."

Helen cast her eyes around the office and saw that Naomi had linked their two desks together in an 'L' shape, and had moved all of the filing cabinets to the back wall. Just inside the front door stood an upright coat stand, a couple of spare chairs, and at various locations around the office, she could see masses of cardboard boxes stacked on top of one another.

On this, her first day, her desk looked almost empty; on it were two three-tier filing trays, a receptacle for holding pens and pencils, a cordless telephone, an A4 notepad, and a steaming hot cup of tea.

"Take your coat off, and drink what passes for tea around here before it gets cold," said Naomi.

Helen removed her coat, sat down, and was surprised by her new, comfy office desk chair.

"I even got you the leather seat that you asked for," said Naomi smiling across at her friend.

Naomi and Helen had become close friends working on an earlier research project trying to discover the truth about the ownership of the old Whitewall Estate on Wordale Moor, and during those investigations, they'd become entangled with an old adversary of Naomi's – the rich and powerful multi-millionaire businessman, Adrian Darke. Both women had come close to losing their lives on his Cragg Vale Estate on the nearby Rushworth Moor when they'd exposed his illegal underground drugs facility, and although most of those issues had been resolved, more than a few had arisen which still required attention.

Prior to accepting her new post, Helen had worked as a conservator at a construction site for the forthcoming Vical shopping centre in Newton, Hyde, but as the months had progressed, and she'd become more interested in carrying out the type of research that Naomi had, she'd jumped at the offer of a job to join her in Walmsfield Borough Council's Historic Research Department.

Naomi was thirty-four years of age and Helen thirty-five; both women enjoyed the same taste in clothes, music, and going out, and whilst Naomi was married to Carlton Wilkes the Head of the Walmsfield Planning Department, Helen was single and in a shaky relationship with her partner Justin, a shift-working security officer whose motivation and work ethic would have ideally seen him employed as a full-time Programme Seller for Coronations.

Both women were experienced researchers and had only met three months earlier, but the experiences and dangers they'd shared in their previous project had brought them closer than either had expected, and now they were together on the first day of their new working relationship.

"Okay boss," said Helen, "what's the order of the day?"

"On a personal note, my biggest desire is to learn more about that old Malaterre Estate under the Dunsteth reservoir, but the most pressing problem is to get that lot catalogued and filed away." She nodded towards the boxes stacked around the room.

Helen looked at them and groaned.

"That was my old life at the Vical Centre," she said.

"Well – you know the definition of a Historic Researcher don't you?" said Naomi.

Helen raised her eyebrows and said, "Go on…"

"A filing clerk with a history obsession!"

Helen nodded and said, "So true – where do I start?"

As Helen busied herself with the filing, Naomi sat back and thought about the Malaterre Estate.

Her first encounter with the name "Malaterre" had been in a dream where she had taken delivery of a large wooden crate, opened it, and had found another box inside; inside that box was another and then another, until at the end she'd found a cigar box. Inside the cigar box had been a small, discoloured cigarette card with the single word, 'Malaterre' written upon it.

The dream had been so vivid that she'd made a note of the name, but hadn't thought anymore about it until within a couple of weeks, and upon the conclusion of her investigations into the ownership of the Whitewall Estate, she'd discovered a small wooden box concealed in a Mausoleum that proved to have a false bottom. To her shock and amazement, two things had been discovered in there; a bronze key with the letter 'M' worked into the bow, and a discoloured cigarette card with the word 'Malaterre' written upon it.

A lady named Daisy Hubert had secreted the box within the mausoleum sometime after March 1869, and had been the sister-in-law to a solicitor named George Hubert who had sent her incriminating evidence against two murderous characters named Abraham and Caleb Johnson; and because he had been afraid of them killing him, he'd asked her to conceal it until she had been in a position to be able to hand it over to the police on his behalf. But subsequent investigations by Naomi and Helen had revealed that Daisy had been murdered by Caleb Johnson before she'd been able to hand the evidence over.

A local search of the name from the Victorian era had shown that there had once been an estate named 'Malaterre' in the Dunsteth Valley, north of Rochdale, which had been flooded in the 19th century to make way for a new civic reservoir.

The things that puzzled Naomi, however, were why Daisy Hubert came to be in possession of the key and cigarette card, what the key fitted, and why she felt the need to hide them in the false bottom of a box already containing incriminating evidence against the Johnsons.

"Penny for them?" said Helen.

"Oh, I'm just mulling over the Malaterre conundrum again."

Helen nodded and pointed towards the boxes, "How about we work together filing this lot, then maybe we'll be have some time to consider that?"

Naomi smiled and said, "All right, I can take a hint, shove one over."

As the time approached 10:30am Naomi said, "All this filing makes me thirsty, do you want a cuppa?"

Helen looked up and said, "Oh yes please, white coffee – no sugar."

Naomi got up and headed for the door, but before she could open it, there was a knock, and her husband Carlton walked in.

"Morning Carlton," said Helen, "have you seen what your slave-driver of a wife has got me doing?"

Carlton smiled and said, "Think yourself lucky, you should try being married to her!"

Naomi slapped her husband's arm and said, "Hey, you'll pay for that later! Now, what brings you down to the bowels of the Council offices?"

"Two things," said Carlton, "number one to welcome Helen to our fold…"

Helen smiled and said, "Thank you."

"…and number two, to tell you about a snippet of news I heard this morning." He paused to make sure that he had both women's attention and then said, "A human bone was discovered on the eastern side of the Dunsteth reservoir."

Naomi's interest peaked; she said, "Really, recent or historical?"

"The reporter didn't say."

Helen said, "I was only reading the other day that the water level had dropped because of successive dry winters and so many more hot summers."

"What?" said Naomi looking across at Helen, "That's a laugh with all the rain that we get around here."

"Nevertheless," said Carlton, "Helen's right, the levels have dropped, and yesterday, a retired doctor walking his dog found the bone near the waterline and reported it to the local police," he paused and then said, "And of course we all know what's under there, don't we?"

"My current obsession," said Naomi, "Malaterre."

Chapter 2

Wednesday 14th June 2006. The Dunsteth Reservoir, Lancashire

Naomi stopped her Honda CRV near to the eastern bank of the Dunsteth reservoir and reached into her handbag. She removed the Clearblue digital pregnancy test kit, held her breath, and looked at the indicator. It was just as she'd seen it the first time; it stated "Pregnant 2-3" demonstrating that she was indeed pregnant and that she'd conceived two to three weeks earlier.

She'd followed the instructions to the letter, waited until the day before her period, and had done the test at her first visit to the bathroom that day. She'd rushed out to tell Carlton but had forgotten that he'd had to leave around 5am to attend a local government cost-cutting seminar in Birmingham.

Now, if the wording on the box was to be believed, it was 99% positive that she was pregnant, and 92% positive about when she'd become so. She clapped her hand up to her mouth and covered a huge, beaming grin.

She and Carlton had been trying for a baby for more than a year, and though both had remained positive, the strain had been beginning to tell; the act of love-making had morphed from a passion-driven desire to consume as much of each other's bodies in as lustful a way as they could, to that of trying to make a baby. The spur of the moment zeal to take one another whenever, had given way to planning and timing, and though both still enjoyed it, it wasn't ever the same as that powerful and gritty act of looking at each in a certain fashion, then jumping on one another and screwing each other's brains out.

But now she had it, the wonderful sum of their planning and love. A less-than-tiny baked bean-sized miracle growing inside of her, and she couldn't wait to tell Carlton.

With a satisfied grin still on her face, she put the pregnancy test kit back into her bag, took out her binoculars, stepped out of her car, and lifted them up to her eyes. She made a minor adjustment to the central focus wheel, and stared at what appeared to be an irregular set of stepping stones breaking the surface of the reservoir in the early morning sunshine.

From a professional point of view the reappearance of the building was exciting, but because of the mysterious circumstances in which she'd first learned about it, it was also chilling, and the more she stared at the innocuous features, the more she wanted to know.

The estate appeared to be within touching distance; she wanted to explore it, to experience what it might have looked like to the last occupants, but because it had been under water for over a hundred years there would be no way of knowing how safe it would be.

"Fascinating isn't it?" said a voice.

Naomi whirled around and saw a man standing behind her; he appeared to be in his late thirties and was dressed in a casual white shirt, blue jeans, and open-toed sandals. He was slim and fit looking, had a full head of dark brown hair, green eyes similar to her father Sam's, and his handsome angular face was clean-shaven. For a split-second she was taken aback because in the instant that she saw him, she felt that she had known she was going to meet him. As though fate had closed a circle that she had known would be closed.

The man saw Naomi's momentary hesitation and said, "I'm sorry, did I startle you?"

"No… Well, maybe a little…"

The man smiled and said, "I suppose that it's these crypt-creeping sandals, and of course my natural ability to be able to move without a sound, especially away from debt-collectors…" He raised his eyebrows in a theatrical way.

Naomi smiled and said, "And *are* you pursued by many debt-collectors?"

"Hundreds!" said the man, "In counties across the entire length and breadth of the land!"

For some inexplicable reason Naomi felt right at home with him and joined in the japery.

"Well," she said, reaching into her handbag for a non-descript piece of paper, "I'm glad that I've found you now, because there is this small matter… " She tendered the folded piece of paper.

The man burst out laughing, held his hands up in the air, and backed away two or three paces. He said, "Okay, it's a fair cop! How much do I owe you?"

Naomi stopped and looked up for a second, and then pushed the paper back into her handbag. She said, "Nothing, I just remembered that it's illegal to collect debts in Rochdale on a Wednesday morning."

The man covered his eyes and said, "Oh my God, if only I'd known, I'd have moved here years ago!"

They both smiled with genuine pleasure until the man extended his right hand and said, "My name's Page, Stephen Page."

Naomi shook the offered hand and said, "Naomi Wilkes."

The same sudden feeling overtook her; a feeling as though he was meant to be there, at that moment in time. Their handshake was different too; it fitted perfectly, and she almost didn't want to let go.

"And what brings you here, Naomi Wilkes?" said Stephen, "Is it the mysterious reappearance of Malaterre?"

Something else clicked inside Naomi's brain; Stephen was the only person to have used the single name 'Malaterre' whereas everybody else had referred to it as 'the Malaterre Estate'. It was nothing that significant, but it indicated familiarity.

"It is indeed," said Naomi giving away nothing of her inner feelings, "I am a professional historic researcher and I'm very interested in this place."

"Is that because of its sudden reappearance, or have you always been aware of its presence?"

Naomi considered her answer before speaking; she said, "I have to admit to knowing nothing of its presence before more than a few weeks ago. I only moved to the North of England at the end of 2000, and everything I know, I had to learn about, instead of growing up with."

Stephen nodded and said, "Ah, I see; so what first brought this place to your attention?"

Naomi felt as though she could tell Stephen about her weird dream, but she opted to keep her cards close to her chest.

"It's a bit of a protracted story which I don't have time to tell you today," she said, "but it is an interesting one." She paused for a second and then said, "But how about you, what is your interest in the place?"

For the first time since they'd met, she saw guardedness show on Stephen's face; he dropped his eyes and hesitated, but then seemed to make his mind up.

"Can I answer your question with a question?"

Naomi said, "Yes, of course."

"You mentioned that you are a professional historic researcher, but you didn't say for whom. Is it a local organisation, and are you here representing them, or do you work somewhere else, and are just showing an interest in the goings on around here?"

"I am the head of Walmsfield Borough Council's Historic Research Department, and whilst I guess that I would be representing them in an official capacity, it is more than just professional interest that has brought me here."

Stephen digested Naomi's reply and then said, "Okay, then there's somebody that I think you should meet."

Out of the blue, Naomi was struck by the speed and ease with which they had become acquainted, and recalled a few lines of Eastern European folklore.

'Little girl, it seems to say,
Never stop upon your way,
Never trust a stranger friend,

No-one knows how it will end.

As you're pretty, so be wise,
Wolves may lurk in every guise,
Now, as then, 'tis simple truth,
Sweetest tongue has sharpest tooth.'

She looked into Stephen's eyes and said, "That's very kind of you but…"

Stephen realised that he had been presumptuous and said, "There's no need to explain, I appreciate that we've only just met. And who knows, I could be a wolf in sheep's clothing."

Stephen's reference to a wolf shook Naomi to the core. She frowned and said, "What made you say that, then?"

"That I could be a wolf in sheep's clothing? Nothing, it was just phrase – why?"

Naomi knew that there was more to it; she couldn't rationalise it, she couldn't explain it, she just knew. She stared into Stephen's eyes and noticed that they had a hazel star around the pupil, similar to her father's; and then she wondered why she had even noticed. She started to feel out of her depth and a bit disorientated.

Stephen picked up on it and said, "I appear to have upset you, and I'm sorry. I've been told in the past that sometimes I'm too forward for my own good." He reached into his back pocket and extracted a black leather wallet and opened it.

Naomi could hardly believe her eyes.

Her father Sam was the most fastidious man that she had ever known when it came to choosing a new wallet. Growing up, she recalled traipsing around endless leather shops in the UK and Spain as he trawled through them looking for just the right one. It had to be black; it had to be a one-fold wallet, with no purse section for coins, it mustn't have zips or masses of compartments; it had to be no bigger than ten centimetres by eight centimetres, and the notes had to be in a billfold, instead of slotted compartments. A tall order indeed – and they had been almost impossible to find!

Now she was staring at an identical one in Stephen's hand. Her already shaken equilibrium took another blow as the coincidences started to mount up.

Oblivious of Naomi's growing unease; Stephen extracted a business card and handed it to her.

"If you'd like to get a potted history of Malaterre," he said, "give me a call and I'll introduce you to somebody whom I'm sure that you'd find interesting."

Naomi looked down at the business card and saw that it stated;

'Stephen G Page
Director
Page & Page Ltd.'

The business address was somewhere that she hadn't heard of in nearby Bury. She said, "Thank you," and then, "Who's the other Page, your wife?" The words flowed out and she couldn't believe that she'd asked such a personal question. She was mortified.

Stephen smiled and said, "No, the other Page is my father; we run a small but specialist bookshop in Bury. But for the record, I'm not married!"

"I'm so sorry!" said Naomi, "I don't know what came over me; it was none of my business…"

"It's nothing," said Stephen.

Naomi felt the need to get away to try to regain some of her composure; she looked at her watch and said, "Look, I'm sorry, I have to go…"

Stephen smiled and extended his hand once again.

Naomi took it, and was overcome by the same inexplicable feeling. She couldn't believe it; something felt so right about holding his hand that she let go of it too quickly.

"Please do give me a call," said Stephen, "I feel sure that you'd be interested in what my mother has to say."

"Your mother?"

"Yes, she's the person who has the inside knowledge of Malaterre."

Naomi's equilibrium calmed as her curiosity kicked in; she looked down at the business card and saw that there were several options for contact including an email address. She looked up and said, "All right, I will, but I need to check my diary first."

Stephen smiled and said, "Excellent, no rush."

Naomi nodded and smiled back; "Okay," she said, "I'll be in touch – bye for now." She turned to head back to her car, when the feeling of a thumb pressing down onto her shoulder, which heralded one of her infrequent psychic experiences, pushed hard down. She heard a woman's voice say, *'S'il vous plaît ne pas aller…'*

She wheeled around and stared at the Malaterre building, and got the second huge shock of the day, for out of the corner of her eye, she'd seen Stephen wheel around and look as well.

For several seconds she didn't know which way to look, at Malaterre, or at Stephen. He appeared to be staring at the building too.

Both had the same puzzled expressions on their faces until Stephen turned, smiled, and then walked away.

Chapter 3

Monday 27th July 1868. The Whitewall Estate, Wordale Moor

Joseph Pickles from Hundersfield District Council stepped out of his Hansom cab, approached the front door of the Whitewall Estate, and looked around; he'd heard tales of a fearful dog named Sugg who belonged to the Johnsons, and he didn't want to be on the wrong side of it. He padded across the courtyard to the front door, cast a last nervous look around, and then knocked.

Within a few seconds the door opened and he was confronted by a hard and intolerant looking man who appeared to have got out of the wrong side of bed for the last six months.

Abraham Johnson looked at the caller, noted the suit, shiny shoes and leather briefcase and then said, "Well, are you going to stand there all day, or are you going tell me what you want?"

Pickles touched the tip of his bowler hat and said, "Mr. Abraham Johnson?"

"Who's asking?"

"My name is Joseph Pickles from Hundersfield District Council, and I wondered if might be allowed to have a word with you?"

Abraham, who was always distrustful of officials narrowed his eyes and said, "About what?"

"I have a proposition that might interest you; that is of course, if you are indeed Abraham Johnson."

Abraham stared at the official for a couple of seconds and then said, "All right, you'd better come in."

He led Pickles through the kitchen into the parlour and pointed to a seat.

Pickles sat down and looked around. The light from the Tudor-style windows didn't fully illuminate the room, but it was adequate; enough for him to see that everywhere appeared to be grubby and untidy. Dirty food dishes and beer mugs lay on the table top, and there was a large box of bandages on the floor next to one of the chairs. He saw Abraham watching him and said, "I hope that nobody was too seriously hurt?"

"What proposition might interest me?"

"I take it then, that you are Mr. Abraham Johnson?"

"Yes, yes," said Abraham, "what proposition have you got for me?"

Pickles was now in official mode, and he wasn't about to be put off.

"And is it correct that you are the current owner of the Dunsteth Estate on Blackstone Moor?"

Abraham went on the defensive; he was aware of the nefarious way in which he'd secured both Dunsteth and Whitewall and he didn't want anybody prying into that.

"Look," he said, "stop prattling about and just tell me why you came."

"I'm sorry Mr. Johnson," said Pickles, "but I do need to know that I have the correct antecedents before I can proceed."

"All right, all right – I own Whitewall and Dunsteth. Now for fuck's sake, spit it out!"

Pickles bristled at the use of bad language whilst he was acting in his official capacity, and had the person opposite been any less intimidating, he might even had said so, but he took one look into the ice-cold, humourless eyes of Abraham Johnson and decided against it.

He cleared his throat and said, "Following several, er, in camera Select Committee meetings, it has been decided that the Hundersfield District Council should progress the procurement of a suitable valley, in which they could site a planned, new, civic reservoir."

Abraham frowned at first, the use of a term like "in camera" was beyond his limited vocabulary, but he grasped the basic meaning. He said, "So what are you trying to say, that you want to buy a whole valley to put your new 'reservoyer' in?"

Pickles raised his eyebrows for the briefest of seconds and then said, "Precisely."

"And that my Dunsteth Estate is in one of the valleys being considered?"

"The Dunsteth Valley is the prime valley being considered Mr. Johnson."

"Do you realise how much revenue I get from that estate?" said Abraham.

"No sir, I don't; but I have been instructed to assure you that if you would consider our proposal, you would be more than happy with our terms."

To the abject surprise of Pickles, Abraham leapt out of his seat, leaned out of the window adjacent to the yard, and yelled, "Caleb! Caleb, get your arse over here boy!" He remained staring into the yard with his head cocked to one side until he realised that he hadn't drawn any response. He yelled once more, "Caleb! Caleb! Are you listening to me?"

Pickles heard some kind of muffled response and then watched as Abraham returned to his seat and plonked himself down.

"Wait a minute mister, er…"

"Pickles,"

"Right," said Abraham, "I want my lad here when you tell me the rest."

A few minutes later the parlour door opened and Caleb walked in.

Pickles looked up at Caleb and felt as though he had been stabbed through the heart. He was big and bulky and appeared to have a permanent scowl upon his face; he was tanned, his hair was brown, thick, and unkempt and he had the most unnerving eyes. They were cruel, and soulless, and they chilled him to the core.

Caleb saw the suited stranger looking at him, and unable to conceal his aggression said, "What are you looking at, toff?"

"Watch your tongue, boy!" said Abraham.

Caleb looked up at his father and said, "Sorry pa, he was…"

"I don't care! Sit down and listen to what he has to say."

Caleb slunk across the parlour and dropped into the chair next to the box of bandages.

Seven months earlier, in November 1867, Caleb had been attacked by Sugg, his own dog, a huge, vicious, and deformed Irish wolfhound, who'd torn away a large chunk of his left calf muscle. His recovery had been protracted and painful, and still caused him to hobble everywhere he went.

The way that Caleb walked across the room wasn't lost on Pickles. He said, "I can see from your injury that the injection of a considerable sum of money wouldn't go amiss, either to ease the burden of your life here at Whitewall by giving you the ability to take on more labourers, or to be able to employ the services of a top doctor to expedite the process of your recovery."

Caleb looked across to his father and said, "What's he on about pa?"

"Yon man," said Abraham, "has come here to ask us some questions about our ownership of Dunsteth."

As with Abraham before, Caleb went on the defensive, knowing full well how they had first tricked his stepmother Margaret into never learning about her rightful inheritance of Dunsteth, and how his father had murdered her when she had found out, and then had taken Whitewall as well.

He cast a quick glance in the direction of his father and thought that he was prompting him to do away with the stranger. He jammed his hand into his coat pocket and grabbed his knife.

Abraham saw; knew what was about to happen, and said, "No boy!"

Pickles saw the exchange and started to feel uncomfortable; everything seemed to be getting tense; he felt as though he was sitting in a basket full of poisonous snakes, and that the wrong move would result in some terrible fate.

"Gentlemen," he said, wishing to get away, "if it would suit you better, I can come back on another occasion."

"Stop being so touchy," said Abraham, "the boy's a bit awkward around strangers and he's lacking in what you'd call social graces, so just tell him why you're here."

Lacking in social graces? thought Pickles; he'd seen more sociable lions at feeding time.

He took in a deep breath, turned to Caleb, and said, "Very well, Hundersfield District Council would like your father and you to consider selling us your Dunsteth Estate, so that we can flood the valley in which it lies, to create a new civic reservoir."

"And they'll pay a cartload of brass!" said Abraham with brimming enthusiasm.

Pickles turned to Abraham and said, "Yes, I feel sure that you would both be more than pleased with our offer."

Abraham turned to face his son with a big grin on his face.

"Do you hear that boy? He wants to buy Dunsteth from us for a cartload of cash!"

Pickles retorted, "Not me personally, you understand..."
He saw Caleb turn and stare straight at him; it felt as though the devil himself was looking into his soul. Without any rational explanation, he started to become edgy and afraid.

"Sounds like my pa's prepared to believe you Pickles," said Caleb in an unsettling way, "so you'd better not let him down – because if you do I'll hunt you down like a..."

"Caleb!" said Abraham, "Stop that! He's here to make us an offer, not to threaten us!"

Pickles watched until Caleb's eyes turned away. It felt as though a huge vice-like grip had just let go of his throat and inner organs and everything inside him wanted to get up and run.

With a hammering heart, he summoned up the last reserves of his courage and said, "I will not be threatened like this! If you cannot dignify this meeting with civility, then I shall leave and take my proposals elsewhere."

Abraham felt the offer starting to slide away; he turned to Caleb and said, "You heard the gent, boy. Don't you open that fucking mouth of yours again until you're spoken to – is that clear?"

Pickles winced inside; he'd never attended a darker or more unsettling meeting in his entire working life.

Caleb said, "Yes pa," and settled back in his seat.

"We don't want Mr. Pickles getting the wrong idea about us!"

Pickles had exactly the right idea about both men; he looked from face-to-face and then said, "Very well, I shall leave my proposal with you to consider; but if I feel threatened or intimidated in any way, I shall leave, and you'll never hear from me again."

"What's to consider?" said Abraham, "you come up with the brass, and the place is yours." He jumped up and extended his hand.

Pickles hesitated.

"What's up?" said Abraham, "Put it there, we have a deal in principle at least."

Pickles looked up at Abraham and said, "It's not quite as simple as that."

Caleb looked across to Pickles and glowered; he opened his mouth to comment, but remembered his father's warning.

"What's not so simple?" said Abraham returning to his seat.

"Yours isn't the only property in Dunsteth Valley Mr. Johnson, and unless we can secure permission from the owners of the Malaterre Estate, we will be forced to look elsewhere."

"And have the owners of Malaterre hinted at what their decision will be?"

"No sir, they have not." He hesitated knowing that his next statement may prove to be contentious.

"Furthermore there may be an added difficulty because they are not all English nationals."

"Not English?" said Abraham.

"No sir, they are of French descent."

"Frogs!" said Abraham, "I thought they were English; they sounded English the last time we crossed words – so which ones are frogs?"

Pickles blanched at the sound of Abraham's 'the last time we crossed words' statement and then said, "The father is French, but the mother is English, and all of the children were born in England."

"So they're English for the most part then?"

"Yes, but I understand that the father, Mr. Etienne Page is the owner, and he is French."

"Fucking frogs!" said Abraham, "How did they end up owning the place?"

"The circumstances of their acquisition are not within my ken, but it is indisputable that Mr. Page senior is the owner, and without his agreement to sell, we will, as I said, be forced to look elsewhere for our reservoir."

Abraham became sullen and the light-hearted mood disappeared in a flash.

"So if the frogs won't sell, we can't either. Is that it?" he said.

"Yes sir."

"Well you'd best make sure that they do."

"Mr. Johnson, if they refuse to…"

Abraham's voice rose as his aggravation increased, he said, "Refusal's not an option Pickles. It would suit me, and my son to sell Dunsteth, so you make them an offer that they can't refuse, do you hear me?"

Pickles started to feel the need to get away again; he said, "We'll do everything in our power Mr. Johnson. I already told you that the Dunsteth Valley is our prime choice, so it is within our interests to secure that land also."

"Right," said Abraham getting to his feet and walking towards the parlour door, "we've got work to do, as I am sure you do, so you go and get those frogs to sign up – and if you have any difficulty persuading them, let us know; perhaps Caleb and me can help them make their minds up."

Across the room, Pickles saw a look spread across Caleb's face. He stood up and walked towards the open door, cleared his throat, and said, "Ahem, yes, well thank you for the offer of help, but I feel sure that we'll be able to manage perfectly well on our own."

Seconds later he stepped out of the kitchen and into the courtyard; he replaced his bowler hat and headed for the waiting cab. Once inside he felt a palpable sense of relief.

As it headed up the long drive he reflected over the meeting and the two men that he'd just left. He wasn't a particular lover of foreigners himself, but the last thing that he wanted was to visit volatile characters like the Johnsons on them, non-English or not.

Chapter 4

Naomi sat at her desk and her mind was in turmoil. Following her meeting with Stephen Page at the Dunsteth Reservoir the day before, she couldn't stop thinking about him – she couldn't rationalise it, but he was the last person that she'd thought about before she'd fallen asleep, and he'd been the first person that she'd thought about, the moment that she'd woken up.

Two things however, stood out the most; one was the strange way she'd felt when she'd been in his company – a feeling as though she'd been one-half of a whole and that he'd been the other. It was a crazy feeling, spooky and uncomfortable, and yet paradoxically, it had been comforting – and none of it made sense. She'd had the darnedest notion that if he'd reached out, taken her hand, and said, "Come with me to Timbuktu," she might have gone, there and then, without thought; and all of this after announcing her pregnancy to a deliriously happy Carlton!

It was ridiculous, she was married, pregnant, happy, and she adored her husband, but for the life of her, she couldn't repress her thoughts and she wondered if her new state and changing hormones might have been in part responsible.

Second was the moment that she'd felt the thumb press down upon her shoulder and heard the voice say, *'S'il vous plaît ne pas aller...'* She'd seen Stephen wheel around to look at Malaterre when she had.

She hadn't known what to say; for several seconds she'd stared at him in shock and disbelief. She recalled him looking at her for what seemed like an age afterwards, but then they'd parted company.

The spooky thing however, was what she'd heard; she'd returned to her office and written it into 'Google Translate' on her laptop, and had received the translation, 'Please do not go...' She still shivered at the weirdness of it and following Stephen's unusual comment about him being 'a wolf in sheep's clothing', she'd wondered whether the voice had implored him not to go, and not her.

That threw up questions; who had asked who not to go? Why had whoever was asking, asked whomever, not to go? It was obvious that Stephen had some sort of link to Malaterre, but was he able to communicate or hear somebody from its past? The questions were endless; she needed information, on him, on Malaterre, on its history, and she wanted to know how she was meant to figure in all of it.

Her dream of finding the cigarette card with the name 'Malaterre' written upon it, and then her discovery of the real card was spooky enough, but the latest goings on were beginning to take the weirdness to stratospheric heights; and she was beginning to feel that she was losing control.

She needed it to level and she needed time to get her head around it all.

"Can I get you a cup of tea?"

Naomi looked up from her desk and saw Helen staring at her.

"Oh, yes – that would be very nice," she said.

"And can I help you with what's troubling you?"

Naomi paused for thought and then said, "I'm sorry Helen, you know how much I love you working here, but a veritable barrage of things are happening to me at the present, and I think that I'm the only one who can deal with them."

"Would it help to talk?"

Naomi looked across to her friend and wanted to tell her about the pregnancy, but she and Carlton had agreed to keep it to themselves until it had been confirmed by the doctor. "Maybe," she said, "but not just yet."

Helen nodded and got up to get the tea.

Naomi watched her walk across to the office door and said, "Hang on a mo, maybe there is something that you can do."

Helen turned and stood where she was.

"Come and sit down." Naomi pointed to the chair opposite her desk.

Helen walked over and sat down.

Naomi sat back and said, "It's no secret that I'm obsessed by Malaterre, but as the days pass by I'm beginning to feel that I'm being caught up in something massive."

"Massive?" said Helen, "In what context, 'massive' as in 'life-changing', or 'massive' as in a big, extended research project?"

Naomi sat and thought for a second.

" 'Massive' as in global."

"Good Lord," said Helen, "global? What, here in Walmsfield?"

"Everything that makes global news is situated somewhere comparatively small," said Naomi, "9/11 was centred on two tower blocks in New York and the massive earthquake in 1985 was centred on Mexico City; both places were small on a global scale, so why couldn't something global happen here?"

"And that's what you think is it? That whatever it is you're being caught up in, will make global news?"

Naomi's confidence took a nosedive; she said, "Oh I don't know Helen! – I'm really confused at the moment. What I can say is that something much bigger is going on here than I have ever dealt with before, and it won't be long until we're all caught up in it."

"What, me too?"

"Yes, you too."

Helen remained quiet for a few seconds and then said, "All right, I'm going for our teas and then I think that we should spend the rest of the day tidying this place up. If we're going to have something massive to deal with, we don't want to be worrying about trivial things such as filing!"

For the first time that day Naomi smiled. She looked at Helen with genuine affection and thought that if she was going to get caught up in something big, she couldn't have wanted anybody better by her side. She reached down to her bag and retrieved a couple of pound coins.

"Go on then," she said, "and while you're at it go down to the food dispenser and get us a Kit Kat Chunky each."

Helen took the coins and looked at them; she said, "So I'm going to have to help you with something massive that could go global, and my sweetener is a *Kit Kat Chunky?*"

"Hey, don't knock it H, this is me pushing the boat out!"

Helen looked at the coins for a second time and then said, "Coracle, more like!"

Stephen Page stood in a climbing equipment specialist's in Stockport, Cheshire, and surveyed his shopping basket; he had a couple of six-step etriers, a cliffhanger skyhook, a grappling hook, some different sized peckers, a talon, and a stubby haul bag.

He knew that he already had an extensive range of climbing equipment back at his home, but adding a few new bits and pieces to his collection was therapeutic to him; it gave him an excuse to visit one of his favourite shops and to immerse himself in his pet hobby whilst also checking out any new bits of equipment that had appeared on the market.

With a satisfied feeling he'd just started to head towards the checkouts when his mobile phone buzzed in his jeans pocket and made a sound informing him that he had just received a text. He put down the shopping basket, retrieved his phone, and read it.

"Arrived safely Les Trois-Ilets.
Going to house tomorrow.
ddadi! xx"

He looked at the 'ddadi!' reference and knew that it was an acronym for 'don't do anything dangerous idiot!' His newly married sister, now Mrs. Kate Starmer, always signed off the same because she reckoned that if somebody else were to read his texts, they would mistake it for an illiterate 'daddy' with a stammer.

He texted back;

"Okay mops!
Take good care out there.
xx"

'Mops!' was his acronym for 'massively over-protective sister!' He smiled, switched the phone back to standby, picked up his shopping basket, and headed once more for the checkouts.

Chapter 5

Rosalind Probus stared down at the bundle on the floor of her hall and cast a quick look at her wall clock; it was 11:40pm. She knew that her long-time lover John Hess would be with her just after midnight and she was sure that she'd been extra careful with the bundle, but she couldn't resist checking it one more time.

She looked at all of the seals along the top and made sure that they were airtight; she then rolled it over and checked the underside. Everything there was okay. She re-positioned the bundle on the nylon-webbing mat and made sure that the carry handles were accessible.

She looked again at the clock on the wall; 11:50pm and the minutes were dragging by.

She stood up and looked at her reflection in the hall mirror.

She was now forty-two years of age and still looked good. She had medium-length blonde hair that complemented her flawless skin. She had full lips, white teeth, and perfectly-proportioned high cheekbones. Underneath her clothes, her body was good too. She had money, only ever wore designer clothes, and she didn't have to work unless she wanted to. All-in-all, she had everything that others would have died for – but that was not what the man in the bundle had died for.

Max Probus had been a generous husband. He'd been wealthy, handsome, dapper, had been charming and attentive, and he had wooed Rosalind to with an inch of her life; and following six gloriously happy months she had accepted his proposal of marriage with open arms.

The ceremony at Hereford Cathedral had been wonderful, the reception had been well catered for, all the guests had been happy, and following a blissful day they had retired to their honeymoon suite for the night.

Rosalind had excused herself and had gone into the en-suite bathroom; she'd slipped out of her clothes and stepped under a hot shower. As the water and creamy soap had spread over her naked body, she'd tingled inside about what was to come and she'd wanted her man – there and then!

She'd rinsed herself, stepped out of the shower, put on the sexy negligee that she'd bought for the occasion, and had walked back into the bedroom.

"Honey," she'd said, "I'm..."

She'd looked around, but he had gone. For two infuriating hours she'd waited in front of the television, sipping the champagne and eating the strawberries that she'd ordered prior to retiring.

Just after 1am he'd returned; he'd walked into their suite with no explanation, had gone straight to the bathroom, showered, and had got straight into bed and gone to sleep without saying a word.

The following morning he'd explained that he'd received a call from the hotel that he'd been the General Manager of, and that he'd had to go there on urgent business.

She'd started to forgive him and, feeling somewhat relieved, and then ever more frisky, she'd pulled off his pyjamas and had rolled him face down onto their bed. She'd reached for a bottle of massage oil, which had been one of their pre-marriage favourites; she'd poured some into the small of his back, spread it across his waist and shoulders, and had then worked down to his pert, hairless backside. She'd poured more oil onto her left hand, had rubbed it into her right hand, and had slipped her fingers between his cheeks. As her middle finger had playfully touched him deep down, he'd jumped, not in a playful or enjoyable way – but in a hurt way.

He'd leapt off the bed and gone into the bathroom without saying a word. Puzzled, she'd followed him, and as she'd opened the door, she'd caught sight of him bending down and applying some cream. He'd leapt up – but it was too late; she'd seen the tell-tale splits around his anus.

At first she'd stood there with a confused expression upon her face, but then the penny had dropped. There had never before been any hint of him being gay, but from that day, until the day that she'd killed him, they'd never had sex again.

There was a sudden, sharp rapping on her front door; she looked up and saw that it was just after midnight. She opened the door and saw John standing there dressed in black, and wearing a beanie hat.

"Are you ready?" he said.

"Yes."

"And have you made sure that the package won't leak?"

"Yes."

John looked around and said, "Right, let's get him into the van."

As planned, John took a hold of the straps at the 'head end', he waited until Rosalind had hold at the 'feet end', and then they lifted.

"Jesus Christ," gasped John, "he ain't light…"

They shuffled through the front door and onto the private drive, worked their way around to the back of the stolen Ford Transit van, and manhandled the body inside.

"Have you got the chains and weights?" said Rosalind.

"They're in the back."

"And are you sure that the dinghy is still there?"

"Yes," said an exasperated John, "I checked an hour ago, and it's still there."

"And did you bring the bolt-cutters?"

"For fuck's sake Ros, give it a rest, I'm not completely stupid you know!"

Rosalind said, "I know, it's just that I'm nervous – I've never done anything like this before."

"And you think I have, do you? Jesus Christ, if it wasn't for you I'd be doing nothing more dangerous than watching porn on my laptop right now!"

"So you watch porn do you?" said Rosalind as she climbed into the passenger seat, "aren't I enough for you?"

"You know what I mean babe," said John, "I was only speaking metaphorically."

Rosalind watched as John switched the engine on and engaged first gear.

"You'd better be," she said, "'cos I'd hate you ending up the same as him." She gestured to the rear with her head.

John frowned and cast a nervous glance in the direction of his partner-in-crime; he said, "If I didn't know you better, I'd think that you meant that!"

Rosalind said nothing; she kept her eyes facing forwards and didn't notice John casting a few odd glances in her direction.

At 00:50am they pulled into the narrow, unmade approach road to the Dunsteth Reservoir and John stopped the van. He looked up at the waning moon, saw that it was high in the sky and giving enough light for them to be able to see without the aid of torches.

He looked in all directions and then said, "Okay, let's do this." He engaged gear and took the van to the edge of the reservoir close to a moored, unmasted dinghy. He jumped out, snipped the security chain with a pair of bolt-cutters, and pushed the dinghy bow first into the water's edge. Once more he looked around to satisfy himself that they were still alone.

He ran to the back of the van, placed the bolt-cutters inside, and with the aid of Rosalind, manhandled the body into the dinghy. He then loaded on the chains and weights, grabbed the oars, and installed them into the rowlocks. He was ready.

He walked back to Rosalind and said, "Right, remember what I said, reverse the van onto the road and then use the brush in the back to erase any sign of tracks whilst I row him out, okay?"

Rosalind nodded and said, "Okay, but try and get him as close to the middle as you can."

"I will, now go!"

He ran back to the dinghy, crouched down, grabbed the transom, and heaved it into the water; as soon as it started to float, he jumped into the stern, sat down, and grabbed the oars. He rowed out several yards, attached the chains and weights to the body, and then made for the centre of the reservoir.

Within five minutes, his arms began to feel tired; he slowed down the rate of rowing and became convinced that the body was getting heavier...

Two or three minutes later he felt water spill into his right shoe; he stopped rowing, looked down, and to his horror saw at least four or five inches of water in the bottom of the dinghy. He looked up and saw how far he'd rowed out, turned around and saw that he was nowhere near the middle of the reservoir; he also saw that he was far enough out, not to be able to make it back if the boat was sinking.

He didn't know what to do; should he try to row harder and get the body further out, or should he dump the body and try to row back? Once again he saw how far he'd rowed out, and in a moment of supreme self-doubt, wondered whether he'd be able to swim that far back.

Without warning the boat hit something and came to an abrupt halt; he fell backwards off the thwart and landed on his back in the water in the bottom of the boat. At the same time, his left oar slid out of the rowlock, into the water, and started to drift away.

He cursed, pulled himself back up onto the thwart, and turned to look at what he'd hit; nothing appeared to be there, only an open expanse of water. He frowned as he tried to figure out what had stopped him, and then noticed the oar drifting away. In blind panic, he grabbed the other oar and tried to paddle the dinghy towards it, but the water in the bottom had grown to six or more inches deep, and the more he paddled, the more water he scooped over the gunwales. The dinghy began to wallow and feel unstable, so he jammed the remaining oar under the thwart, grabbed the body, and hauled it to the side. He attempted to lift the head end, but that was far too heavy so he changed position, grabbed the dead man's feet, and managed to manhandle them over the gunwale.

Then disaster struck. As he attempted to push the body over the side, its weight, and the water in the bottom, tipped the whole dinghy over.

The body sank like stone; the dinghy wallowed about for a few seconds longer and then disappeared below the water. The only things left afloat were he and the loose oar which was now at least twenty-five yards further out towards the centre of the reservoir.

He orientated himself, prayed to God that he would make it, and struck out for the shore and the now-panic-stricken, waiting Rosalind.

Chapter 6

The telephone rang on Naomi's desk; she picked it up and
said, "Walmsfield Historic…"

"Ah Naomi – Bob Crowthorne here."

"Good morning Bob," said Naomi to her favourite
policeman, "To what do I owe this pleasure?"

"I presume you heard the news broadcast about the
discovery of a human bone at Dunsteth reservoir last week?"

"Carlton did, and he told me about it; why?"

"We've received the initial analysis and carbon 14 dating
results, and they indicate that the bone came from a young
woman who died towards the end of the 1800s."

"And now you want my help?"

"Yes please; if you could come up with anything that may
help us to establish who it was, that would be most helpful."

Naomi felt the thumb press down onto her shoulder and
knew that she was no longer alone; she waited for a voice, but
nothing came.

Crowthorne said, "Naomi, did you hear me?"

"Yes, sorry Bob, I was a bit distracted."

Crowthorne was aware of Naomi's 'special capabilities',
and though he had at first been scathing about them, he'd
received far too much inexplicable help dating back to 2002, to
be able to dismiss it out of hand. In the end he'd accepted what
was going on, and had started to hope that Naomi would
occasionally receive some of her 'special help'. It added a
soupcon of intrigue to his investigations and in secret he got
some pleasure from it.

"It isn't, 'you know what' that's distracting you is it?" he
enquired.

"Why Bob Crowthorne!" said Naomi, "You'll be telling me that you believe in all my mumbo-jumbo next!"

There was a slight 'harrumphing' sound at the other end of the line and Crowthorne said, "Well, perhaps I wouldn't go that far, but…"

"But you hope that it is eh?"

"Well it doesn't do any harm to embrace all of the assistance and evidence that we can amass in the course of our duty, does it?"

"Right Bob! And to put your mind at rest, it was one of my 'moments' but so far I haven't had anything concrete."

"Okay," said Crowthorne, "Like I said, we would appreciate *anything* that you can give us."

"All right, leave it with me, and I'll be in touch." She said goodbye and put the phone down.

She hadn't said anything in depth about her psychic side to Helen, but she believed that Helen was already aware that something was not the same with her as it was with other people.

She sat back in her chair and said, "That bone that was found in the Dunsteth reservoir came from a young woman who died towards the end of the nineteenth century."

Helen looked up and said, "Right, so now it's officially our business too?"

"Yes."

"Okay, we'll get stuck into researching Malaterre on Monday, but first; tell me everything that you know."

Naomi put down her cup of tea and leaned back in her chair. She liked Fridays; it felt more like a day of relaxing and reflecting, of looking forward to the weekend, and of socialising with friends. She looked around the office, saw that it was the tidiest that she could remember for years and reflected what an excellent decision it had been to take Helen on.

Another pleasing aspect about Helen was her dress sense; whereas she put clothes on that she purchased from a myriad sources, Helen often wore designer pieces – not anything that she would consider in a million years – but because of Helen's penchant for them, she always dressed in a way that would give her food for thought and would often be the topic of conversation for the first half hour of the day.

"Okay," she said, noting that today's noteworthy item of clothing was a Stella McCartney denim mini-skirt, "I know that the old Malaterre estate covered two-fifths of the land under Dunsteth reservoir..."

Helen interrupted and said, "Excuse me for butting in – but every time that you mention the name Dunsteth, a memory triggers; have you told me about it before?"

Naomi recalled the 2002 investigations into the Whitewall Estate, the most recent discoveries from the Vical Centre, and those from the Elland family mausoleum. The common denominator had been the old Lincoln family who had contested ownership of Whitewall with her great, great, great Aunt Maria, of 'Maria's Papers' notoriety, and their subsequent descendants by marriage, the Johnsons, who had owned the Dunsteth Estate outright.

"It's our old friends the Johnsons..."

"The guys that you told me about at Whitewall?" said Helen.

"Yes; there was a point sometime in the mid-1800s when they owned the Dunsteth Estate which occupied the other three-fifths of the valley, and asserted that they were the true owners of Whitewall." She paused for a second and then said, "And they were the pigs who got Maria locked up in the lunatic asylum."

"But not for long though eh?" said Helen.

"Well we never had definitive proof that she got out..."

"Maybe not, but the old photo you showed me of the supposedly dead Maria from her medical records wasn't *the* Maria was it?"

"No," said Naomi, "it didn't look like her for certain – and I never did find out what happened to her did I?"

"This is what I love about historical research," said Helen, "there's always the possibility that whilst uncovering the truth about one thing, something entirely different could pop up. And who knows, once we start digging into Malaterre, we might find out something new about the Johnsons that could help us to clear up the Maria conundrum."

Naomi sighed and said, "Maybe…" She paused for thought and then said, "Getting back to Malaterre, I know that it, and the Dunsteth Estate were sold to the old Hundersfield District Council sometime around 1868 or 1869, that a dam was built, and that the valley was flooded not long after. Apart from that I have no other information."

"And what about the guy that you met there the other day?"

"Stephen Page?"

"Yes, what has he to do with it?"

Naomi felt a sudden wave of emotion flood over her almost as soon as Helen had mentioned his name, and she didn't reply straight away.

Helen stared at Naomi for a few seconds and then said, "N, are you okay?"

Naomi looked up at the sound of the unfamiliar nickname that Helen had adopted, more than likely in response to her nicknaming Helen 'H'. She gathered her wits and said, "I'm not sure what he has to do with it, but he has asked me if I'd like to meet his mother, whom, it would seem, knows a lot about the place."

"And when are you going to see her?"

"I, er, I'm not."

Helen frowned and said, "Why?"

Naomi felt confused by her sudden rush of emotion again and said, "I don't know… I just haven't made any arrangements."

"Do you have a number to call, or an email address?"

Naomi reached down into her bag and retrieved the card.

"Yes, he said to call him."

"So call him!" said Helen.

Naomi looked down at the card and saw the telephone number; somehow she believed that if she made the call, it would be a pivotal thing. She continued to look at the card in silence until Helen spoke.

"Here," she said, "give it to me; I'll make the call, and if you aren't sure about meeting him, I will."

"No!" said Naomi with too much force.

Helen noticed the change in Naomi's demeanour and said, "N, what's going on?"

Naomi looked at Helen for a few seconds and then said, "All right, I'll tell you; but it stays in this room, right?"

Helen frowned but said, "Right."

"I believe that Stephen Page and I are going to be..." she hesitated, "...to be, somehow involved..."

"Involved?" said Helen, "How do you mean involved? In the investigation – or something else?"

"Something else..."

Helen clapped her right hand over her mouth and said, "Oh my God!"

"Yes, my God," said Naomi.

"But you love Carlton, you'd never become 'involved' with anybody else!"

"I know. That's why I am so hesitant when it comes to making the call."

"So what makes you think that you'd become involved, was it something he said, or did?"

"No, nothing like that, it was when we touched hands..."

Helen clapped her hand up to her mouth for a second time and said, "What? You've already held hands?!"

"No!" said Naomi, "nothing like that, we shook hands when we met."

"And from that, you somehow concluded that you'd have an affair with him?"

Naomi frowned and said, "I didn't say that I'd have an affair with him, I said that I thought we'd become involved."

"Same thing isn't it?"

"No it isn't! There are more ways of becoming involved than having a romantic entanglement."

"Then if you believe that, why don't you make the call?"

Naomi opened her mouth to respond, but then stopped; she looked down at the card, realised how silly she must have sounded to Helen, and then looked back up.

"All right," she said in a resigned tone, "I'll make the call!"

Ten minutes later, Helen deposited another cup of tea in front of Naomi; she looked at her and saw a look of deep reflection in her eyes.

"So," she said, "how did it go?"

Naomi looked up and said, "I'm meeting him on Monday morning at his shop in Bury."

Several miles away, at Page & Page's Book Shop in Bury, the mobile phone in Stephen Page's pocket vibrated and made the familiar noise that told him he'd received a text; he extracted it and read the message from Kate;

'Original house in ruins, but interesting enough.
Dedicated museum typical touristy stuff 'cept for one gruesome artefact.
Can't find anybody who can really help.
Wasted trip info-wise but fascinating 2 c our history!
Returning Kingston 2morrow 2 resume my honeymoon.
Do not disturb!!
Ddadi xx'

He pressed the 'reply' icon and sent;

'Ok mops, it was worth a try.
Interesting developments here though.
Will fill you in when u return.
Have a good time and don't stray off the main roads in Kingston!
I love you even tho u r impossible!
xxx'

He put the phone back in his pocket and headed up to the coffee shop.

At 3:10am, Naomi didn't know what she heard first, the creak on the stairs or the deep snuffling noise. The sound was so alien that at first she doubted her ears – until it happened again. She was horrified, and so frozen with fear that she couldn't wake Carlton.

Whatever it was, it was big; she heard it sniffing and making deep-seated grunting sounds at the doors further down the landing. Her heart rate went through the roof.

She looked up and thanked God that Carlton had closed the bedroom door properly.

The thing moved closer.

Naomi heard it sniff at the bedroom door next to hers. She now believed the animal to be a huge dog, or something like that, and she was gripped by terror.

The creature sniffed at the bottom of their bedroom door, sniffed once more, and then pushed.

Naomi didn't think it was possible to be more terrified; her eyes searched around the room for a weapon, but she saw nothing that would do.

The thing pushed against the bedroom door again, this time with more determination.

Naomi glanced up and saw the bedside light. She grabbed hold of it and attempted to yank the wire out of the base…

With an ear-splitting crash, the creature launched itself into the door and it burst open.

Naomi screamed as she clawed at the wire, desperate to free it from the base.

Carlton woke up; saw what Naomi was doing and said, "Mimi, Mimi, what is it?"

Naomi spun around to face him and screamed, "What do think? Look…" she pointed towards the bedroom door.

Carlton looked across the room and saw only the faint outline of the open door; everything appeared to be just as he'd left it before going to bed.

"What is it darling?" he said, "everything looks okay to me."

Naomi stared into the gloom, and then looked down at the bedside lamp in her hands; she switched it on and realised that she'd just experienced the most horrifying dream that she'd ever had. She put the lamp down, closed her eyes, and fell into Carlton's arms.

"My God in Heaven," she said, "I've just had the worst nightmare ever…"

As Naomi lay asleep in his arms, Carlton kept vigil until the first signs of daylight pervaded their room. He knew what an unusual character his wife was, and he knew that whenever she experienced such things, they rarely came without a sting in the tail.

Chapter 7

"No sir, it is out of the question; my mama would not even consider moving to another location."

Joseph Pickles sat back in his chair in the drawing room and looked around at the elegant surroundings. He then looked down at his feet and back up to Charles. "But sir," he said, "with all due respect, you haven't heard my offer yet!"

Charles Page shook his head and said, "I'm sorry..."

Pickles tried another tack, "And are you all agreed?"

Charles hesitated and then said, "Mostly."

"Mostly?"

"Yes sir, mostly."

Pickles looked at Charles and said, "You'll forgive me for being pedantic, but 'mostly' doesn't quite reach the finishing post does it sir?"

Charles said, "No it doesn't, but we, that is my mama and my siblings Elodie and Monique, believe that our father will respect mama's wishes, and opt to stay here at Malaterre."

Pickles nodded and then said, "And if he doesn't agree?"

"That is not likely, Mr. Pickles."

"But it is not definitive either, Mr. Page."

There was a pause in the negotiations as Charles took stock of the situation.

"Very well, it is clear that we cannot arrive at the definitive answer you require until my father is present."

"And when, may I ask is that going to be?"

"On Tuesday of next week, the fourth of August."

Pickles frowned for a second as he thought about the delay; he said, "And there is no possibility that he will return sooner?"

"No sir, next Tuesday is when my father returns."

Pickles nodded and then said, "I gather that you will need some time to discuss my proposal, so would it suit you if I returned next Wednesday to receive your definitive verdict?"

Before Charles was able to answer, the door to the drawing room opened, and an older lady swept in.

Pickles and Charles stood up and watched as the lady nodded to them in turn, and then sat down.

She was wearing a full-length white dress patterned with tiny roses; the round neckline and short sleeves were edged in red silk and finished off in bows, and around her waist was a red silk sash with two half-length tails.

Pickles waited until the lady was sitting down and then turned to Charles; he said, "Is this your mother sir?"

Charles said, "No sir, she is our nanny, Sabine."

Pickles walked across to her and extended his hand; "How do you do madam," he said.

"I do very well thank you," said Sabine.

"Saba, this is Mr. Pickles, he is from the local Council and wishes to purchase Malaterre from Mama and Papa so that the valley in which it lies can be flooded to make way for a new reservoir."

Sabine frowned and said, "Flooded M'sieu?"

"Yes madam, flooded."

"You must forgive my English M'sieu;" Sabine turned to Charles and said, "What is 'flooded?'"

"Inondé," said Charles.

"Inondé?" said Sabine, "toute la vallée?"

"Yes Saba, the whole valley."

"For a new reservoir you say M'sieu Pickles?"

"Yes madam – that is, if Mr. and Mrs. Page agree to sell Malaterre."

Sabine bristled with indignation, "Non M'sieu Pickles that would be out of the question. We have been here depuis dix-huit quinze – er pardon – since 1815, this is our home, and we all love it here."

Pickles turned to Charles and raised his eyebrows.

Charles said, "Perhaps now you have a taste of the resistance that you will experience from my papa when he returns. We all love it here Mr. Pickles, we love the location, we love the buildings, we love our neighbours, the local shopkeepers, everybody..." He paused and then added, "Perhaps only with the singular exception of the former residents of the Dunsteth Estate, but I am very happy to say, that since they departed last year and took up residence in another estate, even that problem is now resolved."

Pickles recalled his meeting two days' earlier with those 'former residents of the Dunsteth Estate' and shivered at the thought of having to report a negative response from the Page family.

He nodded and said, "Very well Mr. Page; there is nothing more to say until we have an answer from your father. With your permission I shall return next Wednesday."

"That will be fine, but please come after ten of the clock; my father is not an early riser."

Pickles nodded and said, "Of course, and following your decision, I shall convey your wishes to my employers, the Hundersfield District Council."

He turned to Sabine, bowed, said, "Madam," and then extended his right hand to Charles.

"M'sieu Pickles," said Sabine, "have you spoken to the owners of the Dunsteth Estate about their wishes?"

Pickles turned to Sabine and said, "I have, madam."

"And what do they want to do?"

"They wish to sell."

Sabine paused and then said, "Then you have a, a..." she turned to Charles and said, "Une énigme?"

"A conundrum Mr. Pickles," said Charles.

Pickles turned back to face Sabine and said, "Yes madam, it would appear that we do."

Sabine turned to Charles and said, "Have you met with the new owners of the Dunsteth Estate?"

"No Saba."

"Then I think that you should go over to see them tomorrow and ask them why they want to sell their home in such a beautiful location."

Pickles looked at Charles and tried to assess whether he knew who the owners of Dunsteth were.

"If you think so Saba," said Charles, "maybe if they see how much we love it here, they will take a fresh look around and reconsider their decision; that would then encourage Mr. Pickles and his associates to seek an alternative location for their reservoir."

"Bon!" said Sabine.

Pickles looked down at his feet for a few seconds and then looked up and said, "Are you aware that the owners of the Dunsteth Estate are the same now as they have been for the last few years?"

"I'm sorry Mr. Pickles," said Charles, "I don't understand. I was under the impression that new owners had taken over last year."

"No sir; the people incumbent at Dunsteth are but tenants; the owners are still Abraham and Caleb Johnson."

"Saint Mère de Dieu," said Sabine, "those horrible men?"

Charles plonked himself down on the nearest chair and said, "They still own Dunsteth?"

"Yes sir, they do."

"And they are the people who want to sell?"

"Yes sir, they are."

"And have they any inclination that we do not want to sell?"

"No sir, but they have made it very plain to me that they would like you to."

Sabine made a gasping sound and turned to look out of the window; she recalled a promise made to her by her good friend Adolphe and decided that now would be a good time to send a message.

Charles looked at her deep in thought, and then turned back to face Pickles.

"Then I take it that we would be in some sort of conflict if we refuse to sell?"

Pickles tried to sound a lot more placating than he felt. "Perhaps 'conflict' is too harsh a word Mr. Page; I would prefer to use the term 'difference of opinion' for the time being."

Charles nodded and said, "All right, you've certainly given us something else to think about. I shall acquaint my mama and papa with everything that you have told us, we shall consider it as a family, and then we shall give you our decision when you return next Wednesday."

Pickles said, "I understand; I shall see you then, after ten of the clock." He looked across to Sabine and said, "Madam." He turned to Charles and said, "Sir – goodbye for the present," and then left.

Two hours later Pickles walked into the Estates Department of the Hundersfield District Council Offices; he hung his jacket and bowler hat on the wooden coat stand and sat down at his desk with his briefcase.

For the whole of the return journey from Malaterre, his mind had been in turmoil. On the one hand he knew that he was going to have the intransigence of the Page family, and on the other the vehement, vociferous anger of the Johnsons. He racked his brain to try to come up with a solution to the problem because he knew that a lot of the Johnson's ire would be vented on him; and when it came to the Johnsons, that ire and spleen was likely to spill out all over the place and not just within the working environment. It could mean personal threats upon him and his family, at work, at play, in their own home, and anywhere else the Johnsons could think of.

The prospect was horrific and worrying in the extreme.

"Are you all right Joseph?" said a voice from behind him, "You look a bit put upon."

Pickles turned and saw the familiar face of Edmund Turner, his General Manager, "Oh, nothing more than the usual sir," he said, "only perhaps this time, a bit more so."

Turner frowned and said, "You're working on the new reservoir project aren't you?"

"Yes sir."

"Right," said Turner, "are you experiencing some difficulties?"

"You could say that sir…" He went on to explain his dilemma to Turner, but omitted to voice his growing concerns about how dangerous he considered the Johnsons to be.

Turner, who'd taken a seat next to Pickles, rubbed his chin in thought. He said, "Am I right in recalling that the family at Malaterre are of froggy descent?"

Pickles raised his eyebrows at his superior's terminology and said, "The family was originally from France sir, but that was more than fifty years back and all the present children were born and raised here."

"My old grandfather was killed by the frogs in *'la grande terreur'* you know – the French revolution."

Pickles raised his eyebrows and said, "You don't say."

"Yes," said Turner, "he was a landscape gardener who trained at Warwick Castle where old Capability Brown made his name. Good at it he was by all accounts. He got himself a contract working on some Viscount's land near La Rochelle in the 1790s not long after my father was born.

"Bloody silly of him to go there with all that going on if you ask me, but he didn't think that it would spread so far from Paris. However, the revolutionary guard finally arrived to arrest the Viscount and his family; – he wandered around to see what the commotion was about, and got shot by one of the revolutionaries! So much for liberté, égalité, and fraternité eh? Bloody frogs; haven't liked 'em since I heard that."

Pickles looked at his boss and said, "Very interesting sir."

"More than that Joseph," said Turner, "it gives you an insight into the foreigner's mind-set. They aren't civilised the way we English are and you couldn't trust any of 'em; – look at my grandfather!" He paused for a moment to let his imparted sagacity sink in.

"Take those frogs at Malaterre for instance, one minute they'll tell you they don't want to sell; next they could be changing their minds at the drop of a pin. And more than likely after you've put the legwork in trying to find another suitable valley."

Pickles looked at his boss with a mild frown on his face and said, "Are you trying to tell me something sir?"

"Yes," said Turner, "don't go fretting too much about things Joseph, especially when you're dealing with foreigners; things have a way of working themselves out in the end. Dunsteth Valley is our prime choice of location for the new reservoir, and you've told me that the Johnsons who own Dunsteth Hall want to sell, so if you get a negative response from the Pages next Wednesday, go and tell the Johnsons, and let's sit back and see what ensues."

Pickles wasn't a man to be shocked, but the implication of his boss's statement wasn't lost on him at all.

"Are you in any way condoning…"

"Steady Joseph!" said Turner, "I'm not condoning anything. I'm asking you not to be rash in looking for another reservoir venue, when in time, the matter may resolve itself." He paused and then said, "Do I make myself clear?"

Pickles sat back in his chair, looked at his boss, and said, "It couldn't possibly be any clearer, sir."

Chapter 8

Monday 19th June 2006. Page & Page's Bookshop,
Bury, Lancashire

Just after 10:30am Naomi stepped into Page & Page's
Bookshop in Bury and it wasn't at all how she had pictured it.
For some reason she had expected to see somewhere quaint,
with a distinctive library smell, surrounded by shelf-upon-shelf
of old books, and festooned with all sorts of tomes lying about
on worktops and surfaces in wild disarray. But it wasn't like
that at all.

Page & Page's was ultra-modern, not dissimilar to all the
multi-outlet High Street bookstores. It was light and airy,
modern gondolas filled with new releases and popular authors
stood in two rows down the centre of the shop, whilst around
the outsides she could see speciality subject books, magazines,
sweets and chocolate, wrapping paper, writing and drawing
aids; in fact, it had the works.

She picked her way through the numerous people
browsing, and headed towards one of the two tills; she waited
until it was her turn to be served and then introduced herself
and informed the girl behind the counter that she had an
appointment with Stephen Page.

"Mr. Page is expecting you Mrs. Wilkes; he said he'd be
waiting in 'La Café Crème', our coffee shop."

"Ah, okay; this is my first visit here; can you direct me to
it please?"

"Yes, it's at the back of the store, keep heading that way,"
she indicated with a nod of her head, "You can't miss it."

Naomi thanked the girl and walked through the gondolas
until she spotted it; once again she was surprised.

The coffee shop looked like a sumptuous 1920s lounge bar
in its décor; it had big, cream, leather armchairs and sofas, and

comfy-looking leather-cushioned stools sited around an array of low wooden tables. The smell of fresh coffee pervaded the air, but the self-service food counter was stacked with all manner of cakes, fancies and snacks, and the menu of available drinks was one of the most extensive that she had seen.

"Naomi, over here!"

Naomi turned in the direction of the call and saw Stephen sitting at a table for two in the far corner of the cafe. She weaved through the tables and saw him stand up as she approached.

Stephen extended his hand and said, "I've taken the liberty of ordering you a café macchiato before introducing you to my mother, so I hope that is acceptable."

It happened again, in another double-blow. The moment that she shook his hand, the same inexplicable desire to draw close to him overtook her; she could have sunk into his arms and settled down next to him in a cuddle. She breathed him in and loved the smell of his aftershave; he was well groomed and looked faultless. He was dressed in a smart, brown pinstripe suit with a pale yellow shirt, and a perfectly matched tie.

But the second blow was his choice of drink for her. Café macchiato was always her first choice in any coffee bar or restaurant, and he had picked exactly that, out of the dazzling array of options.

She let go of Stephen's hand and said, "Café macchiato's just the right thing, it's my favourite. What made you choose that for me?"

"Oh, I don't know," said Stephen, "just a lucky guess maybe."

Naomi looked at him with mounting suspicion; she still wasn't sure whether he'd heard anything at the Dunsteth Reservoir or not, but one way or the other she felt that something was going on, and him being able to guess her first choice of drinks added to that conviction.

She sat down and said, "I'm very impressed by your shop; I was expecting it to be sort of 'olde-worlde'."

Stephen smiled and his face lit up, "Ah, so you expected my father and me to own some sort of Dickensian book shop thick with dust and cobwebs did you?"

"No – but I must admit that I did wonder."

"And are you disappointed?"

"On the contrary, everywhere looks vibrant and the number of shoppers in here speaks volumes."

"Excellent," said Stephen, he paused and then said, "my mother is waiting for us in the apartment upstairs, and she's looking forward to meeting you."

Without thinking Naomi said, "Is she English?"

It was Stephen's turn to be surprised; he looked at Naomi for a second and then said, "Through and through, why do you ask?"

Naomi saw Stephen's reaction and realised that she'd made a blunder. She couldn't explain that she'd asked because she'd heard the voice in her head speaking in French, but her usual quick-wittedness deserted her. She said, "No reason really, I, er, just wondered…"

Stephen looked into her eyes and nodded.

Desperate to change the subject, Naomi picked up her drink and said, "How is it that your mother is so well acquainted with Malaterre?"

"Because of my father; she loves history and his family historically owned the estate so when she learned about it, it became a passion of hers."

"So why aren't we meeting your father instead of your mother?"

"Because we don't know where he is."

Naomi raised her eyebrows and said, "You don't know where he is?"

"No, he disappeared on a skiing holiday in Switzerland thirteen months ago."

"My God, do you think that he's still alive?"

The thumb pressed down onto Naomi's shoulder and she heard a female voice say, *'Non.'* Her French may have been basic, but she knew what that meant. She opened her mouth to speak, but decided against it.

Stephen hesitated and then said, "I don't know; what do you think?"

Naomi said, "How would I know?"

Stephen stared at her for a few seconds, and then said, "Of course, it was silly of me to ask…" he then tapped his watch, indicated upwards with a nod of his head and said, "Shall we?"

Naomi said, "Yes of course." She finished her café macchiato and followed Stephen through the back of the coffee shop to a door marked 'Private'.

Five minutes later they were seated in the tastefully decorated lounge of the upstairs apartment.

The door opened, Tineke Page walked in, and Stephen introduced her. "Naomi," he said, "this is my mother."

"It's very nice to meet you Mrs. Page," said Naomi.

"Please call me Tineke – my birth name is Christina, but my husband started calling me Tineke not long after we were married and it has stuck. And besides, I like it."

"Yes, so do I," said Naomi. "It is very distinctive."

Tineke turned to Stephen and said, "So this is the young lady that you told me about?"

Stephen nodded and said, "Yes, she's in charge of the Historic Research Department at Walmsfield."

Tineke said, "Ah, not far from Malaterre then?"

"It is in my jurisdiction," said Naomi.

Tineke nodded and said, "Very well; do you know anything at all about the old place?"

"A limited amount – but for the purposes of this meeting, I think that you should consider I know nothing."

Tineke cast a quick glance over to Stephen, who nodded.

"Have you ever heard of Marie-Joséphe-Rose Tascher de La Pagerie?"

Something triggered in Naomi's mind from her distant past, but she couldn't put a finger on it; she said, "Something about the name rings a bell, but for the moment, it eludes me."

"Marie-Joséphe-Rose Tascher de La Pagerie, also known as the Viscontesse de Beauharnais was married to Napoleon Bonaparte in March 1796 and became Empress Josephine of France."

Naomi said, "Oh yes of course, I should have remembered..."

"It's no matter," said Tineke, "but this is. Josephine had a cousin named Stéphanie Tascher de La Pagerie who gave birth to a boy child in 1815 named Etienne. Rumour had it that he was the illegitimate child of one of Napoleon's high-ranking generals, and because she was married to the Duc d'Arenberg at the time, a marriage that had been arranged by Bonaparte, the child was smuggled out of France with Josephine's most trusted friends Armand and Sabine Avrain, to England.

"Because the Avrains were afraid for the life of the child, they decided that it would be safer to live a long way from London, so they purchased an estate, which they re-named Malaterre, or 'bad land' because compared to their beloved Paris, they hated it. It was acquired in 1816, and apart from Armand who died in the 1850s, the family remained there until the valley was flooded in 1869. Furthermore, in order to blend in with the English, and to make life difficult for any potential French assassins they changed their name to Page."

"Why were they afraid of assassins?"

"Parisian society was very different in the early 19th century. Few of the aristocracy remained, but those who had were staunchly proud. They believed that they were the elite, the hoi oligoi, whereas those 'citizens' who had elevated themselves into positions of power following the revolution, were no more than one step above the common rabble, or hoi polloi. So for the Duc d'Arenberg to be cuckolded by a member of the lower orders, despite him being one of Napoleon's Generals, was too much to bear, and it was no secret that the d'Arenberg family thereafter wanted *'les embarras'* or, 'the embarrassments' wiped off the face of the earth."

Naomi was enthralled and then felt a sudden thrill of excitement. She said, "So the bottom line is, you are all related to Empress Josephine?"

Tineke said, "We believe we are, but there is something even more important than that at stake. My husband Renee may be heir to the title of Sixth Duke of La Tascher Pagerie because Renaud de La Tascher Pagerie, who was the fifth and last Duke, died in 1993. What we have to do is to prove a direct line of descent from the Pageries – and up to now, that has been our sticking point. Of course we have lots of anecdotal evidence, and plenty of recorded history to back up our claim, but without definitive proof, it is next to useless."

Naomi nodded and said, "Yes, that has always been the case with claims in the past, and the genealogy buffs are strict about that."

"Quite so," said Tineke.

"So have you brought me here because you think that I might be able to help you with your claim?" said Naomi.

"We aren't sure," said Stephen, "but when we heard that a bone had been discovered in the Dunsteth Reservoir, we wondered if that might help."

Naomi frowned and said, "How? I can tell you that the police have been in touch with me and have confirmed that the bone came from the body of a young woman who died sometime towards the end of the nineteenth century, but in reality it could belong to anybody; so why would you think that it could help you with your claim?"

"We don't know definitively, of course," said Tineke, "but what we do know is that something calamitous happened to the family in 1868, and that it has remained a mystery ever since."

"Now you have me intrigued," said Naomi.

"We are too," said Stephen. "Everybody but my great, great grandfather Charles Page disappeared into thin air that year and we haven't been able to find any trace of them since. Furthermore, according to my grandfather, Charles changed his surname to Preston in 1869 to avoid being hunted down and murdered, and it wasn't until 1938 that my grandfather changed the family name back to Page."

"Good Lord," said Naomi, "that sounds horrific. How many people went missing?"

"Four family members that we know of, but there may have been more. Charles Page, later Preston, is the only member of the family ever recorded after 1869, anywhere."

"Do you have any theories or suspicions about what happened to them or where they went?"

"No," said Stephen, "and the only thing that has been passed down to us with any certainty since that time, is that we are all related to the family who once occupied Malaterre."

"And therefore the Tascher de La Pagerie's," said Naomi.

"Precisely," said Tineke, "but the problem is relating that to the Pagerie family; you see, when the infant Etienne Tascher de La Pagerie was brought to England by the Avrains' and the Malaterre Estate was first purchased, it was all done under the name of Page, and although there are no other known, living relatives of the Tascher de La Pageries, we, according to the genealogists, would still have to provide definitive proof of our lineage via incontrovertible evidence, or a sample of DNA."

The penny dropped and Naomi said, "Ah, so you want me to request that a sample of DNA be removed from the bone found in the reservoir, to see if there is a direct link?"

"Yes please, if possible," said Tineke.

Naomi sat back in her seat and said, "That's a big ask." She thought about it for a few seconds and said, "And it would raise a mountain of questions."

"It might also help us to discover what happened to the rest of the family," said Stephen.

Naomi frowned and said, "So what are you suggesting; that the bone is from one of the missing relatives?"

"Well there are no records of Page family burials anywhere else in the Parish."

"And do you think that is because they could have been buried at Malaterre?"

"It would be most unusual for staunch Catholics to be laid to rest in unconsecrated ground, and downright suspicious if they had," said Tineke.

Naomi nodded and said, "I agree. Could they have gone back to France?"

"Why would they?" said Stephen.

"Maybe they were unaware that their lives could have been in danger by returning?"

Stephen shrugged and said, "It's possible of course, but if they did, why haven't they claimed the ducal title?"

Tineke said, "Forgive me for interrupting your deliberations, but we seem to be going off track. Whether or not there are any other living members of the family is beside the point; we are the ones interested in claiming the ducal title by right of ascension and that is what we will continue to do. If at some time in the future our right is challenged by another member of the family, we shall have to deal with it then."

Naomi nodded and said, "Okay – so, going back to the bone, let us say that we do establish a DNA link, where do you think that it came from? Were there any records of graves at Malaterre, or a private chapel – or mausoleum maybe?"

"None that we know of," said Stephen, "but if the bone is tested, and we do get a match, that would be a start wouldn't it?"

Naomi felt as though she was on the verge of something huge. Direct family links to Empress Josephine of France being discovered by British nationals would be very newsworthy, and even more so if it resulted in Stephen being created a Duke.

She looked at them both and said, "Yes – indeed it would…"

Chapter 9

The Historic Research Department, Walmsfield
Borough Council

Just before 1pm Naomi walked back into the basement of the Council Offices; she'd been up in the Planning Department and had decided with a delighted, but slightly disappointed Carlton, that even though the doctor had confirmed her pregnancy they would keep it a secret from all but her closest family until after the scan at the end of her first trimester.

She should have been collecting Helen and then going to the Ryming Ratt public house for some lunch, but instead, she heard something ahead and stopped. Singing was emanating from her office and she knew just whom it was. A wicked smile crept across her face as she tried to imagine Helen's writhing agony. Postcard Percy had trapped her.

She was well aware of his numerous ruses to collect money for his local charity, but of all of them, his 'singing a song for a pound' was his most excruciating. There was no denying that he had a good voice, particularly for a man over seventy years of age, but it was his dogged determination to sing every last line of the song that had most folk squirming.

She waited until he'd finished, then with a spring in her step, walked down to her office, and entered. She looked across at the anguished face of Helen, and then at the animated face of Percy.

"Good afternoon my dear!" said Percy, "I wasn't aware that you'd taken on such a charming colleague."

"She only started last Monday, but we worked together solving the 'Larkland Fen' case."

"Ah, so this is the young lady that was helping you from the Vical Centre?"

"Yes indeed, and I was fortunate enough to persuade her to come and work here with me."

Percy turned and beamed at Helen and said, "So we'll be seeing a lot more of one another; how delightful!"

Naomi glanced at Helen and saw the look of despair in her eyes; wickedly she said, "Yes you will, and I'm sure that Helen will enjoy your visits as much as I do."

Helen painted a smile on her face and said, "Yes, of course." Her now desperate mind alighted on the drinks dispenser and she said, "Can I get anybody anything to drink?"

"Ooh yes please," said Percy, "Tea, white, no sugar – I'm sweet enough!"

Naomi heard Helen's intake of breath, but ignored it and said, "I'll have a fresh orange please." She smiled and waited until Helen had departed, then sat down at her desk and said, "Percy, you couldn't have come at a more opportune time…" There was a gentle tap on her office door, she said, "Sorry," looked across the room and called, "Come in."

The door opened and a delivery driver stepped inside, "Are you Mrs. Naomi Wilkes?" he enquired.

"Yes."

"Ah good, I have a delivery for you…" he placed a cardboard box half the size of a standard paperback book on Naomi's desk.

Naomi looked at it and said, "Do I have to sign anywhere?"

The deliveryman said, "That isn't necessary – it's just a standard package," he smiled, said, "goodbye," and left.

Naomi pushed it to one side and said, "That can wait, I want to pick your brain."

Percy re-positioned himself and said, "I like the sound of this…"

"Yes, it's about the Malaterre Estate in the…"

"Dunsteth reservoir," said Percy.

"Precisely; I'd like you to dig up everything that you've got on it if you could."

Percy frowned and said, "Is this because of the recent discovery there?"

"Partly," said Naomi, "but there's a lot more to it."

"You're telling me there is," said Percy, "it is one of the great mysteries of the nineteenth century around here."

"So you already know about the place do you?"

"A little; but it's the favourite subject of one of my close friends, Ballseye."

"Ballseye?" said Naomi with a puzzled expression her face.

"Yes," said Percy, "his real name is Marcus, but everybody knows him as Ballseye because he only has one testicle."

Naomi clapped her hand to her mouth and then laughed, she said, "In my entire life Percy, I have never known such a diverse and odd bunch of people as you do!"

"One collects them as one proceeds down life's highway," said Percy with a smile, "and the route is peppered with a rich diversity of characters."

"And if I ever meet him, how should I address him?"

Percy thought for a moment and then said, "You'll meet him all right, so you'd better call him Marcus at first, but trust me, it won't be long before he makes you aware of his clock-weight impediment."

Naomi smiled and shook her head at Percy's reference to part of a man's personal anatomy as 'clock-weights'. She said, "I dread to think…"

The door to the office opened and Helen walked in with the drinks.

"I've just been hearing about Ballseye," said Naomi.

"Ballseye?" said Helen, "What kind of name is that?"

"It's the name of a guy Percy is going to bring in to help us with our research into Malaterre, who only has one clock-weight."

"What?" said Helen, "What do you mean he only has one clock-weight?"

"He only has one testicle my dear," said Percy.

Helen blushed and then smiled, she said, "I can see why Naomi enjoys you coming here if every visit is as amusing as this!"

Percy smiled, and then turned to face Naomi. He said, "And the other thing is his lack of hair. He's very sensitive about it, and although he doesn't have much of it, for some inexplicable reason, he doesn't see it like that. His attempts to disguise it have had my friends and me running for the nearest exit on many an occasion to avoid laughing out loud. So, both of you please be warned."

Helen exchanged a curious glance with Naomi and said, "I can't wait!"

Percy nodded and then said, "Okay, now, I know a bit about Malaterre from memory, and I have more material at home, but I propose that we set a date that will be acceptable to the three of us and Marcus, where we can lay everything on the table."

"Who's Marcus?" said Helen.

"Ballseye," said Percy.

Naomi said, "That sounds like a plan, but in the meantime, what can you tell us now?"

"The Malaterre Estate wasn't always called that; at one time it was named the Blackstone Estate after the name of the Moor upon which it is situated; and yes, before you ask, it was a prominent family, the Blackstones, who used to own the lot.

"Originally it had been used as a coaching inn on the route from Whitworth to Littleborough, but the Blackstones rebuilt and converted it to family use, and they stayed there until the last of them died sometime around 1812.

"I remember that date because of Tchaikovsky's famous overture. The place remained empty until about 1815, and then the Page family moved in and stayed there until 1869 when the valley was flooded to make way for the new Rochdale Civic Reservoir."

Naomi saw Percy stop, and waited until she realised that he'd finished speaking.

"Oh, I'm sorry Percy," she said, "I thought that you were going to continue."

"No, I'm sorry my dear, my speciality as you know is the Whitewall Estate, Gasworks' is Cragg Vale, and Ballseye is the man to speak to about Malaterre."

Naomi smiled as she heard the name Gasworks and said, "How is Gasworks, and has he got his machine yet?" She saw Helen frown and said, "I'll fill you in later."

Percy looked at Naomi and said, "He's fine thank you dear, still has the problem in the, er, chamber of horrors, if you take my drift, and no, he still hasn't got his machine."

Helen was lost and said, "He works in a chamber of horrors does he?"

"No," said Naomi, "unless I'm mistaken I think that Percy is referring to a problem he has with IBS."

"Precisely dear," said Percy, he turned to Helen and said, "I believe that the chamber-of-horrors is also known in less salubrious circles as the 'defarture lounge'."

Helen couldn't help smiling, and started to warm towards Percy.

Percy turned to a grinning Naomi and said, "According to Gasworks, the latest mishap to befall his machine is that the 'end brace' has been positioned in the wrong place, and he's waiting for the engineers to fix it."

Naomi raised her eyebrows and said, "End brace?"

Percy said, "Don't ask 'cos I've no idea."

"And have you found out what the machine does yet?"

"No," said Percy, "but you have to remember that I've only been trying to discover what it does for the past five years or so, whilst there are others out there who have been trying for much longer."

Naomi could see the look of perplexity on Helen's face, and to put her out of her misery, she reached for her diary to arrange their meeting with Ballseye.

Having set the date Percy glanced up at the clock on the wall and said, "Oh my goodness, I have to go girls – I'm supposed to be singing in the shopping precinct."

"But I have some news of my own to tell you about Malaterre," said Naomi, "and it'll be right up your street…"

Percy looked at the clock again and said, "I'm sorry dear, I really am, but I have to go; I'll give you a call at the beginning of next week, and arrange a date to meet you both with Ballseye."

He stood up and walked across to the office door, turned and theatrically said, "Ladies, it's always a pleasure," and departed.

Helen was as surprised as Naomi was at the speed of Percy's departure and said, "Okay, I guess that he meant it then!"

Naomi shrugged and said, "Nothing keeps Percy from his performing."

Helen smiled and said, "Right missy, now you can explain; – machine? Chamber-of-horrors…?"

"Oh no," said Naomi, "I've got far more interesting stuff to tell you about than that…"

"Before you do, what's that?" Helen pointed to the small cardboard box on Naomi's desk.

"It arrived just as you went for the drinks," said Naomi. She picked it up, noted that it didn't have a return address anywhere on the packaging, and then opened it. Inside the box was a single piece of pale blue paper measuring just 7cm by 10cm with the word 'Brahma' written upon it. She frowned, said, "This is weird," turned it over, lifted it to her nose, and smelled it, and then handed it to Helen.

Helen almost mimicked Naomi's actions and then said, "Why would anybody send you this, and what does it mean?"

"I've no idea."

"Is your laptop on?" said Helen.

"Yes."

"Try putting 'Brahma' into Google and see what comes up."

"Good idea," said Naomi. She brought up the Google homepage typed the word 'Brahma' into it, and then said to Helen, "According to the internet, Brahma was the first God in the Hindu Trimurti and was regarded as the senior God, whose job was creation."

"Trimurti?" said Helen.

"Yes, it says here, that the Trimurti is a concept in Hinduism in which the cosmic functions of creation, maintenance, and destruction are personified by the forms of Brahma the creator, Vishnu the maintainer or preserver, and

Shiva the destroyer or transformer, and that the three deities have been called 'The Hindu Triad', 'The Great Trinity' or 'The Trimurti'."

"Well that clears that up then," said Helen.

Naomi expelled a long 'Hmm', took the note off Helen and studied it once more. She looked up at Helen and said, "Any thoughts?"

"None, but considering that you dreamed about a cigarette card with the single word 'Malaterre' written upon it, and then we *found* a cigarette card with the single word 'Malaterre' written upon it, and now we have a piece of blue paper with the single word 'Brahma' written upon it, you do seem to be racking up a plethora of single word conundrums."

"Not the same though is it?" said Naomi, "this was something posted to me by somebody else to draw my attention to a Hindu God for some reason or other."

"And no doubt we'll find out what it's meant to refer to in due course, I suppose." Helen looked down, thought for a couple of seconds, shook her head, and then looked back up again. She said, "Do you know N, – I love working here. My life at The Vical Centre was fascinating enough as a professional archivist, but you, your weird friends, and the situations that we find ourselves in are priceless. I love them!"

Naomi smiled and said, "Good, I'm glad that you're enjoying it but I don't want you saying anything to Carlton about this, you know how protective he gets."

"Yes," said Helen, "and with good reason! It wasn't so long ago that you were being held a prisoner in Adrian psycho Darke's drug facility up at Cragg Vale."

"Whatever," said Naomi, "if anything questionable transpires following this," she pointed to the note, "we'll tell him, but for now we do nothing."

Helen opened her mouth to object but saw the look on Naomi's face, she said, "Okay, but don't make me regret it!"

Later in the afternoon, Naomi decided to call Superintendent Crowthorne about the possibility of trying to extract a DNA sample from the bone found in the Dunsteth reservoir.

She made the call, got past the usual niceties, and without mentioning anything about the 'French voices' she explained the French family connection with the Pages, and then posed the question.

"If what you are saying is true," said an astounded Crowthorne, "and indeed the Page family believe that a relative of Empress Josephine of France, *the* most celebrated French Empress of all time for goodness' sake, could be buried somewhere within the Malaterre Estate buildings, this investigation would elevate to a global level."

The hair on the back of Naomi's neck stood up as Crowthorne used the word 'global', – the same word that she had used to Helen just days before.

"But that, for now," continued Crowthorne, "would be pure speculation. We'd have to trawl through our nineteenth century records for any reported crimes or incidents related to the Malaterre Estate before we would even consider going down that route."

"But would it be such a major task to extract a DNA sample from the recovered bone?"

There was a small pause at the other end of the phone until Crowthorne said, "Not as such, but that kind of puts the cart before the horse doesn't it?"

"How do you mean?"

"Well, if we did get a match from one of the Pages, it would be conclusive proof that they were related to the person from whose bone we had taken the sample, but that doesn't automatically mean that that person was related to the Empress Josephine, does it?"

Naomi emitted an 'Hmming' sound and said, "No I suppose not." She thought for a second or two and then said, "But if there was a match, we would at least have an idea about which family we were dealing with wouldn't we? And then if I'm successful in my research, and we do make the connection, that would make for one heck of an interesting case wouldn't it?"

Crowthorne pondered for a few seconds and then said, "All right, I have no idea whether the bone is in a good enough condition to be able to extract any DNA, but I will make enquiries and if it's at all possible I will request that it is done."

Naomi was thrilled; she said, "Fantastic, you're a star."

Crowthorne said, "Okay, let's just take one step at a time for now and see what results."

Naomi said, "Brilliant, thanks again Bob, it's a pleasure working with you!"

There was a slight pause on the phone until Crowthorne said, "And it's always interesting working with you Naomi – and I suppose that I should be glad there are no ghostly dogs putting the willies up me this time!"

"Oh, you never know," said Naomi with a smile on her face, "the investigation may lead us to Whitewall yet!"

"Don't," said Crowthorne, "that's not even funny!"

Ten minutes later, he picked up the phone and called the forensic laboratory in Rochdale.

"Ah, Superintendent," said the voice at the other end of the line, "I was just about to call you; a closer examination of the bone retrieved from the Dunsteth reservoir has thrown up something interesting."

"Yes?" said Crowthorne.

"Yes," said the voice, "when bones of this age have been exposed to water, or have been submerged in mud or clay, they have a distinctive pattern of deterioration, but this one doesn't conform to any of those patterns at all."

"What are you trying to say?"

"What I'm trying to say is that this particular bone appears to be so well preserved that it could not have come from either of the previously mentioned environments; it would appear that it has not long come from somewhere that must have been very dry for the last hundred-and-forty years or so, and has recently been exposed to water."

Crowthorne felt the goalposts shift. He said, "So what are you implying?"

"I don't know, Superintendent, and I don't know the Dunsteth reservoir other than from driving past it every now and then. But, it would explain things if there was a submerged grave or mausoleum under there that had until now remained watertight, and that had maybe collapsed to such an extent that it had allowed enough water in, to wash the bone out."

Crowthorne began to feel overtaken by a sense of fate, his previous conversation with Naomi started to buzz around his head, and long before he'd finished talking he knew that he would be ordering a full-scale diving operation at Malaterre.

Chapter 10

*'Be sober, be vigilant; because your adversary the
devil, as a roaring lion, walketh about, seeking
whom he may devour.'*

- 1st Epistle of Peter – Chapter 5, Verse 8.

2pm, Wednesday 5ᵗʰ August 1868. The Whitewall Estate

Joseph Pickles alighted from the Hansom cab and asked the
driver to wait. He hoped that he would be out within a few
minutes but knew that he wouldn't. His earlier meeting with
the Page family and their outright decision not to sell the
Malaterre Estate had seen to that.

He drew in a deep breath, walked up to the front door of
the living quarters, and knocked.

There was no reply.

He took two steps backwards, looked up, and saw that one
of the Tudor-style bedroom windows was open; he called out,
"Hello, is anybody at home?"

Nothing.

He waited for a few seconds and then peered all around the
courtyard.

"Hello!" he called for a second time, "Is anybody at
home?" He looked at the driver of the Hansom cab and saw
that he was looking too; their eyes met, and the driver
shrugged his shoulders.

"I can't see nobody neither sir," he said.

Pickles nodded and then walked down the courtyard to the
end of the building. Being August, and hot, he was grateful
that everywhere underfoot was dry.

The Estate, which was essentially a large farm, appeared to
be no different than any other farm he had visited, the

distinctive sounds of insects, sheep, cows and the odd distant bark, allied to the characteristic farmyard smell of animals and animal feed, carried him back to his boyhood days when he had worked on such a farm not long after leaving school.

They had been happy and carefree days; and one of the happiest memories of his life had been of lying on his back on a bale of straw, in the middle of a field, watching the warm day turn into warm night. He'd stared into the majesty of the night sky and had speculated about where he'd be and what he'd see in the coming years, and he hadn't thought for one single moment, that he'd end up being a crusty, middle-aged Council employee, forced to wear a dark suit at all times of the year.

But he knew that there were far worse jobs than his was; he could have been a tanner, or a miner, or a mill-worker, whereas, albeit clad in a dark suit, he was nevertheless walking around a farm in the warm sunshine again, and this time being paid for it. A smile spread across his lips, and he felt as happy as he could be under the circumstances.

He reached the end of the main building, followed it around to the right, and was confronted by a five-barred gate leading to a meadow behind the building. He leaned over it and looked to his right; he could see that there were a couple of open-fronted byres that were tagged onto the main building, causing it to take the form of an inverted 'L'.

He looked across the meadow to see if he could see any kind of activity, but upon seeing none, decided to cross to the other side of the courtyard and inspect the buildings opposite. He turned, took a couple of steps, and then heard some sort of muffled cry. He turned back, leaned over the five-barred gate, and listened.

He made out some sort of noise but couldn't identify it; he lifted up the latch on the gate, walked into the meadow, and closed the gate behind him. He then followed the line of the building, peered into the first byre and saw nothing, then walked along to the second, and looked in.

He was so shocked by what he saw that the effect of it hit him like a hammer blow. His mouth fell open and he gaped into the darkness, unable to believe his eyes.

Against the back wall, and in the gloom of the second byre, stood a large wooden cross with a naked man attached to it. At first he thought that it was a sadistic and life-like depiction of the crucifixion, but to his utmost horror, he realised that it was the real thing.

The man's face was so battered that his features were unrecognisable; he was blood-stained, had multiple cuts and bruises all over his body, and the bloody nails that had been hammered through his wrists and heels to keep him in place were so horrifying to see that he thought he was going to have a heart attack. He reeled back with eyes that were bulging in disbelief. Through a veil of unadulterated horror, he saw the man's chest rise and fall and knew that he was still alive. He clapped his hands over his mouth and didn't know what to do. He was so badly shocked that he couldn't even cry out. He was in turmoil; should he try to help, or should he leave and get the police? He knew that if he left, the man would be dead by the time that he got back, but he was so utterly petrified by what he saw, he couldn't help himself.

He turned and ran – straight into Abraham Johnson.

Five minutes later, the cabby watched as a thickset man limped up to him.

"Your fare has asked me to give you this." Caleb Johnson reached up and handed the cabby some coins.

The cabby looked at the coins and said, "Very generous sir – isn't the gen'leman needing a lift back to town?"

"No – he said to tell you that his meeting is going to take longer than he expected, so we're going to take him back in the trap."

The cabby touched the peak of his cap and said, "Very good sir. Good day to you." He turned the cab around and headed back up the drive.

Back in the second byre, Abraham stood against the back wall with his huge left hand clamped over Pickles' mouth. He had a vicious looking knife jammed into his captive's throat, and he wasn't saying a word.

Pickles thought that his heart was going to burst; it was hammering inside his chest like something gone wild. He was inches away from the cross; he could smell a mixture of sweat, blood, urine, and excrement, and he could hear the laboured breathing and agonised groans from the brutalised man.

In his entire existence he had never been so terrified and he believed that he was living the last few minutes of his life. He felt his legs weaken through fear and lack of breath, but as they began to give way, he felt Abraham pin him even harder against the back wall.

A few seconds later, Caleb walked in and surveyed the scene.

"Fuck me pa," he said, "that was too close for comfort." He nodded towards the man on the cross and said, "I knew that we shouldn't have done him here."

Abraham said, "Yes, yes! Don't go all smart-arse now, you wanted it done as much me."

"I know but…" he hesitated as he saw Abraham begin to scowl at him with disapproval and then said, "…we'll have to feed both of them to the pigs now, and get rid of that cross."

Pickles closed his eyes and didn't think that he could take any more. The screaming, intense pressure inside his head made him think that his brain was going to explode.

Abraham turned, looked at Pickles, and saw that he was standing with his eyes screwed up tight. He removed his hand and said, "What are you doing snooping around here?"

Pickles gasped for air and then said, "I came to tell you that the Page family won't sell Malaterre."

"Fuck!" shouted Abraham, "This day just keeps getting better doesn't it?" He glared at Pickles for a few seconds and then said. "Do you want to die?"

Pickles shook his head.

Caleb heard the question and said, "What? What are you doing? Kill him and let's get cleared up before anybody else sees what's been happening!"

Abraham turned to his son with venom in his eyes and said, "Who *the fuck* do you think you're talking to boy?"

Caleb dropped his eyes and said, "Sorry pa…"

Abraham glared at his son for a few seconds longer and then turned back to Pickles. He leaned closer to him and said, "I said – do you want to die?"

Pickles said, "No…please…"

Abraham yanked him forwards and spun him around to face the man on the cross; he said, "Do you want to end up like him?"

Pickles looked up at the horrific vision in front of him. He saw the man on the cross open his eyes and try to say something – but then give up.

In a pathetic whimper he said, "He's not dead…"

Abraham looked up, heaved Pickles against the back wall, and then stepped up to the man on the cross. He rammed his knife hilt deep under the man's rib cage, yanked it out, and then jammed the same bloody blade under Pickles' throat. He said, "He fucking is now."

Pickles was so petrified that he felt his bladder release. Warm urine ran down his left leg.

"You now have two choices," said Abraham, "die by my hand, or die an old man in your bed."

Caleb couldn't believe his ears, he said, "Pa – *pa?* What the fuck are you talking about?"

Abraham ignored his son and said, "Well, what's it going to be?"

Pickles said, "Die an old man in my bed."

"I thought so," said Abraham, "but there are one or two conditions attached to that."

Pickles stared at Abraham but didn't say a word.

"First, you'll never say a word of what you've seen here or you'll die the same. And don't go thinking that you'll be able to tell the Peelers what you've seen, 'cos even if I do get my neck stretched for it, it won't be before I've paid every murderous, vicious, cruel bastard that I know to do away with you very slowly and very painfully. Do you understand?"

Pickles nodded.

"And second – you'll get those frog bastards out of Malaterre – whatever it takes."

Once again Pickles nodded.

"Now," said Abraham with a dark and threatening glare, "do we have a proper understanding?"

Pickles gulped and said, "Yes."

Abraham stared into Pickles terrified face and then said, "Don't you *ever* go making the mistake of thinking that me or some of my muckers won't be watching you wherever you go... and let me tell you in plain English one last time, if you ever attempt to double-cross me or Caleb, I shall nail you up on a cross, I shall gut you with a *fucking saw*, and then I'll roast your innards in front of your eyes."

He pulled Pickles closer and said, "So – do we have an understanding?"

Pickles nodded his head and said, "We do."

Caleb tried one last time and said, *"Pa...?"*

Abraham wheeled around and said, "One more word from you, boy, and I'll take my stick to you..."

Caleb dropped his gaze and shut up.

Abraham pulled Pickles off the wall of the byre, let go of his clothing and pushed him towards the exit.

"Right, now fuck off, do as you're told, and think on this. If you do as I bid, that'll make you a friend of ours. You'll be safe around here wherever you go, and on top of that, once I get the brass, I might even pay you a small bonus for your trouble."

Pickles nodded and backed out of the byre; he didn't dare to take his eyes off the Johnsons. He exited and then ran across the meadow to the five-barred gate, scrambled over, and set off up the long drive, at a run.

As he put distance between himself and the Johnsons he knew that finding an alternative location for the new reservoir was no longer an option, and that whatever it took, he now had to get the Pages out.

Chapter 11

Thursday 22ⁿᵈ June 2006. Rochdale Police Station,
Lancashire

The phone rang on Crowthorne's desk; he picked it up and said, "Crowthorne."

"Ah, yes Superintendent Crowthorne, this is Inspector Hugh Kearns from the Marine Unit, I wanted to let you know that our chaps will be in attendance at Dunsteth reservoir on Tuesday of next week, the 27th June to be precise."

"Excellent," said Crowthorne.

"Yes, thank you," said Kearns. "Apart from the obvious, are there any special instructions?"

Crowthorne thought for a few seconds and then said, "Not off-hand Inspector, did you receive my brief?"

"Yes sir," said Kearns, "you'd like us to concentrate our efforts on trying to find any recent breaches in submerged structures, paying special attention to all parts of the old Malaterre buildings, is that correct?"

"Yes, correct." Crowthorne paused for a second and then said, "This is the first time that I've had to deploy you chaps; do I need to make any special preparations for you?"

"Not really sir, we're more or less self-sufficient but if we see that we could do with a bit of help, we will call you."

"Very well Inspector, keep me informed." Crowthorne was about to put the phone down when he heard a call, *"Sir!"* He put the receiver back to his ear and said, "Yes Inspector?"

"Sir," said Kearns, "have you got any documentation referring to the structural integrity of the submerged building?"

Crowthorne hadn't thought about that and was taken aback. He said, ""No, I'm sorry, I don't; should I have?"

"Not particularly sir, but when our chaps are diving in the vicinity of old buildings it's always a comfort to know that a marine surveyor has given it the thumbs up first."

Crowthorne was at a loss for words, he said, "I, er…"

Kearns said, "Look, not to worry for the moment sir, our chaps generally know what to look for and what to avoid, so we'll do our preliminaries next week as per, and if we see anything that looks untoward, we'll be in touch to advise you."

Crowthorne's normal exuberant confidence had taken a bashing and he felt a bit inadequate; in a somewhat subdued tone he said, "All right Inspector, you do that, and do be careful."

"We will sir," said Kearns, "we will, TTFN."

Crowthorne put the phone down and sat back in his chair pondering the Inspector's words, when he heard a gentle tap on his office door.

"Come in," he called.

The office door opened and Duty Inspector Peter Milnes walked in.

"Sorry to bother you sir," he said, "but I thought that you should know about this." He held up a report form.

"What is it Peter?" said Crowthorne as he jotted down a memo to himself about the marine surveyors.

"We have a report of a missing dinghy from the banks of the Dunsteth reservoir…"

Crowthorne stopped writing and looked up.

"…which in itself wouldn't be remarkable, but because the owner couldn't find any obvious tyre tracks leading away from where his dinghy had been secured, he wandered around the edges of the reservoir to try and see if it had been sailed to another location on the bank, and removed from there."

"Very resourceful," commented Crowthorne.

"Yes sir," said Milnes, "but although he didn't find any trace of where his dinghy could have been taken out, he did find a single oar washed up on the northern bank approximately two-hundred metres away from where his dinghy had been moored."

Crowthorne closed his eyes and knew what was coming.

Milnes waited until he saw Crowthorne look at him again and said, "So now we are faced with the possibility of a drowning in there."

Crowthorne drew in a deep breath and said, "Bloody marvellous!"

"My sentiments too sir."

Crowthorne pondered for a few seconds and then said, "Did the dinghy owner tell you whether the sails had been left on the boat or not?"

"Yes sir – and they hadn't; in fact the dinghy had been unmasted, leaving only the bare boat there."

"And how had it been secured?"

"With a hefty chain and padlock."

Crowthorne frowned, sat back in his chair, and then said, "So how was the thief able to remove it?"

Milnes held up a polythene evidence bag with half a chain link in it.

"The owner found this on the shore near to where his boat had been moored," he handed the bag to Crowthorne.

Crowthorne looked at it and said, "Bolt-cutters."

"Yes sir."

"And did the owner say whether the found oar had been one of his?"

"He did, and it wasn't."

Crowthorne lapsed into silence and rubbed his chin with his left hand, he looked at Milnes and said, "Puts a whole new light on things doesn't it Peter?"

"Yes sir, I'm afraid it does."

"So now we can rule out an impulse theft, or a drunken idiot's joyride."

"Yes sir, but we cannot overlook the possibility that somebody may have taken the boat deliberately, for whatever reason, and then capsized, losing the oar."

"No," said Crowthorne, "we can't." He stopped speaking for a second or two and then said, "All right Peter, leave it with me for an hour or so, and I'll get in touch with Inspector Kearns from the Marine Unit; they were scheduled to commence operations in the reservoir next Tuesday but I'll see if we can move that forward. In the meantime you'd better check if we've had any reports of missing persons."

"I've already done that sir, and so far, there are none."

"And from neighbouring Forces?"

"Tasha Andrew is on that now."

Crowthorne nodded and then asked, "And how is our newest sergeant – enjoying her stripes?"

"She is that sir."

"Good; well keep me informed if anything else turns up, and I'll get back to you later this morning."

Milnes said, "Very good sir," and headed for the door. He then remembered something, turned back and said, "I take it that you are aware of our latest addition to C.I.D.?"

Crowthorne looked up at the Inspector and said, "No Peter, anybody we know?"

"It's our old friend Phobos."

Crowthorne's face lit up; "Good Lord," he said, "so Leo's back on active duty is he?"

"Yes sir – and he requested to come here."

Brandon Talion Chance, known to all as 'Leo', a hitherto unknown distant relative of Naomi's, had been an undercover officer codenamed Phobos who had helped Naomi to escape from an underground drugs facility run by the notorious criminal Adrian Darke in the grounds of their Cragg Vale Estate and upon completion of the operation had promised to remain in touch.

"And why wasn't I made aware of his transfer to here before now?"

"I think that you'll find that you were sir," Milnes pointed to a stack of paperwork in an overloaded in-tray on Crowthorne's desk.

Crowthorne looked at it, pursed his lips, and then said, "The bane of the job, Peter…"

Milnes smiled and said, "Indeed sir." He headed once more for the door and left.

Crowthorne looked at the overloaded in-tray and, with an exasperated sigh, grabbed hold of a handful of papers.

Twenty minutes later, there was another knock on his door. He looked up and called, "Come in."

The door opened and Sergeant Tasha Andrew walked in; she said, "Sorry to bother you sir, but I thought that you might like to see this."

"Ah, Tasha," said Crowthorne standing up and extending his right hand, "I haven't had the opportunity congratulate you on your promotion."

Tasha shook Crowthorne's hand and said, "Thank you sir."

Crowthorne sat back down and said, "Now then, it's not a report of somebody missing from another area is it?"

"No sir," said Tasha, "we haven't got that back yet, this is something that I've been working on in relation to the Dunsteth reservoir."

Crowthorne frowned and said, "Oh yes?"

"Firstly, I saw that the oar was constructed out of a lightweight alloy and plastic and that got me thinking about how easily it would float." She walked across to Crowthorne's desk and spread a small ordnance survey map in front him. She pointed to a position on the map and said, "This 'X' is approximately where the oar was found; – now, I checked with the Met. Office and ascertained that we have been experiencing South Easterly winds since the dinghy owner last reported seeing his boat in place." She paused as she placed a clear plastic ruler on the 'X' marked on the map.

"Now," she said, "if we align the ruler in a South Easterly/North Westerly orientation, we can get an approximation of where the oar must have come from, when it was lost overboard."

She looked up at Crowthorne who continued to stare at the map in silence. She then retrieved a propelling pencil from her shirt pocket and drew a line back from the oar towards the centre of the reservoir until it crossed back over the south bank. She then turned the map to face Crowthorne, and pushed it towards him.

Crowthorne drew in a deep breath and said, "It cuts straight through the old Malaterre buildings."

"That's right sir," said Tasha, "and with the water level dropping, it just may have been a part of the building that our thief hit that caused a potential capsize."

Crowthorne looked up at his newest sergeant and said, "That was very well done Tasha. Keep up this kind of work and I'll be recommending you for C.I.D."

Tasha thanked him, departed, and walked down to her office with a spring in her step.

Crowthorne reached for the phone and dialled the marine unit number. "Inspector Kearns," he said, "Crowthorne here – about your op. next week, I'm afraid there's been a complication."

Chapter 12

Friday 23rd June 2006. The Dunsteth Valley

The weather was beautiful. It was 10:25am; Naomi was alone in her brand new Honda CRV and in celebration of driving it for the first time that day, she'd put on her favourite summer frock. She slipped a CD into the player and smiled with pure pleasure as the rich tones of Mark Knopfler's 'Quality Shoe' filled the interior from its quad speakers. She enjoyed driving down the single carriageway roads that led to the Dunsteth reservoir because of its breath-taking beauty, and since everything felt fresh and new, she ambled along at a comfortable forty-five miles per hour.

Suddenly, her reverie was broken by the sounding of a horn behind her; she looked into her rear-view mirror and saw that a large, dark blue van was behind her and that two men in the front seats were gesturing for her to move over. She looked at the road in front, saw that there was no approaching traffic and that there were no bends, she slowed down, pulled further over, and switched on her left-hand indicator signalling that it was safe to overtake. Instead, the van driver slowed down too, remained behind her, and kept on sounding his horn. She reduced her speed some more, wound down the window and made a hand-signal for the driver to overtake, but as before, he remained where he was and continued blasting away. She began to feel intimidated until it struck her that something may have been wrong, she decreased her speed, and pulled over onto the left-hand verge.

She watched with curiosity as the unmarked van slowed and then drew alongside, then she gasped as she saw the men. Both were wearing hideous Halloween-type masks.

"You fucking dozy bitch," yelled the driver, "next time I'll ram you off the fucking road!" He stuck the middle finger of his left hand up and then sped off into the distance.

Naomi was stunned; she had no idea what she'd done to upset the occupants of the van and she sat for a full ten minutes trying to regain her composure. Finally she felt settled enough to continue, but for the rest of the journey she watched all around for any further signs of it.

Just after 11am she pulled the CRV off the main road and drove the four-hundred yards down the unmade track towards the edge of Dunsteth reservoir. The wheels crunched on the sand and shingle until she brought it to a stop, applied the handbrake, and switched off the engine.

She shot a glance up the track to make sure that she was alone and then surveyed the scenery. Her previously shaken equanimity resumed its normal level as she marvelled at its unassuming beauty. The sun was high in the sky, there wasn't a cloud to be seen, and because there was no wind, the surface of the reservoir was as smooth as a millpond. The only sounds to be heard were the ubiquitous birds and insects.

She'd pulled off the road at the eastern end of the reservoir and could see the dam in the distance, but even to the untrained eye, the most obvious thing to be seen was the drop in water level. So much so, that the surface of the water no longer hid the topmost parts of the Malaterre estate. They stood out like so many bad teeth in the mouth of an ancient rock giant.

She got out of the vehicle, walked to the water's edge and waited. She wondered whether she'd receive some sort of contact from the French woman, but nothing happened. She tried to centre herself and relax, and half-expected a pressure to occur on her shoulder, but following several minutes of deep concentration, she still had no result.

She looked around at the scenery and tried to visualise what the valley must have looked like before it was flooded, in the days of manual labour and horse-drawn vehicles. She could understand the simplicity and appeal of life then, but when she realised that the journey from her offices to Dunsteth would have taken over three hours each way, she knew which century she preferred to live in.

She took a couple of photographs, and then sauntered around the edge of the reservoir for a hundred yards in either direction, pondering, and hoping to spot something new, but upon finding nothing, she headed back to her CRV with the intention of leaving.

As she opened the door, she had a thought; – it was a beautiful day, she had no other engagements, and she was her own boss. She decided to stay for half an hour in perfect peace and tranquillity by the water's edge. She also justified it by hoping that her extended stay would put more miles between her and the blue van, and that it might encourage the French lady to make contact again.

She walked to the rear of her vehicle, extracted a travel blanket, and ambled over to the water's edge. She laid it out on the soft shingle, sat down, and removed her shoes. The scented air and warmth of the sun were intoxicating; she stared across the shimmering reservoir and let the calm and serenity overtake her.

Within a few minutes she began to feel drowsy. She looked around and saw no other people; she listened to make sure that there were no approaching vehicles, and then lay down on the blanket and closed her eyes. It was wonderful; one of those deliciously decadent periods when she knew that she should have been at work, but instead she was lying on a shingle bank in the warmth of a June day – and she was being paid for it. It was perfect.

Without warning, something yanked her out of her drowsiness and made her frown. She propped herself up on her elbows and looked across the water; she stared for several minutes trying see what had attracted her but concluded that it must have been a fish surfacing and then returning to the deep. She scanned everywhere once more, saw that it looked the same, and then glanced down at her watch. It was 11:25am; she decided that she would stay for another twenty minutes and then head back to her office. Once more she lay back down and closed her eyes.

Several more blissful moments passed by until she heard a plopping sound come from the surface of the reservoir; she lifted up her head, and this time saw one or two bubbles rise to the surface close to the old buildings. She watched for several seconds as the intensity of them seemed to increase, and then in order to be able to get a better view, she sat up half-expecting to see a large fish break the surface. Within a short while however, the bubbles stopped and peace returned to the surface.

She checked her watch again, 11:33am; she looked around, and then resumed her position on the blanket. The warmth of the sun washed over her face once more, and for the second time she felt drowsiness start to overtake her until in the distance, she heard the sound of an approaching vehicle. She jumped to her feet, scooped up the travel blanket, and put it into the back in the CRV.

Seconds later a large white van with the words "North West Police Underwater Search & Marine Unit" came into view; it slowed as it approached and then came to a halt near the CRV.

Inspector Hugh Kearns hopped out of the driving seat and walked across to Naomi.

"Sorry to invade your peace and quiet miss," he said, "we've only come for a quick reccie, and we'll be out of your hair as soon as we can."

Naomi extended her hand and said, "I'm Naomi Wilkes the Head of Walmsfield Borough's Historic Research Department, I'm professionally involved in this investigation."

Kearns shook the offered hand and said, "Inspector Kearns, North West Police Underwater Search & Marine Unit, and er, how fortuitous it was to arrive when we did!" He paused for a second and then said, "So what can you tell us about this place?"

Naomi said, "The two estates were last occupied until 1868, and in 1869 the valley was flooded."

Kearns raised his eyebrows and said, "Right, good – well, nobody will ever accuse you of being too verbose."

Naomi smiled and said, "Sorry – obviously that's the short version."

"Yes right – and what's the long version, three sentences?"

Naomi warmed to Kearns, and said, "I wouldn't go that far…"

"A woman of few words," said Kearns. "Not married by any chance are we?"

Naomi held up her left hand and flashed her wedding ring.

"Typical, all the good ones are taken. Now – about the submerged buildings, do you have any plans or documentation?"

Naomi was caught off guard; she hadn't considered trying to obtain plans, and made a mental note to do so.

"No I haven't," she said, "but I'll find out if there are any still in existence."

"So you don't have anything that could assist us to orientate the structural outlay?"

"No I'm sorry," said Naomi, "but I had no idea that you were coming today."

Kearns nodded and said, "I'm not surprised, the schedules got bumped around and caught us all a bit off guard." He paused and then said, "And do you have any theories about the recently discovered bone?"

"I'm working on that at the moment."

Kearns said, "Okay, we'll…"

Suddenly a 'glooping' sound emitted from the surface of the lake, followed by several large bubbles in a row.

Kearns and Naomi turned and watched until the disturbance subsided, and then continued to stare at the same spot for several seconds afterwards.

"Curious…" said Kearns, "has it done that before?"

"I've only been here for about half an hour, but yes it has. It was one or two bubbles at first, nothing like that lot."

Kearns studied the exact spot on the lake, then said, "Curiouser and curiouser…"

He turned to face the marine unit van and called out, "Okay Ken, bring…"

Another abrupt, but more violent glooping sound emitted from the surface of the reservoir causing them all to turn and watch again.

A series of bigger bubbles spluttered and popped in quick succession and then something surfaced.

Whatever it was couldn't be made out from where they were, but it settled and wallowed in the water near one of the projecting sections of the old building.

"Get the bins Ken," said Kearns to the approaching police diver.

Naomi said, "I've got some too," and walked over to her CRV to get hers.

A couple of minutes later, two sets of binoculars were trained on the surface of the water inspecting the floating object.

Following several seconds of careful scrutiny, Naomi said, "It looks like an oar."

"Yes," said Kearns recalling his earlier conversation with Crowthorne, "I'm afraid that it does."

Naomi kept her binoculars trained on the oar and said, "What on earth is that doing out there?"

An exasperated Kearns removed the binoculars from his eyes, turned to face Naomi, and said, "Making our lives that much more difficult Mrs. Wilkes."

Three-hundred metres further along the northern shore of the reservoir, a third pair of binoculars were withdrawn into the deep gorse bushes, and put to one side.

John Hess said, "Shit," and rubbed his stubbly chin. He'd seen the oar, he'd seen the police marine unit van, and he'd seen the man and woman staring at the floating oar through their binoculars.

For several more seconds he sat in silence deciding upon a course of action; finally he backed his way out of the bushes, crept back the unmade service road along the northern edge of the reservoir, and got into his ex-army jeep.

He pulled his mobile phone out of his backpack and dialled a number.

"Rory, it's John," he said, "I've got a job for you, and it has to be done tonight."

Chapter 13

Friday 7th August 1868. The Estates Department, Hundersfield District Council Offices, Rochdale, Lancashire

"Ah, Joseph," said Edmund Turner, "I trust that you are feeling better today?"

"Yes sir, thank you sir," said Pickles.

"What was it then?"

"I had the most frightful migraine sir, and it renders me unable to see."

"Tsk, tsk," said Turner, "how perfectly inconvenient."

"Yes sir."

Turner paused for a second and then said, "And what kind of reaction did you get from the Messrs. Johnson when you informed them about the Page family's decision not to sell?"

Pickles had had difficulty sleeping since his encounter with the Johnsons at Whitewall two days earlier; the vision of the tortured soul on the cross had been indelibly printed on his mind and he couldn't get rid of it.

He'd gone through the full range of emotions; should he inform the authorities? Should he tell his colleagues? Should he submit to the intimidation of the Johnsons, or should he comply with them and thereby condone what they had done? His mind had been so plagued by the whole experience that he'd been unable to work the following day.

In the end, he'd opted to go along with their demands. On the face of it he had been a coward, and he knew it, but following hours and hours of contemplation, he had realised that the easiest option would be to encourage the Pages to leave Malaterre. And much to his shame, he'd even pondered what form, or monetary amount, Abraham Johnson had meant, when he'd said that there might be a bonus for him at the end.

In due course he'd felt as though he'd been able to justify his stance, and the absolute clincher had been his own superior's attitude towards 'frogs' living there in the first place. Now, he had to get them out.

He looked up at the face of his boss and said, "Frankly sir, they weren't happy."

Turner said, "Hmm," and turned to look out of the office window. He turned back and said, "Joseph, step into my office will you please?"

A minute or so later Turner pointed to a chair in front of his desk and bid Pickles sit down.

"I wanted to speak to you privately Joseph," he said, "because I know that you are a man of the world."

Pickles acknowledged the statement with a slight nod of his head.

"Yesterday I attended a select committee meeting to discuss the planned new reservoir scheme, and it would seem that er …"

Pickles watched as Turner appeared to be searching for a delicate way to say something indelicate.

"…that, hmm…" Turner dropped his head as he puzzled about how to word his next sentence.

Pickles said, "If it helps sir, please be frank."

Turner looked at his subordinate and said, "Yes, very well, I will. It would seem that the members of the committee would prefer to use the Dunsteth Valley for the new reservoir – er, whatever it takes."

Pickles raised his eyebrows and said, "Why sir?"

"It's something about the cubic capacity of the place and the topography of Blackstone Moor. It all gets a bit beyond me when the engineer bods start discussing displacement; angles of run-off, and venting and such like, but according to their combined surveys of everywhere within our district, Dunsteth fully fills the bill, whereas nowhere else does."

Pickles drew in a deep breath and said, "So it appears that we have a dilemma sir."

"Yes indeed, Joseph." He paused for a second as he looked into the eyes of his subordinate and then leaned forwards over his desk. "Can I speak to you in confidence?"

"Yes, of course sir."

"And I have your word that whatever we discuss will remain within these office walls?"

"You do sir."

"Very well; we, that is the committee and I, feel that you should be given special dispensation to encourage the departure of the Page family from the Malaterre Estate."

Pickles frowned and said, "I'm sorry sir; I don't fully grasp your meaning. I have been categorically informed by the Page family that they are not prepared to sell and I cannot see what I could do to change that."

"Ah, now we come to the 'special dispensation' part." Turner leaned over the desk and gestured for Pickles to lean closer.

Pickles conformed and put his head to one side half wondering if Turner was going to whisper.

"We – that is the committee and I, would refute any knowledge of what I am about to say; do you understand?"

Pickles frowned, but nodded and said, "Yes sir."

"Good, good. – Now, we want you to get the Page family out of Malaterre by whatever method you care to employ; foul or fair."

Pickles was shocked; on the one hand he had the Johnsons threatening his life whilst promising friendship and a cash bonus, and on the other, an 'on-the-face-of-it' respectable committee made up of the town's worthies giving him carte-blanche to adopt whatever method he wanted to achieve the same end.

He leaned back in his chair, and said, "This is highly irregular sir."

"Indeed it is my boy," said Turner, "but I suppose one should be flattered that the committee bestows such trust in you."

Pickles raised his eyebrows and said, "Now there's a convoluted form of flattery!"

"There's nothing convoluted about it," said Turner, "why, if the committee hadn't felt that they could entrust you with such a delicate proposal, they never would have. No Joseph, there's nothing convoluted about it at all." He paused to allow his words to sink in and then added, "Furthermore, I have been instructed to inform you that if you do succeed in this delicate endeavour, you will be rewarded. And make no mistake my boy, I mean handsomely!"

Pickles was astounded. Everybody appeared to be counting on him to get the Page family out of Malaterre. He thought about the situation for a few seconds and then said, "Might I be allowed to adopt any method necessary to achieve the requisite outcome?"

Turner balked at giving an outright sanction and said, "We – that is the committee and I, naturally don't condone anything illegal, but on the other hand, if we are not a party to the machinations of such a venture, or if indeed, such a venture had been effected prior to our knowledge, then it would be a case of closing the door after the horse had bolted, what? The end result would be the same."

An idea started to form in Pickles mind.

"And would you mind if I was able to go and visit my sick and aged Aunt for a couple of weeks, sir?" He touched the right-hand side of his nose with his right forefinger.

Turner saw the gesture and said, "Ah, yes – no, of course not dear boy," and then theatrically added, "Wasn't aware she was in such a bad way. When would be a prudent time to go?"

"I think that I should come in to work as normal next week, but it would be very convenient for me to er, visit the dear old thing for the following two weeks."

Turner nodded and said, "Whatever you think old chap." He got up, walked across to the office door, and held it open. As Pickles approached he said, "And don't worry about your pay whilst you're away, I'll square that with accounts."

Pickles smiled at Turner and said, "Thank you sir."

An hour later, he sat in a café with a toasted teacake and a hot cup of tea bemused by the events of the last hour. He'd been given complete autonomy, on full pay, had been given two weeks off work to do whatever he liked, and he'd been promised two financial bonuses – all for removing the Pages from of Malaterre.

The skeleton of a plan had started to take shape and although he hated the idea, he knew that he would have to return to Whitewall to speak to Abraham Johnson.

As he drank the last of his tea, the front doorbell of the café rang and a small man walked in. He weaved through the tables, and much to his surprise, plonked down next to him. He opened his mouth to say something, but then felt something sharp jab into his left side. He winced, looked down, and saw a knife pressed against waist, and then noticed that the man was an oriental.

"My name is Lice," said the man in a quiet, but pronounced Eastern accent, "Flied Lice – an' I'm a flend of Missa Ablaham and Missa Careb. They wanna know what you doin' 'bout bastards in Marraterre? An' don't go rookin' at knife or I stab you in a borrocks – got it?"

Pickles was shocked; nobody appeared to be paying any attention to them, and yet there he was sitting in a café in broad daylight with a knife jammed in his side. He remembered Abraham's warning about being watched all the time, and felt relieved that he had opted to go with them, instead of against them.

He turned to Lice and said, "Tell Abraham that I am going ahead with his request..."

Pickles felt the knife stick further into his side and winced even more.

"Show some fuckin' lespect office boy!" said Lice, "Issa Missa Ablaham to you!"

"Sorry, *Mister* Abraham I mean."

"Atsa betta," said Lice, "Now, what you say?"

"Please tell Mister Abraham that in order to proceed with his request; I need to know the name of his solicitor."

"Wha' you want that for?"

"I need to visit with him."

"Why?"

"That's none of your business Flied Lice…" the penny suddenly dropped as Pickles saw the amusing side to the name and he couldn't hold back a smile.

Lice caught sight of it and said, "You takin' a piss office boy? 'Cos a fuckin' cut you if you are…"

Pickles looked down at the man by his side and saw for the first time how menacing he appeared. He was short in stature, but exceptionally powerful looking and he had a deep scar around his neck, as though somebody had attempted to garrotte him at some time.

"No, I'm sorry, I'm not taking the piss, but please tell Mister Abraham what I said."

Lice stared into Pickles eyes for a few seconds longer, nodded, then slipped away from the table, and out of the door.

Chapter 14

2:00am Saturday 24th June 2006. The Dunsteth Reservoir

"Do you have any idea how much crap I could be in doing this for you?"

John Hess looked at his ex-Army buddy Rory Macready and said, "Yes, course I do, but I wouldn't have asked if I wasn't desperate."

"You must be to ask me to do this hare-brained number." Rory looked out of the jeep window, stared at the waning moon for a second, turned back to John, and said, "And it's hardly as black as a rook's arse out there either."

John looked out of the window and said, "It's not new moon until the twenty-sixth, but by then there'll be coppers crawling all over this place."

Rory wheeled around and said, "Coppers? You never said anything about coppers! Why would they be crawling all over here?"

John realised that he'd made a mistake in mentioning the police, but said, "Surely you've heard about the recent discovery haven't you?"

Rory frowned and said, "Come on, I only got back from Iraq last week; most of my time has been spent in de-briefing, shagging the missus, or sleep, so I've not had time to catch up on the news."

John looked at his watch and said, "Okay, but can we talk about it after you've finished?"

Rory said, "I'm not going in there if there's more to this than you're telling me, so just spit it out."

He sat listening as John apprised him of the bone discovery in the reservoir and then said, "So why do you want me to do this, won't it hamper the police investigation?"

John looked down at the floor of the jeep and then looked back into the eyes of his buddy.

"Because I got involved in something a bit illegal."

Rory said, "Go on…"

"Things had got a bit tough for me since leaving the unit and I agreed to be the driver of a van for a couple of guys who had stolen two antique Chinese urns."

Rory shook his head and said, "You tosser…"

"I know," said John, "anyway, they got the urns and put them in the back of the van, and all I had to do was to drive them to a location in Rochdale for which I would be paid five-hundred pounds. All went okay until the frigging van died a couple of hundred yards from here and it didn't matter what I tried, I couldn't get it started. Didn't help either 'cos the van was nicked."

Rory shook his head but said nothing.

"Anyway, I jumped out and did a quick reccie and found that I was near here; I saw a dinghy pulled up on the bank and figured that if I could get the urns into it and row it out to a safe distance, I could take three transits to log my position, then drop the buggers over the side and retrieve them at a later date."

"And how in hell would you have done that? You couldn't just attach lines and bloody marker buoys…"

"I know," said John, "but the water's not that deep round here, and I could have asked a couple of divers from the base…"

"Yeah right," said Rory, "and they'd just rock on up here and take part in your scam would they?"

John stopped speaking for a second and then said, "All right, maybe I wasn't thinking straight but I wasn't awash with options was I?"

Rory didn't answer; he just stared at John with a resigned look.

John stopped speaking, took in a deep breath, and said, "Anyway, all of that was beside the point because it hit the fan big time. First, because of my desperation to get the job done, I forgot to put the bung in the dinghy drain hole…"

Rory shook his head and said, "Oh for Christ sakes…"

"…and it started to fill with water. Then, I hit something, which I now know was part of the sunken buildings. Anyway, cutting a long story short, the whole damned kit and caboodle sank, except the oars, which are what got the cops looking."

"And now you want me to demolish a part of it so that it buries the boat and the urns?"

"That's the general idea, yes."

"It's a bit extreme isn't? Why don't I just retrieve the urns for you? And wouldn't your partners-in-crime be a bit pissed off if they were destroyed?"

"Like I give a shit what they think! And apart from that they're huge; it would take two of you to get them up, and we don't have the time. When I manhandled them from the van to the dinghy I wasn't wearing any gloves, so I'm not taking chances with the police finding forensic evidence that could lead them to me or them, so they'll understand."

Rory raised his eyebrows and said, "If you say so."

John looked at his friend and said, "You're not having doubts now are you?"

"Course I am you mad bastard – I had doubts the minute you asked me, but that's not what we're about is it? And you know that I can't ever repay you for what you did for me in the Lebanon."

"So you'll do it?"

"Yes – now help me get the gear on!"

Whilst helping Rory with the scuba gear John explained where he believed the boat to have gone down, and which elevation of the building would be best to destroy in order to cover it up. He strapped the bottles to Rory's back and said, "How are you going to do it?"

"Building implosion."

John said, "Christ – does that mean you'll have to go inside to do it?"

"No, nothing like that; building implosion is something of a misnomer but it's the term used commercially for, quote, the strategic timing and placing of explosive materials so that a structure collapses on itself within a matter of seconds."

"Right – and what will you be using, plastic?"

"No, PETN – it's as good as it gets for underwater demolition."

John frowned and said, "PETN?"

"Pentaerythrite Tetranitrate, it's a highly sensitive and very powerful military explosive comparable to nitro-glycerine, but far more stable."

John nodded, scanned the surrounding area, and then helped his buddy to the water's edge.

Rory sat down, pulled on his flippers, and said, "Okay, pass me the blasting caps and demolition charges…"

John handed over the equipment and watched as Rory waded into the water.

Seconds later he was gone from view and the only things that could have been seen to give away his presence were the sporadic bubbles that rose to the surface and popped.

Just after 3:15am, John's tense watchfulness was disturbed as he heard the sounds of Rory returning; the surface of the water became disturbed and then he saw his friend rise up from the depths. He ran to the water's edge watching and listening all the time.

Rory waded up to dry land and pulled his facemask off.

"It's done," he said.

John patted him on the back and grinned.

"Excellent," he said, "now let's get you back to the jeep."

Twenty minutes later John looked out of the window and said, "It'll be daybreak soon, we need to get out of here."

Rory glanced up and said, "Nearly done." He connected the detonator and said, "Okay, we can either do this here, or whilst we're on our way."

John looked at his buddy and said, "I'd like to see it done with my own eyes, so if it's okay with you we'll stay."

"Fine, but we need to get a move on, the longer we're here, the more chance there is of being seen."

John picked up his binoculars and said, "Right, hang on a mo." He checked the surrounding area then turned to Rory and said, "Okay, all clear – do it."

Rory switched on the transmitter, extended the short aerial, and pressed the button.

The first reaction from the reservoir was a deep muffled *"Whump!"* followed by a massive burst of droplets erupting just above the surface; next the epicentre of the explosion caused the water to drop and then suddenly erupt in a disturbed mushroom shape that heaved the surface upwards in a boiling mass. Seconds later, a shock wave similar to a mini-tsunami radiated outwards across the reservoir.

"Okay," said Rory, "job done, let's get out of here."

John switched on the engine, smiled across to his friend and said, "Cheers mate!" He rammed the jeep into gear and then drove them away from the churning, and quickly-discolouring water.

In the dam monitoring station at the western end of the reservoir, the water pressure graphs recorded a massive spike at 3:40am, and then a diminishing pattern of disturbance until returning to normal at 4:12am.

Apart from the graphs, the only evidence to show that something catastrophic had happened was the number of dead fish floating near the old buildings.

At approximately the same time, at Naomi and Carlton's house, Naomi's eyes shot open and she lifted up her head. She could tell from the edge of the lined curtains that dawn had arrived, but the thickness of them blocked out most of the daylight. She'd been convinced that she'd heard a sound downstairs, but being mindful that she'd disturbed Carlton with her nightmare a week earlier, she held her peace and listened.

Although their house was in an urban area, it wasn't close to a main road, and whilst it was possible to hear the odd vehicle every now and then, it was usually very quiet after midnight.

Following a minute or so's intense listening, Naomi lowered her head to her pillow and was about to close her eyes when she heard a faint cough outside. She raised her head again and listened. From somewhere down the street, she heard the engine of a vehicle switch on, and a door close. She slipped out of bed, pulled the left-hand curtain to one side, and saw the rear end of a vehicle turn out of their road.

Her heart rate increased and she frowned as she thought that she recognised the large, dark looking van from the encounter near Dunsteth. She watched it disappear around the corner and then walked out onto their landing and looked down towards their front door. A small piece of paper was lying on the mat.

She walked downstairs, picked it up and looked at it. One side was blank, on the other was written the single word, "hive."

Chapter 15

*Monday 26th June 2006. The Historic Research
Department, Walmsfield Borough Council*

Sitting in her parked car in the multi-storey employee car park
at the Walmsfield Borough Council offices, Naomi opened her
purse and looked at the strange note that she'd found on her
hall floor. She'd opted not to tell Carlton until she'd run it past
Helen but wondered what she would have to say about her
receiving yet another one-word conundrum.

She was well aware of how good Helen was at solving
puzzles after she'd solved most of the two 'contrivances' that
the 19th century Valentine Chance had set for his kin in their
previous investigation – and she looked forward to seeing what
she would make of the latest discovery. The only, but by no
means small, caveat was that whoever had delivered the note
now knew where she lived, and although she wondered if she
was being a paranoiac, she harboured a huge suspicion that the
van she'd seen driving away was the same one that she'd seen
on the way to Dunsteth.

She put the note back into her purse, opened her handbag
to put the purse in, and saw what a tight squeeze it would be
because her fold-up shopping bag was occupying a lot of the
limited space. She removed the shopping bag, placed it in her
glove compartment, shut it, and put her purse into her handbag.
She then stepped out of her car, locked it, and walked across to
her office.

Just before 9am she entered, bid Helen a 'good morning',
and sat down. Before saying anything, she opened her desk
drawer, removed the piece of paper with the word 'Brahma'
written upon it, and saw that it was the same type of notepaper
as the one in her purse. She looked up, opened her mouth to

speak, and then noticed the answer-machine next to her phone. She said, "Good grief!"

Helen looked up and said, *"What?"*

"We've got fourteen new messages on voicemail."

"Is that unusual?"

"Fourteen?" said Naomi, "It certainly is; I'm surprised when I find any more than six or eight – but fourteen?"

Helen raised her eyebrows and said, "Well you'd better grab your desk pad and start writing."

Naomi removed her desk pad from the top of her in-tray, made herself comfortable, and switched on the answer machine.

Messages one-to-seven were received between close of business on the previous Friday to 4:30pm on the Saturday, and were general enquiries. She then pressed the button and moved onto the next message. It stated,

'Message eight, received 6:15am, Sunday, 25th June.
Hi Naomi – Bob Crowthorne here, could you call me as soon as you get into your office Monday morning please. It's urgent. Thanks, bye.'

"That sounds serious," said Helen.

Naomi said, "Hmm," and pressed the switch to access the next message.

'Message nine, received 7:35am, Sunday, 25th June.
Naomi, Bob Crowthorne again, you'll probably be getting a message from the officials at Dunsteth Reservoir soon. Please talk to me before you speak to them. Thanks.'

Naomi glanced at Helen but didn't comment. She pressed the switch again.

'Message ten, received 8:21am, Sunday, 25th June.
Naomi, Stephen here, something major's happened at Malaterre. Can't explain over the phone. We need to meet. Call me please.'

Naomi made a mental note to give Stephen her personal mobile number. She pressed the button again.

'Message eleven, received 10:43am, Sunday, 25th June.
"Message for Mrs. Naomi Wilkes; this is Hugh Kearns of the Underwater Search Unit – Naomi, we need to talk about a new development, please contact me at the mobile number on the card I gave you. Thanks.'

"Crikey!" said Helen, "What on earth has happened?"
Naomi shrugged her shoulders and said, "No idea." She pushed the button again.

'Message twelve, received 3:47pm, Sunday 25th June.
This is Superintendent Kevin Middleton from the Dunsteth Reservoir Control Office; could you please give me a call when you can. Sorry I couldn't leave a direct number, but I could be anywhere on site. If you call our central switchboard they'll transfer your call to me. Thanks.'

'Message fourteen, received 8:35am, Monday 26th June.
Hi Naomi, Bob Crowthorne; give me a call ASAP please.'

"Something's definitely gone on, that's for sure!" said Helen.
Naomi looked up at Helen with a frown on her face.
"Hmm – intriguing," she said.
"You bet," said Helen, "I wonder what it is?"
"Not what's gone on at Malaterre," said Naomi with a frown still on her face, "but here."
"Here?"
"Yes, here."
"I don't understand."
"Our answer-machine jumped from message twelve to message fourteen."
It was Helen's turn to frown; she said, "Are you sure?"

"Positive," said Naomi, "here, listen…" She rewound the messages until it stopped at message twelve, played the dialogue, and then pressed the button once more. The machine announced, *'Message fourteen…'*

"Perhaps it doesn't have the facility to play a message thirteen," said Helen.

Naomi looked at her colleague and said, "Maybe…"

"There are lots of things that don't include the number thirteen, and though I think it's a load of superstitious mumbo-jumbo, it's not that unusual."

Naomi continued to stare at the answer-machine for a couple of seconds longer and then said, "Nevertheless, we need to check it out."

"Okay," said Helen, "but you'd better call all of those people first."

Naomi nodded and said, "Okay, I'll ring Bob first, can you go down to the drinks dispenser and get us a couple of teas?"

Helen agreed and left the office to get the drinks.

Naomi sat back in her chair and listened; the thumb had started pressing down on her shoulder and she knew that something was amiss.

She recalled how only a couple of months earlier, a trusted friend and colleague named Charlotte, who'd been working with her on a previous case, had been discovered leaking information about their investigation in return for money, and though she trusted Helen implicitly, the previous experience had left a scar.

She waited for something to come to her, but when nothing happened, she realised that she hadn't heard much of anything lately. She'd heard the sporadic comments from the French female, but it was almost as though whoever it was was watching over her and assessing what was going on.

She replayed message fourteen, and made a note of the time that Bob Crowthorne had called her, 8:35am, and then deleted it. Next she dialled her office number from her mobile and waited until her voicemail announcement informed her that nobody was there to take the call, and to leave a message. She said, "Me testing," and switched her mobile off.

She waited until she'd heard her answer machine complete its recording and then switched it on to replay the messages; she scrolled through to the end of message twelve, and pressed the button once again. It stated;

'Message thirteen, received 9:23am, Monday, 26th June. Me testing.'

The hair stood up on the back of her neck as she realised that somebody must have entered her office between 3:47pm on Sunday the 25th, and 8:35am that morning.

Suddenly, the French female voice returned and said, *'Votre collègue. Ne pas lui faire confiance...'*

The door to the office opened and Helen walked in with their teas.

"Did you ring Bob?" she said.

Naomi could have spit; she sat back in her chair, snatched up her pen and wrote down, 'Votre colleg. Ne pa looey fair', but then she faltered, for try as she may, she couldn't recall the last word.

"Well?" said Helen placing a tea in front of Naomi, "Did you ring him?"

"What is 'Votre colleg. Ne pa looey fair?'" said Naomi.

Helen frowned and said, "What? – Say it again."

"Votre colleg. Ne pa looey fair."

Helen stopped and thought for a couple of seconds and then said, "Where on earth did that come from?"

Naomi realised that this was the time to tell Helen about her psychic experiences. She sat back in her chair and said, "Okay, I have something to tell you..."

She asked Helen to try to accept what she was saying and to not dismiss it as 'mumbo-jumbo'. She explained how it had all started as far back as 2002 when she had first begun to investigate her great, great, great Aunt Maria's papers and her claim to the Whitewall Estate, and how it had never left her since. She told her about a few of the inexplicable experiences, and about how those around her, including the sceptical Bob Crowthorne, had over time, begun to accept that they couldn't be dismissed out of hand. Finally, she told her about the French-speaking lady who'd been passing on messages that she couldn't understand.

Helen sat with a shocked, but curious look upon her face. She said, "So on all of those occasions when I've seen you acting oddly, such as when that 'apparent bee' flew past your face in my old office at The Vical Centre, and we saw nothing – that was you experiencing 'things'?"

Naomi nodded and said, "Yes, I'm afraid so."

"Afraid so?" said Helen, "I don't know why you'd say that, lots of people would love to be able to experience what you do – me included."

Naomi breathed a sigh of relief knowing that her friend and work colleague had accepted what she'd said.

"It isn't all good," she said, "but I do feel privileged to have this."

Helen nodded and said, "Perhaps you can tell me more over lunch or something, but first, what was it that you said again – and was that one of your messages?"

"Not so much a message, more a statement," said Naomi, "and I don't know from whom, but I believe it's associated with our investigation into Malaterre."

Helen closed her eyes for a second and then said, "Wait a minute; I have to get my head around a couple of things. If you're in dialogue with entities from the other side, why can't you just ask the person who he or she is – and, if he or she…"

"She," interrupted Naomi.

"…okay – if she is linked to Malaterre, why didn't she contact you prior to this, say, two or three years ago when you first started experiencing these phenomena? Surely there are no time constraints. So why has she waited until now?"

"Firstly, I'm not 'in dialogue' with the entities as you put it, I only hear what's being said…"

"What, like somebody talking to you?"

"No, I don't physically hear anything, it's as though somebody made a statement in the immediate past that I can still hear in my head."

Helen nodded and said, "Okay – I think that I can get that, but what about the time thing; if you are a person, being, entity, or whatever on the 'other side', surely you aren't constrained by time like we are?"

"No I don't suppose that they are, but *I* am. I'm not ethereal, I do have time constraints, and if whoever is trying to contact me wants my help with something, they have to wait for me to be somewhere, or to know what they are talking about, or maybe get to know somebody first, or whatever, because if they speak to me about things I have no idea about, none of it would make sense."

"Ah, I think I get it now," said Helen, "so they have to wait for you to be in a position to be able to understand what they want first?"

"Yes, or at least that is my understanding of the whole thing."

Helen nodded and said, "Okay – so what was that French message again?"

Naomi looked down at her pad and said, "It sounded like, 'Votre colleg. Ne pa looey fair', plus something else that I can't recall."

"And couldn't you just tune in and ask the French woman to repeat it?"

"No, I think that she understands me, but maybe that's because she has an insight into a multi-dimensional future…"

Helen gasped and said, "Whoa N, – I can see that you and I are going to be having a lot of interesting conversations in the days to come…"

Naomi said, "I guess so, but up until now I haven't been able to question anybody about anything." She hesitated and then said, "Look, we'll talk in more detail later, but for now, have you any idea what that statement meant?"

Helen looked down at her pad and said, "From the way that you've written it down, I think that whoever it was, was trying to say, *'Votre collègue. Ne pas lui faire'*."

"And what is that exactly?"

" *'Votre collègue'*, – 'Your colleague', *'Ne pas lui faire'*. – 'Do not make it', or perhaps, 'not to do', or something like that."

Naomi frowned and repeated, "Your friend – do not make it, or, not to do? It doesn't make sense."

"No," said Helen, "but then again you did say that you'd heard more…"

"True."

"…and that could make a whole load of difference to the sentence construction and meaning."

"So I'm no better off knowing then?"

"I wouldn't say that – the first part of the message wasn't open for misinterpretation. Your French lady told you that the message was referring to 'your colleague'."

Naomi shrugged and said, "Huh, so that's as clear as mud then? It could be anybody."

"True, but intriguing nevertheless."

Naomi looked down and caught sight of the answer-machine. She said, "Yes – that and our voicemail."

Helen frowned and said, "What about it?"

"While you were out of the office I checked it – and it *is* capable of creating a message thirteen."

Chapter 16

Walmsfield Historic Research Department

Naomi glanced up at the clock on her wall and noted that it was 9:45am. Following her conversation with Helen, she decided to call Superintendent Crowthorne before attending to the other voicemail messages. She reached for her phone, started to dial his number, when it rang. She switched it on and put it to her ear.

"Walmsfield Historic…"

"Naomi, Bob Crowthorne here. Sorry to interrupt you, but there's been an unusual development at Dunsteth Reservoir."

"What kind of development?"

"Part of the old Malaterre building appears to have collapsed."

Naomi couldn't believe her ears; she said, "What? How much?"

"We haven't established that yet, but Inspector Kearns is down there with his team this morning to reconnoitre."

"But how could that have happened?" said Naomi.

"We have formed an opinion but it's too early to air it, though I must say, if our suspicion proves to be right, it would have serious consequences for this investigation."

Naomi looked across the office and saw Helen frowning; she covered the mouthpiece of the phone and whispered, "Part of Malaterre has collapsed!" She saw the look of shock appear on Helen's face and then continued her dialogue with Crowthorne.

"Are you telling me that you suspect foul play?"

Crowthorne paused and then said, "I'm sorry Naomi, it's too early to say."

"So – do you need anything from me?"

"That's why I called. We need a list of everybody you've been speaking to with regard to Malaterre, and I do mean everybody; that includes office staff, your friend Percy Johns, Postcard Percy I think you call him; his acquaintances, your personal friends, and anybody else you can think of."

"This sounds a bit over-the-top Bob – just because part of the old building has collapsed."

Crowthorne considered his words and then said, "Very well, because of your unique position I'm happy to divulge more to you, but for now it has to be for your ears only; is that understood?"

Naomi said, "Yes."

"There's an outside possibility that a body may be down there."

Naomi sat back in her seat and said, "Considering our find, I'd have thought that was a high possibility!"

"No," said Crowthorne, "I don't mean a historical body, I mean a recent one."

Naomi was stunned; she said, "No! Have you any idea whose?"

"Whoa, wait," said Crowthorne, "I didn't say that there *was* a body down there, I said that there is the outside possibility of one being down there."

"But what's happened to make you suspect that?"

"I'm sorry Naomi, I'm not at liberty to say anymore, and indeed I may have already overstepped the mark by saying what I did, so please help me now by gathering as much information as you can."

Naomi agreed, said 'goodbye' and put the phone down. She sat back in her chair and looked at the honest and inquisitive face of Helen and decided to confide in her.

"All right," she said, "Bob asked me to keep this to myself but..." She told Helen everything that had passed between them and then extracted a promise from her not to let it go any further.

Helen agreed and then said, "Are you going to tell him how you feel about Stephen, and about the French 'voices'?"

Naomi rankled and said, "What do you mean, 'how I feel about Stephen'? I don't feel anything about him!"

"You know what I mean," said Helen, "your special relationship with him."

Naomi frowned and said, "Hey, let's get this straight, there is nothing between…"

Suddenly the thumb pressed down on her shoulder and a voice said, *'Nous sommes libres…'* She stopped speaking and stared into space waiting for more.

Helen realised that something unusual was happening and stared in silence at her friend.

A few seconds later, Naomi looked at Helen and said, "What is *'nous sommes libres'*?

Helen said, "Shit, did you just hear that?"

"Yes – what does it mean?"

"*'Nous sommes libres'* means, 'we are free'."

The hair stood up on the back of Naomi's neck; she looked at Helen and saw that she was experiencing the same thoughts.

"Are you thinking what I'm thinking?" she said.

"Malaterre?"

"Yes," said Naomi, "We've got to get down there."

"To do what?"

"I don't know – we've just got to get down there."

Helen said, "Wait N, I know that all of your instincts are urging you to head down there right now, but in reality, we could be more effective staying here and calling people."

Naomi stared at Helen for a few seconds and then said, "Okay, you're probably right, but, after we've made the calls, we're going down there, and no arguing!"

Helen agreed and said, "Who do you want me to call?"

Naomi gathered her thoughts and despite an irrational desire to call Stephen herself, which made a mockery about there being nothing special between them, said, "You call Stephen Page and try to arrange a time today, when we can meet him at Dunsteth Reservoir."

Helen nodded and reached for her phone.

Naomi picked up hers and dialled Bob Crowthorne.

"Crowthorne."

"Bob, it's Naomi here."

"Yes Naomi, how can I help you?"

"I've heard one of my voices again." There was an extended pause on the line and she knew that Crowthorne would be wrestling with his cold, hard logic. She heard him say, "Okay, what have you heard?"

"It's not what I heard that's important, it's what it implies."

"All right – but first please tell me what you heard."

"Nous sommes libre."

Once again there was a pause on the line and then Crowthorne said, "You heard that?"

"Yes."

"In French?"

"Yes."

"And did you understand it?"

"Not at first, but Helen deciphered it for me."

Crowthorne said, "Helen?"

"Yes Helen Milner, she works with me now at Walmsfield; she was the conservator who helped me with the Cragg Vale investigation a few weeks ago."

"From the Vical Centre?"

"Yes, we work together now."

"Ah," said Crowthorne, "and she speaks French does she?"

"Yes."

"Then you'll know that the voice said, 'We are free'?"

"Yes."

Crowthorne expelled a long humming sound and then said, "And of course you are somehow linking this to the Malaterre investigation and the Tascher de La Pagerie connection?"

"How else would you explain it?"

"You know my scepticism about that type of thing..." Crowthorne paused for a few seconds and then said, "But, having said that, I – I don't suppose it would do any harm to take on board outside possibilities."

Naomi remained silent until she realised that Crowthorne wasn't going to expand further, and then said, "So what do you propose now, with my extra bit of info?"

Crowthorne expelled a *'pah'* that sounded dismissive and he realised that he might have upset Naomi; he tried to cover it up by apologising and saying that he was blowing on a hot coffee.

Naomi remained silent.

Crowthorne reasserted himself and said, "I'm sorry, I don't mean to be offensive, but three French words that you heard in your head doesn't constitute new evidence."

Naomi took offence and said, "I thought that we were getting past this, Bob!"

"I'm trying, I really am; but I have to deal in practicalities. I can't be questioned at some time in the future by the press or by one of my superior officers and justify my actions by psychic messages."

"Why not? There have been lots of instances where psychics have helped the police in the past."

Crowthorne faltered and then said, "All right, let's just say for a minute that I do believe you, and everything that the message could imply. What are you suggesting that I do?"

"Drain the reservoir."

The three small words had a stunning effect on both Helen and Crowthorne. Naomi saw Helen spin round and look at her with an incredulous look upon her face, but was then distracted by hearing Crowthorne gasp, *"What?!"*

"You heard me – drain the reservoir."

"Have you any idea of the enormity of that?" said Crowthorne.

Naomi remained silent.

"We're talking about water diversion and management, weeks of planning, a full scale police operation that would cost thousands of pounds, and upon completion of our investigation, re-stocking the reservoir." He paused and then said, "And all because you heard a voice say, *'nous sommes libres'*?"

Naomi listened patiently and then said, "You know that it isn't just the Tascher de La Pagerie thing. There's the bone, the mysterious oars, and your…"

"Just a minute Naomi," interrupted Crowthorne, "somebody's knocking at my door."

Naomi heard muffled voices on the other end of the phone, and then she heard Crowthorne say, "Very well, keep me informed." There was a brief pause and she heard him say, "You still there?"

"Yes," said Naomi, anxious to resume what she was saying, "and to get…"

"Wait a minute," said Crowthorne, "before you go any further, there's been another development at this end."

"Yes?"

"Yes, you recall the oars that were discovered at the reservoir two days ago?"

"Yes."

"Following their discovery we put out an enquiry to see if there were any reports of missing persons from outside of our area, and one just came back.

"A lady named Julia Probus reported her son Max missing five days ago to the Greater Manchester force. According to Mrs. Probus, her son was in the habit of telephoning her every day and visiting her every Tuesday, but on June the fifteenth the calls stopped. Furthermore, her son didn't visit her last Tuesday either. She reported that she'd called her son's wife, one, er…Rosalind Probus, and was told that her son had gone on a business trip to Europe and would be back within a week, but when she phoned her son's office, nobody knew anything about the trip, and nobody had seen him since Monday the fourteenth either. So, she called the Greater Manchester force and reported him missing."

"And has he shown up?"

"No, and suspiciously enough," said Crowthorne, "the Manchester force received a missing person's enquiry from Mr. Probus's secretary, but they've heard nothing from his wife. They sent an officer round to see her, but he reported that the family home appeared to be deserted, so now a notice has been sent out to all UK exit points to apprehend her if she attempts to leave. "

"Ooh, suspicious indeed," said Naomi, "but what relevance does this have on our investigation at the Dunsteth Reservoir?"

"The Probus household is just two miles from there."

Naomi stopped, drew in a deep breath, and said, "So now will you consider draining the reservoir?"

Crowthorne hesitated and then said, "I don't know. I'll have a word with Inspector Kearns and see what he advises, but given the new developments, it's not now out of the question."

As Naomi put down the phone she looked up at Helen and said, "Bob may do it..."

"Why? That sounded like one hell of an ask to me!"

"Because they've received a report of a missing person from a property located a couple of miles from the reservoir."

Helen said, "It's still a big ask; when people go missing, the police don't normally consider draining reservoirs as a first resort."

"No," said Naomi, "but with everything else that's going on..." she recalled the pieces of paper and reached down for her handbag, "...the case for draining it has got to be mounting."

She saw Helen nod, extracted the note, placed it under the one with 'Brahma' written upon it and pushed them across to her. "Here," she said, "I know how much you like these."

Helen picked up the notes, looked at the first, and then saw the second; she said, "My God – you've got another?"

"Yes, it was pushed through my letterbox at home in the early hours of Saturday morning."

None of the seriousness of the situation was lost on Helen, she said, "Please tell me that you've told Carlton and Bob Crowthorne?"

"No I haven't, I..."

"N, said Helen, "are you crazy?"

"I thought..."

"No, you didn't think," said Helen, "because if you had you would have done exactly that!"

Naomi put her hands in the air and said, "Okay, okay, perhaps it was silly of me, but I wanted to let you see them first."

"Sometimes I wonder about you;" said Helen. "You do realise that the very act of pushing a note through your own front door for Christ's sake, is a loud and clear message saying, *'I know where you live!'*"

"Yes I do, and I will tell Carlton and Bob as soon as you've looked at the pieces of paper and stopped lecturing me!"

Helen recalled that apart from being a good friend, Naomi was still her boss; she said, "Okay, as long as you know that my frustration is only because I care…"

"I know that, and I'm sorry if I'm causing you any stress, but I know that you're good with puzzles, so what do you make of the latest one?"

Helen looked at both pieces of paper and said, "Same paper, different pen, different handwriting."

Naomi hadn't considered those points; she said, "Let me see."

Helen pushed the notes back.

Naomi studied them and then said, "Same paper, different pen, but could the person who wrote these have swapped hands to write one?" She pushed the notes back to Helen.

"And thereby leaving us to assume that we're dealing with more than one person? Interesting."

Even though she'd mooted the idea, Naomi wasn't happy about it; she kept seeing images of the retreating van and likening it to the one she'd had the bad experience with on the way to Dunsteth. She looked at Helen and said, "There may be something else too…"

She explained the encounter and watched with concern as Helen's exasperation level rose.

"And you thought it best to keep this to yourself too?" said Helen.

Naomi opened her mouth to speak but was cut off.

"And you didn't think it in the least suspicious that the men just happened to have a couple of Halloween masks to put on?"

Naomi looked down and said, "I…"

"No, don't," said Helen, "let's not even go there. From this very second on, we will do everything – absolutely everything, by the book. We'll adopt the principals that we learnt as researchers; we'll record each and every event, happening, find, and experience as it happens, and we'll leave nothing out." She paused and looked at Naomi as though she was chastising a wayward child. "And," she said, "we won't keep any secrets from those who should know, including each other! Agreed?"

Naomi looked up and said, "Agreed."

Helen stared angrily at Naomi for a few seconds and then looked back at the second note. She saw the word 'hive' written upon it and said, "That's interesting too." She pushed the note back to Naomi and said, "On the first note the word 'Brahma' is written with an upper case 'B' but the word 'hive' has a lower case 'h'."

Naomi looked at the note and said, "That's because Brahma is the name of the Hindu God."

"A noun, yes," said Helen, "but hive is a noun too, so why doesn't that have an upper case 'H'?"

Chapter 17

The young female receptionist from the front desk knocked,
entered the Estates Department, and walked across to Joseph
Pickles' desk.

"Begging your pardon sir," she said, "there's an oriental
gentleman in reception asking for you."

Pickles winced at the sound of 'oriental gentleman' and
gathered that it could be Lice. He nodded at the receptionist
and said, "Very well, tell him that I'll be down presently."

The girl looked awkward, and instead of walking away,
hovered by Pickles' desk.

Pickles frowned, turned in her direction, and said, "Was
there something else?"

"Begging your pardon again sir, the oriental gentleman
was very adamant that I urge you to come down straight
away."

Pickles stared at the girl in silence for a second and then
said, "Very well." He got up and followed her down to the
front desk, and saw Lice loitering in a quiet corner. He glanced
around, saw that he wasn't attracting any attention, and then
sidled up to him.

"You took your fuckin' time office boy!" said Lice in an
aggressive way.

"What do you want?" said Pickles.

"You gotta appointmen' with Missa George Hubert, a
soricitor in Hyde, rater 'is mornin' got it?"

Pickles frowned and said, "I'm sorry, what did you say?"

Lice turned to face Pickles, took a couple of steps closer
and grabbed hold of his penis and testicles.

Pickles tried to recoil as Lice applied the pressure.

"You fuckin' heard me office boy, George Hubert, soricitor, in Hyde at ereven-thirty sharp. Got it?"

Pickles nodded.

Lice stared at his hapless victim for a couple of seconds longer and let go. He then checked to see that he hadn't attracted any unwanted interest, and disappeared out of the front door.

Pickles straightened his face and his attire and then turned to head back to his office. He saw the young receptionist looking at him in an odd manner, but he ignored the inquisitive looks, nodded at her as he strode past, and went back to his office.

Ten minutes later he looked at Turner's office door and decided upon a positive approach. He got up, walked over to it, and knocked.

"Come," called Turner from inside.

Pickles entered, closed the door, and walked across to his superior's desk.

Turner looked up and said, "Ah, Joseph, what can I do for you?" He winked and said, "Not about your sick Aunt is it?"

"No sir, I have an appointment with a solicitor in Hyde at eleven-thirty this morning."

Turner looked at his pocket-watch and then at Pickles with a puzzled expression on his face. He said, "And of what significance is this to me?"

"It's in connection with the Malaterre estate."

Turner replaced his watch in his waistcoat pocket and said, "Ah, right – and what has a solicitor in Hyde got to do with this?"

"He's the Johnson's solicitor sir, and I want him to inform the Messrs. Johnson that legally, there is nothing that he, or we, can do to make the Page family reconsider their decision to sell Malaterre."

Turner sat back in his chair and reached for his tobacco pipe; he extracted a match from a small desk container, struck it, and lit the leaf. Through one or two clouds of scented tobacco smoke, he said, "And you think that this will help do you, Joseph?"

"To use the vernacular sir, it will certainly put the cat amongst the pigeons…"

Turner nodded and looked down; he considered what he'd been told, then looked back up and said, "Very well. Thank you, Joseph."

Pickles stood in silence waiting for more, but when he realised that he'd been dismissed, said, "I thought…"

"Yes, thank you Joseph…" interrupted Turner, "…it is considerate of you to keep me abreast of ongoing developments, but as far as your sick and elderly relative is concerned, I am aware of your tragic circumstances and it won't be necessary to involve me any further."

Pickles looked blankly at his superior for a few seconds longer until the penny dropped. He said, "Yes sir, thank you sir," and walked out.

At 4:30pm George Hubert knocked on the front door of the Whitewall Estate, he heard the sound of approaching footsteps, and braced himself.

The door opened and Abraham Johnson said, "George, what are you doing here?"

"I need to talk to you about something."

Abraham raised his eyebrows and said, "It sounds serious – you'd better come in." He led Hubert into the parlour and said, "I'll go and get us a beer each while you sit yourself down."

Hubert said, "Thank you Abe – that would be most agreeable."

A few minutes later, Abraham re-appeared with two beers, placed one in front of Hubert, and said, "If it's that serious, should Caleb be present?"

Hubert had a deep-seated fear of Caleb; despite having an explosive temper, Abraham could for the most part be amiable and approachable, but not Caleb. It took nothing to make him surly and ill tempered. He felt that his hold on life was right on the edge each time that he was with him, and that if he made one wrong move, or said the wrong thing, it would be curtains. And the dreadful injury that he had sustained to his left leg after being attacked by Sugg, his monstrous and bad-tempered dog, hadn't made him a less dangerous man; it had turned him into a foul-tempered, sadistic, and heartless brute that would kill for no more than a wrong look.

He looked across to Abraham and said, "It might be the most practical thing to do."

Abraham nodded, and then disappeared. Five minutes later he re-appeared with a suspicious looking Caleb and another beer; he said, "Right, sit yourself down lad, and let's hear what George has got to tell us."

Hubert looked with apprehension at the Johnsons and got straight to the point; he said, "The Page family won't move out of Malaterre."

A surreal sort of silence descended upon the room and then almost too calmly, Abraham said, "Say again George."

Hubert cleared his throat and said, "I'm sorry to be the bearer of such bad tidings gentlemen, but the Page family have opted to stay put at Malaterre."

"And who told you that?" said Abraham.

"A Mr. Joseph Pickles from the Hundersfield District Council Estates Office."

Abraham lowered his head, looked at Caleb, looked back at Hubert, and said, "Oh he did, did he?"

"Yes Abe."

Abraham nodded but remained quiet as he pondered.

Hubert felt the tension in the room rise, and decided that then was a good time to leave.

"Right then gents," he said rising up from of his seat, "I do have other calls to make, so if you'll forgive me…"

Abraham said, "Stay where you are and finish your beer."

Hubert faltered and sat back down. He picked up the tankard, quaffed the last of the beer, and then looked from face to face. He said, "Look, I'd like to help but…"

"But you won't," cut in Abraham.

"It's not a case of that Abe, you know that my…"

"I know that I pay you a lot of money to watch my back and get my legal problems sorted," said Abraham.

"And this isn't a legal problem, this is…"

"This is a fucking balls-up, that's what it is!"

Hubert drew in a deep breath and wanting to keep matters calm said, "Abe, I know that you and Caleb want to sell Dunsteth, and I know that Hundersfield District Council want to buy it, but…"

"So fucking sort it out!" said Abraham.

"There is nothing to sort out! If the Page family refuse to sell Malaterre, there is nothing that we or Hundersfield District Council can do about it!"

Abraham slammed his fist onto the parlour table and shouted, "And what do we pay you for – to piss away our chances whilst they have you dancing round like an organ-grinder's monkey?"

Hubert shifted back in his seat; he knew how dangerous it was to cross either of the Johnson men, and both were sitting in the parlour glowering at him. He cast a furtive glance in the direction of Caleb and saw his ice-cold, pale blue eyes boring into him and it felt as though an ethereal tendril reached across the room and threatened him with the direst and cruellest of consequences if he looked at him for one second longer.

He dropped his gaze and then turned to face Abraham.

"It, it's not as simple as that…" he said.

"Yes it is!" bellowed Abraham, "You get those frog-eating bastards out of there, or we'll do it for you!"

Hubert closed his eyes; the monthly stipend from the Johnsons was a generous and welcome one under normal circumstances, but when they wanted their pound of flesh, refusal wasn't an option. Solicitor or not, long-term personal advisor or not, and notwithstanding nearly one-hundred years of loyal service to the Lincoln/Johnson family, he knew that not doing their bidding didn't just result in a terminated arrangement; it could result in unbelievable levels of pain and suffering.

The walls of the parlour appeared to advance whilst the door seemed to retreat. He called on the last of his withering reserves and said, "I have stood by you for years; I have supported you in all of your questionable endeavours, and with my help you have evaded all sorts of legal problems, but what you are asking me to do now is something out of my control. I cannot argue a legal point about their undisputed ownership and therefore their right of decision; it is theirs to make, and theirs alone."

Caleb turned and shifted forwards in his seat; he opened his mouth to speak, but saw his father point a finger at him, and was quelled in an instant.

Abraham turned to face Hubert and said, "And you've been paid well for everything that you do."

"Nevertheless," said Hubert, "I am restricted by things that can be achieved using the letter of the law, and as long as my position within the right side of it remains immutable I will always be in a position to help and advise you, but if you start requiring me to operate outside of it, you will turn me into a common criminal and ergo, weaken your own positions."

"Ergo him out the fucking door pa!" said Caleb, "We can…"

"Shut up boy!" yelled Abraham. "Speak when you're spoken to!"

Caleb sat back in his seat and said, "Sorry pa."

Abraham turned back to Hubert with venom in his eyes and said, "So that's it then, you refuse to help us?"

"No, of course not; I'll always help you, but it has to be within the law."

"Right," said Abraham with a snarl, "get out before I lose my temper."

Hubert looked at Abraham and gagged at the thought that this was he *before* losing his temper? He wasted no time, reached down for his leather briefcase and brought it up onto his lap.

"I'm sorry," he said.

"I said; *get out* before I lose my temper!"

Hubert stood up, nodded at the seething Caleb, and departed.

Outside in the yard, he clambered into the seat of the waiting Hansom cab and instructed the driver to head for Rochdale railway station.

With every distancing foot from Whitewall, the pressure lifted from his shoulders. He'd survived another encounter with the Johnsons, but he knew that the clock was ticking...

Back in the parlour, Caleb turned to his brooding father and said, "So what now pa?"

Abraham looked at his son with pure evil in his eyes, and said, "Get the old gang together; we've got a job to do."

Chapter 18

Naomi, Helen, and Crowthorne said their goodbyes to the marine surveyor and waited until Stephen accompanied him back to his car.

Naomi had introduced Stephen to Crowthorne and Helen, and they had listened with interest to Stephen's account of Malaterre and the Tascher de La Pageries, and during the conversation, Helen had ruffled Naomi's feathers by mouthing, "He's gorgeous!" to her.

Crowthorne waited until the men were out of earshot and said, "I have to agree with Helen about those notes and the incident with the two men in the van; you should have told me. What did Carlton have to say about it?" He looked at his watch and saw that it was 11:40am.

Naomi screwed up her face and said, "Not happy…"

Helen felt that a second chastisement was imminent and spared Naomi by saying, "So what do you think Superintendent; could the masked men be associated with the notes?"

"Highly likely."

"And have you formed any theories?"

"Not from what little we've got." He looked at Helen and said, "Weren't you the person who solved those old nineteenth century contrivances a few months ago?"

"I was, but 'El Fuego de Marte' could still be lying in the graveyard of St. Andrew's Church in Charleston for all we know."

"El Fuego de Marte," repeated Crowthorne, "The Fire of Mars. A grand name for a ruby that – I like it."

Out of the blue, Naomi felt a pressure on her left shoulder; she blinked and saw that she was looking out of a car windscreen. She was in the right-hand, front seat, but it was the passenger seat, and she could see that the car was light grey. To the left and right of her were low-hanging tree branches festooned in Spanish moss, and on the car radio she heard the words, *"the day that hell broke loose just north of Marietta, all along the Kennesaw line,"* in a distinctive country & western song.

"And the notes?" said Crowthorne to Helen, snapping Naomi out of her psychic episode.

"I agree with you that the van men and the notes could be linked, and I don't think that we have enough clues yet to work out what it's supposed to mean." She paused and then added, "But unless I'm mistaken, I don't think that it'll be long until we get some more. Someone appears to be trying to draw Naomi's attention to something, but whether it's ominous or not, is a different matter."

Crowthorne said, "What about you Naomi?"

Naomi had jotted down the lyrics of the country and western song with the intent of trying to find it on the internet later that evening and Crowthorne's question brought her back to the present. She said, "I've no idea, but if I get any more, I'll let you both know straightaway."

Crowthorne smiled and said, "Good." He looked up, saw Stephen returning, and waited until he'd joined them. He said, "Well that's it then, I don't suppose that we have much choice other than to drain the reservoir now do we?"

Before anybody could answer a white van with the logo 'United Utilities' emblazoned on the side pulled up close to Crowthorne's car. A uniformed man stepped out and walked across to them.

"Ladies, gentlemen," said the man, "I'm Kev Middleton the Rochdale Dam Superintendent, has the surveyor finished his initial inspection?"

Crowthorne introduced everybody and then said, "In answer to your question, the surveyor has had a quick look, but only from the surface. He used an underwater remote camera and has informed us that we aren't to go anywhere near the old building until the dam has been drained."

"Ooh that's a bugger," said Kev, "and did he say what caused the collapse?"

"He wouldn't elucidate."

Kev turned, stared across the water and said, "It's going to be a hell of a job." He continued to stare towards the dam for a few seconds longer, then turned back, rubbed his chin, and said, "Have you formulated any theories, Superintendent?"

Crowthorne had, but opted to keep his cards close to his chest. He said, "None that I'd care to air right now."

Kev made an 'Hmming' sound and looked back over the water.

"Have you got any theories, Kev?"

All eyes turned to Naomi.

Kev turned to look at Naomi and said, "Not as such, but I do have what you might call an oddity." He looked at the gathered faces and then said, "It was something that I noticed on the banks."

Nobody spoke.

Once again Kev looked from face-to-face and then said, "I've been hawking around this reservoir for longer than I care to remember and I've seen it in all sorts of conditions; low, overflowing, drought, and even drained when we were forced to effect some necessary maintenance work on the inner dam wall, and in all of my time here I've never seen such a high water mark as produced by this collapse.

"The bank inclines from five to forty-five degrees in some places, but the same as a harbour wall, you can always see evidence of where it got to through the bits of washed-up foliage and the like."

He looked at each fascinated face, and then continued, "But what went on last Saturday night defies all belief. I mean, I have no idea how much of that old building collapsed, but it must have been a bloody big chunk to create such a huge wave up the banks."

"That's pure conjecture though isn't it?" said Helen, "Look at the effect of tsunamis when undersea earthquakes occur."

"I take your point Miss," said Kev, "but a tsunami is generally created when a huge void is opened up in the ocean bed causing the sea to first to drop inside it, and then well back up with titanic force, or alternatively, when an earthquake drives a huge section of land upwards displacing the sea.

"What we have here is different. The submerged building had already displaced the water by volume, and almost regardless of how big a chunk had become detached, it was only falling down a relatively low distance, and through water."

"But that's also how tsunamis are caused; what about Santorini?"

Kev hesitated because he didn't want to get too drawn into a subject that he loved without being able to give it the time that it deserved. He looked at Helen and said, "The Santorini caldera is probably a bad example of what you're trying to say, but I take your drift. There have been many instances of land above the water being dislodged and crashing down through natural events, and they do cause tsunamis, but what we have here is different."

He looked around until he saw two similar sized stones and picked them up.

"Here, come with me," he said.

Everybody followed Kev to the water's edge.

"Now watch the ripples once I've thrown this first stone in." He threw the stone into the water a few feet away from where they were standing; it went in with a heavy *'plop'*. The water sunk over the top of the stone and then rose up, creating the small ripples that ensued.

"There's our 'Santorini' type tsunami. Now," he said holding up the other stone, "if I was to wade out into two feet of water, hold this stone just below the surface and let it go, do you think that we would re-create that?"

"I wouldn't have thought that we'd see any effect would we?" said Naomi.

"Precisely Miss," said Kev, "the stone has already displaced the water by volume and the viscosity of the water would slow the stone's descent too." He stopped and looked once again at the attentive faces and then said, "So it's much the same with the old building over there. I believe that the water isn't much above forty to fifty feet in depth at that point, and we have to assume by the size of the new high-water mark that it must have been a substantial piece to fall, but it couldn't have all come from the top of the old building, it must have fallen off in a kind of wedge, so that would have had two effects. One, it would have created less resistance as it fell through the water, and two, it may not have had that far to fall. So how in buggeration did it produce such a shock wave?"

Crowthorne, who already had his suspicions decided to bring the speculation in to check.

"That's an interesting theory, Superintendent…"

Kev looked around and said, "Please call me Kev, I'm comfier with that than the rank thing…"

"Very well, Kev, as I was saying, it's an interesting theory, and one that I shall put to my Marine Inspector when I next see him, but as you mooted earlier, it is still an oddity which will no doubt be resolved once we've been able to drain the reservoir."

"So you will do it then?" said Stephen.

"Yes sir," said Crowthorne, "it would seem that we have no other option."

Stephen looked down, thought for a minute, and then said, "Superintendent?"

Crowthorne and Kev both looked at him.

"Superintendent Crowthorne that is," he said, "I wonder if I might…"

The conversation was brought to a halt upon the approach of a boat; everybody turned around and saw the Marine Unit rib approaching at high speed. Within a few feet of the bank the engine was cut, the rib drifted up the shingle, and came to a halt. Hugh Kearns and a diver jumped out and walked up to the gathering.

"Afternoon chaps!" said Kearns, "Lovely day what?" He looked at Kev and said, "You're the Dam Superintendent fellah aren't you?"

"I am – Kev Middleton."

Kearns shook hands with Kev and pointed out across the reservoir, "Well I'm sorry to say old chap, but we'll need you to pull the plug out."

"If only it was as simple as that," said Kev.

Out of the corner of her eye Naomi saw a little boy chasing a dog. Several yards behind, a man was following and calling something indiscernible to the boy, but as they drew closer, his calls became more distinct.

"James!" shouted the man, "Don't go any further!"

Naomi watched, as the boy appeared to disregard the instruction and continue to chase the dog.

"James Anthony Hanna! Stop now and do as you're told!"

The boy turned and shouted something back.

"I don't care, stay where you are now or we'll go straight home!"

The altercation attracted everybody's attention and they all watched in silence as the boy stood still whilst the dog kept on running.

As it drew closer, Naomi could see that the dog was holding something in its jaws, but she became distracted as the man shouted again.

"Sit! Sit!"

The dog faltered, turned its head, and then started to run back to the man. As it passed the boy, he made a lunge for the object in its mouth, but the dog sidestepped and continued running until he got to the man's side. Once there he dropped the object, the man picked it up and threw it, and the dog set off again in pursuit.

Stephen tapped Crowthorne on the shoulder and said, "Superintendent, can I ask you something?"

Crowthorne turned away from the boy and the dog and said, "Of course Mr. Page."

"I am an experienced diver and rock climber; I have climbed all sorts of things from natural structures to manmade ones, and given my knowledge and attachment to Malaterre, I wondered if you would consider allowing me to be a part of the team that enters the building if indeed it would be safe to do so?"

The thumb pressed down on Naomi's shoulder and without hearing a single thing, she wanted to say, 'No!'

Crowthorne hesitated and then said, "I don't know Mr. Page," he shot a glance towards Kearns who shrugged and raised his eyebrows, "all of this is new to me and I doubt that I will end up choosing who will be on the team." He turned to Naomi and said, "And indeed we do have one other very experienced diver back at the station too…"

Naomi frowned but didn't speak.

"…and you know him."

Naomi said, "I do?"

"Yes, your old friend Leo."

"Good Lord," said Naomi, "I had no idea! But isn't he on…" she wavered as she considered her choice of words, but was beaten to it by Crowthorne.

"No, he has been assigned to C.I.D. at H.Q."

Naomi recalled how much she was in debt to Leo after he had saved her life and rescued her from an underground drug manufacturing facility on the estate of one of her most dangerous adversaries, the once rich and powerful Adrian Darke, who thanks to her, was now languishing in prison somewhere at Her Majesty's leisure.

Stephen broke her reverie and said to Crowthorne; "So do you think that I could be considered for the team?"

"Like I said, I'm not sure Mr. Page, this is very much Inspector Kearns' domain and in the end it will be up to him who he chooses."

Stephen turned to Kearns and said, "What do you think?"

Kearns said, "We do tend to use our own, Mr. Page, but if you have a unique knowledge of the Malaterre Estate, that could be most useful. Let me have a list of your qualifications and previous dives and I'll consider your request."

Out of nowhere, the dog that had been running in front of the man and boy suddenly shot past everybody and caused Helen to jump to one side.

"Sit! Sit!" shouted the man. He ran up to the gathering and said, "Sorry folks, I didn't mean to disturb you, Sit has a mind of his own when he gets into the countryside."

"Sit?" said Helen.

The man turned to her and said, "Yes, it's an odd name, but James here," he patted the boy's head, "said 'sit' to him so often whilst he was a puppy, and at all the wrong times, that he thought that was his name. He'd never sit, but whenever we called out 'Sit', he'd come running."

Helen smiled and said, "Bless."

The pressure on Naomi's shoulder increased and the French voice suddenly said, *'Regardez!'*

Naomi turned, looked at the dog, and her eyes widened in disbelief.

"Oh my God," she said.

Everybody turned and looked at the dog too.

"That's a human femur in its mouth!"

At 11:20pm Naomi walked into her office at home and switched on her computer. She called up to Carlton, "I'll be up in a few minutes," and heard him acknowledge her. She brought up the Google search engine and typed in, *'the day that hell broke loose just north of Marietta, all along the Kennesaw line'*. She saw that the words formed the lyrics of a song by a man named Don Oja-Dunaway, and that they had originally been taken from a Confederate letter written during the American Civil War.

She sat back in her chair and wondered why she had seen and heard what she had earlier in the day, and what the words of an old Confederate letter, in the form of a song, had to do with any of it. For several minutes she sat in silence but nothing more came to her, and then as a final act before going to bed, she clicked onto her email account and pressed the 'send/receive' icon. She watched as several emails flagged up, none of any real interest until she saw the name 'Alan Farlington."

She opened the email and read.

'Hi Cuz & Carlton,

Debs and I have been invited by our best friends Julie and Steve Robiteaux to their outdoor Thanksgiving Day celebrations in Gainsville this November and they've asked us if we'd like to invite any friends. Subsequently, we recalled how much you and Carlton enjoyed your brief stay here in 2002, and we wondered if you'd like to come visit, and attend their celebrations as our guests?

It would be a blast if you could, and especially if you could make it for a couple of weeks or so, 'cos we could take you up to old St. Andrew's Church in Charleston and show you where The Fire of Mars or 'El Fuego de Marte' is supposed to be buried, amongst other things. What do you think?

Lots of love
Al & Debs xxx'

Naomi felt the wheel of fate grind round and then recalled the date of her pregnancy. She knew that she wouldn't be allowed to fly by the time November arrived. She printed out the email, switched off her computer, and went upstairs to where Carlton was reading in bed.

Carlton saw the paper in Naomi's hand and said, "Everything okay pet?"

Naomi patted her stomach and said, "Guess where this little monkey has stopped us going this November…"

Chapter 19

At 9:30am the telephone rang on Naomi's desk. Helen walked over and sat down in Naomi's chair; the phone rang again. She reached over and picked it up.

"Walmsfield Historic Research Department, Helen Milner speaking."

"Good morning Miss Milner, Superintendent Crowthorne here, is Naomi available please?"

"And good morning to you too Superintendent; no I'm sorry, she had a meeting in Rochdale at nine o'clock and I'm not expecting her until ten-thirty. Is there anything that I can help you with?"

Crowthorne hesitated for a few seconds and then said, "Yes please; could you tell her that the human femur we retrieved from the dog came from a woman aged about seventy years old? And that according to the carbon 14 results, she died in the latter decades of the 1800s."

"Latter decades, couldn't we get a better result than that?"

"Yes, and we will. To get a date with a ten or fifteen year accuracy, we need a very good measurement of the isotope ratios and two samples from the same source – but in order to progress matters quickly I asked the lab to let me have the results of their initial test, that's why it's not as accurate as it could be just yet."

"And is there a familial link to the other bone found in the reservoir?"

"I don't have the DNA results to date, but I wouldn't bet my last pound against it." He paused and then said, "Another thing; this latest bone also appears to be in the same state of preservation as the first indicating that it too had only just been exposed to water."

"That's curious," said Helen, "I could understand one burial being disturbed if it was a tomb or such, but two burials suggests something more."

"Like what?"

Helen thought for a second or two and then said, "Perhaps the bones came from some hitherto unknown and undisturbed mausoleum somewhere on the old estate?"

Crowthorne pondered and said, "It's a possibility I suppose; has Naomi got the plans for the old place?"

"She's ordered them from the Land Registry Office, but they haven't arrived yet."

Crowthorne said, "Okay, please let me know when they do, 'cos I'd like to have a squiz too."

"A *squiz*?" said Helen, "What the heck's a squiz?"

"A squiz – a look, you know…"

"No – I don't."

"Everybody's heard of a squiz!"

"In your pre-diluvial world maybe." Helen paused and then for fun added, "But then again I suppose that I wasn't around whilst Inspector Abberline scoured Whitechapel for Jack the Ripper."

The normally-reserved Crowthorne smiled and said, "Cheeky monkey!"

"Yes," said Helen, "and I'll bet you saw a few of those too – on top of barrel-organs!"

Crowthorne couldn't help himself; he laughed out loud and said, "Okay, *young* Miss Milner. Please ask *young* Mrs. Wilkes to let *old* me have 'a look', aka 'squiz', at the architectural plans of Malaterre when they arrive."

"I will, Superintendent Crowthorne, I will." She paused and then added, "Shall I ask her to bring the monocle too?"

To Crowthorne's delight he found the banter with Helen most agreeable. He said, "I can see that I'm going to have trouble with you…"

"Moi?" said Helen, "No…"

Crowthorne made a 'Hmming' sound and then said, "I've also received an email from Kev Middleton about their plans for draining the Dunsteth reservoir and it would appear that it isn't going to be as straightforward as they'd hoped because of the need to preserve water."

"Will this hold up our investigation?"

"To a certain extent; the plans are to divert the water to Haslingden Grane, just west of Haslingden, where the Calf Hey, Ogden, and Holden Wood reservoirs are situated, but because of carrying capacities, and several other problems it would appear that we will only be able to drain two-thirds of Dunsteth at any one time."

"And will that stop us?"

"Not as such. Once drained, the water below us will be fifteen to twenty feet deep, but of course this means that unless Kev and his team can come up with another solution, we will have to rely on Inspector Kearns and his chaps to carry out any research at the lower levels of the Malaterre buildings."

"Okay Superintendent Crowthorne," said Helen resurrecting a little of their past repartee, "I'll pass the info to young Mrs. Wilkes."

There was a slight pause on the line until Crowthorne said, "Look, everybody and his dog calls me Bob, so please feel free to do the same."

"Thank you Bob, and of course you must call me – a taxi."

There was another pause on the line as a grinning Helen heard Crowthorne say, "I beg your pardon?"

"I'm sorry Bob; just me having a little fun at your expense. Please call me Helen, not, a taxi."

Crowthorne clicked and said, "Okay, okay, not many people joke with me anymore so I'm a bit out of practice."

"In that case," said Helen with an impish grin, "I'll have to see what I can do about that…"

Crowthorne made one of his customary harrumphing sounds, and said, "One last thing, Taxi…"

Helen smiled and said, "Ooh, touché!"

"…could you please advise Naomi that we won't be able to proceed with any of the works at Dunsteth until at least the tenth of July? The water won't have finished draining until then."

"Okay, I will, thanks for calling Bob."

Helen put the phone down and smiled; she knew that she would be having fun in the future with the not-so-crusty policeman.

At Rochdale Police Headquarters Crowthorne too put the phone down and was still smiling when he heard a knock at the door.

"Come in," he called.

Inspector Peter Milnes walked in and said, "Sorry to disturb you sir, but I thought that you'd like to know that the Probus woman was detained at Dover East docks half an hour ago."

"Ah," said Crowthorne, "has anybody questioned her?"

"No sir, the Port Authority Police are awaiting instructions from you."

"I see; and was she accompanied?"

"Not that I have been told, no sir."

Crowthorne thought for a couple of seconds and then said, "Very well, let's get her back here then, and we'll question her."

Milnes said "Very good sir," he turned and walked towards the door and then stopped. He turned back to face Crowthorne and said, "I understand from the lads at Dover that she's something of a looker sir."

Crowthorne looked up, frowned, and said, "Go on…"

"And petite."

Crowthorne said, "And your point is?"

"If she did have anything to do with the goings-on at Malaterre, or indeed, even if that wasn't related and she had anything to do with the alleged disappearance of Mr. Probus, her physique would indicate that she must have had help, and more than likely from a man."

Crowthorne sat back in his seat and said, "I don't mean to be rude Peter, but that didn't require the services of Sherlock Holmes to work out, did it?"

"No sir it didn't, but in my cack-handed way, what I'm trying to say is, wouldn't it be prudent to release her and let her board the vessel?"

Crowthorne put down his pen and said, "Oh, I see…"

"As long as the ferry is within UK territorial waters our police will have the power of arrest, so if we let her go aboard and keep tabs on her, we may see her meeting somebody else."

Crowthorne leaned back and said, "Not likely though is it Peter? If, and it's still a big 'if', she's had a hand in any of this, her accomplice could have been a hired help, or even a paramour, and he or she may have been instructed to keep well away until the dust had settled."

"True enough," said Milnes, "but is it worth a shot?"

Crowthorne thought for a few seconds and then said, "Have the Port Authority boys told her why she's been detained?"

"They made some excuse about having a problem with a piece of her luggage."

"And what time does her vessel sail?"

"10:40am sir; it's 'The Pride of Dover' bound for Calais."

Crowthorne looked at his watch and saw that it was 9:55am; he looked up at Milnes and said, "All right, let her board and ask Dover to put a female plain-clothes officer on her – then ring P & O and Dover Port Ops to tell them that before she enters French waters we'll be instructing 'The Pride of Dover' to return to base."

"Even if she remains alone sir?"

"Yes. We don't want her disappearing into thin air on the continent, that'd be a nightmare."

"Not a good advert for détente sir," observed Milnes.

Crowthorne raised his right eyebrow and said, "Quite…"

At 11:25am Naomi entered her office with her hand over her mouth and an *'Oh-My-God... '* expression on her face.

Helen saw it and said, "What?"

"I've just seen Percy and a guy whom I presume to be Ballseye or Marcus – whatever, and I know that I've been known to partake of the odd 'bitch and tonic' in the past, but wait 'til you see for yourself."

Helen glanced up at the clock on the wall and noted the time; she said, "They're due here at eleven-forty-five, where are they?"

"Up on the ground floor talking to one of the girls from reception."

Helen said, "I thought that you'd be back by ten-thirty; what delayed you?"

"Oh, don't get me started!" said Naomi taking her seat at her desk, "Some complete spanner blocked me in at the Exchange shopping centre car park."

"I thought that you had a business appointment in Rochdale?"

"I did; with Messrs. Marks and Spencer, two of my special clients."

Helen raised her eyebrows and said, "I see, it's all right for some…"

"Well it was until I got back to my car and saw that the total fidiot…"

"Fidiot?" interrupted Helen.

Naomi looked up and said, "Yes – *effing idiot…*"

Helen nodded and said, "Okay…"

"…had parked his car right across the back of mine. I couldn't believe it; I went back into M & S and got them to put out an announcement – that drew no response, then I went to the shops and stores each side, again with no response, then in a high state of dudgeon I went back to my car so that I could wait and bollock the numpty, but when I got there, he or she had gone!"

Helen grimaced and said, "Annoying or what?"

"Right," said Naomi, "and on top of that I had to buy a new shopping bag."

"Why did you have to do that?"

"I'm trying to wean myself off plastic bags so I'd bought myself a fold-up sort that I'd sworn I'd put in my glove compartment but when I looked it had gone."

"Perhaps Carlton had taken it?"

"Carlton with a fold-up M & S shopping bag?" exclaimed Naomi, "I don't think so!"

Helen shrugged and said, "It's no biggy though, N – if it'd been a Harrods bag or something like that it would have been different."

"Hey, it's a biggy to me! I liked my M & S bag, that's why I had to buy another."

Helen shrugged and then told Naomi about her telephone conversation with Bob Crowthorne, omitting the jokey part.

"So," said Naomi after digesting it all, "now we have two bodies from the nineteenth century?"

"Yes, and if Bob's suspicions are proved to be correct, there may be a third from the twenty-first."

Naomi sat back in her chair and said, "It's annoying about the delay in draining Dunsteth; the sooner we can get people down there better I'd like it."

There was a sudden loud knock on the door, Helen looked up and saw that it was 11:45am on the button. She nodded and said, "That'll be Percy and Marcus…"

Chapter 20

*10:00pm Friday 21ˢᵗ August 1868. The Monkey Pit
Public House, Rochdale*

The landlord of The Monkey Pit Public House was an ex-bare-
knuckle boxer named Bill Sampson, but because of his
enormous build and physique everybody called him Bull. He
had been dishonourably discharged from the 47ᵗʰ Lancashire
Regiment of Foot after he had killed a man with his bare fists
in a bar fight in Malta when the regiment had been deployed
there in 1856. He had seen all sorts of action, military and
otherwise, and few men posed a threat to him, but as he
glanced across to the darkest corner of the public bar, even he
felt apprehensive.

Rochdale and vicinity was known to harbour some
dangerous and psychotic characters, some convicted, some not,
but seldom had so many of the terrifying and unstable men
ever been gathered in the one place before.

He looked across to where they were sitting and made sure
that none of them saw him looking.

In the farthest corner was Abraham Johnson, the chairman
of the meeting, on his right, sat his son Caleb; to the right-hand
side of Caleb sat the short-tempered Chinaman, Lice. On the
left-hand side of Abraham was an empty seat, but to the left of
that sat a sometimes–unhinged, murderous lunatic nicknamed
Squeaker, a name that he had been given because of the
hideous sounds his victims made whilst he was garrotting
them. And to Squeaker's left was the aggressive and syphilitic
fighting dwarf known as Squat.

Bull shook his head and hoped that no-one from the local
police force would walk in and that nobody else would even
look sideways at them.

The group appeared to be speaking in hushed tones and Bull knew that something major was going on, but the empty seat next to Abraham intrigued him.

The door to the bar opened and his inquisitiveness was answered. He closed his eyes and groaned as a slight-looking man known as 'the pastor' walked in.

"Bless you Brother Bull," said the pastor as he walked by.

In terms of dangerousness, Caleb was way above the others, but in terms of instability and the high chance of meeting a swift end in a darkened alleyway, the pastor was the man. He nodded and watched as the pastor took the empty seat at the table.

"Beers all round Bull!" called Abraham.

Bull nodded, set about his task, and left them to their business.

"Wha' you want with us boss?" said Lice.

Abraham looked around and saw a lone man sitting at a nearby table; he nudged the pastor and nodded in the direction of the man.

The pastor leaned and looked over Lice's shoulder; he nodded to Abraham and walked across to the man.

"Good evening brother," he said.

The man, a big, surly looking miner looked up and saw the fake dog collar at the pastor's neck and said, "What do you want?"

"I want you to leave."

The miner leaned back in his seat, looked at the slight figure of the pastor and said, "Yeah?" he turned and looked at the men in the corner and saw that one was Chinese and another a dwarf, and said in a loud voice, "And I'd like to fuck your mother but she probably committed suicide when she gave birth to you, so piss off back to your flock of freaks."

Three heads turned around and looked at the miner.

"Did that ugly bastard just call me a freak?" said Squat.

"Yes I did, half-pint," said the miner, "so what are you going to do about it, kick the shit out of my knees?"

Caleb saw Squat attempt to leap to his feet but restrained him. He leaned forwards, turned, and looked at the miner.

The miner opened his mouth to say something but then saw that it was Caleb Johnson. He leapt up, knocked his seat over, and started to back away, in doing so he noticed that the other man was Abraham Johnson. He gasped and felt his sphincter muscle loosen; he held his hands in the air and said, "Sorry gents, I didn't mean to offend…" He looked at Caleb's eyes and thought that his bowels would let go at any minute.

"Please, gents, sorry – let me get your beers…" He wheeled around to head for the bar and walked straight into the pastor. He recoiled and started to back up, but was pushed backwards until his retreat was halted by the wall. He looked down into the pastor's ice-cold eyes and said, "I'm sorry, I…"

The moment that he spoke he felt two sharp pains; one in his lower stomach and the other in the top and left-hand side of his penis. He winced and tried to lean forwards but couldn't move through being pressed against the wall.

The pastor looked up into the eyes of the distraught man and said, "That's right brother, I have two knives pressed by my reckoning about a quarter of an inch into your flesh. With two simple pushes my beautiful babies will enter your lower intestine and your cock; then with two slashes, one up, and one down I'll kill you *and* I'll cut you're fucking cock off."

The panic-stricken man said, "No, I'm really sorry, please don't…"

The pastor looked into the eyes of the miner and said, "Do you live in Rochdale, brother?"

The miner said, "Yes."

"Are you married?"

"Yes."

"And do you have any daughters?"

"No, I don't have any children."

"Shame," said the pastor, he looked across to Abraham and said, "Do you want him to die, brother?"

Before Abraham could answer, Bull walked back into the public bar with the first of the beers, saw what was happening and said, "Hey! What's going on? You know that I don't allow…"

Lice and Squeaker jumped up from their table, squared up to Bull, and said, "You don't allow what?"

Bull stared for a second at the fearful looking duo and felt his resolve weaken, and then, as if that wasn't enough, Caleb stood up, pushed Lice and Squeaker to one side, and said, "You don't fucking allow what?"

Bull swallowed hard, put the drinks down on the table, and retreated.

Caleb turned to Abraham and said, "Do you want the pastor to gut this piece of shit in the back alley pa?"

Abraham got up out of his chair and walked across to the miner; he stared into his petrified eyes for a second, then turned back to the others and said, "No, come on boys, the gen'leman wants to buy us all a drink," he then turned back and glared into the miner's eyes, and said, "And after that he's going to *fuck off...*"

The miner felt his bladder begin to lose control, he looked at Abraham and said, "Yes, yes, that's what I want to do, thank you Mr. Johnson."

Abraham turned to the pastor and said, "So you put your babies away and let the good man go to the bar, and I feel sure that he'll apologise for any offence he may have caused."

The miner looked down at the pastor and said, "Yes, yes, I'm really sorry, I, I..."

Before withdrawing the blades, the pastor looked up into the eyes of the miner and said, "If ever I walk into a bar, and you're there, you walk out; if ever you walk into a bar and I'm there, you walk out; and if ever you see me anywhere in the street, you cross over to the other side and don't even look at me, do you understand?"

The miner nodded and said, "Yes."

"Because," said the pastor, "if you don't do as I say, I shall be having a lot of fun with you and that wife of yours, do you understand me, brother?"

"Yes, yes, I do..."

The pastor continued to stare at his hapless victim for a few seconds longer and then backed away.

The miner glanced down but saw no sign of the knives; he edged out of the way of the pastor and headed straight to the bar to buy the drinks.

On his way there, he passed a lone man sitting at a table the farthest away from the group; his back was to them all and he kept his capped head staring down at his drink.

Abraham looked at his cronies and said, "Right, let's get seated and not draw any more attention to ourselves."

Everybody sat down and waited until Bull and the miner had delivered their drinks and departed.

"Right boys," said Abraham, "I've brought you all together again because I've got a job needs doing that suits all of your individual skills."

The men glanced at one another and either smiled or raised their eyebrows.

"You'll all be paid plenty, you'll all get free accommodation, free food, and free beer until we've finished the job, and as soon as you tell me you're in, there'll be five quid each to keep you going."

Lice, Squeaker, the pastor and Squat gasped and looked at one another again; as if with one voice they said, "We're in!"

Abraham looked from face to face and said, "You know the routine though – if you're in, you're in. If you get caught and you blab, you'll die; if you ever implicate Caleb or me you'll die, if you let us down, you'll die, and if any one of you double-crosses any of the others, you'll die such a fucking horrible death, as you'll wish you'd never been born. Is that understood?"

Everybody nodded.

"Right," said Abraham, "those who are with us shake my hand now."

Each man shook Abraham's hand in turn; he reached into his pocket and pulled out a large brown leather bag, and gave Lice, Squeaker, the pastor, and Squat five pounds each.

"There's four Inns around Rochdale and you're already booked in under different names. Caleb will tell you which they are and what names are booked at each, so it'll be up to you to decide where you want to go. Like I said earlier, everything there will be free, but I don't want you to get into any trouble." he turned to Squat and said, "And that especially applies to you."

Squat frowned and opened his mouth to object but saw Caleb glaring at him.

"Yes boss," he said.

Abraham looked at each of the faces and said, "I mean it! If any one of you fucks this up by not behaving, I'll consider it a let-down, and I just told you what would happen if you did that." He looked at each face again and saw them all nod.

The pastor said, "You must have been confident that we'd all say 'yes' to go booking the rooms in advance brother."

Abraham turned to the pastor and said, "You think I don't know you? You've all agreed to do the job, you've shaken my hand and taken the five pounds, and I haven't even told you what's required yet."

Once again the four men looked at each other and then at Abraham and Caleb.

Lice said, "We all rike workin' for you boss, so nobody gonna ret you down."

Nods all round.

"So what is the job?" said Squat.

Abraham leaned forwards and said, "It's a removal job with fringe benefits."

"Removal job?" said Squeaker.

"Yes," said Abraham, "we're going to permanently remove a family."

Squat's eyes lit up; he said, "Are there any women involved?"

Abraham looked at Squat and said, "This is serious Squat – don't you let that fucking syphilitic knob of yours start ruling your brain, or I'll be the one to cut it off, do you understand?"

Squat looked down and said, "Yes boss, sorry."

Abraham continued staring at Squat for a few seconds and then said, "Right, finish your drinks, sort out between you where you're staying, and wait there until you receive word from me." He looked at each face and then said, "And don't none of you let me down or you know the consequences, right?"

Once again nods all round.

Abraham looked at everybody and then picked up his tankard and said, "To us."

"To us," was echoed back.

A few minutes later he leaned towards Squeaker and said, "Do you know that piece of shit who bought us the drinks earlier?"

"I know of him, but I don't know his name."

"Right, there's an extra five shillings in it for you if he's gone before the end of the week."

Squeaker's face contorted into a sadistic smile and he said, "Care to add another half-crown to that and I'll do his whole family?"

"No," said Abraham, "he's the only one who's seen us all together."

"What about the landlord?"

Abraham pondered for a few seconds and then said, "Maybe later."

At the table in the farthest corner, the lone man in the cap picked up his drink and downed it. He got up, pushed his seat under the table, shot a quick glance at the group in the corner, and departed.

Chapter 21

Friday 30th June 2006. The Historic Research Department, Walmsfield Borough Council

Naomi looked at Helen with anticipation, said, "Are you ready for this?" saw Helen nod, and then called, "Come in."

The door opened and Percy stepped inside in front of Ballseye.

"Good morning ladies," he said, "I trust that we aren't late and that you're both in good spirits and health." He stepped to one side and said, "This is my friend Marcus, whom I hope will be able to help you with your research into Malaterre."

Helen looked up and only just managed to stop her mouth falling open.

Ballseye appeared to be at least six feet two inches tall, was thin and willowy-looking; he wore cheap-looking clothes, dirty off-white trainers and a trilby hat that appeared to be at least a couple of sizes too small. All unremarkable except for one thing – sticking out from under the trilby was the worst looking ginger wig that either girl had ever seen.

The tightness of the hat had pinched the dome of the hairpiece, causing its edges to protrude upwards over Ballseye's ears, accentuating the shock of straggly grey hair sticking out below.

"Aw right," said a sullen-looking Ballseye.

Naomi shot a glance towards Helen and then stood up and extended her right hand.

"How do you do Marcus," she said, "Percy's told me all about you."

Ballseye ignored the proffered hand and said, "What, me doin' that bastard what done me mum?"

Naomi frowned and said, "I'm sorry…"

"Well he fu…" Ballseye saw Helen staring at him with a fascinated expression on her face and moderated his language, "…he started it," he said.

"Who started what?" said Naomi withdrawing her hand and sitting back down.

"He did!" said Ballseye, "The bastard what done me mum; an'…" he pointed down towards his crutch and said, "it's a good job I've only got one plum or 'e'd have done me too. Bastard!"

Percy grabbed the break in the conversation and said, "Any chance of a cuppa, girls?"

Helen was engrossed in Ballseye's opening comments and didn't register Percy's request at first; she looked at Ballseye and said, "Who started what?"

Ballseye looked at Helen for a second, flopped down onto a chair, and then turned to Percy; he said, "I thought you said they was all savvy in here?"

Helen took exception and said, "Hey, wait a minute…"

Naomi interrupted and said, a bit louder than she normally would, "I know that Percy drinks tea, white, no sugar. Marcus, what would you like?"

"Just a go."

Naomi paused, frowned, and then said, "A go?"

"For Christ's sake," said Ballseye turning to Percy once again, "They're as bad as one another!"

It was Naomi's turn to take exception, she said, "Wait a minute Marcus, you're the one who's come in here talking in riddles – so we can do without the sarcastic comments, okay?"

"You sound like my sister," said Ballseye, "she's always having a go."

"Nobody's having a go," said Helen, "we don't know what the bloody hell you're on about."

Percy raised his eyebrows at the sound of a 'lady' swearing, but said nothing.

"I thought you'd heard all about me?" said Ballseye.

"Well we haven't," retorted Helen.

Ballseye turned to Percy and said, "So you didn't tell 'em about me doing that bastard?"

"Why would I?" said Percy, "It has nothing to do with Malaterre."

Ballseye looked back at Naomi and said, "So this is all your fault then?"

Naomi said, "What is?"

"You saying that Perse had told you all about me when he hadn't!"

"It was just a turn of phrase! I didn't mean that he had *literally* told me everything about you."

Ballseye turned to Percy and said, "See, this is what I have to put with, people lying. Why can't anybody just be straight with me? That's why I lost my last job."

Naomi looked at Helen and then looked at Ballseye. She had become accustomed to Percy's bunch of oddball people over the last few years, but most of them had been light-hearted and amusing. Ballseye was something else; intense and serious and she wondered whether she'd be making a mistake getting involved with him. She said, "Okay, let's start again." She extended her hand and said, "I'm Naomi, and this," she said pointing towards Helen, "is Helen. We're pleased to meet you, and we'd be delighted if you could help us with our enquiries into Malaterre. Now, would you like something to drink from our drinks dispenser?"

Ballseye weakly shook Naomi's hand, nodded, looked at Helen and nodded, and said, "I'll have a hot chocolate, and can I take my hat off? It's warm in here."

"Sure, you can put it on the coat-hanger by the door," said Naomi.

Ballseye stood up, removed his hat, and hung it over the top of Helen's coat.

Helen glanced up and nearly screeched; Ballseye had inadvertently pulled his wig off too, it had fallen out of his hat, and it sat like a deformed orang-utan inside the collar of her best Karen Millen coat. She leapt up and said, "Jesus Christ Marcus, get this bloody thing off my coat!"

Ballseye turned, saw his wig, and said, "All right, keep your hair on; it's only a fucking syrup."

"Me keep my hair on? That's rich coming from you! Get it off my coat now, please!"

"That's another thing," said Marcus sitting down and rubbing his bald patch, then looking at his greasy palm, "More people lying to me. The stupid bints in the hairdressers' told me that the glue would hold it in place for at least eight hours."

Helen's anguish raised a notch, she said, "Marcus...?"

Naomi frowned and said, "Bints? *Bints?* That's a bit un..."

Percy looked down and shook his head.

"Exactly," said Ballseye, "I told 'em, just be honest with me, will it do the trick? And now look, it's probably got cheap perfume all over it and I'll end up walking round smelling like a tart."

No one person in either Naomi's or Helen's life had ever got them so exasperated and affronted in such a short time; they were both so stunned by Ballseye's comments that they didn't know which offensive remark to respond to first.

Ballseye got up, snatched the wig off Helen's coat, and put it up to his nose.

"Yep," he said, "I knew it..." he thrust the wig into Percy's face and said, "sniff that Perse – it smells like I've spent the night with a fucking prozzie."

Percy recoiled as Ballseye continued to push the wig under his nose.

"All right, that's enough!" Naomi looked at Percy and said, "I think that you should leave and take Marcus with you."

Ballseye ignored the statement and said, "Have you got a mirror I can use?"

Naomi looked at Percy and said, "Well?"

Percy opened his mouth to speak but was cut off.

"Come on," said Ballseye, "One of you birds must have one; you all preen yourselves so much."

"We're women," said an infuriated Helen, turning from extracting nylon ginger hairs from her coat collar, "we're not birds, or tarts, or bints – women!"

"I know you are," said Ballseye, "that's why I asked *you* for a mirror and not Perse."

Helen was flabbergasted, she looked across to Naomi and opened her mouth to speak, but she too was cut off.

"Just look at this," said Ballseye holding the dishevelled wig out towards Helen, "which way round is it supposed to go on?" he paused and then said, "Perhaps you can figure it out while your mate gets me that hot chocolate she offered."

Naomi looked at Percy and saw him raise the palms of his hands in perplexity.

"I haven't got all day you know," said Ballseye looking at Naomi, "and I presume that you weren't lying to me too when you offered me that drink."

"All right," said Naomi, "I'll go and get the drinks!"

She stepped out of her office and headed down to the dispenser whilst trying to calm her jangling nerve ends. She determined to give Ballseye his drink and then have nothing more to do with him, but as she wrangled with her emotions, the thumb pressed down on her shoulder and a voice said, 'No…' She frowned and continued walking, still determined to sever all ties with Ballseye but the thumb pressed harder and the voice repeated, 'No…' She wasn't sure what 'No' meant; 'No' don't take him a drink; 'No' don't consider severing ties with him, or 'No' to something else.

She walked up to the dispenser, got everybody's order, headed back towards her office and then to her amazement heard peals of laughter coming from within. She opened the office door and saw Helen and Percy laughing at a puzzled-looking Ballseye.

In Ballseye's top pocket he had a notebook with three golf balls on the front cover formed to appear like a pair of eyes over a nose, and in his frustration, he had stuffed his wig into that pocket and it hung over the notebook causing it to look like a small, unkempt ginger animal peering out.

It looked so amusing that even the aggravated Naomi couldn't help grinning.

Ballseye held up the mirror that Helen had given him, looked at the reflection of the 'small animal', and turned round to face them all.

"It looks better on him than it does me – and he doesn't have *any* bollocks!" he said.

Naomi placed the drinks on Helen's desk and everybody helped themselves.

Ballseye sat down and slurped his hot chocolate until Percy said, "I've already told the girls about Malaterre's previous ownership, why don't you tell them what you know?"

Ballseye put down his plastic cup, wiped his mouth on the sleeve of his jacket, and said, "Right. It was constructed out of our local sandstone and built on a substrate of the same; that's why it doesn't make sense that any of it should have collapsed. Nothing about the size of the ashlars..." he saw Percy frown and said, "...ashlars Perse, the stone blocks used for constructing the building."

Percy said, "I know what ashlars are Marcus, I was frowning because I hadn't given any thought to *why* part of the building should have collapsed."

"Right," said Ballseye, "nothing about the size of the ashlars, which were considerable in volume, lends itself to collapse. Of course there would be a degree of deterioration to the sandstone and the sacrificial lime mortar joints, but nothing to make the building alter its shape so much that it could occasion collapse. Then there are the wooden window frames, doors, and maybe even a priest door, but even if they'd all rotted away, that would have just left empty portals and fenestration holes, nothing that should have caused a collapse."

Naomi, Helen, and Percy were amazed at the change in Ballseye; he sounded so different.

Unaware of everybody's fascination, Ballseye continued.

"The construction was Elizabethan in style with the front of the building facing northeast. This allowed for the maximum amount of sunshine at the rear which suited the lifestyle of the extravagant Blackstone family who regularly invited village locals up to the then named Blackstone Hall for annual church festival feasts.

"At the time of the valley flooding, the estate belonged to the Page family who had disappeared, some say back to France from where they'd originated, but that has never been verified as far as I'm aware. There were no graves, mausoleums, outhouses, or follies in the grounds, but there was an orangery that lay about two-hundred feet, southwest of the main building in the ornamental garden.

"Lady Charity Blackstone was celebrated as having one of the finest collections of European ornamental flora and fauna, which I believe was removed to Chatsworth House in Derbyshire before the valley was flooded.

"The valley in which the Malaterre Estate was situated also contained the old Dunsteth Estate that belonged to the Lincoln family, but that too was sold off prior to the flooding. Up until the recent developments, I understood that both buildings had remained untouched and in a safe condition, which was in fact confirmed by a marine surveyors report, available to view online at one of the dot gov sites, dated..." he reached into the back pocket of his black jeans, extracted a piece of folded paper, read it, and said, "...the fourteenth of November, 2005."

Naomi was astounded; Ballseye was like a living encyclopaedia. She said, "That was amazing Marcus, do you know anything more about the Page family?"

Ballseye leaned back in his chair and looked right up at the ceiling; he appeared to be studying it as though he'd seen some sort of aberration. A few seconds later he looked down and said, "No, but I can research them if you'd like."

Naomi thought that Ballseye's research into the Pages might make a fascinating addition to what Stephen and Tineke had already told her, and with a bit of luck even unearth something that they didn't know. She said, "Yes, I would appreciate that if you don't mind."

Helen was equally astounded by the change in Ballseye and said, "Do you know anything about the family that lived at the Dunsteth Estate?" she looked sideways at Naomi and knew that it was the Johnsons from Whitewall infamy, but wanted to know if Ballseye knew anything about them too.

As before Ballseye looked up at the ceiling for a few seconds, and then said, "The estate was owned from as far back as I have researched by the Lincoln family; they were succeeded by their in-law relatives the Johnsons, two nasty bastards, father and son I recall, the father Abraham ended up being mauled to death by a dog in the Roch Valley in 1869, and the son was rumoured to have been killed by the same dog on the Whitewall Estate in 1870…"

"What?" said Naomi, "How did you know that?"

Ballseye turned to Naomi and said, "I didn't say that I knew that; I don't tell lies. Other people tell me lies like that bastard what done me mum, but I don't, so don't accuse me of it."

It was as though somebody had pressed a switch and the offensive, belligerent Ballseye had returned.

Naomi said, "I'm sorry, I should have said: where did you hear the rumour?"

Ballseye looked straight up at the ceiling for a few seconds and then said, "From the old belongings of a Victorian policeman, an ex-Police Inspector named Brewster; he made an unsubstantiated note in a private pocket book."

Naomi was intrigued. She said, "Do you remember whether or not there were any other observations in the pocket book?"

"There were lots, but they were only his private notes, and so couldn't be proved."

"Were there any others relating to Whitewall?"

Ballseye said, "When it comes to Whitewall, Perse is your man."

"Ah," said Percy, "that's where we differ Marcus, I only deal in hard cold fact, you take on board all kinds of information and form opinions – I don't."

"But I don't lie about 'em," said Ballseye, "I say whether it's a rumour, or urban legend, or unsubstantiated, and I only ever tell people the truth."

"Fair enough," said Percy.

Naomi was keen to hear if Ballseye had any more info on Whitewall. She said, "Were there any other observations in Brewster's book about Whitewall?"

Once again Ballseye looked up. A few seconds later he said, "Yes, according to Brewster he'd become friends later in life with a man named Simeon Twitch who'd worked at

Whitewall with his wife until 1892. It was Twitch who confided in Brewster that he'd buried the remains of Caleb Johnson in a copse behind Whitewall in 1870, when he was employed by tenants Mary and Silas Cartwright. Only Mary Cartwright wasn't who she pretended to be; her birth name, according to Twitch was Chance; Maria Chance, and she'd married Silas Cartwright and concealed her real name from public record, because she'd been an escaped patient from a lunatic asylum in Macclesfield."

Naomi was stunned on two counts; she recalled the discovery of the remains of one man and one woman from the copse in 2002, but she'd had no notion that the male could have been the elusive Caleb Johnson; – and she'd seen the post-mortem photograph issued by Parkway Lunatic Asylum purporting to be Maria Chance. She hadn't believed it to be the same woman as the only other known photo of Maria, and now she'd been proven to be correct – apparently – according to the unsubstantiated account of the old Police Inspector.

But it fitted very neatly together and all the pieces of the jigsaw puzzle appeared to have been put into place. She was happy to accept it as being the final chapter in the Maria Chance saga, and she couldn't wait to inform the rest of the family, unsubstantiated or not.

Everybody in the office had been reduced to silence by the revelations, and the first to break it was Percy when he said, "Well I'll be damned."

Naomi stood up, walked around her desk and kissed a shocked Ballseye on the cheek, she said, "Thank you Marcus, you've made my day."

Ballseye blushed and said, "Don't be getting the wrong idea about me; I know I'm a young-looking forty-two-ish, and I've been told that I can be a babe magnet, but I'm not available 'cos I'm in a serious relationship."

Helen nearly choked; she looked at the unkempt, lanky, balding figure of Ballseye, dressed from head-to-toe in black with a ginger wig sticking out of his top pocket, she considered that he looked more like sixty than forty-two-ish! And she wondered where in hell he'd been told that he was a babe magnet.

Naomi smiled and said, "I'm sorry if I embarrassed you, but your info on Whitewall has closed a book that has remained open for far too long."

Ballseye nodded and said, "Okay, but just to finish what I was saying about the Dunsteth Estate, the Johnsons sold it in December 1868, and flooding commenced in December 1869 after the completion of the prize-winning dam wall."

"Prize-winning?" said Helen.

Marcus turned to her and said, "Yes, for the speed of its construction."

Naomi looked from face to face and said, "That was amazing; and it deserves another hot chocolate."

Ballseye sat upright, pulled the wig from his pocket, and wiped his mouth on it.

"Any chance of a Mars bar with that?" he said.

Chapter 22

At 10:35am there was a knock on Crowthorne's door. He called, "Come in."

The door opened and Sergeant Tasha Andrew walked in.

"Good morning sir," she said. "We don't often see you here on a Saturday."

"No, and I don't intend making a habit out of it either. I'm missing a good game of golf followed by a hearty lunch with a good friend."

"Sorry to hear that sir, is there any particular reason why you had to come in?"

"This blasted Malaterre business, amongst other things."

"Ah, I understand sir, if at some time in the future I could help, I'd be delighted to give it a go."

Crowthorne said, "Thank you, and your offer is something that I shall consider, but let's see how things develop." He paused for a second and then added, "Now, you wanted to see me?"

"Yes sir; first, we've received a message from the Dover Port Authority informing us that Rosalind Probus has been detained at Dover Police Station…"

"Ah, yes, and did she meet up with anybody on board the Pride of Dover?"

"No sir, but we did cause something of a kerfuffle. We weren't aware, but protesting French fishermen had planned a blockade of Calais which would have seen the Pride of Dover making it through before it was put into place, but our request to return the Probus woman to Dover delayed the ferry's arrival time at Calais, and they had to be diverted to Ostend, a diversion that met with widespread disapproval and a shed-load of angst by all accounts."

Crowthorne pulled a face and said, "Ouch!"

"Ouch indeed sir; anyway, with your approval we'll send a car down to pick her up."

"Yes, that's fine," said Crowthorne.

"Now sir, number two – we've received the DNA results extracted from the femur discovered last Monday, and they don't match those of the other bone tested."

"Oh, that's a surprise," said Crowthorne.

Tasha frowned and said, "Why so sir?"

Crowthorne realised that he hadn't spoken to anybody else about Naomi's 'Tascher de La Pagerie' link, and that he should have kept his remark to himself. He said, "I had formed a theory that they might be from the same family."

"That's not such a large stretch sir," said Tasha, "considering that they both indicate a termination of life at around the same time."

Crowthorne nodded, and made a mental note to be more careful with his remarks in the future.

"And the other thing sir," said Tasha, "once again we had a comment returned stating that the bone was in very good condition and not at all indicative of it being exposed to water for such a long time."

Crowthorne sat back in his chair and said, "Yes, I was aware of that from an earlier communication with the lab personnel."

Tasha nodded and said, "It will be interesting to find out where the bones came from, and whether they were isolated bones, or whether they were part of two full sets of skeletal remains."

"Yes," said Crowthorne, "but none of that helps us with our enquiries into the missing Probus man does it?"

"No sir," said Tasha, "and the mysterious collapse."

Crowthorne recalled Tasha's earlier offer and said, "Have you come up with any thoughts?"

"I have sir, but so far it's only conjecture."

"And?"

"I think that it had to be an underwater explosion sir."

Crowthorne was impressed. He said, "Interesting, but there is a niggling problem with that scenario. If the collapse had occurred before the discovery of the first human bone that may have been one thing, but it wasn't, the bone was found first." He paused and then said, "So, was the collapse a deliberate act to cover up a historical secret..." his mind flashed to the Tascher de La Pagerie conundrum again, "...or has another historical secret – the discovery of the second bone – been uncovered because of the collapse, or could we be dealing with three separate events?"

"It would be hard to associate the disappearance of Mr. Probus with anything historical at Malaterre sir," said Tasha.

"Indeed it would..." Crowthorne's inquisitive mind kicked in, he said, "...or would it?" A frown appeared on his face and he sat back in his chair; he picked up his pen and started tapping his teeth with the capped end.

"Sir?" said Tasha.

Crowthorne looked at his sergeant and said, "Just a thought – but what if Max Probus was involved..." he reached across to his old-fashioned A4 desk diary and flicked back a few pages. He looked up at Tasha and said, "The first bone was discovered at the reservoir on Monday the twelfth of June, and the first indication we had that he was missing was just three days later on the fifteenth. What if it was he who took the dinghy, for whatever reason, dived the site and somehow started this whole shemozzle?"

Without being invited, Tasha sank down onto a chair in front of Crowthorne's desk; she sat pondering the question for a few minutes and then said, "My first instinct was to dismiss that thought, but it isn't that far-fetched. I knew that the first bone had only just been exposed to water, but I hadn't given any consideration to *why* it had. The first oar was found on the northern bank of the reservoir on the twenty-second, but it could have lain undiscovered for days. So it may be a far-fetched notion at the moment, but to consider that Max Probus started this whole episode isn't beyond the wildest stretches of imagination."

The two police officers sat in silence for a few minutes until Crowthorne said, "Tri-dimensional chess, Tasha."

Tasha said, "Sorry sir, I don't follow."

"It was the fictional game of 3D chess played aboard the USS Enterprise between Spock and his fellow officers in the Star Trek series. It appeared to be impossible to fathom, and even the playing boards appeared to be randomly positioned at the commencement of each game."

Tasha took the point, looked at Crowthorne, and said, "Fascinating..."

Crowthorne shot Tasha a questioning look because he recalled that word being used by Spock on numerous occasions in the series, and he wondered whether or not she was subtly taking the mickey.

"...tri-dimensional chess – yes sir," said Tasha without giving anything away, "and Max Probus just may have made the first move."

Without removing his inquisitive gaze Crowthorne said, "Yes, indeed."

Tasha got up, walked across to the door, and turned before exiting. She said, "I'll give some more thought to your theory sir."

"Okay, but don't waste too much time on it, it's only speculation."

Tasha opened the door, stepped through and then re-appeared. She waited until Crowthorne looked up, then she held her right hand straight up with her four fingers parted in the middle.

"Live long and prosper," she said, then closed the door.

A big grin spread across Crowthorne's face; "You asked for that!" he thought.

Across town at the Rochdale Exchange shopping centre, Naomi exited the Marks and Spencer store with her shopping and walked back to her car. She'd been so pleased with the fit and style of the trousers that she'd purchased the day before that she'd bought some more in a different colour. She'd left home to hit the store early and her foray had been successful;

she'd managed to get the trousers, and to secure the right size of an outfit that she'd craved for some time.

As she neared her vehicle her heart sunk, for parked right behind her was another car, once again blocking her in. She walked up to her vehicle, deposited her clothes in the rear, and then stared all around for signs of the miscreant driver. As with the day before nobody appeared – she looked at her watch, saw that it was just after eleven o'clock and wondered what to do. She looked into the offending vehicle, saw nothing to indicate who may have been driving it, and then to her delight, saw that the vehicle displayed no Road Tax licence.

She nodded her head and then rang Bob Crowthorne's direct line.

Twenty minutes later a police patrol car sporting an ANPR (automatic number plate recognition) camera, pulled up behind the offending car and two uniformed officers stepped out.

"Mrs. Naomi Wilkes?" said the first officer.

"Yes, that's me."

The officer smiled and said, "Sorry to tell you this but our ANPR camera has detected that it's a stolen vehicle."

Naomi shook her head and said, "Brilliant. So what does that mean?"

"It means that we can get it taken away, but it will be about an hour before it's gone."

Naomi looked at her watch and said, "Okay, at least I'll be home for lunch I suppose."

The officer looked at his watch and said, "Yes, we should be well out of your hair by twelve-thirty."

Naomi recalled the previous day's episode and said, "This is the second day on the trot that this has happened to me here."

"Really?"

"Yes, some plank blocked me in yesterday too."

"That's most unusual if you don't mind me saying," said the officer, "because this is the first time that we've ever had to come here to sort anything like this out."

"And of course it would happen to me!"

The officer smiled and said, "Well, if you can give us another hour, we'll have it sorted for you."

"Do you guys carry cards with direct line numbers on?"

"No, why do you ask?"

"In case this happens again."

The officer smiled again and said, "Sorry no, but in my opinion being blocked in here would be possible once, unusual twice, and almost impossible a third time, so it's doubtful that you'd use the card anyway."

Naomi shrugged and said, "Okay, thanks for your help guys; I'll hit the shops for another hour."

"And from the look on your face madam, I'd say that was no hardship."

Naomi glanced back over her shoulder and said, "Can a girl *ever* do too much shopping?"

The two policemen smiled and set about their business.

At 12:55pm Naomi pulled up outside of her house; she got out of her CRV, opened the tailgate, and extracted her shopping. She closed the tailgate, picked up her bags, aimed the electronic key at the passenger door, and pressed the button. The familiar clunk as the doors locked confirmed that the vehicle was secure, but to be certain, she got hold of the passenger door handle and pulled. Satisfied that the vehicle was indeed locked, she turned, and headed through her gate towards the front door of her house.

She didn't even give a second glance to the young man who appeared to be engrossed in his mobile phone as he strode past her with his left hand in his baggy trousers pocket.

At 2:05pm Helen walked into Page & Page's bookshop in Bury with her partner Justin and looked around; she too was taken with the modernity of the place and stared in amazement.

"Do we have to come in here babe?" said Justin, "there's a match on this afternoon and I want to get back in time for it."

Helen baulked at the idea and was becoming more and more disenchanted with her relationship. Almost everything that Justin did aggravated her and she'd thanked her lucky stars that she'd chosen not to set up home with him.

She turned to him and said, "It's a rugby match for crying out loud, you don't even support one of their teams, so what's so important about it, and why couldn't you record it and watch it later?"

Justin shook his head and said, "Women! You'll never understand."

"No, and you'll never understand women. I don't often ask you to accompany me to places that I'd like to go to, so if you'd rather leave, I think that'd make us both happier right now."

Helen's obvious annoyance went straight over Justin's head; he looked around at the interior of the bookshop and couldn't begin to understand what the attraction of books was in a digital age. He shuddered, and jumped at her offer.

"Well if you think so babe?" he said.

"Yes I do."

"So are we still on for tonight?"

"Tonight?" said Helen.

"Yeah, me stopping over."

Helen thought about that too and recalled Justin's habit of refusing to dress and shave until at least lunchtime on a Sunday, and whilst that had been acceptable at the early stages of their relationship, it had become much less so of late.

"No, I don't think so," she said.

"Why not?" said Justin glancing at his watch, "We can get a few beers in, send for a curry, and have an early night."

Helen looked at Justin; he was wearing a dark purple football team polo shirt, dark blue jeans, and clumpy black shoes, his growing beer belly had become more evident and he hadn't shaved. She wondered what on earth she was doing with him and said, "No, sorry Just – and please don't call me either, I want time to think about this relationship."

"What?" said Justin, "Just 'cos I don't want to walk around a friggin' bookshop, you're calling time?"

"No, not just because you don't want to walk around a friggin' bookshop! It's everything else beside."

"Oh fucking charming, princess, and I suppose that you think you're all it too?"

Helen hated Justin swearing in public and winced; she said, "Look, just leave will you? I'm sick and tired of you embarrassing me."

Justin looked at Helen from top to toe and said, "Yeah – well fuck you too, you're dumped," and walked out of the shop.

"Hello Helen."

Helen wheeled around and saw Stephen Page standing behind her.

"I overheard that unpleasant exchange and wondered if you required some assistance."

"To deal with Justin?" said Helen, "no, his bark was always worse than his bite, but I must say that a hot drink wouldn't go amiss right now."

Stephen smiled and said, "Well allow me to escort you; I have just the thing to bring a smile to your face."

Helen looked at Stephen; he was wearing a black suit, a crisp white shirt with cuffs that protruded below the level of his jacket sleeves, a pale blue silk tie, and shiny, black, moccasin-style shoes. He was shaven and clean looking, he smelled pleasantly of aftershave, and he couldn't have been more different to Justin.

Stephen offered up his right arm and waited until Helen linked it; he led her up to the coffee shop, sat her down at a table for two, and said, "Wait there, and please allow me to choose."

Helen was fussy about her drinks and wondered what kind of excuse she could make not to seem rude or unappreciative if Stephen got it wrong.

A few minutes later she saw him approach with a tray held at shoulder height; he weaved through the tables, stopped in front of hers, and deposited the tray on the table. She looked at the contents and her mouth fell open; sitting there was a mocha, a pain au chocolat, and a cappuccino.

Stephen turned the tray around making it obvious that the mocha and pain au chocolat was for her.

"Whoa, that's my idea of indulgent Heaven!" said an astonished Helen, "How on earth did you know that I'd like those?"

"Just one of my secret skills," said Stephen with a smile, he looked down at Helen's bag and said, "That's nice, is it Versace?"

Helen was impressed; she said, "Yes, I picked it up in Milan a couple of years ago."

"Have you ever been to Puerto Banus in Andalusia?"

"No I can't say that I have."

Stephen nodded and said, "There's an avenue there named the Avenida de la Ribera that runs along the front of the marina, it's filled with designer outlets selling the most outrageously over-priced goods, next to numerous delightful but over-priced, open air restaurants overlooking the multitude of millionaires' boats; and looking at your clothes and accessories, I'd say that that would be your idea of Heaven, not just a drink and a pain au chocolat!"

Helen looked at Stephen and said, "Mmm – yes..." She mulled over the scene, and then thought to herself, 'And especially with a guy like you...'

Stephen immediately looked down, and then looked back at Helen. He said, "Now – thank you for coming in response to my call."

"You have me intrigued, what's so important that it warranted me coming to see you in private?"

Stephen reached into his jacket pocket, extracted a sealed envelope, and handed it over; he said, "This is for you and Naomi. It contains a photocopy of the only known private family plans of the Malaterre estate. There are other plans held by the Land Registry Office, but they aren't anything like as detailed as these. These show secret passageways, rooms, priest holes, and that kind of thing."

"Wow," said Helen, "intriguing."

"It is, and even these aren't thought to be comprehensive."

"So there could be other bolt-holes that you don't know about?

"Indeed."

"Wow – what I wouldn't have given to be let loose in there before it was flooded!"

"You and me both," said Stephen.

Helen put the reins on her imagination and said, "Why didn't you give this to Naomi?"

"I tried to contact her this morning, but she hasn't responded and I have to go to London on business this evening."

Helen said, "Oh I see – and when will you get back?"

"In a few days' time, five at the most."

Helen nodded and picked up the envelope. She placed it into her handbag, and said, "Okay, I'll give this to her first thing Monday. Now, tell me more about Puerto Banus…"

Chapter 23

'Was none who would be foremost,
To lead such dire attack:
For those behind cried, "Forward!"
And those before cried, "Back!"'

- Baron Macaulay.

10:00pm Friday 4th September 1868. The Monkey Pit Public House, Rochdale

The interior of the public bar of The Monkey Pit pub was not a pleasant place. The decoration hadn't been attended to for years; the paint and lime-wash walls were peeling and creating an unusual pattern of shadows above the only two wall-mounted gas-lamps. Lit candles stood on those tables that the gas-lamps shed no light over, and the air was thick with tobacco smoke, fumes, body odour, and the smell of stale beer. Several groups of men sat around tables' playing card games or chatting and drinking, and every now and then a heated discussion would erupt into a quarrel, which Bull the landlord would soon quell. And the only two rules that applied were unwritten ones.

First – whenever the Johnson men were in the public bar don't sit at the table in the corner, and second – don't do anything to upset them. The consequences of breaking the first rule could be intimidating enough, but the consequences of breaking the second rule were downright life threatening.

Abraham, Caleb, and Lice waited at their table until Bull had deposited their beers and departed.

Lice then leaned towards Abraham and said, "Whass up boss?"

Abraham looked around and said, "Have you heard anything from Squeaker?"

Lice frowned and said, "We was not supposed to be seeing each other before the job boss."

"Yes, yes, I know, but it's been two weeks since I last saw you all and he was supposed to be doing a small job for me; I want to know if he finished it."

Lice looked up at Abraham and didn't know how to respond, he shrugged his shoulders and said, "Wha' you wan' me to say boss?"

Abraham frowned and picked up his tankard, he took a deep drink of beer and put it back down on the table. He wiped his mouth on his left coat sleeve and said, "Do you know which Inn Squeaker went to stay at?"

"Yes – issa Led Rion in Rawton Stleet."

Abraham turned and glared at Lice; he said, "What did you say?"

"The Led Rion in Rawton Stleet boss."

Abraham looked up at Caleb and said, "Bloody chinks, I'll never get the hang of what they're saying."

"The Led Rion in Rawton Stleet!" repeated Lice.

Abraham turned to him and said, "Yes, I get that he's at the Red Lion, but where the fuck is Rawton Street?"

"It's Lawton Street pa," said Caleb, "that's how these slanty-eyed bastards speak."

Abraham gritted his jaw and took another swig of ale.

"At's why I never wanna stay there boss," said Lice.

"What?" said Abraham.

"At's why I never wanna stay there."

Abraham frowned as his legendary short-temperedness started to arise; he turned to Lice and said, "Why don't you want to stay there?"

"'Cos of a names boss."

"What about them?"

"A can't say 'em plopery."

"You can't say anything fucking properly," said Abraham.

Lice realised that this wasn't the time to continue this line of conversation and said, "Yes boss."

"So," said Abraham, "have you seen Squeaker or not?"

"No boss."

Abraham looked at Caleb and said, "Remind me again, where is Lawton Street?"

"About a quarter of a mile from here, just off Market Street."

Abraham nodded and said, "Is Galloping John in the next bar?"

Lice said, "A go an' check boss." He got up and disappeared for a few seconds and then came back; he sat down at the table and said, "Garroping John is in a pub boss, but he's gone upstairs with Rirry."

Abraham frowned and said, "Rirry?"

"He means Lily pa," said Caleb,

Abraham shook his head and said, "Not Lifting Lily?"

"Yes boss," said Lice.

Abraham thought for a few seconds and then said, "That might work in our favour; she might only charge tuppence a go, but she'll have cleaned John out before he's got his pants back on."

"So what's on your mind pa?" said Caleb.

"We'll wait 'til John comes down, then send him off to the Red Lion to ask about Squeaker."

"What do you want to know?"

"I want to know if he finished that guy who pissed the pastor off the last time we were here."

"And was he meant to?" said Caleb.

"Yes, and I want to know if it's done; I don't want any loose ends flapping about before we do the job."

"And do you want John to ask Squeaker if he finished him off?"

"No, of course not," said Abraham, "just get him to go to the Red Lion and ask Squeaker to meet us here at nine o' clock tomorrow night."

Out of nowhere, a commotion broke out in the next bar.

"*Oi*, you thieving bitch, what have you done with my money?"

"I haven't touched it, you pencil-dicked moron!"

"Oh yes you have, and you'd better hand it over or I'll fetch the peelers!"

"You can fetch the fucking Pope for all I care; I haven't got your money!"

Abraham looked at Caleb and said, "You'd better get in there before Lily's husband gets involved."

Caleb nodded and walked into the next bar.

Galloping John was half-way down the back stairs with his pants over his arm, and he was gesticulating like a madman towards Lifting Lily.

"I'm warning you, you saggy-titted cow, hand my money over or you'll feel the back of my hand!"

A burly-looking man stood up from one of the tables and said, "What did you just say to my wife?"

Galloping John looked down at the man-mountain and gulped; he called, "She just stole my money!"

"I said – what did you just say to my wife?" The burly man picked up his tankard and emptied the contents onto the bar floor, wetting the feet of nearby drinkers who hastily backed away.

Galloping John remained frozen on the stairs and said nothing.

The burly man held his pewter tankard up in the air and shouted, "See the shape of this? This is going to be the shape of your fucking face two minutes from now if you don't apologise."

Caleb pushed his way through the backing-up throng and sidled up to Lily's husband.

"Ned," he whispered in his ear, "pa wants Galloping to do a job for him."

Ned spun around, saw who was standing next to him, and said, "Sure thing Caleb."

"So be good and sit down 'til Galloping's done pa's errand, then you can re-arrange the shape of his face if you want to."

Ned looked at Caleb and said, "Sure, anything you say."

Caleb called up to Galloping John, "Get your pants on then come into the back, pa wants a word."

You could have heard a pin drop in the bar; whenever either of the Johnson men spoke, above all Caleb, everybody else shut up, it was more than their life was worth not to.

Galloping John started to pull his pants on and called, "Coming Mr. Caleb, coming."

Everybody parted to make way for Caleb and Galloping John as they disappeared into the public bar, and nobody, but nobody, would have swapped places with John right then.

Ten minutes later, Galloping John threaded his way through the tables and chairs and disappeared out into the street with his instructions from Abraham.

Seconds later, a lone man who had been drinking with his back to Abraham and company finished his drink. He pulled the peak of his cap down over his eyes, stood up, and followed John out of the pub.

Abraham pulled his pocket-watch out of his waistcoat pocket and flipped it open; it was 11:30pm and John hadn't returned, he turned to Caleb and said, "Galloping's been gone a while, if he's pissed off and not done as I bid, I'll…"

Caleb patted his shovel-sized right-hand on his father's left knee and said, "Don't fret pa, he's not been gone that long."

"I get you another beer missa Ablaham," said Lice, "then if John's not back in a half hour, I go rookin'."

Abraham nodded in agreement, but some inexplicable thing started to nag away at him; as Lice stood up, he grabbed hold of his elbow and said, "Wait, fuck the beer, just get down to the Red Lion and find out where he is."

Lice acknowledged the order and slipped away.

The minutes ticked by until at close to midnight Lice returned and sat down at the table; he picked up his beer, gulped down a draft, and just stared at Abraham.

Abraham said, "Well, where was he?"

"He wasn't nowhere boss."

"What do you mean nowhere? He only left here just over an hour ago, he can't have just disappeared."

"Nobody's seen him boss."

"What, nobody from the Red Lion?"

"Yes, an' that's not all boss…" Lice took another drink of beer.

Abraham and Caleb stared at him until he'd put the tankard back down, and saw him shift uncomfortably in his seat.

"'Cos a couldn't find Garroping John, I went into Led Rion an' asked for Squeaker…" he looked from face-to-face and then said, "an' he never checked in."

Caleb frowned, leaned forwards, and said, "What? Nobody's seen Squeaker since our last meeting?"

"A don' know about that missa Careb, but nobody's seen him flom a Led Rion."

"And nobody from the Red Lion saw Galloping either?" said Abraham.

"No boss."

Abraham cast a suspicious glance to Caleb, frowned, and then turned back to Lice; he said, "Right, first thing tomorrow go over to the pastor's place and see if he's all right, then get him to go and check on Squat. After that make some discreet enquiries about Squeaker and meet Caleb and me here tomorrow night at half-past-seven. I want to know what the fuck's going on."

Chapter 24

Monday 3rd July 2006. Naomi & Carlton Wilkes' house

At 8:10am Naomi climbed into her car in preparation for going to work, she placed her handbag on the passenger seat, glanced at herself in the vanity mirror, fastened her seatbelt, and started the engine. She engaged gear, released the handbrake, and pulled forward the few yards to the end of her drive; she then stopped before pulling out into the road, to check that no traffic was coming. As she did so, her full handbag rolled over and almost fell into the passenger foot well. She applied the handbrake, disengaged first gear, and picked up her handbag with the intention of putting her fold-up shopping bag back into her glove compartment. She removed the bag, opened the glove compartment, and sat staring at it with her mouth open.

There in the compartment was an identical fold-up M & S shopping bag. For what seemed like minutes, she never moved; she remembered telling Helen that she'd misplaced the bag and had had to buy a replacement for it – but there it was, as large as life, and in the same place as she'd last seen it. With a puzzled expression on her face she placed the second fold-up bag next to the first, closed the glove compartment, and headed for work.

At 8:55am Naomi entered her office, said to Helen, "Don't question my actions, just come with me." She led Helen from the Council offices to the multi-storey car park and said, "Do you recall me telling you that I had to buy a replacement bag for the one that had gone missing?"

Helen said, "Yes."

Naomi extracted her car keys from her bag, clicked the button, and unlocked her car.

"Well look at this." She opened the passenger door, reached in, put her hand on the glove compartment catch, and stepped to one side so that Helen could see. She pressed the catch, opened the compartment, and said, "See?"

Helen looked in and said, "Yes, what about it?"

"What do you mean what about it?" She gestured towards the compartment and said, "Look, there are…" She turned and saw that there was only one bag in there.

"What?" she exclaimed, "How the hell…?"

Helen frowned and said, "Am I missing something?"

"Too right you are, I got into my car this morning, went to put my new bag into the glove compartment and found the original one there."

"What?"

"Yes 'what?'," said Naomi, "so where is it now?"

Helen looked at Naomi and wasn't sure what to say; she knew that Naomi would object to her challenging her grip on reality, but she was stumped too. She looked at her watch and said, "What time did you get here?"

"Not more than ten minutes ago."

"So presuming that you aren't losing your marbles…"

"Hey!" said Naomi with an edge to her voice, "Not you!"

Helen regretted saying the offhand remark and said, "Sorry…" She paused until she saw Naomi nod her acceptance and then said, "So, within ten minutes of you leaving your car, somebody has got inside, opened the glove compartment, removed the original bag, closed the glove compartment, locked the car, and disappeared?"

"Right."

"So why – and how?"

Naomi said, "The 'how?' I don't know. The 'why?' – maybe to make me think that I'm losing it?"

Once again Helen stared at Naomi in silence; she thought about whether she could be under strain following the receipt of the two strange notes and the episode with the van men, but then realised that if Naomi was right, something sinister was going on. She wheeled around and said, "Does this car park have any closed circuit TV cameras?"

"Yes it does."

"Then we need to get over to security and check them out."

At 9:20am Crowthorne heard a knock on his office door. He called, "Come in," and watched as Inspector Peter Milnes walked in.

"Yes Peter?" he said.

"Good morning sir," said Milnes, "We've just charged Rosalind Probus with the murder of her husband."

"My word, that was quick."

"Indeed it was sir, totally unexpected."

Crowthorne put down his pen and sat back in his chair.

"Did she have a motive?"

"Secret lover sir."

"Did she say that he was involved in the murder?"

"No sir, she overdosed her husband on sleeping tablets and he died in his sleep."

Crowthorne let out a gasp and shook his head. He said, "And were we right in assuming that it was something to do with Malaterre?"

"Yes sir, her long-time-lover attempted to row the body out into the middle of Dunsteth Reservoir, but for some reason the boat capsized."

"Hence our discovery of the oars?"

"Yes sir," Milnes paused and then said, "it never fails to amaze me how many people meet the same end for the same reason."

Crowthorne nodded and said, "And has she named the other party?"

"Yes sir."

"Anybody we know?"

"Not as such; but we do know of him. He was something of a minor celebrity round these parts a few years back. His name is Hess, John Hess, and he was an N.C.O. in the Duke of Lancaster's 4th Battalion based at Preston who was part of an undercover rescue mission in The Lebanon.

He and several others pulled out a small group of captured squaddies and a Papal Missionary. Hess was awarded a bravery medal because his C.O. had been killed and he had taken over."

Crowthorne said, "Oh yes, I remember the man – bald-headed, swarthy-looking guy. Didn't he end up with a gammy arm or something?"

"Yes sir, that's him. He got a massive electric shock when his parachute snagged a pylon on a night training exercise."

"Ooh nasty."

"Put him in hospital for months by all accounts…"

"And the Probus woman has implicated him?"

"Yes sir, we're issuing a warrant for his arrest."

"Is he still in the service?"

"No sir, he was honourably discharged about two years ago."

Crowthorne emitted an exasperated sigh and said, "Stupid sod; all that kudos and he's given it up for what?"

Milnes said, "There's better men than him gone down the same route sir."

"All right, do we know where he is?"

"No sir, and to be frank, if the Probus woman was on her way to France, he may already be out of the country."

Crowthorne nodded and said, "Yes, very well, put out the usual alerts."

"One other thing sir."

"Yes?"

"Yes sir, one of our lads in 'B' Division was in the same outfit as Hess, and he's brought something to our attention that might have a bearing on proceedings."

"Go on," said Crowthorne.

"According to the P.C. from 'B' Division, Hess's best buddy was a chap from the Duke of Lancaster's Battalion too named Rory Macready, an underwater demolition expert."

Crowthorne didn't think that he could have been more shocked. He said, "Good God, that puts a whole new complexion on things."

"It does indeed sir."

"We'd better get him in for questioning too."

"It's already underway."

Crowthorne thought of something else; he said, "And we'd better let Inspector Kearns and his marine chappies know about this too. If the collapse at Malaterre was caused by a deliberate underwater explosion, that could make the whole structure much more unstable."

A knock at the door interrupted the conversation.

"Come in," called Crowthorne.

Sergeant Tasha Andrew walked in and said, "Sorry to disturb you sir, this just arrived in the morning post."

Crowthorne watched as Tasha placed a thick-looking letter in front of him.

"It's a copy of the Marine Surveyor's report sir."

"Ah yes, thank you. Are there any surprises in it?"

"No sir; they're advising us that in their opinion it was indeed an underwater detonation that triggered the collapse of the Malaterre buildings and that the immediate surroundings are highly unstable."

"Enough to hinder our investigations?"

"Not up to me to answer that sir," said Tasha.

"But in a nutshell?"

Tasha paused and then said, "In a nutshell sir, they want us to keep well away from the damaged area. It would seem that whoever perpetrated the act appeared to have been successful in covering up whatever it was he or she may have been trying to conceal, whilst also rendering that part of the building so unstable that it would be tantamount to suicide to disturb anything anywhere near it."

Crowthorne sat back in his chair and looked from face-to-face. He said, "So that's it then, we're buggered?"

Tasha looked down and raised her eyebrows.

Milnes said, "Looks that way sir."

Tasha emitted an 'Hmming' sound and looked back up.

"Tasha?" said Crowthorne.

"I don't want you to think that I'm any kind of expert on how to deal with submerged buildings and the like, but I am an avid watcher of all things historical if they're marine related."

"Such as?" said Crowthorne.

"Such as what's left of the villages around the edge of Santorini, or the remains and relics of Queen Cleopatra's harbour in Egypt, and similar programmes."

"And the point being?" said Crowthorne.

"Well, as I said earlier sir, it's not up to me to answer such questions, but I have seen cases where it has been necessary to destroy part of an unstable structure in order to stabilise the rest of it."

Crowthorne shook his head and said, "Sergeant Andrew, you continue to amaze me."

"Me too sir," said Milnes nodding and looking at Tasha with raised eyebrows.

"Have we heard how the drainage is progressing?" said Crowthorne.

"Ahead of schedule sir," said Tasha, "Kev Middleton rings every day to give us an update, and though he is pleased that things are progressing so well, he remains adamant that he won't be able to remove enough water to give us much less of a depth than eighteen to twenty feet at the best."

"That doesn't sound too bad," said Crowthorne.

"But not too good by all accounts either," said Tasha, "because the severest damage is in the bottom ten feet of the building on the easternmost tip of the south wing, where paradoxically, its highest point is too.

"By all accounts the building is Elizabethan in design which should have meant that the traditional 'E' shape layout would have seen the north and south wings with an equidistant height, but according to the plans we've been able to obtain, the latest occupants of the estate, the Page family, had an observation tower built on the southern wing to accommodate one of the family members penchant for stargazing. This in effect, added another fifteen feet to that wing, now giving it the appearance of a tower projecting above the water."

"So how much will be above the waterline once it's drained?" said Milnes.

"It's a three-storey building except for the additional tower on the south wing. The ceilings are twelve feet high per storey, and therefore it will be about forty feet high. We should be able to see at least half of it above water."

"Which means that the entire ground floor, most of the first floor, and nearly all of the damage will be below water," said Crowthorne.

"Yes sir, it will."

Crowthorne leaned forwards, picked up his pen, and started tapping it on a desk pad in front of him. He looked up and said, "We won't be able to keep the public away from the reservoir as such, nor do I see an apparent need for it at this juncture, but I will speak to Inspector Kearns about setting up an exclusion zone around Malaterre."

"Very wise sir," said Milnes, "and if you don't mind my tuppence worth, I suggest that we only allow the public onto the southernmost bank of the reservoir until we've completed our investigations, and the buildings have been made safe."

"Yes, good thinking Peter," said Crowthorne, "make it so." He looked at Tasha as he realised that he had used another saying often voiced by Captain Jean-Luc Picard from the Star Trek series, and saw that she was looking at him with half-raised eyebrows. He quickly dismissed it by saying, "Okay, we all have work to do – has anybody anything to add before we wind this up?"

Neither Milnes nor Tasha spoke.

"Very well, thank you both," he looked at Tasha and said, "and I shall be passing your interesting stabilisation comments on to Inspector Kearns."

Tasha said, "Thank you sir, but I doubt that he won't already have considered those measures."

Crowthorne watched as his two subordinates departed; it had been the second time in quick succession that he'd been impressed by Tasha. The seeds of an idea started to form, and the more he thought about it, the more sense it made.

He leaned forwards, picked up his telephone, and dialled Leo Chance's number in C.I.D.

Back at Walmsfield Borough Council Office's Security Department the officer-in-charge, said, "I know that it's frustrating ladies but I can't access today's recordings until six o'clock tomorrow morning."

"But that's ridiculous," said Helen, "what if the police wanted access to it today?"

"That would be different…"

"Then why can't *we* see them today?" said Naomi.

"Because, Mrs. Wilkes, you aren't the police."

"So?" said Helen, "We believe that somebody broke into Naomi's car and the longer we leave it, the more time they'll have to get away!"

"Oh, I see," said the officer, "did the thief get away with much?"

Before Helen could stop herself she blurted out, "Naomi's shopping bag!"

The security officer said, "Was there anything of value in it?"

"No, it was just the bag, but that's beside the point."

The security officer frowned and said, "This bag, was it valuable?"

Naomi and Helen looked at each other, until Naomi said, "No, it was a fold-up M & S bag."

The security officer hesitated and then said, "So somebody broke into your car to steal a fold-up M & S shopping bag; is that right Mrs. Wilkes?"

"More or less, yes."

"More or less?"

"They didn't exactly break into my car…"

"You left it unlocked?"

"No, whoever it was had a key."

Once again the security officer paused, he pondered for a couple of seconds and then said, "And are you the only person who has keys to the vehicle?"

"Obviously not Sherlock," said Helen, whose disdain with ex-boyfriend and security guard Justin still bore the scars.

The officer turned to Helen and said, "I don't think that there's any need for sarcasm Miss, I may seem like an inconsequential 'job's-worth' to you here, but as per the situation now, we do have our uses."

"I'm sorry," said Helen, "but it's obvious that Naomi doesn't have the only keys otherwise whoever got into the vehicle wouldn't have been able to!"

"Not so Miss. Entry could have been gained using a grabber."

Naomi frowned and repeated, "A grabber?"

"Yes Mrs. Wilkes. It's a device no bigger than a matchbox. People operating those devices usually wait in shopping centre car parks or at street corners, or wherever, and then press a button on the grabber when they see somebody aiming an electric key at a vehicle door to lock it. The device will then 'grab' the signal and store it. Thereafter, they can gain entry to the vehicle by using the grabber."

"Good Lord," said Naomi, "whatever next?"

"Yes Mrs. Wilkes. That's why you should always lock your car door by inserting the key into the lock whenever you're leaving it in a public place."

"Good grief," said Naomi, "talk about live and learn."

Even the acerbic Helen began to moderate her ideas about the security officer after learning that useful piece of info.

"Now," said the officer, "having said that, does anybody else have a set of keys?"

"My husband does, but why would he go to my car and take out my shopping bag?"

"Begging your pardon Mrs. Wilkes, but why would anybody take the risk of accessing your vehicle, maybe with the knowledge that the car park has CCTV installed, to steal a fold-up M & S bag?"

Helen opened her mouth to object but was suddenly cut off.

"Bugger – no!" said Naomi as she turned and ran out of the door.

Helen exchanged puzzled glances with the security officer and then set off behind Naomi.

With a thumping heart Naomi ran as fast as she could to her office, burst in and came to a dead stop.

Seconds later Helen ran in behind her and said, "N, what is it?"

Naomi pointed towards her desk.

Helen walked past her and saw a small piece of paper on Naomi's desk. She picked it up and looked at it.

Written upon it was, "2 Delta 2."

Chapter 25

*The Historic Research Department, Walmsfield
Borough Council*

"I'm starting to get pissed off now," said Naomi, "who the bloody hell's doing this, and why?" She paused and then said, "And what in Christ's name is '2 Delta 2' supposed to mean?!"

The phone rang on Naomi's desk; she snatched it up and said, "Naomi Wilkes."

"Mrs. Wilkes this is Mike Pomeroy in security…"

"Yes Mike?"

"Can you come back here? I have something to show you."

Naomi shot a glance at Helen and said, "We'll see you in a couple of minutes." She put the phone down and said, "The security guy wants us to go back over there."

Five minutes later Mike turned around when he heard Naomi and Helen enter; he said, "Thank you for coming. Following our conversation I went into the video monitoring room, which thanks to government cutbacks is not now manned," he shrugged and then said, "and I checked the camera overlooking your part of the car park. I think that you should see this." He got up from his seat, walked across the office, and held open the door.

"This way please ladies," he said. He escorted Naomi and Helen the short distance to the next room, unlocked the door, and went in. He walked across to a bank of monitors situated atop a large workstation, pointed and said, "This is camera CP3 which covers your area of the multi-storey car park."

Naomi and Helen looked to where Mike pointed, and saw that the screen was black.

"What's happened to it?" said Naomi.

Mike looked at the control panel and said, "According to this, the camera is still operational, so something must be blocking the lens."

"Well there's only one way to find out," said Helen, "let's go over there."

As the two friends and the security officer walked over to the car park, the Venetian blinds of an upper level office parted and a pair of inquisitive female eyes followed their progress.

"Good Lord," said Helen a few minutes later, "look at that!"

Naomi and Mike looked up at the CCTV camera and saw that the lens had been capped with a makeshift plastic bottle top.

Helen walked up to the camera and reached up.

"No, don't touch it Miss," said Mike, "let's leave it to the police."

"I wasn't going to remove it," said Helen, "I wanted to see if I could reach it." She looked up and then extended her arm, but saw that she was a full twenty-five centimetres short. She turned to Naomi and said, "You're taller than me, you try."

Naomi walked across to the camera, reached up, and saw that she too was unable to reach the cap.

"So somebody had to come here with a cap and a device for getting up to it," said Helen.

"Somebody who knew exactly where you parked your car," added Mike.

"And who knew where the cameras were," said Naomi.

Helen turned to Naomi and said, "It has to be somebody who works here."

"It doesn't follow that it *has* to be a Council employee," said Mike, "because in reality anybody could walk up here without drawing attention to themselves – but this *is* a staff-only car park, so if an outsider has done this, he or she may have had to reconnoitre the ground prior to doing it. And if they have, they may have been caught on the same camera looking."

"How long do you keep the CCTV recordings?" said Naomi.

"Two months."

Helen turned to Naomi and said, "And when did you get the first note?"

"About a fortnight ago."

"So if somebody was caught, we'll still have the footage?" said Helen to Mike.

"Yes Miss."

Naomi looked at Mike and said, "And how long would it take you check out the footage?"

"From when?"

Naomi turned to Helen and said, "What date was it that Percy came to see us before he brought Balls…" she hesitated as she saw Mike look at her, "…Marcus?"

Helen looked down for moment and then said, "The nineteenth of June – I remember it because it was just one week after I started. And that was when you got the first note too."

"Right," said Naomi. She turned to Mike and said, "From the nineteenth of June."

"A fortnight then," said Mike. He saw the friends nod and said, "Okay, in theory it should take a full seven days because we can only speed up the footage 'times two' otherwise we might miss something. However, if in the first instance we concentrate only from say, 0600 hours to 2000 hours that will cut out ten hours per day and reduce the overall watching time to a total of…" he removed his mobile phone from his pocket, clicked to a calculator app, tapped in the figures and said, "…just over four days if we monitor it non-stop, twenty-four hours per day."

"That's ridiculous," said Helen.

"And do you have the capability of monitoring it twenty-fours per day for the next four days?" said Naomi.

Mike shrugged and said, "Not a chance, unless we pay somebody overtime to do it."

Naomi said, "Brilliant! *We* can't authorise that, and if it is somebody employed by the Council, we can't ask anybody else to authorise it, in case it alerts them."

Mike thought about the situation for a few minutes and said, "I'm the Chief Security Officer here and there are two of us employed to cover the time from 0600 until 2200, Monday to Friday, and one guard from 0800 to 1600 Saturdays and Sundays. If you're happy with the arrangement, I'll make sure that the footage from CP3 is monitored whenever we've got any spare time; we'll start from 0900 today and we'll work our way backwards at double-speed, and see what we come up with."

Naomi looked at Helen, and then back to Mike; she said, "Thank you er…"

"Mike – Mike Pomeroy, Mrs. Wilkes."

"…Mike, I would appreciate that, and please call me Naomi."

Helen stepped forwards and extended her hand, she said, "And I'm Helen Milner, I started work here with Naomi three weeks ago, I'm sorry about the sarcastic 'Sherlock' comment I made earlier."

Mike smiled and shook the offered hand, "That's all right Miss," he said, "I get it all the time."

"And Helen's just fine too, thank you Mike."

Mike nodded and smiled.

At Rochdale Police Headquarters, twenty minutes later, Bob Crowthorne said, 'Brahma', 'hive', and 'two delta two', two notes written on the same paper, each note written in a different hand, one delivered by an unknown courier, one pushed through your home letterbox, and one left on your desk; is that it?"

"And somebody getting into my car and messing around with my property," said Naomi.

Crowthorne sat back in his chair and said, "This is serious Naomi; whoever is doing this knows where you live, where you work, where you park your car, how to get into your car, and how to get into your office."

"Maybe not that," said Naomi, "when Helen and I went across to the security office, I couldn't swear that we locked it."

"Nevertheless, it would be prudent given everything else, to presume that the perpetrator or perpetrators may have access to that too."

"But why would anybody do this to me? If they meant to harm me, surely they wouldn't warn me first."

"Intimidation Naomi; somebody is trying to get inside your head and mess with it."

"And to a certain extent it's working. I'm becoming very wary about where I go, and everything I do." She recalled the two occasions with the cars blocking her in at the Exchange shopping centre and the unnerving experience with the men in the van and said, "And what about those cars that blocked me in, and the two guys in the van, could they be part of this too?"

Crowthorne thought for a second and said, "Yes, maybe – probably."

There was a short silence as Crowthorne and Naomi pondered until Naomi said, "So what do you advise?"

"Do nothing for the next hour; stay in your office and don't venture out except for the calls of nature etc."

"And then what?"

"I'll ring you back and advise you further."

Naomi nodded and said, "Okay, I've got Helen here with me, so we'll both wait for your call." She said goodbye and put the phone down.

It rang again.

Naomi wasn't in any mood for niceties; she picked up the phone and said, "Walmsfield Historic Research Department."

A soft-spoken female voice at the other end said, "Could I speak to Mrs. Naomi Wilkes please?"

"Yes, speaking."

"Ah Mrs. Wilkes, we noted that you didn't respond to our message left last Monday as per your request?"

Naomi frowned and said, "What message, what request?"

"Your request to call you at work, last Monday."

Naomi tried to think if she'd forgotten something, but nothing came to mind. "I'm sorry," she said, "I'm still in the dark, what request are you referring to?"

Helen, who'd been taking in one side of the conversation looked up and frowned. She tapped the top of her desk with her pen and mouthed, "Who is it?"

Naomi covered the mouthpiece of the phone and mouthed back, "No idea."

"You asked us to call this number at 8am last Monday, and leave a message if your request was acceptable; but if you never received it…"

Naomi suddenly recalled the missing Message 13.

"…I apologise, so let me re-iterate, I have checked with the Directors, and the answer to your question is, 'Yes'."

Naomi said, "Okay, I get that the answer is 'Yes', now can you tell me who you are and what the question is?"

There was a pause at the other end of the line, and then the caller said, "I'm sorry, haven't I made myself clear?"

"You have," said Naomi, "but I still don't know who you are, and what the question is supposed to be."

Helen put down her pen and sat back in her chair fascinated by the conversation.

"I'm Jacqueline Williams; I'm one of the personal assistants at Messrs. Parslow and Turner."

"And the question was, Ms. Williams?"

"About the arrangements… "

"Arrangements?"

Helen frowned but listened intently.

"Yes Mrs. Wilkes, the Directors have confirmed that we will collect your husband's body from Manchester Royal Hospital next week."

Naomi dropped the phone, jumped up from her chair, and knocked it over backwards.

A startled Helen saw the look of horror on Naomi's face and said, "N, what is it?"

Naomi looked at Helen and shrieked, "This is too much now! Get that fucking woman off my phone… "

Chapter 26

At 7:30pm Assassin Agent Spécial, Capitaine Nicolas Durand sat in the corner of the public bar with a newspaper, and listened.

Because of his pronounced French accent he'd given everybody in, and associated with, the public house the idea that he was a deaf mute, one of the skills that he had acquired so that his nationality wouldn't be given away, whilst affording him the ability to be able to listen to conversations without being suspected. He had been taught not to react to any kind of sudden sound, and on one occasion, when Caleb Johnson had crept up and banged a pewter tankard on a table behind him, as per the training he'd received at l'Ecole Spéciale Militaire de Saint-Cyr, the Special Military School of Saint-Cyr, he'd shown no sign of hearing it, and had convinced everybody in the pub that he was indeed profoundly deaf and dumb.

He had disposed of the men referred to as "Squeaker" and "Galloping John," but he'd been careful not to endanger the rest of his mission by being exposed before he'd found out what their plan for the Page family was.

He huddled over the top of his newspaper, pulled his cap down over his eyes and took everything in.

Across the room Abraham looked around and saw that the only other person in the bar was 'the deaf mute'. He leaned across the table to Lice and said, "Right, let's have it."

Lice also looked around the room and then said, "A went to see the pastor, an' he checked on Squat an' they was both awlight boss."

"And has anybody heard anything about Squeaker?"

"No boss."

Caleb leaned forwards and said, "What nothing at all?"

"No Missa Careb."

"And what about Galloping?" said Abraham, "Did he show up?"

"Rirry says he's no ronger about."

Abraham leaned back in his chair, turned to Caleb, and said, "I know that my hearing isn't what it used to be, but sometimes this Chinky bastard beats me."

"Rirry says Garropin's no ronger about boss, a couldn't make it simprer!"

"He said that Lily says Galloping's no longer about pa," said Caleb.

Abraham wheeled around to Lice and said, "What? Why not? Where's he gone?"

Caleb remembered Ned's threat to re-arrange Galloping's face after he'd insulted Lily, and without saying a word got up and went into the lounge bar. He saw Ned, and then sat down next to him at his table.

Ned turned to object and then saw who it was; he said, "Howdo Caleb, anything up?"

"Did you put Galloping into hospital after I told you to leave him be?"

With no little amount of concern Ned said, "Course not! I wouldn't do that."

"Then where is he?"

Ned looked left and then right, and then leaned closer towards Caleb; he said, "We don't know. He disappeared on that night you and your pa were last here, and he hasn't been seen since."

Caleb frowned and said, "Right – any ideas?"

"We wondered if it was one of you, so nobody's said a thing."

Caleb frowned, said, "It wasn't any of us, so if you do hear something, tip me the wink."

"Will do."

Caleb nodded, thanked Ned, and walked back deep in thought to the public bar; he sat down at the table and conveyed his conversation to Abraham and Lice.

Abraham leaned back in his chair and stroked his chin; he looked at Caleb and said, "Something's going on." He thought about the pastor and Squat and he knew from past experience that they wouldn't have said anything to anybody. Next he considered the miner whom they'd crossed swords with a couple of weeks' earlier.

"And what about that arsehole who upset the pastor, has anything been seen of him?"

"A couldn't lightry say boss, 'cos a don't come here all a time."

Abraham thought for a few seconds and then said, "If Squeaker had gone on his own I might have understood that, but for something to happen to Galloping too is too much of a coincidence, so somebody knows something."

"Can we manage without Squeaker?" said Caleb.

"Not really," said Abraham, "what I'd got in mind was pushing it even with him, so unless Squeaker turns up, I think that we need to send for you-know-who."

Across the room Nicolas fractionally turned his head to pick up the info.

Caleb looked at his father and saw him gesture towards his back with his right thumb. The penny dropped, his mouth fell open, and he said, "You're not saying…"

"Yes."

Caleb said, "What! Harry the Camel – he's as mad as a farmyard rat!"

"And Shake," said Abraham.

Caleb flopped back in his seat and said, "Come on pa, the fucking Wenderliks – you can't be serious?"

Abraham leaned forwards and said, "It's either them or Gogs so what choice do we have? We have no idea how many people we'll be dealing with, so we have to be prepared."

"But they're both complete bloody lunatics – nobody can control Camel when he's off on one, and Jake's not called

'Shake' for nothing. He can have a fit if he doesn't put matching socks on."

"So would you prefer Gogs?"

"I would have done if he could see all right, but he's as blind as a bat without his specs on."

Abraham leaned closer to Caleb and said, "Well make your mind up boy, 'cos we ain't exactly awash with murderous lunatics are we?"

Caleb leaned back and said, "We've got to get some better help."

"Yeah," said Abraham, "and where do you suggest we look for it?"

Caleb groaned and then had a brainwave; he said, "What about Grinner?"

Abraham raised his eyebrows and said, "Whoa – now you're pushing it, he's downright odd."

"But what if we could get him working for us?"

Abraham pondered awhile and then said, "Maybe as a last resort, but I heard that he was working somewhere the other side of Manchester – Stockport, I think."

"Are you sure he would be good to have on a gang boss," said Lice, "he's, he's…"

"Weird?" said Abraham.

"Yes boss."

Abraham made up his mind, turned to Caleb and said, "No, let's get Camel and Shake in first, they're working in Bolton at the moment, so if we can keep them off the booze before the job, they'll be all right."

Lice sat with a frown on his face until there was a lull in the conversation, he then leaned forward and said, "Can a say something boss?"

Abraham looked down and said, "What?"

"At's a same man what's sitting in a corner as rast time we was here."

Abraham turned, looked at the back of Nicolas and then leaned across to Caleb – he said, "He's the mute isn't he?"

Caleb said, "Yes, why?"

Abraham looked at Nicolas again and then leaned over to Lice, he said, "So what are you getting at?"

"A dunno boss, maybe nothin', maybe somethin'?"

Abraham pondered for a few seconds and then said, "Do you think that he's listening to us?"

Lice looked up and said, "A dunno boss, it's jus' odd 'at he's here again."

Abraham shot another quick glance at Nicolas and said, "Right, let's not take any chances – when he leaves, do him."

Lice said, "Awlight boss."

"Wait," said Caleb in a hushed tone, "if we're doing those frogs we don't want to be attracting any attention to ourselves, and, if anything goes wrong we can't afford to lose any more men, especially if we already have to call on idiots like the Wenderliks."

Abraham nodded and then leaned across to Lice, he said, "All right, but when he leaves, follow him and see where he goes. Then if necessary we can do him later."

Lice nodded and said, "So what's a plan boss?"

Abraham looked across towards Nicolas and then leaned towards Lice, he said, "Today's the fifth and we need time to arrange the Wenderliks so you get the pastor and Squat to meet us here on Friday the 18th and we'll make the final arrangements."

At 9:50pm Nicolas finished his beer, folded up his newspaper, stuffed it into his jacket pocket, and exited the bar.

Across the room, Caleb gave Lice a dig.

Lice finished his beer and walked out into Henry Street; he looked left, and then right, but saw no sign of Nicolas. He walked across to the other side and looked towards Suffolk Street and then towards Millstone Road, but as before he saw no sign. Because Suffolk Street was closer, he set off at a run, hoping that his quarry had opted to go that way, and that he wouldn't have to report to Abraham that he'd lost him so soon.

Back in the public bar Caleb did a double take when to his amazement, he saw Nicolas walk back into the bar with a mug of ale, sit back at his table, and re-commence reading his paper. He looked at Abraham and said, "The mute's back."

Abraham turned around and saw Nicolas engrossed in his paper and said, "You dopey arseholes, he went for another drink."

Caleb looked at Nicolas and said, "So where's Lice?"

"Probably chasing his shadow," said Abraham, "no doubt he'll be back when he realises he's lost the mute."

Caleb continued staring at the back of Nicolas and said, "Hmm, I don't know pa – I'm getting an odd feeling about him now."

Half an hour later Lice came panting into the bar and almost stopped dead when he saw Nicolas; he frowned, went back to the Johnson's table, and sat down.

"How the fuck he do that?" he said.

"What? Get another drink?" said Abraham.

Lice glared at Nicolas's back and said, "I ain' stupid boss, 'at fucker wasn't inna bar when a reft."

"Maybe he went for a piss?" said Abraham.

Caleb looked suspiciously back at Nicolas and said, "I don't know; – perhaps we should let Lice do him after all."

Abraham said, "All right, but not too close to The Pit, we don't want Bull getting suspicious."

Fifteen minutes later, Nicolas finished the last of his drink, stuffed his newspaper into his pocket, and exited once again.

Lice was up like a flash; he crossed the bar, pushed through the few people milling around the door and went out into Henry Street. Once again he saw no sign of Nicolas.

"Fuck!" he spat out, "Not again…" He ran across the street and looked towards Suffolk Street and Millstone Road but as before, saw nothing.

"Fuck!" he said again. He ran back into the bar, saw no sign of Nicolas, and then charged into the urinal – and saw nobody.

With a tortured look upon his face he returned to the public bar and sat down at the Johnson's table.

"'At bastard's disappeared inna thin air again," he said, "what is he a fuckin' irrusionist?"

"You've lost him again?" said Caleb.

Out of character, Lice said, "You fuckin' deaf? A said so didn' a?"

Caleb reacted instantly; he grabbed hold of Lice's jacket and yanked him out of his chair. He opened his mouth to speak, but felt something sharp sticking into his neck just below his Adam's apple.

"You gonna make me stick you Careb?" said Lice.

Abraham yanked the two men apart as Bull walked into the room.

"Is everything all right with you boys?" said Bull.

"It's just a little disagreement," said Abraham.

"You know that I don't allow fighting in here."

"And I told you that it's just a disagreement. They weren't fighting!"

Bull stared at all three men who glared back in defiance – he held their gaze for a few seconds then nodded, and retreated into the lounge bar.

Lice looked at the Johnson's and said, "I'm solly boss, an' Missa Careb, but 'at deaf fucker made me pissed off vanishing rike 'at. 'Ere's something funny about him, a know it."

Caleb glared at Lice for a second, turned to Abraham, and said, "He may be right."

Abraham said, "All right, let's say that you're both correct and that there is more to the mute than meets the eye, what do you think it's about? Do you think he's spying on us for some reason?"

Caleb and Lice didn't answer.

"And if he is spying on us, why?"

Caleb said, "How many years have we been coming in here pa? Yet, it wasn't until about a week ago that we started seeing him – maybe it is something to do with what we've got planned?"

Abraham pondered and then said, "All right, if he's somehow overheard us he'll be expecting us to meet here on Friday the eighteenth right?"

Both men nodded.

"So," said Abraham, "let's meet here as arranged and if he turns up, we'll know that something's amiss."

"Unless he's become a regular," said Caleb.

"Right, so have a word with Ned and ask him to let you know how many times he comes in from now on, and if possible get Lifting Lily to give him a pull and steal his wallet. That might tell us who he is and where he's from."

"Why don' a just fuckin' knock it outa him boss?" said Lice.

"Because you'd have to find him first – and after tonight's performances I doubt you could find your cock with both hands."

Outside in Henry Street, Nicolas stepped out of the shadow of a deep doorway and ran towards Millstone Road.

He realised that the Johnsons were now suspicious of him and that they were planning to do something that required a lot of people. He knew that it was about the Pages and that it could be at Malaterre, but what was being planned, and when, were still a mystery to him.

He now needed to do two things; find the Wenderliks in Bolton, and be in the public bar of The Monkey Pit on the eighteenth.

Chapter 27

'Nine-hundred-and-ninety-nine can't bide
The shame or mocking or laughter,
But the Thousandth Man will stand by your side,
To the gallows-foot – and after.'

\- Rudyard Kipling

Monday 3rd July 2006. The Historic Research Department, Walmsfield Borough Council

"It's all right Naomi," said Crowthorne, "I understand your anguish and following the call from the undertakers, I'm getting a copy of their phone records plus I'm taking positive action."

"What kind of positive action?"

"For the next couple of weeks I'm assigning a man to you for protection."

"What about Carlton? It's *his* life that was being threatened, not mine."

Crowthorne paused and then said, "I don't think so. Of course we'll keep a weather eye on him and proceedings, but I think that this is all about you, not Carlton."

"But why, what the hell have I done?"

"We can speculate all day long, but it would only ever be that, so until whoever it is emerges from under their stone we'll keep you safe."

"And will they emerge from under their stone, or do you think that they'll remain anonymous?"

"They'll reveal themselves in time. These types of games have to have a payoff; the antagonists usually derive a perverse pleasure from tormenting their victims and then letting them know who their tormentor was."

Naomi said, "I don't like the sound of that."

"Quite so – but the measures I'm putting in place should keep you out of harm's way."

"Should?"

Crowthorne hesitated and then said, "From a professional standpoint I can't offer you more. You know that I'll do everything in my power to protect you, but there's always the unforeseen." He opted not to air his suspicion that in Naomi's case, he was expecting an unforeseen.

"Thank you Bob," said Naomi, "you know that I appreciate what you do for me, but do you think that we could be overreacting a bit?"

"I'm not prepared to take any chances. We've seen that whoever is behind this has access to your vehicle and place of work, and they even know where you live, therefore I feel justified in taking these steps."

"So does that mean that somebody will be parked outside my house every night for the next two weeks, even when I'm at home in bed?"

"Yes, but it won't be so obvious; and there are other more advanced techniques of surveillance available to us if we need them."

Naomi hesitated before answering and then said, "And will I have different people following me, or will I be like the Queen and have some guy with me 24/7?"

Crowthorne smiled and said, "I am assigning one particular officer to you for the most part, but it won't be just him; and no, I'm afraid that you won't be getting the level of security that Her Majesty gets."

Naomi blushed and said, "Course not, sorry." She then asked, "Will I get to meet my new escort before he starts looking after me?"

"You already have."

"Oh, who is it?"

"Your old friend Leo."

It felt as though a weight lifted off Naomi's shoulders; she said, "Leo Chance?"

"Yes."

Naomi smiled and leaned back in her seat; "That is so good to know," she said, "will he accompany me, or follow me, or what?"

"He'll accompany you wherever you go, and there'll be a different type of more discreet accompaniment whenever you're apart."

"But won't his presence be a bit too obvious to whoever's trying to scare me?"

"Maybe so, but that's the idea."

"Okay," said Naomi, "so when can I expect to see him?"

Crowthorne looked at his watch and said, "Anytime soon, I despatched him half an hour ago."

Almost on cue, there was a tap at Naomi's office door; Helen got up, opened it, and was for a few intense seconds, distracted by the good-looking man standing in front of her.

Detective Sergeant Brandon Talion Chance, known as 'Leo' to all of his friends and acquaintances was six feet tall, slim, suntanned, and very fit looking. He had short, dark hair, a handsome angular face, and perfect white teeth behind an engaging smile.

"Good morning madam, you must be Miss Milner," he said.

Naomi looked up and saw Leo; she beamed and said to Crowthorne, "He's here!"

"Good," said Crowthorne, "once you've finished catching up, try to concentrate on the reason for Leo being with you, follow his instructions to the letter, and don't hesitate to contact me if anything else unusual happens."

Ten miles south of Walmsfield, an unlisted mobile phone sprang into life; the owner picked it up, clicked the symbol, and said, "Yes?"

"It went as you said."

The owner of the phone nodded slowly and said, "Good. Go four now, then five in three."

"Very good."

The phone owner terminated the call and then dialled another number.

"Yes," said the person who answered.

"Check for UFOs. If any, go level three, post zero two alpha. Understood?"

"Understood."

The phone owner terminated the call, deliberated for a few seconds, then reached for a different phone and pressed the number one.

"Yes sir," said a female voice.

"I'll be out this afternoon."

"Okay, anything I can do in your absence?"

"No thank you, just hold the fort."

"Will do."

At 2:45am the following morning Sergeant Tasha Andrew sat with D. C. Roger Walburn in the rear of an unmarked observation vehicle, parked around the corner from the Wilkes' house, watching the monitors of two high-powered night-vision cameras covering both directions to Naomi and Carlton's home.

The approach of dawn was starting to alter the appearance of the night sky, and both colleagues were beginning to feel the first stages of tiredness.

Tasha's new appointment to the C.I.D had come as an unexpected surprise, and when she'd been informed that surveillance of the Wilkes' house was to be undertaken with immediate effect, she'd volunteered for the first night without question, despite a protest from Crowthorne – and having started duty at 14:00 hours the previous day. In the end her ebullient enthusiasm had overcome all objections and she'd been allowed to do the first night.

"I've got a bit more coffee if you'd like some," said Roger.

Tasha turned and said, "If you're sure, I came on at two this afternoon and although I catnapped at the station for a couple of hours, I'm starting to feel it."

Roger said, "Talk about glutton for punishment!"

Tasha smiled and said, "This is my first night in C.I.D. so I wanted to show some willing!"

Roger smiled back and said, "This is my third year, so trust me, most of it is bloody boring." He reached down into his bag, retrieved his flask, and poured some of the lukewarm liquid into the lid.

"Here you are, it's…" Roger hesitated as he caught sight of a faint movement on camera one out of the corner of his eye.

Tasha saw Roger's distraction and turned towards monitor one. Almost immediately camera one appeared to fall and then blank out. Both colleagues turned and stared into monitor two. They watched for several minutes but saw no movement.

"What do you think happened?" said Tasha.

Roger kept staring into monitor two and then said, "I'm not sure; it looks as though the camera has fallen."

"Where was it placed?"

"On the side of a telegraph pole seventy-five yards from the Wilkes house."

The colleagues continued to stare at the monitor for several minutes longer but saw nothing suspicious.

"Maybe it got dislodged by a squirrel or something?" said Tasha.

"I wouldn't be surprised," said Roger, "when you've been doing this as long as I have nothing shocks you anymore."

Tasha glanced away, reached for her lukewarm coffee, and then monitor two blanked out.

"Shit!" said Roger, "something's up!"

Without thinking Tasha snatched open the side door of the van and ran straight into a huge clenched fist encased in a silk glove. The searing blow knocked her straight out and opened up a deep gash from her right eye socket to halfway down her cheek.

Roger saw what was happening, attempted to get to his feet, and was hit in the chest by a 50,000-volt taser. His convulsing body arched backwards until all went black.

At 5:00am Naomi and Carlton were wakened by somebody ringing on their front doorbell; Naomi got up first and looked out of the window. To her surprise she saw two police cars with flashing blue lights stopped outside.

"Crikey," she said, "what the hell's going on?"

Carlton walked to the window and looked out too; "You get some clothes on," he said, "and I'll go and see what's happened."

Two minutes later he opened the front door and saw Bob Crowthorne standing there.

"Bob!" he said, "what on earth are you doing here?"

"Do you mind if I come in?"

"No, not at all." Carlton pulled the door opened wider and stepped to one side to let Crowthorne past; as he did so, he stepped onto something. He looked down and saw a small piece of paper sticking out from below his left foot. He reached down got hold of it, and looked at it. One side was blank, on the other was written the word, 'male'.

Chapter 28

Tuesday 4th July 2006. The Dunsteth Reservoir

At 05:17am, and for the first time in living memory, the water level of the Dunsteth Reservoir dropped below the thirty-foot marker. A full ten feet of the main Malaterre Estate buildings now lay exposed to view, plus the extra seven feet of the walls of the observation tower on the roof of the south wing. The windows were all missing, as was the eight-foot high glass dome.

As the water had drained away, the building had become exposed to the warm summer air; the sandstone ashlars and the lime mortar joints had started to dry, and they'd started to contract. Under normal circumstances the natural drying process wouldn't have presented any particular dangers or problems to the structural integrity, but in the case of Malaterre, the circumstances weren't normal by any standard.

At ground floor level, on the easternmost corner of the south wing, a ten-foot diameter hole had been blown into the masonry causing a further six feet high by ten feet wide section of the stonework directly above, to become very unstable indeed. And as more and more of the masonry above began to dry out, the tiny by comparison stresses that applied to the joints escalated that instability, and hairline cracks started to form around the area of destruction. Tiny pieces of stone and jointing material became dislodged and floated down to the reservoir bed, and every now and then bubbles broke the surface of the water adjacent to the south wing.

On the southern bank of the reservoir a young back-packer who'd slept in his one-man tent emerged into the sunshine dressed only in a pair of Calvin Klein cotton underpants. He stretched his arms into the cool early morning sunshine, yawned, and then stuffed both hands down the front of his underwear. He took hold of his testicles in his right hand and his semi-hard penis in his left. He looked all around, checked to see if anybody was present, and then squeezed and massaged until he became fully hard. Once more he looked around, and then satisfied that he was alone, he stepped out of his underwear.

He looked down at his naked body and felt a thrill of excitement. There was something wonderful and exhilarating about being out in the open, naked, and hard, and he relished every delicious, naughty, moment of it.

With his manhood sticking proudly out in front of him, he walked to the water's edge and considered going in for a swim. He touched the water with the toes of his right foot and remained motionless whilst he decided what to do.

Thirty feet below, at the eastern corner of the south wing of Malaterre, multiple stress fractures suddenly failed and a huge piece of the building became detached. It plummeted down and a large crack snaked up the south-eastern wall, breaking open joints, splitting sandstone ashlars, and cracking windowsills. The heavy falling masonry dropped onto an interior stone floor, split it open, and continued its descent into a basement room.

Seconds later another piece of masonry disconnected from the lower levels of the first floor, hit the jagged edges of the gaping hole at ground floor level and arced over to the left. As it cascaded into the basement behind the first piece, a huge chunk smashed into the basement floor and smashed a three-foot by four-foot hole into it. A second crack shot up the exterior of the south-eastern wall and continued upwards to the roof level of the first floor. At the same time, a mirror crack followed the identical route up the interior. But that crack didn't stop at the first floor; it continued on up, out of the water, to the ceiling level of the second floor.

On the banks of Dunsteth Reservoir the naked young man heard a sharp crack that resembled a gunshot. The sound spread out across the surface of the water, and then echoed with a second lesser crack as it hit the dam wall in the distance. Mesmerised by the sound, and staring in all directions he jumped back as a small wave engulfed both of his feet and continued up the bank for another three or four feet behind him.

In front he could see the outline of the first building sticking out of the water, and in the distance he could see the outline of another, but he had seen nothing to indicate where the sound could have come from.

He snatched up his underpants and pulled them back on, fearful that a warden or local poacher may have seen him. He ran to his tent, dressed, and packed everything away. Thirty minutes later, there was no sign that anybody had ever been near the reservoir to witness the momentous occurrence.

In the submerged basement of the Malaterre Estate, the churning, disturbed water began to clear, and as it did so the top of a door could be seen through the hole in the basement floor; a door with a shiny bronze escutcheon plate in the top right-hand corner.

Chapter 29

Friday 11th September 1868. Trinity Street, Bolton, Lancashire

Nicolas Durand stood in the doorway of the new Railwayman's Arms public house with a small beer in his hand, and stared down the road towards the Trinity Street Railway Station construction site.

He pulled his watch out of his waistcoat pocket and flipped it open; it was 7:55pm. He knew that the current shift would end at 8pm, and that both of the Wenderliks would be finishing then. He'd learned that they were in the habit of calling into the Railwayman's Arms for a drink after work, and especially after payday, and he also knew that the Chinaman Lice intended calling to see them with Abraham's proposal the following day.

It had taken him three full days to find the Wenderliks, and then another two to find out where they were living and employed; not an easy task for a man with a French accent, and without wanting to draw attention to himself.

His biggest ally had turned out to be Bull, the landlord of The Monkey Pit. He'd seen the look of stress on Bull's face following the altercation between Lice and Caleb, and he'd followed him to market in Rochdale the next day. He'd taken a huge risk, approached him, revealed his true identity, and had prayed that the English dislike of Frenchmen wouldn't compromise his position. But he needn't have worried; he'd come to the conclusion that Bull would have sided with Napoleon himself, if it would have helped him to get the Johnsons out of his pub and his life.

The whistle from the construction site sounded signalling the end of the shift, and within a few minutes, men started to wander off the site.

Nicolas walked back inside, sat down at a table facing the bar, and spread a newspaper on the table in front of him. He leaned down and made sure that the knife he'd placed in his right boot was just where he wanted it.

At 8:15pm the door opened and the men from the construction site poured in; he'd been puzzled by Harry Wenderlik's nickname 'Harry the Camel' until a large man with a hump on his back walked in, followed by a smaller man with similar features, but minus the hump.

"I'm ready for this," said Harry, "so get 'em in lad." He propelled Jake towards the bar.

"Do you want a saucer of peas?" said Jake.

"Yes, you get us them, and I'll get some bread and cheese for us snap later."

Jake nodded and waited for his turn at the bar.

Without making it obvious, Nicolas watched each man from the site as he paid for his food or drink, until he saw the man that would suit him best. He was a thick set, tough-looking man with an intolerant face, who appeared to be trying to conceal his pay packet whilst paying the barman.

He shifted his position in his chair, and saw that the man's wage packet seemed thicker than the others, leading him to speculate that he may have either been a foreman or boss with more pay, or that he may have been in receipt of some sort of bonus. Regardless, he saw that the man was being very careful not to put his wage packet on display.

He took in a deep breath, stood up, and called, "Attendez Messieurs!"

At first nobody took any notice, he then banged on his table and called, "Gentlemen, s'il vous plait – wait. Don't pay for your boissons…er, pardon – 'ow you say – drinks."

Everybody turned to look at him with curious looks upon their faces.

"I am sorry to interrupt you all, but you will hear from my accent that I am French, and in my country we have a tradition when somebody close dies, we celebrate their passing. So, because I am the only member of my family here, and my loving mother is now resting with God, I would like to buy everybody a drink to wish her 'bon voyage' – d'accord?"

At first you could have heard a pin drop, but then one-by-one the workmen cottoned on and started calling their orders over the bar, and most of the men started ordering drinks that they would never have paid for themselves.

Within half an hour Nicolas was being celebrated as a 'decent bloke', in direct contrast to the 'bloody frogs' living in France, and to add to the 'bon camaraderie' he paid for a few bottles of red wine, which he knew would react how he wanted with the copious amounts of beer being consumed.

Amidst plenty of backslapping and commiserations for the loss of his dear mother, he extracted the pay packet from the pocket of the thickset furtive man, removed three pounds, and stuck it in the jacket pocket of Jake Wenderlik. He then confirmed his elevated position of being 'one of the good 'uns' by paying for bread and cheese all round with the money that he'd just stolen.

To wish everybody *'une bonne nuit',* he bought everybody a whisky and then, amidst a general call for him to stay, he departed.

He walked out of the Railwayman's Arms, wandered down towards the Railway Station construction site, found a comfortable place to sit, and waited.

The first indication that the party had deteriorated was when Jake Wenderlik came flying through the public bar window of the Railwayman's Arms followed by the thickset man whose wages had been lifted. He leapt onto the prone figure of Jake and commenced beating him about the face with his fists.

The animal roar that preceded the appearance of 'Harry the Camel' Wenderlik was awesome. He came raging out of the pub and started laying into the thickset man who was beating his brother. Within minutes all hell had let loose with fists and bottles flying around, until the police had arrived.

Most of the participants had been arrested; others had been sent to hospital with injuries to their faces and bodies, and the three men with the most serious injuries had been the thickset man whose wages had been relocated, Harry, and Jake Wenderlik.

Nicolas got up from his makeshift seat and ambled back to his small hotel to get an early night; – he wanted to be up in time for the morning train back to Rochdale.

At 2:00pm the next day, Nicolas walked into the drawing room of Malaterre with another man; he nodded at the gathered family and then turned to Sabine.

"Madame Avrain," he said, "je suis Nicolas Durand – un capitaine de l'armée française, anciennement de l'Ecole Spéciale Militaire de Saint-Cyr, et ceci est mon compagnon Sergent Philipe Moreau."

"Please, Capitaine Durand, my English is good now," said Sabine.

"Then in that case Madame, I am Nicolas Durand, a Captain in the French Army, formerly of the Special Military School of Saint-Cyr, and this is my companion Sergeant Philipe Moreau. We have been despatched here by Brigadier General Niel, with instructions to protect you all.

Charles Page was astounded. He said, "To protect us, – from what? And who is Brigadier General Niel?"

Sabine said, "Adolphe Niel is the Minister for War in France and he is one of my oldest and dearest friends, he knows about our family connection and I informed him about our situation."

"But was that necessary Saba?" said Charles's father, Etienne.

"When I heard that the family might be going into direct conflict with the horrible Johnson men, I wasn't prepared to take any chances."

"But surely they wouldn't do anything physical to us?" said Charles's younger sister, Elodie.

"I am not saying that they will, but I didn't want to risk it."

"And so that is why we are here," said Nicolas, "Philipe will be staying with you until we are sure that the danger has passed, and I shall be trying to discover what, if anything, is being planned, and trying to stop it before it happens."

"Do you think that we are in danger M'sieu?" said Monique, Charles's youngest sister.

Nicolas thought about his answer for a second and decided that honesty was the best policy. He said, "It is possible Mademoiselle."

Charles's mother Marie-Francoise said, "And what makes you suspect that, Capitaine Durand?"

Nicolas turned to her and said, "I have been in England for just over two weeks Madame, and I have been gathering information on some kind of move against you all, but I have not yet been able to establish what form it will take, and when it will take place."

"Then I insist that you escort the family out of Malaterre to somewhere safe, Capitaine," said Sabine.

"That of course is one of our considerations," said Nicolas, "but if the estate is being watched by our adversaries, and they discover where we have relocated to, the family would be in just as much danger there."

Charles said, "Why? If we've moved out of Malaterre, then the Johnsons would have achieved what they wanted, so why would we still be in danger?"

"Because we will still own the estate wherever we are living," said Etienne, "and we can still refuse to sell it to Hundersfield District Council."

"That is correct," said Nicolas.

"So what do you propose?" said Marie-Francoise.

"I know that the Johnsons are meeting with some other men on the night of Friday the eighteenth, next week, and I shall try to find out what is being planned. In the meantime, Philipe will stay here with you. I will check in with him every day before noon, and if any of you need to leave the estate, it should be with me."

"And what if something happens to you Capitaine?" said Etienne.

"Then Philipe will know because I will not have reported to him and he will escort you out of harm's way – to France if necessary."

Just after 4pm Nicolas prepared to leave; he was escorted to the door by Etienne, Charles, and Philipe. He shook the hands of Etienne and Charles, bid them *'au revoir',* and walked to the stables with Philipe.

"This is a far more dangerous situation than I have told the family Philipe, so you must remember the Brigadier General's orders."

"I know," said Philipe, "to get Charles out of Malaterre at all cost."

Nicolas looked at his friend of many years and said, "I know you Philipe, we have fought too many battles for me not to understand how your mind works, and I know that you will do everything in your power to save the women; but, if it comes to a direct choice, you have your orders."

Philipe put his hand on Nicolas's shoulder and said, "I know my friend, and if it comes to it, I will carry them out as instructed."

"Bon," said Nicolas, "now I have to figure out how to go back into that foul Monkey Pit drinking house without being seen."

Chapter 30

*Wednesday 5th July 2006. The M20 motorway,
Ashford, Kent*

Stephen Page assessed the speed and pace of the traffic ahead,
adjusted his speed, and then clicked the Mercedes' cruise
control on. He felt the minute surge as the car's computer took
control, then removed his right foot from the accelerator and
put it into a more comfortable position. It was 10:05am, it was
going to be a long journey back to Bury, and of all of the car's
numerous functions, cruise control was his favourite.

He reflected upon the last few days. His visit to a select
London-based book fair had been a success. He'd managed to
secure three of the seven volumes that he'd wanted, and he'd
made a few useful contacts. But the most enjoyable aspect of
the trip had been when he'd visited his sister Kate, and had
seen the look of happiness on her face, upon her return from
honeymoon.

Apart from the expected account of every minute of every
day, as per the norm with his sister about every holiday from
as early as he could remember, she'd also told him about the
diversion to Martinique and Les Trois-Ilets, and the visit to the
original birthplace of their distant ancestor. She'd explained
how the original house was now a shell and all-in-all
unremarkable. She'd shown him the touristy leaflets supplied
by the museum in Empress Josephine's memory, and she'd
promised to tell him about 'the gruesome artefact' on display
there – but at that precise minute, her shopping, previously
ordered via the internet, had arrived. Dinner followed delivery,
drinks followed dinner, and bed followed a bit too much
alcohol and she still hadn't told him about the artefact.

He decided to make a note in his Filofax diary to call her
that evening; a simple letter 'K' would suffice. He let go of the

steering wheel with his left hand, reached across to the Filofax on the passenger seat and attempted to remove the propelling pencil from the integral belt loop. For a split second he took his eyes off the road…

Five-hundred metres ahead, in the middle lane of the motorway, Alf Newton, a short-tempered, aggressive truck driver was yelling a tirade of profanities at the female driver of a Citroen people carrier who hadn't moved over to let him pass. He had seen from a distance that the she appeared to be talking on her mobile phone, and as he'd approached the back of her vehicle he'd flashed his headlights several times and sounded his horn.

Kerry Jackson, the driver of the Citroen was oblivious to what was going on behind her. A recording of Meatloaf's 'Bat out of Hell' was playing on her CD player, she held a lit cigarette in her left hand whilst she steered with her right, and she was having an animated conversation on the mobile phone that was jammed into her left ear with her left shoulder with her best friend Tracy about the guy that they'd both coveted that she'd managed to *"cop off wiv"* the night before.

Newton pressed his foot down on the accelerator; ten tons of tractor unit pulling forty-one tons of loaded trailer surged forwards. Within less than a metre from the back of the Citroen, he moderated his speed, and continued drawing closer then dropping back at fifty-plus miles per hour, whilst flashing his lights.

Under cruise control, Stephen's Mercedes continued at seventy miles per hour in the outside lane and drew one hundred yards closer to the tractor/trailer unit. The propelling pencil remained fast in the Filofax belt loop and he looked down to see what was impeding it…

In the Citroen, Kerry decided to open the driver's door window to let out some of the cigarette smoke. She took hold of the steering wheel with her left hand, the one holding the cigarette, and pressed the electric button set into the armrest of the driver's door.

Through being distracted, she tapped the wrong button, the wrong way, and the passenger window fully opened. A blast of air travelling at fifty-five miles per hour, Storm Force ten on the Beaufort scale, blew the cigarette out of Kerry's hand and into one of the ruffles on the front of her cotton mini-skirt.

With the wind still surging in, she let out a shriek, dropped the mobile phone, and started batting like crazy at her skirt. She took her eyes off the road, lifted her foot off the accelerator, and started to turn left...

In the huge red MAN tractor unit, Newton yelled, "About fucking time!" He accelerated. The truck sped forwards and started to overtake the Citroen...

In the right-hand lane, Stephen's Mercedes was now two hundred metres behind the truck and closing fast...

In the Citroen, Kerry looked up and saw that she'd veered out of her lane, and yanked the wheel over to the right.

In the tractor unit Newton saw the Citroen veer right, yelled, "What the fuck?" and yanked his steering wheel over to the right too. In doing so, he caught sight of the fast-approaching Mercedes in the door mirror, said, "Shit," and yanked the wheel back over to the left. Now in panic, he saw that he was going to hit the rear of the Citroen and instinctively slammed his foot onto the truck's air brakes.

All eighteen wheels locked in a blinding blizzard of blue smoke. The trailer unit started to skid into the right-hand lane, and the tractor unit screeched towards the corner of the slowing people carrier.

With complete horror, Newton watched as it slammed into the Citroen, at first knocking it around to the right, and then rolling it, over and over, whilst it disintegrated into thousands of shattered car parts across the entire motorway.

In the left-hand lane, a company rep who was late for his next appointment had been staring at the screen of his mobile phone whilst trying to send a text. He looked up, saw the hell unfolding in front, dropped it, and hit the brakes. The ABS kicked in and his brand new BMW went into a rapid, controlled deceleration – but not so for the large lorry behind him who had no chance of stopping in the same distance.

The lorry smashed into the back of the BMW, ploughed over the top of it, and killed the rep outright.

The phone suddenly rang on Stephen's Garmin satnav. He looked up, saw the trailer unit slewing around to the right in a blur of smoke, and then he saw a huge chunk of lorry tyre arc up in the air and come screaming straight down at his windscreen. With a lightning reaction he yanked the wheel left and veered into the middle lane.

The tread slammed through the windscreen of a car that had been tailgating him, and killed the driver. That car then ploughed into the back of the trailer unit and buried itself bonnet deep under the back axle, almost beheading the already-dead driver.

Stephen's Mercedes shot across the motorway, roared around the back of the lorry on top of the BMW, and passed in front of an old VW Camper that was skidding out of control towards the mayhem. As it miraculously made the emergency lane he spun the wheel right, yanked on the handbrake, released it, then accelerated and missed the metal crash barrier by a hair's breadth.

Seconds later the car screeched to a stop one hundred metres ahead of the horrific crash scene with the phone still ringing on the satnav.

Two-hundred-and-fifty miles northwest in the Walmsfield Historic Research Department, Helen removed the plans of the Malaterre Estate and spread them out on her desk. In the wake of the numerous occurrences since Stephen had given them to her, she'd forgotten about them. She cast her eyes across the blueprints and shrugged because she had nothing to compare them with; nothing appeared to be out of the ordinary, and from the legend she could see that the plans and design had been drawn up by a long-gone firm of architects named "Messrs. Syracuse, Syracuse and Athlone" in 1722.

She looked at them for ten minutes and then gathered up the three sheets, folded them and placed them on Naomi's desk. She looked up at the clock on the office wall and saw that it was 10:30am. Naomi had told her that she would be in around ten o' clock and she began to feel uneasy. She looked at her watch, confirmed the time and then reached for her mobile phone and dialled Naomi's number. It was engaged.

She decided upon a cup of coffee, collected a few coins from her purse, and headed towards the office door. As she reached for the handle, the door opened and Naomi stepped inside whilst talking to somebody on her mobile. She stopped when she saw the anxious look on Naomi's face and stepped to one side to let her past.

"And you're sure that you're okay?" said Naomi.

Pause.

"Oh my God – *Oh my God*, how horrific."

Pause.

"Okay, okay, we'll see you the day after tomorrow at ten-ish in my office. Take care, bye."

Naomi looked up at Helen and said, "Stephen's been involved in a horrific accident on the M20 near Ashford in Kent."

Helen was stunned and said, "Christ – is he okay?"

"He is, but he thinks that at least two, maybe three people have been killed."

Helen said, "Good Lord, how awful." She saw the look of concern on Naomi's face and then said, "Are you okay?"

"I'm not sure."

Helen frowned and said, "Has something happened?"

"Yes and no; I don't know."

Helen frowned again and said, "What?"

Naomi walked across to her desk, sat down and took some coins out of her purse. "Here you are," she said handing them to Helen, "go and get us some drinks and I'll explain."

A few minutes later Helen deposited the drinks on their desks and said, "Right, let's start again."

Naomi took a sip of her coffee and said, "I was on my way in when I heard someone shouting something in my head. At first it didn't make sense, but it sounded like a woman with a French accent and I kept hearing the name Stephen."

"And what did you hear?"

" *'Naomi, appel Stephen maintenant! Stephen maintenant!'* I knew that 'maintenant' meant 'now' and I wasn't sure about the rest, but with the intense pressure on my shoulder and the voice repeating, 'Stephen maintenant!' in such an urgent way, I dialled his mobile number."

"And that was the right thing to do wasn't it?"

"That was, yes. Stephen told me that by calling him it made him look up and see what was happening in front, and that it had saved his life."

"And that was a good thing, so why the hesitation?"

"Because the French woman in my head used my name."

Helen was puzzled and said, "So what?"

"I've been experiencing these odd things for more than four years now, and in all of that time nobody has called me by my name."

Helen was even more confused and said, "Sorry, I don't get it, what's the big deal about somebody using your name?"

Naomi's mind was going ten-to-the-dozen and she wasn't sure about the connotations either. She thought for a few seconds and then said, "It's what it implies."

Helen said, "Implies?"

"Yes – in my past I have been confused about what I hear. I've always felt that my mind has somehow tapped into a kind of timeless collective – a bank of gathered information that I can access on occasion, and that at other times, it can somehow impart information to me. And although the contacts or information are personal to me or my circumstances, I have never seen it as a personal service, only a wonderful ability to have an insight into what is there." She stopped and looked at Helen and then said, "Sorry if this sounds a bit confusing, but what I'm trying to say is that by somebody from some other place, time or dimension, calling me by my name, it implies that they know me. And if they are already dead or living memory bytes floating around the ether, and I'm still here in terrestrial form, how can they? Does it imply an ability to communicate across space and time with the living, and how is time measured in eternity? Do ghosts have calendars and watches? How did that woman know when to contact me? Or is my entire existence some kind of weird spatio-temporal logic of the self?"

Helen sat back in her chair and said, "Good grief N, what on earth is going on in that brain of yours?"

"Trust me," said Naomi, "that's only scratching the surface of what I've been trying to figure out."

Chapter 31

Thursday Morning 6th July 2006. The Town Clerk's Office, Walmsfield Borough Council

Morag Beech looked across at Gabriel Ffitch, the Town Clerk of Walmsfield and said, "I don't like this babe, we're going to get caught."

Gabriel put both elbows onto his desk and rested his forehead on the palms of his hands, he looked across to the blousy, overweight figure of his personal secretary and said, "And just what are we supposed to do about it? AD's got us by the balls and he calls the shots."

Morag stood up, walked to the back of the Town Clerk's chair, and started to massage the back of his neck and shoulders.

"Tell him to go fuck himself – what can he do from where he is?"

Morag and Gabriel weren't in a personal relationship but they'd spent a lot of time together, in and out of work, and though both suspected that something might happen one day, to date it had not.

Morag's surname was Beech, but she always referred to the two of them as 'Ffitch and his bitch'. She dressed in black, was overweight, and plain looking. She had a diamond stud in her nose, and she gave the impression of being imposing and unapproachable. On the plus side however, she was fiercely loyal to Gabriel, and she was an excellent P.A.

Gabriel was a dapper man; he was handsome, one inch shorter than Morag, he was slim and well-dressed and he looked the total opposite to her, but something gelled between them, and he loved being in her company.

They'd been wheedled into Walmsfield Borough Council as Town Clerk and P.A. through the devious machinations of Adrian Darke, so that they could warn him if any moves were being planned against him by the Council. And in return for their loyalty they'd both received generous annual payments.

But Darke's illegal activities and illegal substance factory situated on his Cragg Vale Estate had been exposed with the help of Naomi Wilkes, and he was awaiting trial in Manchester's Strangeways Prison, bearing a grudge the size of Mount Everest.

Gabriel turned and stared at Morag. He said, "Are you kidding? If he can pull this stunt with the Wilkes woman, what do you think he'd do to us if we turned traitor? Jesus Christ, it doesn't bear thinking about."

Morag continued massaging Gabriel's shoulders and shrugged. She said, "Maybe. But without us he'd be stuffed."

Gabriel turned around again and said, "What did you put in your coffee today, fairy dust? You don't think for one minute that we're his only outside contacts do you?"

Morag grabbed the sides of Gabriel's face in her ham-sized hands and turned it to face forwards.

"What about FA Cup, Hinchcliffe, and Dominic Sheldon? None of them were arrested after the bust at Cragg Vale." He paused and then said, "And what about that bloody animal Hayley Gillorton?"

Morag wasn't a woman to be intimidated, but the thought of Hayley Gillorton wasn't a pleasant one. She said, "And do they all still work for AD?"

"Well none of his businesses ceased trading – except maybe Darke Desires, so yes, I'd guess that most of them still do."

"I mean the nasties."

Gabriel pondered for a second or two and then said, "I wouldn't bet against it, and I wouldn't like any of them to be coming after you or me, that's why we've got to do what he says."

Morag remained silent for a while and then said, "Okay, we'll do what he wants for now, but I've got an idea."

Gabriel tried to turn his head again but was restrained by Morag.

"Don't go doing anything stupid," he said, "I mean it! And thinking about it, don't do anything *at all* without running it past me first."

"I won't, I promise," said Morag.

Fifteen minutes later, she returned to her own office and sat down. She eyed the daily box of cream cakes perched on the end of her desk, extracted a chocolate éclair, and ate it. An idea was starting to take shape in her mind and the more she thought about it, the more she considered that it would work.

She unlocked her bottom left desk drawer and extracted the mobile phone that had been given to them by Adrian Darke. She switched it on and dialled the private number.

A male voice said, "Yes?"

"Can't initiate five without being compromised."

There was a momentary pause and then the male voice said, "We'll be in touch." The phone clicked off.

Morag's satisfied smile disappeared off her face; – she'd lied to Gabriel for the first time since they'd met, and it felt like a real betrayal.

Following the events of the past few days Naomi wanted to regain some of her normal fortitude and equilibrium; she recalled the doctor telling her that by the time she'd taken the pregnancy test she'd been about four weeks pregnant. That had been on the 14th of June, this was now the 6th of July, and she wondered just how much her hormones were beginning to affect her rationale.

She'd reported in to the office first thing, but had announced to Helen that she planned to go to Dunsteth Reservoir to 'check things out'. Helen had aired her concerns, but she'd prevailed, and she'd asked Leo to follow from a discreet distance so that she could have the time alone to centre herself.

Unknown to Naomi had been Carlton's involvement. Following the horrific assault on police officers Tasha Andrew and Roger Walburn, the whole surveillance programme had been altered.

Crowthorne had visited Carlton, and had assured him that Naomi would be watched twenty-four hours per day. In return, Carlton had confided that Naomi was pregnant, but on the strict understanding that Crowthorne didn't let Naomi know that he knew.

Naomi turned into the narrow, unmade approach to the eastern end of the reservoir, drove to the water's edge, and stopped her vehicle. She wound down the window and listened. For several seconds she tried to pick up the sound of Leo's unmarked police car, but when she heard nothing she felt vulnerable again. She wound up the window, looked all around, and in doing so, caught sight of herself in the rear view mirror. She let out an exasperated sigh and said, "For crying out loud Naomi Wilkes, what's the matter with you? Get out of the damned car!"

She stepped out of the CRV, closed the door, and lifted her face up to the warm sunshine. It felt wonderful.

Dressed like a typical rambler, John Hess had seen Naomi arrive and had dropped down behind a gorse bush. He'd been walking along the northern path of the Dunsteth Reservoir near to where he'd found the dinghy, and had been unable to believe his eyes. In the distance he'd seen the outline of the old Dunsteth Estate buildings, and he could see the top half of the building that his pal Rory had partially demolished, but from where he was, he couldn't see any sign of damage.

He'd heard a television news item about the draining of the reservoir because of a police investigation, and later in the same broadcast, he'd heard that Rosalind Probus had been charged with the murder of her husband, and that the police wanted to question him. He'd done as much as he could to alter his appearance whilst he considered how to get out of the country.

That day he wore a pair of thick-soled brown leather boots, fawn coloured socks, three-quarter length beige trousers, and a green T-shirt, and in the three weeks since disposing of Max Probus's body he'd allowed his facial hair to grow into a moustache and small beard. He'd also shaven his head and taken to wearing bandanas.

Out on the main road adjacent to the reservoir, Leo Chance sat back in his unmarked Volvo V70 after surveying the area through a pair of binoculars and satisfying himself that Naomi was alone. From his vantage point in the car, he could see her and her CRV through the foliage and he was able to watch the entrance to the unmade approach road, should any other vehicles attempt to drive in.

What he hadn't seen was the figure of John Hess on the northern bank.

John watched Naomi for a while and then without any warning some pollen blew up his nose and he sneezed.

Naomi's first instinct, brought about by several weeks of growing paranoia, was to run back to her vehicle and get inside, but as she saw the harmless-looking man rise to his feet and wave, her nerves steadied and she waved back.

Leo saw Naomi wave, grabbed his handgun, stuffed it into his trouser pocket, and started to make his way towards her under cover of the trees.

John opted to play it cool. He ambled across to Naomi and said, "Lovely morning isn't it?"

Naomi said, "Yes it is."

"Sorry if I startled you back there but I'd bent down to tie my bootlace and something went up my nose," he smiled and then pointed to it and said, "mind you, with a conk this size, it's not surprising."

Naomi smiled back and relaxed.

John extended his hand and said, "I'm John and this is one of my favourite bird-watching haunts."

"Ah, a great British twitcher."

John smiled again and said, "Not quite, I do believe that a twitcher is defined as 'a type of birder who seeks to add as many species as possible to their life list in as short a time as possible', whereas I, apart from turkey at Christmas, confine my studies to wildfowl."

Naomi noted the lack of equipment and said, "And you do this with just your eyes do you?"

John was rocked by the Naomi's acuteness but gathered his wits and said, "I do find that eyes can be useful – but when I'm 'watching' I'm usually in a hide with a whole host of equipment."

Naomi smiled at John's speedy retort and extended her hand, she said, "Touché! I'm Naomi Wilkes, and I'm the reason the reservoir is being drained."

John didn't know how he managed to control his emotions, but in as casual a way as he could muster, he looked around, stepped closer, and said, "Really – how fortuitous to meet you."

From the cover of the nearby trees Leo watched as Naomi approached the man with her arm extended and for no discernible reason, alarm bells started to ring. He made a mental note of what the stranger looked like, how he was dressed, his approximate size, weight, and age, and then he removed a slim, twenty-megapixel digital camera from his pocket, zoomed in, and took three photos of him.

Watching all the time, he returned to the car, contacted Control, and informed them that he wanted an immediate photo-search carrying out. He removed the SD card from the camera, inserted it into a card reader in the car's instrument panel, transmitted the photos to H.Q., and then turned to look back at Naomi.

He couldn't see her.

He frowned, altered his position, and with a horrible sinking feeling in the pit of his stomach said, "Shit, no!" and leapt out of the car. He charged through the trees, broke out to where she'd been standing, but she'd gone.

Chapter 32

Friday 18th September 1868. The Monkey Pit Public House, Rochdale

Abraham and Caleb Johnson walked into the lounge bar of The Monkey Pit, and as usual, it had an immediate effect; people averted their eyes and one by one either stopped talking, or did so only in hushed tones.

From behind the bar, Bull, who'd been looking down and serving drinks, noticed the change, and then saw the Johnsons.

"Gentlemen," he called, "best if you stay in here tonight."

Abraham frowned and said, "Why?"

"The chimney sweep's coming tomorrow morning and I've not been able to light the fire in the public bar."

Abraham cast his eyes around the busy lounge bar and said, "That's all right, we'll go where we normally do."

"As you wish gents," said Bull, "but let me make it up to you by bringing you one of my hot toddies each – on the house."

Caleb looked at his father, raised his eyebrows, and nodded.

Abraham said, "All right, but bring us a beer as well."

Bull waved an acknowledgement and carried on serving.

"I don't know why he bothers with a fire yet anyhow," said Caleb as they walked into the public bar, "it's still only September, and it's not cold."

Abraham said, "July and August are the only months he doesn't light it, and I'm not saying no to one of Bull's hot toddies, I've heard that they're worth having."

The two men settled down at their usual table and made small talk until they saw Lice arrive.

Lice sidled up and sat down; he looked around and then said, "Mute not here boss?"

Abraham looked over Lice's shoulder and said, "I haven't seen him, did you find anything out about him from Ned or Lily?"

"Nothing. Sripperly bastard's not been seen here since that night a lost him."

Abraham frowned and said, "Have you been coming here every night then?"

"Course not boss, I asked Ned like you instlucted, an' he told me."

Abraham nodded and said, "Right, well that answers that then." He shot a quick last look at the empty place that had been occupied by Nicolas and leaned closer to Lice.

"Did you go and see the Wenderliks?"

"No boss."

"What?" said Caleb, "Pa told you..."

"A couldn't missa Careb."

"Why?"

"'Cos they was both in hospital, with a porice guard, awaiting allest for fighting in a rocal pub."

"What near here?"

"No missa Careb, in Bolton."

"Damn!" spat out Abraham, "Those fucking Wenderliks, especially Camel. They can't keep their fists to themselves and they're always in trouble with the Peelers."

Caleb looked at his father and said, "Can't say I'm surprised – and can't say that I'm sorry either, they're both arseholes. We could never have relied on them, and we'd have been wondering right up to the night of the deed whether they'd be there."

Eight feet up the chimney, Nicolas Durand, who'd strapped himself to one of the internal metal climbing rungs now knew that whatever was being planned was going to be at night.

"And what are we supposed to do now?" said Abraham, "We can't do those frogs with just five of us."

Lice looked up at Abraham and said, "Can we do it with six boss?"

Abraham turned to Lice, paused, and then said, "Maybe – have you got somebody else in mind?"

"Yes boss. When a rearned the Wenderiks were in hospital a didn't just come back to Lochdale, a went to Stockport an' found Glinner."

"You found what?"

"Glinner boss."

Abraham frowned and said, "Grinner?"

"Yes boss."

Abraham looked at Caleb, emitted a "Hmm," and raised his eyebrows; he then turned to Lice and said, "And what did he say?"

"He said he'd do it, but he wants two guineas a day for each day he works for you."

"And did you tell him what we'd be doing?"

"He said for two guineas a day, it didn't matter."

"But did you tell him?"

"A told him we was going to get lid of a famiry of flogs out a big house in a cuntly an' he said he'd he could do that."

"Famiry of flogs in a cuntly?" repeated Abraham, "What?"

"A family of frogs in the country," said Caleb.

Abraham turned back to Lice and said, "You're a canny bloke Lice, but sometimes I'm buggered if I can understand the chinky shit that comes out of your mouth."

"Thank you boss," said Lice.

Caleb said, "And did you tell him *how* we were going to get rid of 'em?"

Nicolas leaned to the right to listen to Lice, and in doing so dislodged a piece of soot. It dropped down into the empty hearth, disintegrated, and sent a small shower of dust across the nearby stone floor.

As Lice and Caleb turned and looked, Bull walked into the bar with the hot toddies. He saw the soot fall, and his heart missed a beat. He changed direction, swept some of it to one side with his shoe and said, "Sorry gents, it's been doing that for the past three days, are you sure that you don't want to sit in the lounge bar? I'll clear a table for you."

Abraham said, "No, but you can get Lice a hot toddy too."

"All right gents," said Bull noticing another small piece of soot fall, "and can I get you a refill while I'm at it?"

Abraham and Caleb nodded and watched in silence until Bull had departed.

Up the chimney, Nicolas cursed his stupidity for not sweeping the chimney more thoroughly, and made a mental note never to make the same mistake again.

Caleb leaned over to Lice and said, "Well?"

Lice looked puzzled and then answered, "Yes thanks missa Careb."

"No you dopey bugger, I meant, well, did you tell Grinner how we were going to get rid of the frogs?"

"No."

Abraham looked at Lice and said, "So he doesn't know what's involved?"

"No boss – first off a couldn't tell him 'cos a don't know what we gonna do, but, when Glinner heard that it was you an' missa Careb in charge, he knew that it wasn't going to be no tea celemony."

Abraham looked across to Caleb and said, "I don't know, what do you think?"

Caleb put his hand up to his mouth and chewed things over for a second or two. He said, "I don't know either. Have you met him?"

Abraham looked around, saw that the bar was still empty, and said, "Not close up but I did see him once, just before he was released from Leicester Gaol; he was working in the prison laundry at the time. Most of the inmates kept well away from him, even the arse bandits; he had a reputation for being dangerous and short-tempered if anybody disagreed with him."

"What was he in for boss?" said Lice.

"He'd been locked up for putting two blokes in hospital in a pub fight."

Caleb said, "We've done worse than that."

"Yes," said Abraham, "but it's just, him…"

"You aren't afraid of anybody," said Caleb, "and me neither if it comes to it, so if he gets out of line we'll just kick the shit out of him."

Abraham cast his mind back to the episode in Leicester Gaol and recalled how he'd felt when he'd first seen Grinner. He'd been folding washed linen in a side room off the laundry and he'd heard the weirdest laugh; he'd stepped to one side, looked in the laundry, and had seen him. Grinner had been short, stocky, and powerfully built; he'd had a bald head and had been clean-shaven except for a short tuft of black hair under his bottom lip. As he'd looked, Grinner had seen him looking and had turned to face him; the grin had disappeared off his face and he'd stared right back. For the first time that he'd ever been able to recall, he first averted his eyes, and within seconds he'd heard a muffled comment from Grinner followed by another extended weird laugh.

His apprehensive recollection was disturbed by Lice.

"Why was he called Glinner boss?"

"Because he was always grinning," said Abraham, "not in an amusing way, but in a weird way. His real name was Dan Jonbury and whenever he did anything bad, or was planning to hurt anybody, or whatever, he had this evil grin on his face. And his laugh was even worse; I only heard it a couple of times but it sounded like somebody stabbing a monkey."

Caleb saw the look of apprehension on Abraham's face and said, "If you ain't sure pa…"

Abraham looked at his son and re-asserted himself, he said, "No, you're right, we'll use him, and if he gets out of line we'll kick his arse and see if he laughs that off."

Caleb gave a determined nod and said, "That's more like you; now, do you think he can be trusted with a job like this?"

Abraham remained silent for a couple of seconds and then said, "Buggered if I know – but it doesn't look as though we have much…"

Something happened in the lounge bar. At first an audible gasp went up, then it went silent, and then everybody started asking questions at once.

Abraham turned and frowned, he said, "What's going on?"

Caleb said, "I'll go and see." He got up and walked into the lounge bar. At first, all he could see were people gathered around a man, and that they all appeared to be firing questions at him at the same time. He pushed through the throng until he saw who was standing there, and then said, "Stone the bloody crows!"

He went back to the doorway of the public bar and called, "Pa, you'd better come in here."

A puzzled Abraham got up, followed by Lice, and walked into the lounge bar. People parted as he approached, but he stopped dead when he saw who was there. He looked at the dishevelled man and said, "Christ, you look like shit. What happened to you, and where have you been?"

Galloping John said, "London."

"What the fuck were you doing in London?"

"I didn't go there by choice."

"I gathered that," said Abraham, "so how did you get there?"

"In a wooden crate."

Even the stoic Caleb said, "A wooden crate? What were you doing in a wooden crate?"

"I was knocked out, gagged, tied hand and foot, wrapped in an old carpet and some hessian sacking, stuffed into a crate, and then put on a train to London."

"Then what?" said Abraham.

"Then because I couldn't move, and because I was gagged so tight, I was taken to a warehouse in Whitechapel and left for three whole bloody days. I thought that I was going to die there."

"So how did you get out?" said one of the onlookers.

John looked down for a few seconds and then said, "'Cos of the smell."

"What smell?" said the onlooker.

John turned to the hapless man and said, "What do you think, you tit?"

A few people smirked once the penny had dropped, but that angered John even more.

"You can laugh," he said, "but you'd all piss and shit yourselves if you were tied up in crate for three days."

"And when did all this happen?" said Abraham.

"On the night you sent me to ask about Squeaker."

"But that was two weeks ago," said Caleb.

"I know! It's taken me that long to get back 'cos the bastard who did it took my money too."

"And did you see who did it?" said Abraham.

"Oh yes, and if I ever see him again I'll do him good and proper, you mark my words."

"Do we know him?" said Caleb.

"You all do; it was that deaf mute who sat in the public bar reading the newspaper a couple of weeks back."

Momentary shock ensued until Caleb blurted out, "Bastard! I fucking knew it!"

"Me too boss," said Lice, "a said he was sripperly."

Abraham's eyes blazed, he said, "Right, has anybody seen him around?"

A small bead of sweat broke out on Bull's top lip, which he quickly wiped away.

Silence reigned.

"I said," repeated Abraham, "has anybody seen him around?"

One or two voices said 'No' but nobody else spoke.

Abraham looked from face-to-face, and with pure venom in his eyes, said, "I'm warning you, if anybody is holding out on me they'll pay for it with their fucking lives."

Once again nobody spoke.

Abraham continued staring around the room for a few seconds and then turned to his men and said, "Right – you three – next door," he pointed towards the public bar and then looked at Bull, "and you get us beers all round."

Bull said, "Right away," and silently prayed that Nicolas, who he'd helped, wouldn't be discovered.

The four allies walked into the public bar.

"That sneaky bastard sure had us fooled," said Caleb.

Abraham cogitated and then said, "Yes, but what's he up to? Why did he do that to John?"

"Maybe 'cos of Maraterre Estate boss," proffered Lice.

Abraham turned and stared at Lice; he said, "Maybe, maybe. Last time we were here Caleb said that we hadn't seen him 'til we'd started planning to do the frogs."

He turned to John and said, "Did you make it to Squeaker that night?"

"No, he got me before I had a chance."

Abraham said, "So it may have been him who disappeared Squeaker too…" He fell silent for a few minutes and then said, "Right, in case the mute got wind of any of our plans, let's move them up and get it done." He turned to John and said, "Are you up for a bit of work if I pay you? I'll make up for your last couple of weeks too."

"I need to sort myself out first, but I can be ready by Sunday."

"No," said Abraham, "most people go to church of a Sunday, so we can't guarantee they'll be in when we want them; we'll wait until Monday night. The moon'll be right too." He turned to Lice and said, "Monday morning go and see Pickles and tell him to keep away from Malaterre, after that, contact the pastor and Squat, and meet us by the burnt Ash on Blackstone Moor at 11pm. Got it?"

"Got it boss."

Abraham turned to John and said, "You go and get Grinner, meet me and Caleb here at ten, then we'll meet up with Lice and the others at eleven."

"Don't you want us to go to the burnt Ash the same?" said John.

"No, three blokes heading out on to the moor at that time would be bad enough, but five would be downright suspicious, so we'll do it my way after dark, understand?"

"Yes."

Bull walked in with the beers and cast a furtive glance towards the chimney; he said, "Here we are gents," placed the beers on the table and left.

Abraham picked up his jar of ale, held it up, and said, "Right, here's to a good night slicing frog throats."

Up the chimney, Nicolas had heard it all. An idea had started to take shape in his brain, but whether he and Philipe would be able to cope with an attack by seven of the most dangerous men that he'd ever come across was something else altogether.

He remained as still as he could and prayed that they would all soon leave.

Chapter 33

Friday 7th July 2006. Bellthorpe Grain Mill, Castleton, Rochdale

Naomi regained consciousness and tried to open her eyes but the blindfold was so tight that she couldn't see a thing. Her ankles were tied, her wrists were bound behind her back, and she was gagged.

She could tell that she was on a bare concrete floor, and she knew that she was somewhere very large and hollow because the slightest sounds echoed around the room. She also picked up a distinctive smell. She coughed, listened, and then coughed again, but drew no response. She made a loud "Hmming" sound, but that too was fruitless.

She had no idea what time it was, or even what day it was.

The last thing that she remembered was being spun around – dragged to an old jeep with a hand clamped over her mouth, and then something being jabbed into the side of her neck.

Now, she was hungry, bound, shoeless, and lying on her right-hand side. She adjusted her position, sat up, and banged the back of her head against something hard. She cursed, drew her knees up, rocked forwards, and then attempted to stand. She got halfway up, but her ascent was halted and she dropped back to the floor and banged the base of her spine.

She rubbed it and then fiddled about behind her back until she found a length of rope tied to her wrist bindings. It was linked to a metal 'H' frame girder which she presumed to be a roof support. The linking rope felt about twenty-five millimetres thick, was soft, and greasy. She'd felt rope like that before, but couldn't recall where.

She adjusted the position of her hands and established that the girder was rusting; that was a bonus.

Out of the blue she heard something. She remained still and listened. It was the distinctive 'chug' of a boat engine. She'd heard numerous throughout her life, and she knew that she was listening to a canal boat. That was encouraging too, because the sound may have been coming from the Rochdale canal.

She waited until silence had descended, and then wasted no time. She began to abrade the rope against the base of the rusty stanchion.

Fifty metres away, John Hess watched as his hostage had emerged from her near twenty-four hour coma through a pair of night-vision binoculars equipped with an infrared light. He'd seen that she'd started to abrade the rope, and he was pleased that she appeared to have adapted to her situation. He didn't want to cause her unnecessary suffering, but he did need to have her captive if his plan was to succeed. He estimated that it would take her at least four to six hours to cut the ropes holding her to the stanchion, but then she'd have to saw away at the thick plastic cable ties around her wrists and ankles. An overall time, he estimated, that would take at least six to seven hours. This would give him ample time between visits to re-secure any bindings that she'd freed.

He watched for a few minutes longer and then said, "Nod if you can hear me." The words echoed around the empty room.

Naomi froze; she tried to assess the direction from which the words had come, but it was difficult in such a place. She didn't respond, hoping that the statement would be repeated so that she could have a second shot at it.

"I said nod if you can hear me."

Naomi had learned a trick from her father Sam whilst dinghy sailing. He had told her that it was always possible to establish the direction of the wind in relation to the boat and sails by using her ears. He'd told her to turn her head until she could only feel the breeze on one ear, and then to turn it until she could feel the breeze on both. Thereafter, by turning her head left and right to make minor adjustments, she had learned the art of establishing an accurate wind direction.

She now applied the same knowledge to the voice and was surprised to realise that it was easier to establish from whence it came with the blindfold on rather than without. She nodded and made fine adjustments.

"I have no intention of hurting you but you will be my captive for the next three or four days dependent upon the police. If I am apprehended, I shall tell them where you are and you will be freed. Before I leave I will remove your gag and blindfold but you will see that it is pitch dark in here. Three times a day I shall feed you, give you something to drink, and I'll give you the opportunity to use the bathroom. But, I should warn you; you are being held captive at the very top of a disused grain silo and the individual grain chutes no longer have protective covers. There are four of them, and each one is two hundred feet deep. If you fall down one in the dark, you will not survive.

"My advice to you is to stay where you are, and within four days at the most, you will walk out of here unharmed. Nod if you understand."

Naomi didn't respond at first; her mind was going ten-to-the-dozen.

"I said nod if you understand!"

Naomi nodded.

"Good – then I shall come over, remove your gag and blindfold, give you something to eat and let you use the portable lavatory that I have brought for you."

Naomi shuddered at that thought, but knew that she could cope. It had been less than three months since she'd been in almost the same situation in the underground drug factory at Adrian Darke's Cragg Vale Estate, but there, she had feared for her life.

John put the binoculars into their carrying case, placed them on the floor, and removed a small but powerful Cree torch from his pocket and switched it on. He walked cautiously around the grain chutes, only once shining the light down one, but it looked so deep and menacing that he kept well clear. He looked at his watch, noted that it was 11:06am, and knew that the police would already be responding to the message that he'd sent one hour earlier.

He saw Naomi react as he approached and said, "Keep still, I'm going to remove your gag and blindfold."

Seven miles away at Rochdale Police Headquarters, Carlton and Leo sat in Crowthorne's office.

Carlton's raging anger at the incompetence of the police had subsided, and he'd begun to settle.

Crowthorne had been tempted to suspend Leo for his part in the disastrous debacle, but had realised that that would have been a knee-jerk reaction that would have been self-defeating, because despite the current unacceptable situation, he was still one of, if not *the* best officer he had for this kind of case.

Leo was less forgiving; much less forgiving, and was determined to return Naomi to safety whatever it took.

Crowthorne pushed the note he'd received via email across his desk towards Carlton.

Carlton picked it up and read;

'My name is John Hess; I am wanted in connection with the murder of Max Probus which I did not do. I was however, responsible for the demolition, by controlled implosion of the Malaterre Estate in Dunsteth Reservoir to conceal Mr. Probus's body. This I admit.

Naomi Wilkes has been secured with a sensitive explosive device in the second floor room below the observation tower of the Malaterre Estate building.

My demands are these; first, stop draining the reservoir with immediate effect because another explosive device operated by a gravity switch has been placed three feet below the waterline directly under where she has been secured.

Once I've received confirmation that the drainage has stopped I'll inform you where that device is and how to disarm both of them. In exchange for this, I demand safe passage out of the UK to a destination of my choice.

Reply with your answer and know this; you know who I am, and you know that I can do this, so please don't endanger the life of Ms Wilkes by fucking me about.

Hess.'

Carlton finished reading and looked up at Crowthorne; he said, "Can this be true?"

Crowthorne shook his head and said, "He's done it once, so there's no guarantee that he couldn't do it again."

"But wasn't anybody monitoring Malaterre?"

"There was no reason to do so."

"I beg to bloody differ," said Carlton.

"Mr. Wilkes," said Leo, "I accept full responsibility for this situation, so with Superintendent Crowthorne's permission I think that you should be venting your frustration on me."

"Frustration doesn't even half cover it Sergeant, I'd like to wring your bloody neck for what you've done!"

Leo looked down and then back at Carlton, he said, "No more than I do, sir."

Carlton looked at the crestfallen Sergeant and then recalled that he had saved Naomi's life once before. His anger subsided and he said, "I'm sorry Sergeant, I can't begin to thank you enough for what you did for Naomi and me a few months ago and perhaps I'm being a bit too harsh now, but I'm sure that you can understand my ire."

"I can indeed sir."

Carlton turned to Crowthorne and said, "You told me a couple of days ago that you would be organising another type of surveillance for Naomi – what were you referring to?"

"Satellite surveillance."

Carlton was shocked; he said, "So that's not just film nonsense?"

"No, it's not. The Hollywood version bears little resemblance to the real thing, but the technology is there and it's being used far more than the public know."

"So do we know that she's definitely in the Malaterre building?"

"No we don't, because we weren't deploying it during those times that she was being watched from the ground."

"Brilliant," said Carlton, "just bloody brilliant." He sat in silence for a few seconds and then said, "So now what?"

Crowthorne reached for the email, looked at it again and said, "You know that we won't accede to this demand don't you?"

Carlton nodded and said, "Yes, but what will you do?"

"I've already called Kev Middleton, the Superintendent in charge of draining the dam, and asked him to stop; next I'll speak to Inspector Kearns from the Marine Unit and see what he advises, but if Hess is to be believed, and he has placed an explosive device with a gravity switch just below the waterline it's doubtful that he'll want to go anywhere near there with a boat in case it triggers an explosion."

"What about a helicopter, could we deploy one of those and drop somebody into Malaterre?"

Leo said, "We couldn't sir, because of the down draught, especially if the building's unstable."

Carlton let out a "Gah!" sound and said, "This just keeps getting better and better doesn't it? And all the time my beautiful wife is at the mercy of God knows what kind of deranged bloody moron." He looked at Leo and said, "I swear Sergeant, if anything happens to her, I will not be held responsible for my actions…"

Leo looked down but didn't respond.

"Carlton," said Crowthorne hoping to pour oil onto the troubled water, "there's no guarantee that Naomi is in the building…"

"And there's no guarantee that she isn't!" retorted Carlton.

"No, but, given the short time from Naomi's disappearance to the receipt of the demand, Hess would have had to work a minor miracle to achieve what he says."

"And that's beside the point," said Carlton.

"Yes, I agree, and we will take all of the necessary factors into consideration, but we have limited options given the unique circumstances of this case and we'll need to proceed with the utmost care whichever course of action we take."

Carlton opened his mouth to respond but was interrupted by a knock on Crowthorne's door.

Crowthorne raised his eyebrows at Carlton and saw him nod in approval; he called, "Come in."

The door opened and Inspector Peter Milnes walked in.

"Sorry to disturb you sir, but you need to see this." He walked across to the small flat screen television on one of Crowthorne's units and switched it on to BBC North West.

The screen switched on and showed a news reporter standing on the southern bank of the Dunsteth Reservoir; the sound then came on.

"...so just to reiterate," said the reporter, "BBC North West has received a tip-off that a young woman believed to be Naomi Wilkes, the Head of Walmsfield Borough Council's Historic Research Department, has been taken hostage and secreted with an explosive device in one of the rooms of the emerging Malaterre Estate. So far we are unaware of why she's been placed there, and what action the police will be taking, but this appears to be either the product of someone's very sick imagination, or the start of an extremely hazardous and dangerous situation." The reporter paused and stepped to one side whilst the camera zoomed into the estate building; he then said, "This is Roy Bright reporting live from the banks of the Dunsteth Reservoir near Rochdale in Lancashire – now over to Lynne Hampson in the studio."

Crowthorne was the first to respond; he looked at Milnes and said, "How the bloody hell has this happened Peter, and who's responsible?"

Milnes shook his head and said, "Sorry sir, I haven't the foggiest."

Ten miles south in the executive offices of Darke Industries, Garrett Hinchcliffe, Dominic Sheldon, and Hayley Gillorton sat with open mouths listening to the news report.

Hinchcliffe turned to the others and said, "Is this anything to do with us?"

Sheldon turned to Gillorton and raised his eyebrows.

Gillorton, in her usual abrasive way said, "What are you looking at me like that for? I know sod all about it."

"Well who does?" said Hinchcliffe.

Silence.

"Come on people," said Hinchcliffe, "somebody knows something."

"Come on people?" repeated Gillorton, "Where the fuck do you think you are, the conference room of the TUC?"

Hinchcliffe glared at Gillorton and said, "No but from the sound of your language, I'd say your mother and father's house."

"Don't you bag my parents," said Gillorton rising to her feet, "or I'll fucking lay you out."

"Stop it you two!" said Sheldon, "In case you'd forgotten we're supposed to be on the same team!"

"Well…" said Gillorton.

"Hayley!" snapped Sheldon, "Please!"

Gillorton sat back down and glared at Hinchcliffe.

"Something's going on and we need to know what it is before AD gets wind of it."

"Unless he already has," said Sheldon, "he does have a TV in his cell."

"Could it be that fu…?" Gillorton saw the disapproving look of the two men and moderated her language, "could it be the work of that bloody Neanderthal, FA Cup?"

"Leander Pike?" said Hinchcliffe, "He wouldn't do anything without AD's consent."

"And are you sure that he hasn't had it?" said Gillorton.

Hinchcliffe hesitated and then said, "What stage were we at with the Wilkes woman?"

Sheldon said, "We received a call from Morag Beech yesterday telling us that she couldn't deliver note five without being compromised."

"All right," said Hinchcliffe, "don't do anything further until I've spoken to AD. You two meet me here on Monday at 2:30pm and Hayley, be aware that Pike will be here so keep it calm and don't wind him up."

"Fucking brilliant," said Gillorton. "That's all I need…"

Chapter 34

10:00am Saturday 9th July 2006. Dunsteth Reservoir

As the police car carrying Carlton, Leo, and Crowthorne turned into the eastern approach road to Dunsteth Reservoir the driver's mouth fell open. Without thinking he said, "Oh I don't believe this…"

Crowthorne leaned and looked over the driver's shoulder and he too was shocked.

Parked on both sides of the approach road were dozens of cars. People were removing fold-up chairs, picnic hampers, and cool-boxes and making their way to vantage points all around the edges of the reservoir.

"…what do they think this is, a bloody theme park?" said the appalled driver.

Carlton was horrified; he said, "My God, that's my wife supposed to be in there, do they think that it's some kind of sick entertainment?"

"That's the press for you Mister Wilkes," said Leo, "they're a damned scourge."

Crowthorne tapped the driver on the shoulder and said, "Get onto Control, and get a couple of cars down here. I want the whole northern and eastern banks cleared of people and I want a temporary closure on this approach road."

"Do you want them all cleared away sir?" said the driver.

Crowthorne looked at Carlton and then said, "I'm sorry Carlton, I should have seen this coming, that reporter has a lot to answer for."

"Have you found out who tipped him off yet?"

"No, but he should have come to us with his knowledge, not run the story to grab a few more viewing figures."

Carlton was more philosophical and said, "At least he was only doing his job, the guy who should be strangled is the idiot who tipped him off."

"If it was a guy," added Leo.

"Sir, the people – do you want them cleared away?" reiterated the driver.

Crowthorne thought for a few seconds and then said, "If we attempt to keep the whole reservoir clear of people it'll take dozens of men to police it, but if we allow the public access to a limited area, they'll more or less police themselves and we'll only need a couple officers down here at any one time."

"So you're going to let members of the public watch what's going on," said a horrified Carlton, "with my wife tied hand and foot in that building? Where do you think we are, the Roman bloody Colosseum?"

"Please, Carlton," said Crowthorne, "you know me by now. Do you think that I would advocate such a course of action just to sate the public's morbid curiosity?"

Carlton abated and said, "No of course not, but nevertheless..."

Crowthorne made a sweeping gesture with his hand as the police car came to a stop close to the water's edge, he said, "Just look around you. The area around the reservoir is huge; it's heavily foliated, it has a public right of entry across the dam wall, and it has numerous access points all around. If we try to force an exclusion zone around this whole area the cost would be enormous and we'd still have determined people getting through, in particular, members of the press."

Carlton looked about and saw the enormity of the problem.

"And on top of everything else," said Crowthorne, "we're not sure that Naomi is in the building. Indeed if pushed, I'd put my money on her not being there."

"The Superintendent's right sir," said Leo, "the press alone, which I'm convinced already have a presence here right now, are a devious bunch, and we could end up chasing them all day and night at this time of year. By giving everybody an allocated place, we can exercise much more control."

"All right," said Carlton, "whatever…"

Crowthorne turned to the driver and said, "Did you get that?"

"Yes sir. You want everywhere except the south bank cleared of people and you want the eastern approach road closed."

"Correct. Restricting the number of parking places will help to reduce the numbers too, plus of course, this is the weekend, so lots of people will be back at work by Monday."

"And do you want the cars removed from the approach road today too sir?"

"No, just close it down, and don't allow any others in."

The conversation was interrupted by a tap on the nearside rear passenger window.

Crowthorne wound it down and saw Stephen Page standing there. He said, "Mr. Page, this is a surprise, what are you doing here?"

"I don't mean to be rude Superintendent, but I'd have thought that was obvious."

Crowthorne's feathers ruffled; he said, "And I don't mean to be rude either sir, but I didn't expect to count you amongst a bunch of thrill-seeking day-trippers."

Stephen soaked up the pique-laden riposte and said, "Sorry Superintendent, please accept my apologies for my ill-considered reply, it was unforgiveable."

Crowthorne nodded and climbed out of the back seat, he shook hands with Stephen and said, "Apology accepted. Now, shall we start again? What are you doing here?"

"I gathered that you'd show up this morning, what with all the furore engendered by those irresponsible television reports, and I wanted to offer my services."

"Your services?"

"Yes, I am a fully qualified and very experienced climber. For eight years I was a senior member of the Llanberis Mountain Rescue Team which goes to the aid of those in need on Snowdon, and I am also an experienced rock and edifice free climber."

"And your offer is what?" said Crowthorne.

"I want your permission to enter the Malaterre Estate to see if I can help Naomi."

Crowthorne was flabbergasted; he said, "No I'm sorry Mr. Page, that's out of the question. First we haven't established whether or not she's there, second we have our own people who can do this, and third, nobody knows how safe that structure is."

"And I don't mean to be pushy," said Stephen, "but the first point of me entering the building is to establish whether Naomi's there; second, I am exactly the kind of person the force calls upon to execute this type of operation, and third, if nobody knows how safe that structure is, how will you ever establish it without the aid of an experienced climber?"

All of Crowthorne's cards had been trumped; he thought for a few seconds and then said, "And what would you do if you saw that she was wired up to an improvised explosive device?"

"If I saw any hint of an I.E.D., I'd call for help and be able to advise the bomb disposal guys of the safest route in."

"And how would you gain access if there is a second underwater device below the tower?"

Stephen reached into his pocket and pulled out a folded plan of the estate; he spread it across the bonnet of the police car and pointed to the northernmost tip of the south wing. He said, "By approaching here and scaling the exterior of the wall."

Crowthorne studied the plan and said, "And why wouldn't you just climb into the building via the north wing and choose the safest route across?"

"You said it yourself; nobody has an idea how safe that building is, and if it has been partially demolished by a controlled detonation, any part of it could collapse at any time. By climbing into the south wing from the north elevation I would be accessing that wing from the safest place, and I would be entering the building at a point closest to where Naomi is believed to be being held captive."

Crowthorne remained silent for a few seconds and then said, "I'll have to verify your credentials and clear it with the Chief Constable first, but if he has no objections I'll put you in touch with Inspector Kearns of the Marine Unit and you can work out a strategy between you."

Stephen smiled and extended his right hand; he said, "Thank you Superintendent, this is very important to me."

Crowthorne shook the proffered hand and said, "And thank you Mr. Page, it is heart-warming to come across people willing to risk their lives for others, though if you've spent eight years with the Llanberis Mountain Rescue Team, you'll be no stranger to that."

"No sir," said Stephen, "I'm not."

"Very well, I'll check things out as per, we'll clear the north and east banks of the reservoir, and if I could get you some professional help would you want it?"

"Not on this occasion. I do most of my climbing alone, and I wouldn't want to endanger anybody else's life."

Crowthorne nodded and said, "Okay, how much time would you need?"

Stephen looked at his watch and said, "I could be here by 2pm."

Crowthorne looked at his watch too and said, "No, make it 3:30pm. That'll give us both plenty of time, and my officers time to clear the undesignated area and seal off the approach road."

Stephen nodded in agreement and said, "Right, 3:30pm it is"

"And," said Crowthorne, "if I get a negative response from anybody, I'll call you on your mobile."

Standing huddled close to a public telephone in Strangeways Prison, Adrian Darke was blazing. He said, "What do you mean, you've no idea? You're supposed to be my top man for Christ's sake!"

Garrett Hinchcliffe winced and said, "Sorry AD but it's taken us all by surprise."

"How far did you get with the, er…" Adrian wasn't sure whether the phones were being tapped or monitored and chose his words with care, "…recent strategy we planned?"

"Level five."

"So the client won't yet have drawn any conclusions. Is that correct?"

"At present, yes."

"So our strategy could have been misconstrued as somebody else's?"

"Yes, it could."

Adrian thought for a few seconds and then said, "Do you recall that meeting we had in Grozny?"

"Yes."

"And the farm equipment we bought?"

Hinchcliffe knew that Adrian was referring to a deal between his little known 'Darke Desires' company which ostensibly traded in 'objet d'art', but in reality brokered illegal arms deals, and he knew that the 'farm equipment' purchased from the Chechens in Grozny had been Russian RPG-7 rocket propelled grenade launchers with fragmentation, heat, and high-explosive warheads.

"AD," said Hinchcliffe full of misgiving, "I'm not sure about the suitability of that equipment…"

"I said, do you recall it?"

"Yes, of course."

"And do we still have much in stock?"

"AD…?" said Hinchcliffe again.

"Will you shut up and answer the question?! Do we still have much?"

"I believe that we do, but only for level three work."

Adrian knew that that was the high-explosive warheads; he said, "Perfect, then I think that you should put some of it to good use before it gets rusty."

Hinchcliffe felt a sinking in the pit of his stomach and said, "Er… And did you have any particular clients in mind?"

"The ones whose strategy we'd been working on."

"But…"

"But nothing, that's my decision, are you going to argue with me?"

Hinchcliffe paused and then said, "And is there anybody in particular that you'd like to put in charge of the project?"

"Not my problem – and that's what I pay you for. Just get it done."

Hinchcliffe drew in a deep breath, and said, "How soon?"

"ASAP."

"What? You're not suggesting…?"

Adrian leaned closer to the phone and hissed, "You're beginning to piss me off now Hinchcliffe, so if you can't do what I ask, I'll be forced to consider your retirement package and find a replacement. Is that understood?"

Hinchcliffe knew all too well that disloyal staff from Adrian's inner circle didn't just leave his employ with a pat on the back and a pension for past service; they left with a quarter ton concrete boot set around their feet for a deep-sea diving experience. He said, "There's no need for that AD, I'll expedite your instructions with immediate effect."

"Yes," said Adrian, "with *immediate* effect." He slammed down the phone.

At Darke Industries H.Q. Hinchcliffe removed a white cotton handkerchief from his trouser pocket and wiped small beads of sweat from his brow; he closed his eyes for a few seconds and said, "Shit…"

He waited until his emotions had steadied then dialled his secretary and said, "Get me Mr. Pike."

Chapter 35

Monday 21st September 1868. Hundersfield District Council Offices, Rochdale

Joseph Pickles' mind was in turmoil; he stared at his notepad and tapped it with the tip of his pencil. It had been six weeks to the day since he'd heard anything from the Johnsons, his two weeks off work to visit his 'sick old relative' had long since passed, and although his boss Edmund Turner hadn't made any specific references to Malaterre he had, on two separate occasions within the last two weeks, asked him if the he was any nearer to a decision about the siting of the new reservoir.

He leaned back in his chair and felt nonplussed. His last visit to Whitewall had been such a traumatic affair that he felt no inclination to go there to ask the Johnsons what was happening, but he concluded, if he'd heard nothing by the end of the week, that's what he'd have to do.

He looked up at Turner's door, determined his course of action, walked over to it, and knocked.

"Come in," called Turner. He watched as Pickles entered and then pointed to the chair in front of his desk. "Joseph," he said, "sit down."

"Thank you sir," said Pickles.

"Now, what can I do for you my boy?"

"It's about the problem…"

Turner cut in and said, "You're not about to tell me that the trust placed in you by the select committee was misplaced are you?"

Pickles dropped his gaze, thought for a second and then looked into the eyes of his boss. He said, "To be honest sir, I don't seem…"

Turner cut in again; he said, "Haven't we given you enough er, 'freedom' to be able to sort out this problem?"

"It's not that sir, it's…"

"Joseph, Joseph," said Turner, "today is the twenty-first of September, 1868. By Christmas 1869, Hundersfield District Council will be the proud owners of a brand new reservoir constructed to meet the demands of its growing population.

"I am the Head of this department and I employ people, competent people, to execute the plans of the town's worthies, which includes, at the forefront, the select committee who has chosen you to lead their campaign. We – that is, the committee and I – appreciate the uniqueness and complexity of the task we have set you, but we have every faith that whatever it takes…" he paused, lowered the timbre of his voice, and repeated, "…*whatever it takes* – you will prevail."

Pickles watched as Turner lowered his head and stared up at him through raised eyebrows. He felt jammed between the devil and the deep blue sea, but as his boss's gaze bore into him, he drew in a deep breath and said, "And I won't let you down."

Turner leaned back in his chair, placed the fingertips of his hands together, and said, "Excellent my boy! That's the kind of spirit that sorted the bloody frogs out at Agincourt, and though I am in no way belittling your task, it's not exactly in the same league, what?"

"No sir, it's not."

"Now then, what was it you wanted to see me about?"

Pickles said, "Given the extended passage of time since you – that is, the committee and you…," he couldn't help repeating the expression used by his boss, but put no trace of sarcasm in it, "…handed me this task, I was beginning to wonder if you were coming under pressure from above, to conclude this business."

"Ah, I see," said Turner, "very thoughtful of you Joseph. The answer to your question right now is, no, but that state of affairs won't remain the same indefinitely. We – that is, the committee…" he hesitated as he recalled Pickles' use of the same terminology seconds earlier, then said, "…you know…" he saw Pickles nod, and continued, "have scheduled another meeting for…" he reached for his large desk diary, turned the pages and said, "Monday the second of November, at which, I am hoping to be able to report that we will have secured their favoured location."

Pickles nodded and said, "Very well sir, I'll…"

The conversation was interrupted by a knock on the door.

Turner said, "Excuse me Joseph, I'm expecting some important papers…" he called, "Come in."

The door opened and a young female receptionist stood in the doorway; she said, "Begging you pardon Mr. Turner sir, but there's a gentleman to see Mr Pickles in reception."

"Expecting somebody Joseph?" said Turner.

"Not that I was aware sir."

Turner looked at the receptionist and said, "Very well, be off with you and tell the gentleman that Mr. Pickles will be with him forthwith."

"Yes sir, I will sir."

Turner waited until the door had closed and said, "Will that be all Joseph?"

Pickles thought for a few seconds and then said, "In light of your scheduled meeting with the select committee, it may be prudent for me to spend a little more time away with my ailing relative sir."

Turner nodded and said, "Yes, of course, take as much time as you need." He saw the look of apprehension on his subordinate's face and realised in what a difficult position he'd been placed. He said, "Look Joseph, this is all highly irregular and I appreciate the intense pressure that you've been put under, but if you do pull this off, I promise you, not only will you receive a sum commensurate with your supreme effort, but you will be in line for a promotion and an incremental increase in remuneration."

Pickles was surprised; every time he spoke to somebody about the Malaterre Estate the rewards seemed to mount. He now had the offer of friendship and cash from the Johnsons, a bonus, pay rise, and promotion from work. His spirits lifted. He said, "Thank you sir, I shall give it my undivided attention from this day forward."

"Well said," said Turner, "now, I have work to attend, and you have somebody waiting in reception."

Pickles got up, said, "Thank you for your time sir," and went back to his desk. He picked up his diary to see if he had forgotten any meetings and saw that it was blank.

He walked down the stairs to reception and approached the front desk.

"Yes Mr. Pickles sir?" said the young girl.

"There's somebody to see me?" he said.

"Yes sir, over…" the receptionist looked over Pickles' left shoulder, frowned, and said, "…sorry sir, the gentleman was over there."

Pickles turned, looked through the meandering folk arriving and departing the Council Offices, and said, "What does he look like?"

"A very distinctive gentleman sir – he was oriental, Chinese I believe, wearing a brown jacket and corduroy trousers."

Pickles turned as his heart rate increased, he looked all around the reception area and saw no sign of whom he took to be Lice. He turned back to the receptionist and said, "Where was he the last time you saw him?"

The receptionist pointed to the same quiet corner in which he'd had the previous unpleasant encounter. "Over there on that chair sir," she said.

Pickles looked again but saw no sign.

"Perhaps the gentleman had to avail himself of the W.C. sir?"

"Maybe," said Pickles, "I'll go and wait on that seat. If he comes to you in the meantime, direct him over to me."

"Yes sir."

Pickles walked over to the seat, perched down, and kept his eyes peeled. He remained seated for two or three minutes and was about to remove his pocket watch when a commotion broke out from a corridor leading off the right-hand side of the reception. He heard raised voices, and then a small feminine scream. He jumped to his feet and followed the sound of the noise.

In the corridor, he saw a small group of men and women gathered around a prone figure; he pushed through and saw that it was Lice. He said, "What's going on here?"

A young man, who'd taken off his jacket and rolled up his shirtsleeves, removed a bloodied hand from the back of Lice's neck and looked up; he said, "I don't know how this has happened, but I'm an ex-Army Medical Officer and this man is dead."

Pickles was stunned. He stood with his mouth open for what felt like an age. All around him people were scurrying about; he heard a man directing somebody to fetch the police, and he felt others bump into him in their haste to do something useful, but he was shocked into complete immobility.

His mind was racing; he knew that Lice was involved with Abraham and Caleb Johnson and he wondered what their reaction would be when they found out that he was dead. He wondered if he'd be implicated in some way, whether they'd hold him responsible or even worse whether they'd try to exact revenge against him.

He walked back to the seat and plonked down. He tried to figure out how Lice had died; had he fallen onto something sharp? Had an ulcer burst? Or horror of horrors, had somebody killed him?

He dropped his head into his hands and didn't care about the extra remuneration, pay rise, or promotion anymore; he wished that he'd never got involved with any of it.

"Mr Pickles sir, are you all right?"

Pickles looked up and saw the young receptionist staring at him.

"Would you like me to get you a hot sweet cup of tea? My father told me that it was good for shock, and you look like you need it."

Pickles said, "Yes please, that would be nice."

"You sit here and make yourself comfortable while I make it then, no doubt it won't be long before the police arrive and want to speak to us all." The receptionist smiled and walked off.

The horrific thought of police involvement spread across Pickles' realisation like a hammer blow; he needed to do something, and to do it fast.

Five minutes later, the receptionist walked back to the seat with a piping hot mug of tea; she stopped, looked around, and then walked back to her desk with a puzzled expression on her face.

"Strange," she said to her female companion, "I made Mr. Pickles some tea but he seems to have vanished."

"Yes he did," said the companion, "I saw him leave."

"Leave?"

"Yes, and it must have been important because he went without his hat."

On the opposite side of the reception area, a young woman dressed in a dark blue, full-length skirt and matching jacket tightened the ribbons of her bonnet under her chin. She cast a quick look around, waited for the opportune moment, and then slipped out of the building.

Chapter 36

'The vilest deeds, like prison weeds,
Bloom well in prison-air,
It is only what is good in man,
That wastes and withers there.'

- Oscar Wilde.

2:25pm, Saturday 9th July 2006. Bellthorpe Grain Mill, Castleton, Rochdale

On the top floor of the Bellthorpe Grain Mill Naomi sat opposite John Hess as they picked away at a double portion of fish and chips.

"I've bought us a couple of balm cakes and some Coke too," said John reaching for his backpack, "would you like some?"

Naomi nodded and looked into the face of the man opposite. Although the only illumination was from the pale white light of a battery-operated lantern on the floor, she could see that he didn't appear to be anything other than considerate and attentive. He'd provided her with a mattress, blankets, and even an old chair, and as per his promise, he'd fed and watered her, allowed her to use the portable toilet in privacy, and he'd brought her several packets of moist wipes to keep herself relatively fresh.

She looked across at his handsome face and said, "You don't strike me as a bad man, so why have you done this?"

Hess looked down and said, "I think I'm a bad man, but I don't mean to be. I fell for a beautiful woman, got caught up in her life, and here I am."

"Using me as a bargaining piece?"

"I suppose so, yes."

"And is it the police you are bargaining with?"

"Well, trying, at least."

"You do know that they never acquiesce to blackmail don't you?"

John handed Naomi a balm cake and a Coke and then said, "What else could I do? I'm an ex-military man who's discredited my unit by my actions, I've disposed of my lover's husband's body in Dunsteth Reservoir, I'm responsible for the partial demolition of that old building to cover it up and now I've added kidnapping and demands by threats to my crimes. How much worse can it get?"

Naomi was shocked, she said, "Are you kidding? If you proceed with this line of action it could get much worse, you could even end up being shot."

John looked down and said, "That might not be such a bad thing…"

"Oh do me a favour," said Naomi, "if you handed yourself into the police without harming me and my baby…"

John's head snapped up, he said, "Oh my God, you're pregnant?"

"Yes, but only by a few weeks."

John was mortified; he couldn't believe that he'd allowed himself to sink so low. He said, "I'm so sorry, I had no idea."

"How could you?"

John looked down and said, "I've been such an idiot…what the hell's the matter with me? Harming or endangering the life of women is something that I abhor."

Naomi surprised herself by reaching out and touching the back of John's hand, she said, "It's not too late."

She remembered reading about a condition known as Stockholm Syndrome where captives developed feelings for their captors, and she started to understand why. Alone and in the darkness of their stark surroundings, it felt as though the only man that mattered right then was the one sitting opposite. She looked at him and said, "What's your name?"

"John – John Hess." He hesitated and then said, "It's actually Johann Hess, but everybody calls me John."

"Johann Hess? It sounds German – you're not related to *the...?*"

"I believe so, but our connection goes way back. My grandfather's name was Burkhard, not Rudolph. He was a tank commander in a German Panzer Division in World War Two."

Naomi said, "Interesting – thank you for telling me, I had heard about you from a colleague of mine when we were discussing the complications of getting into the Malaterre Estate."

John frowned and said, "Getting into the Malaterre Estate?"

"Yes, hadn't you heard that a couple of bones had been discovered there?"

"No – but they couldn't have come from the guy whose body I dropped there because he's probably under tons of rubble and he's not been dead that long."

"They're not; the carbon 14 results showed that they belonged to people who died sometime around the 1870s."

"Crikey," said John, "did my idiocy destroy a crypt or something?"

"No, the bones were discovered before your involvement."

"So on the day that I saw you surveying the scene with a guy from the Marine Unit, you weren't on to me?"

"No, it was because of the discovery of the old bones."

John shook his head and said, "Would you bloody Adam and Eve it? Then I come along like a complete plank and get half the building blown up!"

Naomi pushed the container holding the last chip across to John and said, "Like I said, it's not too late."

John saw the gesture, pushed the container back, and said, "Give that to junior."

Naomi smiled, said, "I will," and ate it.

John considered their situation, and then thought about the unborn baby. He jumped to his feet and said, "This isn't right; – it's time to man up." He looked at Naomi and said, "First I'm going to get you out of here and then I'll hand myself in to the police – do you need to use the loo or anything before we go?"

Naomi said, "I wouldn't mind."

"Stick your hands out."

Naomi complied.

John removed a lethal-looking knife from his right-hand coat pocket, flipped it open with one hand, and severed the rope holding her left wrist to the metal stanchion. He then cut through the cable tie around her ankles. He handed her a small LED torch from his bag and said, "Take this and watch where you're going, I don't want you or that baby coming to any harm."

Several minutes later Naomi returned and saw that John had packed away most their belongings. She said, "Are you sure about this?"

John was surprised and said, "Christ, you're one of a kind. I kidnap you; subject you to a living hell in almost total darkness, you have to put up with feral pigeons flying around and all sorts of monstrous creepy-crawlies, and you ask me if *I'm* sure?"

Naomi jumped and looked around, she said, "You never said anything about monstrous creepy-crawlies! God, if I'd known that I'd have chewed through the gag and screamed the place down!"

"Good job I didn't tell you then," said John with a wry smile. He untied the rope from the stanchion, tied a bowline onto one end, looped it into a slipknot around his left wrist, and then tied the other end around Naomi's waist. He checked that the knot was secure without being too tight and then said, "I don't want to take any chances with you falling, and this rope's a bit long, so gather it up and stay close behind me. There are four huge grain chutes in here, so you'll need to be very careful until we get to the other side of them."

Naomi said, "Okay," – left a decent length of rope between them, and then twisted some around her left wrist and clung on to it.

"Are you ready?" said John.

"Ready."

Because of the sheer darkness of the vast room, and because the LED lantern was poor at directing light forwards, John's view was restricted. He inched forwards twenty metres or so, then stopped, and said, "Okay, keep well over to the right now – the openings are about fifteen to twenty feet from here so keep your torch pointed down in front of your feet, stay behind me, and look out for any loose items on the floor."

The words echoed around the room, and somewhere in the distance Naomi heard the flutter of wings.

"Do we have to go anywhere near those birds?" she said as John started to lead her forwards.

"Not until we get to the other end of the room."

Naomi looked around and said, "I'm not keen on things flying around me. How did they get in here? I can't see any windows."

"Dunno, most of them are pigeons; maybe parent birds laid eggs on the floors below and the young flew up here and became trapped."

"And are they what's causing that unpleasant smell?" said Naomi.

"That and old grain, I should think."

Naomi followed John and moved to his right until she came up against the wall; she kept the beam of the torch in front of her feet, and in doing so, failed to see an area of thick wooden shelving above her head. She cleared the first stretch without incident, and then walked face first into a thick spider's web.

Something heavy fell onto her forehead and attempted to scuttle into her hair. She let out an ear-splitting scream, jumped to the left, crashed into John, and dropped her torch as she tried to batter the hellish monster off her head.

John staggered sideways and landed his left foot onto a small length of discarded scaffold pole. The pole rolled to the left, he yelled, *"Shit!"* and started to do the splits. As he lost his balance he threw the lantern up into the air and saw it sweep upwards and outwards. He followed it with his eyes and in a moment of pure horror, saw it disappear into the open grain chute inches away from his feet. In the blink of an eye, he was over. He screeched as he dropped, gripped the rope, and then felt it suddenly tighten.

Around the perimeter of the chute was a six-inch steel rim with small gaps in it; the rope slipped into one and kinked.

Above and to the right, Naomi was wrenched to her left and slammed to the floor before the rope could jump out of the gap. It shredded the skin of her left wrist as it unravelled, and then tightened with immense pressure around her back and waist. She felt as though she was being cut in two.

Down in the chute, John hardly dared to breathe. He stayed as still as he could until he heard Naomi gasp in pain and then remembered that he'd tied the other end of the rope around her waist. In a moment of regained chivalry he let go of his end, but the slipknot tightened around his left wrist and he stayed put. He tried to grab the knife in his pocket, but the angle at which he was suspended made it impossible to reach. With a herculean effort, he wrenched himself up with his left arm, plunged his hand into his right pocket, and got it.

Up above, Naomi felt the rope slacken and re-tighten, and then with excruciating pressure, drag her sideways across the concrete floor. She screamed out as fingernails and fingertips broke and tore as she tried to clutch at anything to stop her momentum. She then slammed into the steel rim and gasped again as the full weight of John's body exerted its pressure across her stomach.

From down in the chute she heard John shout, "I'm so sorry; I hope that you'll forgive me for this one day…" and then she felt the rope go slack. She screamed and shouted, *"No! – John, no…"*

From somewhere deep below she heard a muffled thump, and then all went silent.

She didn't know how long she lay on the floor sobbing, but as she sat up and removed the rope from around her waist, she felt an unpleasant sensation in her lower abdomen. She waited until it subsided and then picked up the small torch and backed away from the chute. She edged her way to the right-hand wall and followed it until she reached the door leading to the stairs.

As she descended it got lighter, she looked down at her clothes and saw that they were torn, dirty, and blood-stained.

Her left wrist was bleeding, she had burst blisters, loose skin, and broken fingernails and both her hands were covered in blood and dirt.

She reached the ground-floor level, attempted to push open the doors that led to freedom, and saw that they were locked with a heavy padlock and chain. She could have screamed; she looked around and saw that the windows were so small that even with the glass removed she couldn't have climbed out.

She dropped to her knees, sobbed, and then lifted her head and shouted, "*Help me* – somebody, please!"

Five-and-a-half miles away in Bury, Stephen Page's head shot up as he was making final checks of his climbing gear. He stood up and said, "Don't worry, I'm coming…"

Chapter 37

3:10pm Saturday 8th July 2006. Bellthorpe Grain Mill, Castleton, Rochdale

Drained, hurting, and mentally scarred, Naomi headed back to the staircase that led to the top of the grain mill and went up to the first floor.

She'd walked all the way around the ground floor and had seen the bases of the grain chutes, each shut off by a large, metal, sliding door. She'd walked across to the one that contained John, had called out several times, and had banged on the door, but none of it had drawn a response. She'd made a mental note of where it had been and had then continued her search for an exit. She'd found four other doors that led to the outside, but all had been locked except one. With a huge sigh of relief she'd burst through it only to find that she was in an enclosure with a fifteen-foot high wall and no exit.

She pushed open the door on the first floor level, walked in and looked around; the layout looked similar to the ground floor with the chutes dominating the space. Once again she noted that the metal-framed windows were too small to climb out of, even they'd been safe to do so.

Feeling ever-wearier, she pressed on until she found a small office in the far corner almost diagonally opposite the staircase. With no expectation of finding the door unlocked, she turned the handle, pushed it open, and then recoiled and jammed her left hand up to her face. The cloying, sickly-sweet stench was horrendous; it seemed to bypass her nose and settle onto the back of her throat.

Through screwed up eyes she saw a grubby-looking sleeping bag covered by an old grey blanket, empty beer cans, discarded fast-food containers, and several girlie magazines. In the corner was an old wooden table atop which were more beer cans, a couple of empty vodka bottles, and two part-burned candles.

Her first instinct had been to step backwards in case she'd disturbed somebody, but it soon became apparent that nobody had occupied the room for several weeks. She stepped inside.

Lying on the table was a discarded evening newspaper that had been wrapped around an old packet of fish and chips; she peeled back the pages, found a publication date, and saw that it dated from the end of May that year.

She looked across to the far corner of the office and saw another door. With her nose still gripped as best as she could, she made her way across to it. She was about to step onto what appeared to be a small piece of cloth, when the thumb pressed down on her left shoulder and a voice said, 'Stop!'

With her left foot hovering, she stopped and then placed it down next to her right. She looked at the cloth and saw that it appeared to be suspended around one centimetre above the wooden floor. She dropped to her haunches, looked closer, then ripped a clean page out of a girlie mag, used it as a glove, and lifted the cloth.

To her horror, she saw that somebody had pressed dozens of used hypodermic needles through a thin piece of dense sponge, had laid it on the floor just inside the door, and had placed the cloth over it to trap any unsuspecting soul. The sheer volume of needles, so closely packed together, and some still blood-stained, could have penetrated all but the hardiest footwear, and could have infected any hapless victim. It was a testament to the horrific depravity of the office's previous occupier.

Careful not to let anything touch the broken skin on her hands, she picked up the lethal trap with the torn out page, and cast it into a wooden box underneath the table. Half expecting it clatter into the receptacle; she was surprised to hear that it fell silently into it instead. Her curiosity took a hold; she leaned under the table, and pulled the box into the open. Lying in the bottom was the cause of the horrific smell, a small dead dog. She jumped up, said, "Jesus Christ!" grimaced, and pushed the box back with her right foot.

Now desperate to get out, she turned and inspected the floor for other nasties, walked across it, stepped out of the door, and onto a small landing. To her left was a lift door; to her right was the door to a fire escape.

She pushed the button to call the lift, but nothing happened. She then walked to the fire escape door, pushed the metal bar, and stepped out onto the rusty, grilled landing. She drew in several deep lungs full of fresh air in an attempt to purge the stink of the decaying dog, and then set off, downwards.

A few minutes later, she reached the bottom of the fire escape and emerged into a long-deserted piece of open ground adjacent to the Rochdale Canal. She crossed it and then followed a wire mesh perimeter fence until she found an area that had been breached; she then pushed through it into the trees, and discovered that she was on the side of the canal that had no towpath.

She looked across to the other side but nobody was there; she then pushed her way through the trees until she reached a low brick wall, squeezed around the end it, and stepped into a short unused, unpopulated, side road named Bow Street. She ran down it to its junction with a main road named Queensway and saw a fish and chip shop on the opposite corner. She ran over to it, but saw that it was closed. She was about to commence knocking on the doors of the terraced houses next to it, until through a stroke of luck, she saw a taxi heading down Queensway towards her. She raised her arm, hailed it down, got in, and instructed the driver to take her to her home address.

Naomi's unkempt and bloodied appearance wasn't lost on the middle-aged Pakistani cab driver; he stared through the rear-view mirror, and said, "Are you all right Miss, you look as though you've been…"

Naomi cut the cabbie off and said, "I'm fine, can we please go?"

The cab driver continued to stare through the rear-view mirror for a few seconds longer and then said, "If you're in some kind of trouble…"

"No, I'm not! Can we please just go?"

The cab driver then became suspicious; he started to wonder if Naomi had done something to somebody else; he looked at her through the rear-view mirror one more time, nodded his head, and set off, determined to contact the police once he'd arrived at their destination.

4:05pm Dunsteth Reservoir

Crowds of fascinated onlookers gathered along the southern bank of Dunsteth Reservoir and followed the various proceedings in the warm afternoon sunshine.

Since seeing the dramatic television report, several hundred had gathered there including numerous news reporters, and all were vying for the best place to watch after being corralled to the south bank by the police. What was annoying to most was the odd angle of the Estate building because a lot of the police activity appeared to be concentrated on the northern side of the south-western wing which was out of sight.

What they could see were three rib-type police launches – two circling the building to prevent over-enthusiastic boaters entering their buoyed exclusion zone, and one that appeared to be used for ferrying people and equipment to the out-of-sight northern elevation. There was a lot of police activity, a mobile ops van on the eastern approach road and numerous small craft sculling around the southern and western sides of the building. The other two sides were off limits. The more observant onlookers would also have been able to pick out people from the press in some of the small boats presenting, reporting, or pointing cameras at the building and surrounding areas.

On the south-western wing, Stephen Page, adorned in his professional climbing gear, was free-climbing up the northern face. His powdered, strong fingers and toes, covered in soft specialised climbing shoes, gripped the deep joints between the sun-dried ashlars, and propelled him upwards. On his back he had a soft bag containing a VHF radio with a fitted ear and mouthpiece attuned to the police frequency, a powerful digital camera that could relay live images, a bottle of water, and a banana. The latter items had been his idea in case Naomi was in the building and in need of food or drink.

Below in the now motionless third police rib were Inspector Hugh Kearns, and one of his best divers, Constable Aaron Reay. Kearns watched Stephen's progress through a pair of image-stabilising binoculars and listened to his comments as he made his way up the building.

On the eastern approach road Crowthorne sat in the mobile ops van with an anxious Carlton, and listened via a loudspeaker to Stephen's progress reports. Aimed at the northern elevation were two cameras atop the ops van, following Stephen's measured progress.

Roy Bright, the BBC North West reporter who'd first broken the story of Naomi's capture stood on the southern bank of the reservoir. Life hadn't been easy for him since that day and he knew that his job hung in the balance. He stood poised in front of the outside broadcast camera as he listened to his studio link introducing him, and then saw the red light come on.

He lifted the mic up to his mouth and said, "Good afternoon from the southern bank of Dunsteth Reservoir. As we speak a professional free-climber..." he looked at his pad, more for effect than need, "...named Stephen Page is scaling the northern elevation of the tower just over my right shoulder, though because of the orientation, we cannot see him. We understand that he is in constant communication with the police mobile ops van, and that we will be kept abreast of any developments as they occur.

"The man in charge is Superintendent Bob Crowthorne of Lancashire County Police and earlier today I spoke with him. This is what he had to say..." He broke off as the studio indicated to him that the short digital VT was running and he looked at his watch. He had two minutes and thirty seconds.

At a densely foliated section of the southern bank, two of Adrian Darke's henchmen manhandled a large metal crate

271

towards the water's edge. Happy that they were out of sight, they removed the lid and extracted the Russian RPG-7V2 rocket propelled grenade launcher. They loaded the high-explosive warhead, and laid it down ready for use.

Seconds later Leander Pike appeared and checked that all was in order. He pointed to the crate and said, "Right – take that back to the van, and wait for me."

The two men picked up the crate, and left.

Pike picked up the heavy RPG and pushed through the foliage until he could see his target. He saw that he was within range, lifted it to his shoulder, aimed, and squeezed the trigger.

The gunpowder booster charge launched the grenade in a cloud of grey-blue smoke and then the rocket motor ignited. Seconds later the stabiliser fins deployed and it screamed across the water towards its target.

At exactly the same time, the VT stopped, and BBC North West handed transmission back to the outside broadcast unit at Dunsteth.

Everybody watching saw Roy Bright suddenly spin around – duck, and then yell, "Jesus Christ! *What the fuck's that?"*

Chapter 38

Abraham Johnson moved out from the cover of the burnt Ash, snatched his pocket watch out of his waistcoat pocket and held it up to make use of the available moonlight. It was 11:30pm, and he was blazing mad. First because he'd given strict instructions to Lice that he, Squat, and the pastor should meet him at 11pm, and second, that he was being made to look a fool in front of Grinner.

With a gritted jaw he walked back to the Ash and stood seething.

Caleb sidled up and said, "You all right pa?"

"No I'm not. I'm going rip that fucking chink's head off if he ends up making me look like an idiot in front of Grinner!"

Caleb dropped his gaze and then looked back up; he said, "Don't you worry about Grinner pa, if he even dares to badmouth you he'll have me to deal with."

Abraham looked at his ever-faithful son and felt genuine affection for him; he said, "You're a good lad Caleb."

Once again Caleb looked down; he didn't often hear kindnesses from his father, but when he did, he was touched. The moment passed, he looked back up and said, "Time's a passing."

Abraham expelled an exasperated snort through his nostrils; he looked to his left and saw that Grinner and Galloping John, who were sitting with their backs to the trunk, were beginning to look restless. He shook his head and almost hissed, *"Fuck!"*

"Can we do it with just us?"

"Not a hope."

Caleb pondered for a few seconds and then said, "This isn't like Lice pa. Maybe something bad's had happened to him."

Abraham frowned and said, "Like what?"

"I don't know, but think about everything that's happened in such a short time. Squeaker's disappeared off the face of the earth, Galloping got put onto a train to London, the Wenderliks have ended up in hospital and now Lice hasn't turned up with Squat and the pastor. It's too much of a coincidence."

Abraham stared into his son's face and said, "You could be right…"

"And another thing," said Caleb, "we know that the mute from The Pit was responsible for doing what he did to Galloping, and we knew that he'd given Lice the run-around too, so just because we haven't seen him lately, doesn't mean he still isn't around. He could be the one who's fucked us up tonight."

Abraham remained silent and then walked away.

At first Caleb wondered if he'd said something wrong, but a few seconds later he saw his father walk back.

Abraham said, "If what you say is true, the mute'll think that he's buggered us up good and proper right?"

Caleb said, "Go on…"

"And he'll more than likely expect us to abandon what we'd planned, right?"

"Yes."

"So what if we trump his cards and go ahead anyway?"

Caleb was shocked, he said, "I thought that you said we wouldn't have a hope of doing it with only four of us?"

"And if you're correct that's what he'll be thinking too, right?"

"I suppose so, but it's a big risk, and I don't want you taking it out on me if I'm wrong."

"Don't be such a cloutnut, 'course I won't! In fact, the more I think about it, the more I think you could be right. Just 'cos we can't see the mute doesn't mean that he hasn't buggered this up with his planning, scheming, creating smoke screens and the like."

"So what now?"

Abraham removed his watch from his pocket again and said, "It's quarter-to-midnight, it's obvious that the others aren't coming, so we'll go and do the job on our own."

"Shit pa, that's really risky…"

"And has that ever stopped us before?"

Caleb hesitated and then said, "No it hasn't. I'll rouse Grinner and Galloping and you can explain your plan as we go."

Abraham turned to Caleb and said, "Plan? What plan? We're going there to kick Frog arse and then leave."

He looked across at Grinner and Galloping John, called them over, and said, "Right listen to me. We've had our plans screwed up but we're still going ahead with the job."

Without warning Grinner laughed out loud and said, *"Yes! – That's what I'm talking about!"* It was the weirdest laugh that Caleb and John had ever heard and made them both look at him as though he was demented.

They exchanged questioning glances until Abraham glared at Grinner and said, "and you can keep that bloody silly racket under control? Or you'll wake up half of Blackstone Moor."

Grinner laughed again, but louder and more forced – and nobody saw an ounce of humour in his eyes.

Abraham waited until the sound had subsided and then said, "As I said – we're still going ahead with the job, but under no circumstances are any of you to steal anything. Is that understood?" He looked at each man in turn and waited until he'd had an acknowledgement; then he said, "This job is about getting rid of a whole brood of frogs, men, women, and children, so I don't want any of us being caught and implicating the others because he's got sticky fingers. We do what we've got planned, and then we get the fuck out with nothing but frog blood on our blades. Got it?"

Once again he waited until he'd had an acknowledgement. He then turned to Grinner and said, "You haven't worked with us before, so there's something you should know. If anybody, *ever,* betrays me, or Caleb, they'll die. Whoever of us is left, will track down the traitor, however long it takes, and however far they go, even through the bowels of hell itself, and we'll get them, and when we do, they'll die the most gruesome and painful death they could ever imagine."

Grinner backed up half a step as Abraham drew closer.

Abraham said, "Do we have an understanding?"

Grinner nodded his head and wanted to laugh, but nothing came. For the first time that he could remember, he felt threatened by another man.

Abraham stared at Grinner and heard John gulp. He then backed up, looked at each face in turn, and said, "Right, let's get this done."

Eighty miles away at Railway Dock in Hull, Etienne, Marie-Francois, Charles, Elodie, and Monique Page stood on the deck of the Pénélope Class French Frigate *Jeanne d'Arc* with Nicolas.

"You should all be safe now," said Nicolas, "I have requested that one of Brigadier Niel's men meet you in Boulogne to escort you to Paris, where you will be his guests until somewhere suitable is found for you to live."

"Boulogne, not Calais?" said Marie-Francois.

"No Madame, the railway line from Boulogne to Paris via Amiens is quicker."

"But how does the Brigadier know that we're coming, Capitaine?" said Elodie.

Nicolas turned to the beautiful girl and tapped the side of his nose; he said, "We special agents have our secrets mademoiselle!" He saw the look of hurt on Elodie's face, relented, and said, "Very well, but you must never tell the English or they may try to copy us..." he leaned closer and whispered loud enough for all to hear, "...French carrier pigeons."

Elodie blushed as everybody else laughed.

The only person who remained unamused was Charles; he took Nicolas by the elbow, led him to one side, and said, "Capitaine, may I have a word?"

"Bien sûr Charles, how can I help?"

"I'm not happy about leaving Saba at Malaterre and I want to go back with you."

Nicolas stared into the concerned face of Charles and then said, "But Philipe is with her and it's doubtful that an attack will be made on her now."

"You can't be sure of that Capitaine."

Nicolas recalled his earlier foray dressed as a woman in the offices of Hundersfield District Council, and how he had despatched the Chinaman. He said, "Naturally Charles, it is impossible to guarantee that the Johnson men won't attempt an assault on Malaterre, but I have taken steps to make sure that such an escapade would be foolish."

"Nevertheless," said Charles with growing fortitude, "unless we can be absolutely sure, I'd still like to go back."

"But you know why it is so important that you all leave."

"I do Capitaine, but that alters nothing. The very thought of leaving her there at the mercy of those Johnson men and their vile colleagues fills me with a deep foreboding and I would never forgive myself if anything happened to her."

"And I am under strict orders to make sure that you are safe M'sieu."

Charles hesitated and then said, "Then you will need to come with me to Malaterre."

"And there is nothing that I can do to persuade you to stay aboard?"

"No Capitaine, I have made up my mind."

Nicolas thought about the situation for a few minutes and then said, "Very well – we'll leave on the first train tomorrow morning."

At 12:30am, six masked men, dressed in black, left a tavern in Bury. Without saying a word to one another, they mounted their horses, and set off for the eight mile ride to Malaterre.

Chapter 39

4:10pm Saturday 8th July 2006. Dunsteth Reservoir

The rocket propelled grenade screeched across the water, climbed, and then slammed into the second floor level of the south wing, directly below the observation tower. The explosion was deafening.

Stephen Page was blown off the north-eastern face, dropped thirty feet into the water, and disappeared below the surface.

Shattered pieces of stonework shrieked into unsuspecting members of the public, tearing at flesh and clothing, and a huge pall of smoke climbed skywards whilst everybody watched, mesmerised by the horrific turn of events.

Inside the mobile ops van Carlton yelled, *"No! Naomi!"* He leapt to his feet, jumped out of the van, and ran to the water's edge oblivious of the small pieces of masonry raining down all around him.

In a state of pure shock, Roy Bright forgot that transmission had been handed back to him and said, "Jesus Christ…"

Leander Pike stared at his handiwork with an impassive look, and waited to see what he'd achieved.

The two closest police officers saw Pike on the bank, jammed their craft into gear, and headed towards him…

The smoke started to clear the second floor level and then the impact of the explosion began to manifest itself. Hundreds of cracks began to merge into big ones, the big ones merged into bigger ones, and then two huge cracks snaked up either side of the eastern corner. Two more cracks opened up at roof level and zigzagged towards the observation tower, thirty feet apart. The intense pressure became too much for the building to withstand and with an ear-splitting crash the second floor level of the wing collapsed.

People stood in awe until they saw the police rib come into view below the breaking masonry. As if with one voice they started yelling at the hapless officers, who themselves only had eyes for Pike.

The massive section of building slewed out and plummeted down.

The marine officer piloting the rib looked up, rammed the gear lever forward, and attempted to speed away as the falling masonry cascaded into the reservoir beside them. Both men were launched out of the rib and into the raging water.

Roy Bright saw what was happening and yelled, *"Oh no...oh God – they've got to be dead..."*

Crowthorne leapt out of the ops van and ran to Carlton. The scene before him was almost biblical. The wave created by the falling masonry surged up the bank and soaked them both to knee level but neither moved. In that one moment, it looked as though the whole of creation had stopped moving. And then, as the wave withdrew it was as though an unseen god turned up the volume switch. In a tumultuous uproar, hundreds of voices started yelling, screaming, and crying; – until another huge crack rent the air, and the volume switch was turned off again.

Everybody turned. Another piece of masonry, this time from the south-eastern side of the observation tower, slaked off, and fell straight into the same section of water as the first piece. It hit the surface with a thunderous crash and sent another wave surging up the bank.

A second police rib appeared and the crew started picking people out of the water, whilst gesturing for others to back off.

Hugh Kearns turned to Aaron Reay said, "Shit mate – that was close..." and then a jagged piece of stone the size of a house brick hurtled down from the second floor level, bounced off a projecting section of wall, and buried itself into the crown of Aaron's head.

Blood sprayed into Kearns' face. His mouth fell open in shock, and then he caught sight of a woman on the shore gesticulating upwards. Without thinking, he dived over the side as another huge piece of masonry dropped through the bottom of the rib, inches from where he'd been standing.

Roy Bright suddenly remembered he was on air and said, "I have never seen anything like this before. I'm almost lost for words…people are injured everywhere and part of the building has been blown away by some sort of weapon. At least two policemen may have died, maybe more…" He turned and looked into the crowd as the screaming of a near-hysterical woman cradling a young girl with a huge gash on the side of her head pierced his ears. He felt the emotion rise. He turned back to the camera and said, "This is just terrible, awful…"

On the Eastern bank, four marine officers launched two more ribs and headed out towards the mayhem.

At 4:20pm, the taxi carrying Naomi home arrived at her house. She jumped out without speaking, ran up the short front path, and punched the numbers into the private key safe situated just inside their porch.

The taxi driver got out and called, "Missus – hey missus, my fare…"

Naomi ignored him, let herself in, and shouted, *"Cal, Cal…"* She listened for a couple of seconds and realised that he wasn't there. She looked down at her bloodied hands and wiped them on her top.

Outside the suspicious taxi driver waited until Naomi had run indoors, and then requested his control to get the police.

Naomi didn't know what to do first; she saw the phone lying on her kitchen table and snatched it up. She was about to dial 999 when it rang. She nearly dropped it and said, "Bugger!" The phone rang a second time. She clicked the button and said; "Yes, who are you?"

"Shit – Naomi?" said a flabbergasted Helen, "Is that you? We thought that you could be dead!"

"What? Why? – and where's Cal?"

"I thought that he was at home, that's why I was calling."

"He's not."

"Maybe he's at Dunsteth."

Naomi was confused; she said, "Why? What the hell is he doing at Dunsteth?"

"Christ," said Helen, "have you no idea what's happened at Malaterre?"

"Course I haven't! What *has* happened?"

Helen said, "You need to get to a TV and switch it on to BBC North West now."

"What," said Naomi, "Why?"

"Just do it, then ring me back on my mobile and I'll call the police for you."

Naomi stared in disbelief as she realised that Helen had terminated the call.

With a puzzled expression on her face she walked into her lounge, dropped down onto her sofa, picked up the television remote, and clicked onto BBC North West.

The news reporter appeared to be on the verge of tears.

"In all of my years reporting," he said, "I have never witnessed anything like this."

The camera panned around and showed horrified onlookers gathered around the southern edges of the Dunsteth Reservoir staring at the Malaterre Estate buildings.

Naomi watched in amazement as three police launches pulled people out of the water and gestured to others to keep clear.

Without warning, a loud rumbling penetrated the air and everybody looked up.

"Oh no, please God, not again..." shouted the reporter.

Nothing appeared to happen for a few seconds, and then in frozen silence the first floor level on the corner of the south wing became detached. Directly below was a police rib with two occupants staring upwards too.

Men and women started screaming at them to move, but it was too late. In what looked like slow motion, it smashed down onto the rib.

People screamed as they watched more panic-stricken individuals in the water thrashing about in all directions.

"No, no, no..." sobbed the reporter.

The thumb pressed down onto Naomi's shoulder and a voice said, "I'm sorry – he's gone…"

Naomi leapt to her feet and said, "No – not him…"

She dropped the remote onto the floor, ran towards the door, and a searing pain shot through her lower abdomen. She gasped and bent double as the excruciating feeling spread into her back. She clutched at her stomach, dropped to her knees, and the last thing that she saw before all went black was the shadowy outline of a man staring in through the front window…

Dunsteth Reservoir was a scene of utter despair. Everywhere people were crying and trying to console weeping children; others were injured to varying degrees, and everybody seemed to be shouting at the same time. The only thing that seemed to be being ignored was the motionless Pike.

Further down the southern bank a lone man saw him and yelled, *"You bastard! You did this!"* He picked up a handful of stones and started throwing them, whilst keeping up a tirade of abuse.

Several other people clicked, and took up the tirade too.

A marine officer in a nearby rib caught sight of what was happening, saw the lone man on the bank, and headed towards him.

Roy Bright saw Pike too and yelled into his mic, "That's the guy whose done this…he's the one who created all this carnage…"

The cameraman turned and zoomed in but it was too late. In the flash of an eye Pike had gone.

With people yelling abuse, and the police closing in, Pike lumbered through the trees and foliage, broke out onto the southern perimeter approach road, and clambered into the waiting van. Seconds later the van screeched away before anybody could identify it, or him.

On the eastern bank of the reservoir, a shocked and disorientated Stephen Page emerged from the depths and waded up the bank, unable to believe his luck and his eyes. He gathered his wits for a few seconds and then saw Carlton and

Crowthorne. He staggered across to them and said, "Good God in Heaven – what happened?"

Carlton looked at Stephen with a wild look in his eyes, then turned and ran back to the ops van. He ran up the steps and launched himself into Leo Chance. He said, "I'm going to kill you…"

Crowthorne leapt into the van, grabbed Carlton from the rear, and shouted at him just as the phone rang.

A startled monitoring officer in the van snatched it up, listened to the voice at the other end, and shouted, "Guys, guys – stop! Mrs. Wilkes is alive…"

Deep in the swirling and troubled reservoir the waters began to clear. The damage to the southern wing had been catastrophic and immense, but the rest of the building had stabilised.

The two biggest pieces of falling masonry had landed in the same place and had broken open more of the submerged basement. The left-hand wall that had concealed the door with the bronze escutcheon plate had been ripped away, and for the first time in one-hundred-and-thirty-eight years, the door stood exposed, accessible, and ready to give up its vile secret.

Chapter 40

Sunday 9th July 2006. The Neonatal Intensive Care
Unit, The Royal Oldham Hospital, Lancashire

Carlton looked at Naomi and could have broken down. She was battered, bruised, and both hands were bandaged – but it was the haunted look in her eyes that did it.

Being an ex-Army officer, he was used to controlling his emotions, but even he'd been brought to the edge of tears when he'd heard that his beautiful wife had lost their baby. He wasn't a violent man, but he wanted someone to blame, someone to vent his anger on, and he wanted to rip the head off the man who'd caused all the loss of life and damage at Dunsteth.

He saw Naomi staring up at the ceiling, brought his chair closer to the bed, and gently placed his right hand over her left. He gathered resolve and said, "We didn't know whether…"

"It was a boy."

Carlton hesitated and then said, "A boy? How…?"

"It was a boy..."

Carlton looked at Naomi's face, opened his mouth to speak, but was cut off.

"…just before I collapsed at home, I heard a woman say, 'I'm sorry, he's gone'."

Carlton gathered that Naomi didn't mean that she'd physically heard the voice. He said, "But couldn't that have meant something else pet?"

Naomi shook her head and said, "No. At first I wondered if it could be Stephen Page, but somehow I could still feel his presence…"

Carlton frowned and said, "How?"

"I don't know, I just did." She paused, looked at Carlton, and said, "He is okay isn't he?"

"He was as shaken up as everybody else of course, but according to the police, only four people were known to be killed."

Naomi turned to look at her husband and said, "Four? My God."

"Yes, two marine officers in a rib, Inspector Kearns' close friend and colleague P.C. Aaron Reay, and a female member of the public on the south bank. All hit by flying or falling masonry."

Naomi leaned her right hand over the side of the bed and pressed a button on her remote control unit. The head of the bed rose until she was in a comfortable sitting position. She said, "Has Bob formed any theories about why anybody should have done what they did, or maybe who did it?"

Carlton thought about his answer and said, "No, not yet."

Naomi recalled Helen's remark before passing out and said, "And why did Helen think that I could be dead?"

Carlton wanted to be frank with Naomi, but he was concerned about her emotional and physical condition, and he didn't want to put pressure on her. He said, "I expect it's because you were kidnapped."

Naomi looked at Carlton again and said, "You're keeping something from me."

Carlton hesitated, but it was too long.

"What Cal?"

Carlton looked down, then into the eyes of his wife. He said, "Don't you think that we should talk about this when you're feeling stronger?"

"I hope to be getting out of here today, so a couple of hours won't make a difference."

Carlton stood up and walked across to a water dispenser. He turned to Naomi and said, "Want some?"

"No thanks."

Carlton poured himself a plastic cup full of water, drank it, and said, "All right. We aren't sure, but, the target may have been you."

"Me? *Me?*" Naomi was shocked. She said, "What have I done, and who would want to do that to me?"

"That's what we have to establish. Lancashire police received a note from the Hess guy informing us that you'd been placed on the second floor of Malaterre, near the observation tower, and that you were wired up to an explosive device. He must have then leaked it to BBC North West."

"John Hess did all that?"

"Yes, he was blackmailing the police in an attempt to get out of the country."

"He told me that he was using me as a bargaining piece before he died, but he never said anything about me being supposedly tied up in Malaterre."

Carlton recalled the message that he'd received from Bob Crowthorne earlier that morning and said, "They got Hess's body out of silo 3 by-the-way. He didn't survive the fall."

Naomi looked down and said, "It's crazy I know, but I liked him, and I believed him when he said that he was going to give himself up."

"Hmm," said Carlton, "maybe, but if it wasn't for him, you may still be..." he stopped short and looked at Naomi.

"Pregnant? I know, but if it hadn't been for a last gallant act from him, I could have gone down that silo too."

Carlton wasn't in the mood to hear praise about his son's killer, and said, "Perhaps we can agree not to talk about that man…"

Naomi looked down, and then back up. She said, "So has Bob any theories about who fired the grenade?"

"None that he'd share with me, but there was something about his pensiveness that got me thinking."

"And how about you, do have any thoughts?"

Before Carlton could answer, one of the senior nurses walked across to Naomi's bed and said, "Excuse me Mrs. Wilkes, Mr. Leonard will see you later this morning, and if all's well, you'll be able to leave afterwards."

Naomi smiled and thanked the nurse. "It'll be nice to sleep in my own bed for a change," she said. She thought about the episode with the two surveillance officers, waited until the nurse had departed, and said, "Could whoever have fired that rocket have anything to do with those strange notes?"

"We think so."

"We?"

"Yes, Bob, and me – and even that bloody moronic Leo Chance."

Naomi felt protective towards Leo and said, "That's not fair, especially after…"

"Especially nothing! If he hadn't been so lax in his duty, none of this would have happened and all of those people would still be alive."

Naomi looked down and lapsed into silence.

Carlton relented to a degree and said, "I know that you're grateful to him for saving your life a few months ago, but he could have cost you your life this time!"

"That wasn't likely…"

Carlton felt his pent up frustration and anger rise. He said, "Don't be so naïve Naomi. Hess could so have done to you what he did to that poor guy in the Dunsteth reservoir!"

Naomi said, "And he's paid the price now…"

"Quite right too! If I'd seen what he'd done to you at the top of that mill, I'd have pushed the bastard down the silo myself."

Naomi was shocked to hear her mild mannered husband speak with such vehemence. She said, "No you wouldn't."

"Oh yes I bloody well would have!"

Naomi watched as Carlton walked across to the ward window with his right hand up to his mouth. She realised that he was still hurting from the news of losing their baby. She said, "John didn't *'do'* anything to me at the top of the mill, but I take your point."

Carlton wheeled around and said, "Oh, so it's *'John'* now is it?"

Naomi let Carlton simmer for a few seconds and changed the subject. She said, "So who do you, Bob, and 'the moronic Leo' think is behind this?"

Carlton looked at Naomi and said, "You can quit with the digs Mimi, 'cos I'm not in the mood."

Naomi knew that Carlton loved every bone of her, and that his anger was as much to do with losing the baby as it was to do with her being placed in danger. She said, "Sorry Cal."

Carlton turned from looking out of the window and walked back to his chair. He sat down, took hold of his wife's hand and said, "I'm sorry too, but I get so, so bloody furious when I think that somebody maybe trying to harm you."

Naomi took hold of Carlton's big strong hand in both of her bandaged hands and said, "I know darling, and I love you." She waited for a few seconds and then added, "So who do you think is behind it?"

Carlton looked up into Naomi's beautiful, big brown eyes and said, "We haven't got a clue, but, if whoever fired that grenade was planning to kill you, he may now think that you're dead, and, and…" he paused.

"And what?"

"…and Bob wants to put out an announcement that you died at Malaterre."

Naomi was stunned; she said, "And who'd know that I was still alive?"

"The hospital staff, Helen, Bob, Leo Chance, and me."

"And the ambulance driver, and the taxi driver, and Stephen Page…"

Carlton frowned and said, "Stephen Page? How would he know?"

Naomi didn't know how to explain. She said, "Trust me, he knows."

"You're not telling me that he's…"

"Yes, I am. And he knows – along with the taxi driver and the ambulance driver and any other person who may have seen me…" She thought about something else. "And what about mum and dad, would you tell them that I was dead too?

"For a short while, yes, but…"

"But nothing Cal – I am not putting them through that!"

Carlton knew better than to argue. "Okay," he said, "I told Bob that you wouldn't agree, but trust me young lady, there isn't a place that you'll be going from now on without accompaniment, and it will stay that way until we catch those ba… – people – who tried to do this to you."

Naomi cast her mind to Dunsteth and said, "Was much damage done to Malaterre?"

"On the southern wing yes – but we'll know the full extent tomorrow. A team of marine surveyors, Hugh Kearns, and his divers are there today, and they're all reporting to Bob tomorrow morning."

Out of the blue, the thumb pushed down onto Naomi's left shoulder and a female voice said, *"Naomi, obtenir la clé."* She frowned and put her hand up to her shoulder.

Carlton saw the action and the change in Naomi's expression. He said, "What is it?"

Naomi looked at Carlton and said, "What is, *'obtenir la clé?'*"

"It's French and it means, 'get the key'. – You heard that?"

Naomi felt her head swim and said, "Whoa Cal, this is weird…"

"What key, and what's weird?"

"Le sous-sol à Malaterre…"

"Shush, Cal…"

Carlton ignored Naomi and said, "Sweetheart, what's weird?"

"Naomi – le sous-sol à Malaterre…"

Naomi frowned, rubbed her left shoulder, and said, "Weirder…"

Carlton said, "Please, Mimi, what is it?"

"What is *'le sous-sol à Malaterre'*?"

Carlton pondered for a second and said, "The basement at Malaterre…" He paused, the penny dropped, and he said, "No, no, no – don't even think about it…"

Naomi looked at Carlton and said, "You know that we have to do this."

"But…"

"But nothing …" she recalled the key that she'd found in the mausoleum with the 'M' in the bow, turned to Carlton, and said, "…We're on the verge, honey."

Carlton felt full of trepidation. He said, "I don't know about this Mimi – and what's so weird?"

Naomi looked into Carlton's eyes and said, "Whoever's communicating is French. She's female, and for a reason that's way beyond my comprehension, she knows my name, and I think that she'd been listening to our conversation…"

Chapter 41

Following the best day that the servants of Malaterre could ever remember, every one of them entered a bedroom of their choice, upstairs.

Sabine and Philipe sat in the drawing room enjoying a glass of cognac before she retired, watching the flames dance around the burning logs in the fireplace.

Philipe put down his glass and said, "That was most generous of you to give the servants the clothes."

Sabine took a sip of her cognac, savoured the taste for a second, and then swallowed it. She felt the familiar golden liquid warm her mouth and throat and then said, "And what else should I have done M'sieu? The family is on its way to France, and they were restricted in what they could take. The clothes would have ended up somewhere, maybe with somebody we don't know – so why not give them to people who served us so well over the years?"

"An admirable sentiment Madame, but generous nonetheless."

Sabine smiled and said, "In two more nights they will return to a more realistic way of life, so I am happy that they can enjoy the next two like ladies and gentlemen."

Philipe lifted up his head and listened. He heard the sound of girlish laughter from one of the upstairs bedrooms and said, "And I think that they are enjoying having free reign of the upstairs bedrooms too!"

The chime of the grandmother clock struck and Philipe noted that it was 12:30am. He finished his drink and said, "If you'll excuse me Madame, I must make a check of the estate."

"Is that really necessary? The family have gone now."

"I'm afraid so Madame. I have strict orders from my Capitaine, and I would feel more comfortable knowing that everybody is…"

A dog barked outside, then another, and then another.

Philipe jumped up from his seat and said, "Madame – please, go to your bedroom and lock the door."

Sabine nodded, and exited.

Philipe ran across to a cupboard, extracted his Fusil modèle 1866, breech loading, Chassepot rifle, his leather belt containing his ammunition and bayonet, two of the brand new French Galand revolvers, and a cross-belt housing six throwing knives. He fastened everything in place and then ran up to the roof of the north wing.

Sabine had not obeyed Philipe, and had run to the room from which she'd heard the most noise.

Upon entering she'd found three of the young female servants frolicking about on the bed dressed in the nightclothes of their previous employers. Her presence quelled them in an instant. She looked at the eldest, a housemaid named Martha, and said, "Martha, find Mr. Gedge and tell him that we may have unwanted visitors."

Martha jumped off the bed, nodded, and bowed her head. She said, Yes Ma'am," and left.

A couple of minutes later , the Butler, Able Gedge, an ex-military man, with the Head Gardner and a boot boy met Sabine on the landing and saw the worried look upon her face.

"How can we be of service, Madame?" said Gedge.

Upon arriving at the Malaterre Estate, Abraham had already been harbouring huge misgivings about their planned operation. The walk up Blackstone Moor had taken its toll on Caleb's injured leg, and although he hadn't complained, he could see that his son was limping.

The drive to the front of the house wasn't long, but the foliage was sparse and it was very exposed.

They entered the grounds. Abraham instructed Caleb to conceal himself behind a bush, and to watch the façade for prying eyes whilst he inspected the windows. He then told

Grinner and Galloping John to spread out and check the rear for entry points. His final instruction had been to meet them at the southern corner to listen to their findings before attempting an entry.

John opted to go left, and circled around the south wing keeping close to the wall. The ground floor windows were all sash-type and closed. He worked his way along to the rear door accessed by half a dozen steps up a grand terrace surrounded by a neo-classical balustrade.

He waited for a couple of minutes half expecting to see Grinner approach from the opposite direction, but when he saw nothing, he made his way back to the rendezvous point.

At the front of the house a frustrated Abraham made his way from window-to-window but found none accessible. He returned to Caleb with mounting concern, and then they proceeded to the meeting place.

At the north wing it began to unravel.

Grinner crept along the northwest elevation, and in direct contradiction to what Abraham had instructed, tested each of the windows by trying to raise them up. As he tried the last window at the end of the wing, unlike all of the others, it appeared to give some way, but because it was a large window, and because the latch couldn't be seen from where he was standing, he climbed up onto the window ledge to see what was what.

He saw that the catch hadn't been pushed fully into place, and that there was enough room to slip the blade of his sheath knife between the frames, to ease it open. And once again in contradiction to Abraham's instructions, he decided to open the catch before reporting to the others.

Inside Malaterre, Able Gedge entered the same darkened room and saw Grinner standing on the window ledge, attempting to open the latch with a vicious-looking knife. He edged his way around the inner walls and cocked the dragon blunderbuss in his right hand.

At the southern corner of the south wing, Abraham looked at Caleb and John and said, "Where's Grinner?"

John said, "Dunno boss. I waited a couple of minutes near the back terrace but he didn't show up so I came here."

Abraham turned to Caleb and said, "And did he show up at the front?"

"If he did, I didn't see him."

Abraham pursed his lips and glared along the length of the building but couldn't see the other side of the raised terrace. He pulled his pocket watch out of his waistcoat, noted the time, and turned back to John.

"Right," he said, "go and see what that lobcock's up to and get back here."

John nodded and set off along the rear elevation, keeping close to the wall. As he reached the terrace he opted to climb over the balustrade instead of going around it.

In the room on the end of the north wing, Gedge saw Grinner slide the catch open. He stepped in front of him, raised the dragon, and fired point blank into his chest.

The thunderous blast blew Grinner off the window ledge and killed him before he hit the ground.

Up on the roof of the north wing, Philipe ran to the western corner, looked down, and saw Grinner lying flat on his back. He looked left and saw John climbing over the balustrade. He raised the Chassepot, took careful aim, and squeezed the trigger. The cartridge entered John's left shoulder, plunged into his left lung, and killed him too.

Abraham and Caleb saw John fall and gathered that Grinner had been shot too. They looked at one another and ran as fast as they could towards the main gate.

Up on the roof of the north wing, Philipe inspected each side trying to locate any other intruders. He ran to the northeast side and saw two figures running towards the main gate. He noted that the one at the rear appeared to be hobbling. He raised the Chassepot, took careful aim, and fired once more.

Near the main gate, Caleb's injured leg suddenly gave way and he crashed to the ground. The cartridge screamed over his head and thudded into the grass in front of him.

Abraham heard his son gasp as he fell; he turned, ran back to him, yanked him to his feet, and almost dragged him towards the large stone gateposts.

Up on the roof, Philipe waited until he could see the men again, he aimed at the uninjured one, took a deep breath, held it, and was about to squeeze the trigger, when the boot boy burst out onto the roof.

In an instant, thinking that another assailant was behind him, he dropped to the floor, spun the Chassepot around, and aimed at the innocent boy.

"Mister, Mister, don't shoot – it's me, Daniel..." he pleaded.

Philipe saw who it was, leapt to his feet, and looked back towards the front gate, but nobody was there.

Less than a mile away from Malaterre, the six masked riders heard the shots in the still night air. The lead rider held his right hand up and the others reined in their horses. A short discussion was held, and five minutes later they resumed their ride towards Malaterre, at a walk.

Chapter 42

Tuesday 25th July 2006. Dunsteth Reservoir

Hugh Kearns and his two support divers, Richard Kershaw and Julian Merrifield, followed the line of the building down, and despite it being seventeen days since the destruction of part of the south wing; the water clarity was still not good. Most of the suspended matter that had resulted from the catastrophic event had had time to settle, and there had also been enough time for the water to re-oxygenate, but it still left a lot to be desired.

As they moved down, the divers inspected the areas that had been stabilised and preserved in accordance with the SASMAP initiative, (to Survey, Assess, Stabilise, Monitor and Preserve Underwater Archaeological Sites) of CORDIS, the European Commission 'Community Research and Development Information Service', because they knew that it was their lives on the line if anything had been missed.

Everything seemed to be in order, and Kearns gave the thumbs up to Richard and Julian to descend the last fifteen feet to the reservoir bed.

The three companions switched on their underwater lamps and swept them around, peering into voids that had, until days before, been unspecified rooms within the estate building. They had studied the plans in the week before the dive, but technical drawings viewed in a warm, dry office bore little resemblance to the submerged actuality of the present day Malaterre.

Kearns was the first to touch bottom. He made a sweep of the surrounding area with his lamp, and was immediately drawn to something reflecting light back. He made his intention known to Richard and Julian, and indicated to them to stay put.

Both men nodded their understanding and gave him the thumbs up.

Kearns carefully lifted off the reservoir bed in an attempt to reduce sediment, and swam towards the object reflecting his lamplight.

Prior to the dive Naomi had given him the bronze key with the 'M' in the bow and had requested him to look for anything that it might fit. He'd taken the key, but he'd voiced his scepticism about any locking mechanism that had been submerged for so long remaining in working order.

Moving at a snail's pace and watching in all directions, he swam through the gloomy water until he saw what was causing the reflection. It was a shiny bronze escutcheon plate, in the top right-hand corner of a door.

He reached out and touched the door with his ungloved hand; it felt like new. He backed up a few feet, examined it, and saw that it showed no sign of having been submerged. With a puzzled expression on his face he inspected the damaged masonry to the front and sides of the door, and was able to establish that it must have been walled up, and watertight.

The door stood in a shallow recess, some sixty centimetres behind the bottom course of a row of newly broken stone ashlars, and it appeared to open outwards. This would present an access problem.

He looked down into the gap between the door and stonework and saw differing sized lumps of masonry lying on the old stone floor. He indicated for Julian to approach, and for Richard to stay where he was.

He made Julian aware of what he wanted, and the two divers cleared all the broken masonry from in front of the door. They then waited a few seconds until the sediment had settled.

He indicated for Julian to back away a few feet, and then retrieved the bronze key from his carry bag. He held it up to the lock, and it appeared to fit. He inserted it, and then turned to look at his companions. He saw them both carry out a quick reccie of their surroundings, and then give him the thumbs up. He twisted the key to the left, and the locking mechanism opened.

Every curious fibre in him wanted to reach down, take hold of the door handle and open it, but he knew better. He turned the key to the right, locked the door, and indicated to his companions that they should return to the surface.

Crowthorne, Naomi, Carlton, and Stephen Page, stood on the east bank of the reservoir and stared at the Malaterre estate buildings. The approach road had been closed to the public since the events of the fateful Saturday, and Kev Middleton had continued draining the water until two days prior to the dive. From where they stood the shored up damage looked extensive but sound. The specialist company of archaeological masons and conservators had done an outstanding job in stabilising the structure, and now everybody wanted answers.

In accordance with Naomi's wishes, the news of her rescue had been announced and everybody had been happy except Adrian Darke. He had been furious that his request to finish her off had failed, but due to the heightened police interest in everything around and about her, he had called a temporary halt to his intimidation agenda.

Numerous cameras, witnesses, and mobile phones had been in attendance at Dunsteth on the day of the explosion, but none of them had been able to identify who had launched the grenade. Leander Pike had been sent on a month's paid holiday to Tenerife the next day.

The four colleagues watched as Kearns and his support team emerged from the depths and made their way to the eastern bank.

As soon as Kearns removed his headgear Naomi said, "Did you find anything that the key fitted?"

Kearns raised an eyebrow at Naomi and said, "Steady on, old thing. I've still got the taste of half a pint of our erstwhile drinking water swishing around my north and south which won't go away until I've had an equal amount of orange juice."

Almost by magic, one of Kearns' support unit men appeared at his side with a glass of freshly squeezed orange. "Your orange, boss," he said.

Kearns took the orange juice, said, "Thanks Jim." And downed it in one go. He looked at Naomi and said, "Now I can talk. In answer to your question, yes I did."

Naomi squealed with delight and said, "Yes! I knew it..."

"And furthermore it opened the locking mechanism as though it had been installed yesterday." He went on to explain his findings in detail, and how he and Richard had cleared away the rubble from in front of the door to allow partial access for the forensic archaeologists.

"And so we wait again?" said Naomi to Crowthorne at the end of Kearns' narrative.

"Only until tomorrow," said Crowthorne, "I received an email from English Heritage earlier today advising me of their ETA."

"And when is that?" said Naomi.

"They should be here at eight o' clock tomorrow morning."

Naomi cast a quick glance at Carlton and said, "And Helen and I will be here just after nine."

Carlton knew that it was pointless to argue; instead he looked at Crowthorne who confirmed that the police would be in attendance too.

"Inspector Kearns?"

Everybody turned and saw Stephen pouring over a sheet of paper spread across the bonnet of Crowthorne's police car.

"Yes?" said Kearns, ambling over with everybody else.

"Can you confirm on this old blueprint exactly where that door was?"

"Certainly," said Kearns looking down, "it was..." He looked at the plans, hesitated, and then said, "May I?"

Stephen nodded as Kearns swivelled the plans around to face him. Following several seconds' scrutiny he called Richard and Julian over and said, "Am I missing something guys, or does this look different to what we saw?"

Richard and Julian looked at the plans and both frowned.

"Is that the correct floor plan?" said Julian.

Stephen double checked the grid and said, "Yes."

"Well I'm sorry to say old chap, but that doesn't look like what we saw," said Kearns.

Richard turned to Julian and said, "Jules, how many floor levels did we pass on the way down?"

Both Julian and Kearns answered, "Three."

"Three?" said Stephen, "That isn't possible."

"Why not?" said Crowthorne.

Stephen pointed across to Malaterre and said, "Look at the old building. It's three storeys high plus a basement and what's left of the observation tower on the roof of the south wing. Most of the first, and the entire second floor is above water. According to these blueprints, we have the ground floor level and basement below the waterline. So you would only have had to pass two floors to get into the basement."

Richard looked at Julian and said, "Jules?"

Julian remained silent for a second and then shook his head. He looked at Kearns and said, "I know what I saw boss, how about you?"

Kearns too remained silent for a second, then turned to Stephen and said, "Could those blueprints be incomplete?"

Stephen looked at the grid in the bottom left-hand corner of the blueprint and saw that the legend read, "Basement Level – Level One of Four." He spread each of the other sheets out and consecutively read, "Ground Floor Level – Level Two of Four" – "First Floor Level – Level Three of Four" and "Second Floor Level – Level Four of Four." He looked up at the others and said, "According to these plans, you shouldn't have been able to pass three floor levels on the way down."

"Nevertheless," said Kearns, "we did."

Stephen folded up the blueprints and said, "Intriguing, that means that a hitherto unknown level has opened up..." He turned to Crowthorne and said, "Do you mind if I show up here tomorrow morning too?"

Chapter 43

10:00am Wednesday 26th July 2006. Dunsteth Reservoir

The forensic archaeologist and police divers were ready.

During the first hour and a half they'd all been engaged in removing loose masonry, getting rid of the stone ashlars that were preventing the basement door from opening, and recording and photographing everything that they'd seen or touched. Underwater lighting had been positioned, and now all that remained was to gain entry.

The project leader, and the most experienced underwater archaeologist, Professor Benedict Brooks, signalled to his support divers and received a 'thumbs up' from each. He nodded and swam up to the basement door. He then inserted the bronze key into the lock and turned it. He was aware that air might have been trapped at ceiling level if the room had remained watertight all the years, and with that in mind, he cast a final look upwards to make sure that a sudden expulsion wouldn't dislodge anything above him. Satisfied that all was well, he took hold of the door handle, twisted it to the left, and pulled.

Nothing happened.

He exerted more pressure on the door, but as before it remained in position. He signalled for Kearns to join him, and indicated that he should try turning the key in the lock.

Kearns first turned the key clockwise and felt the locking mechanism move. He then turned the key anti-clockwise and once again felt the mechanism move. He twisted the key anti-clockwise again in case it was a double locking mechanism, but the key wouldn't turn any further. He turned to Brooks and nodded.

Brooks swam forwards, took hold of the door handle, whilst Kearns kept hold of the key, and at a signal from Brooks, both men pulled.

Nothing happened.

They looked at each other, and then with a nod from Brooks, both men pushed.

Nothing happened.

Kearns indicated for Richard and Julian to bring the lamp closer, after which, a careful examination of the door, jambs, and architrave gave no indication why the door wouldn't open.

Puzzled by the event, Brooks signalled everybody to surface.

On the east bank of the reservoir, Naomi, Carlton, Helen, Crowthorne, and Stephen saw the divers surface and climb into the support boats.

Full of anticipation Naomi watched as the boats approached and then beached in front of them. She saw from Kearns' face that something was amiss. She walked up to him, and said, "What's wrong?"

"Technical hitch, I'm afraid – the door won't open."

Brooks walked over as everybody gathered together. "Hugh's right Naomi, we could both feel the mechanism shift in the lock, but for some reason, the door wouldn't open."

"Couldn't you just force it?" said Stephen.

Several pairs of disapproving eyes turned and looked at him.

Stephen realised that he'd made a gaffe and said, "Sorry guys, I let my enthusiasm engage before my brain."

Crowthorne said, "I trust that you eliminated the obvious?"

"We did sir," said Kearns, "we cleared away all the debris from the collapse, Ben and his guys removed the two stones that had been cemented to the floor in front of the door, and we turned the key in the lock, but the blighter stayed shut. The weird thing though, was where the lock was." He saw the inquisitive looks on the faces of Naomi and Helen and said, "It was in the top right corner of the door."

Naomi frowned and said, "Why do you think that it was placed there?"

"To stop young hands reaching it?" proffered Helen, "Especially if it was some sort of cold store or pantry, or somewhere that alcohol may have been kept."

"Or maybe even guns or gunpowder," added Carlton, "shooting was very prevalent in the nineteenth century."

"So why wasn't it shown on the plans?" said Julian.

"It could have been constructed years after the place was built," said Carlton, "so it wouldn't have shown on those blueprints." He thought of something else and turned to Kearns. He said, "I know that this might sound silly but did you push and pull the door?"

All eyes turned to Carlton and Kearns said, "Yes sir – we did."

Carlton said, "Sorry, I just thought…"

"Nothing to be sorry for sir – sillier mistakes have been made in the past."

Carlton felt sheepish and said, "I'm sorry, I wasn't implying…"

"Cal," said Naomi, "it's okay – Hugh gets the point."

"Given the violent circumstances that caused the exposure," said one of the other archaeologists, "could some kind of pressure on the door frame be holding the door shut?"

"Or could the wooden door have swollen?" said Helen.

Brooks turned to Helen and said, "That's a good thought Miss, but it isn't the case. The wood is oak by the look of it, and it hasn't been exposed to water long enough to cause it to swell that much." He then looked at his companion archaeologist and said, "And the door appears to be unaffected by pressures from the frame, so I think that can be ruled out too."

"Could something have been forced under the door from the inside?" said Crowthorne.

"It's possible sir," said Kearns, "but not likely. Any trapped air would have been expelled from an upper vent such as the keyhole, and water ingress would have more likely occurred at a lower point, which by rights, should have seen anything at floor level being pushed into the room, not out of it."

Crowthorne said, "Hmm, I see." He paused and then added, "It would help if we knew whether there were any more doors to that room." He turned to Stephen and said, "Are the plans you have the only ones?"

"I'm afraid so," said Stephen.

Crowthorne turned to Naomi, he said, "What about Walmsfield Council – do they have any?"

Helen said, "Not on file. The ones we got came from the archives of the old Lancashire Land Registry, which preceded the current Land Registry Office, and they aren't even as detailed as the ones Stephen showed us."

Stephen looked at Crowthorne and said, "Are you suggesting that there might be more rooms at that level?"

Crowthorne said, "Not necessarily, but it might answer things if there was another door."

"How?" said Helen.

"Because somebody may have bolted our door from the inside, and have exited from another door."

"Of course," said Helen.

Naomi felt the thumb press down on her shoulder. She didn't acknowledge it by moving in any way, but stepped back from the throng, and listened. At first nothing happened, and then a quiet female voice with a French accent said, *"Naomi – la clé."*

She frowned; – she gathered that whoever was contacting her knew that she had the key, but she couldn't understand why that person didn't know that they'd already tried it in the door.

Knowing that she couldn't communicate by thought alone, she excused herself and said that she was going to get a packet of tissues from her car.

With her head held down, and her back to everybody else, she said in a hushed tone, "We've tried it, and it doesn't work."

No response.

Naomi continued walking towards her car, and said, "We've tried the key in the door, and it doesn't work."

No response.

She tried repeating the statement several times over, and in different ways, but she still drew no response. With a puzzled frown upon her face, she reached her car, opened the tailgate, and removed a packet of tissues from her handbag.

She looked across to the gathering and saw Stephen staring at her – and then to her amazement, she heard Stephen's voice in her head say, "Wait there."

Seconds later Stephen walked up to her and said, "She can't understand you."

Naomi was shocked. She'd suspected from their first meeting that Stephen had heard the woman's voice at Malaterre, but he'd never confirmed it, and had always changed the subject when she'd broached it.

"So you can hear what I can?" she said.

"Not everything," said Stephen, "but I can hear the French voices from Malaterre."

"And that's why you think that you're related?"

"One of the reasons, yes."

"And what else can you hear like me?"

"I doubt that I can hear anything else that's personal to you, just like you can't hear anything that's personal to me."

Questions started to flood into Naomi's head. She thought about the numerous voices that she'd heard, but try as she may, she couldn't think of a single statement that may not have come from a member of her family. She frowned and said, "That's one heck of a thought…" She suddenly came up with a jolt. "Wait a minute," she said, "if what you're saying is true, how come I can hear you, and the French voices?"

"Now that's the big question isn't it?" said Stephen.

Naomi clapped her hand up to her mouth and said, "Good grief, you're not implying that I could be related to Empress Josephine too, are you?"

Stephen shrugged and said, "It would explain a lot wouldn't it? And the family similarities too…"

Naomi looked at Stephen's eyes again and saw how much like her father Sam's they were, she recalled their same taste in wallets – Stephen knowing which coffee she liked and everything else, and she wanted to flood him with questions, but she looked over his shoulder and saw Helen approaching. She said, "We've got to carry this conversation on at a later time…"

Helen walked up and said, "Is everything okay with you two?"

Naomi said to Stephen, "Helen knows about my, my…"

"Gift?" said Helen.

Naomi turned to Helen, and said, "Yes, gift…" she turned back to Stephen and added, "and I've told her about your 'ability' too."

Stephen looked at Helen and smiled. He said, "In that case, I hope that it hasn't put you off me – me being a weirdo and all?"

Helen felt a tingle of excitement at even such a minor implication and said, "No way."

The comment ruffled Naomi's feathers and she changed the subject. She looked at Stephen and said, "When you approached me, you said that the French woman couldn't understand me?"

Helen raised her eyebrows.

"I'll explain later," said Naomi.

"No she couldn't," said Stephen, "because she only understands French."

"So what should I be saying?"

"Try, *'Nous avons essayé la clé et la porte ne s'ouvre pas'*.

Naomi said, "What?"

"Nous avons essayé la clé et la porte ne s'ouvre pas!"

Helen smiled and said, "He's saying 'we tried the key and the door doesn't open…"

Stephen looked at Helen and said, "Impressive…"

Helen blushed, smiled, and tingled again.

Naomi rankled again and said, "If you were right in your earlier submission, then the French woman must have heard *you* already."

Before anybody could respond, Naomi heard, *"Tourner la clé vers la droite."*

She looked at Stephen and he said, "Turn the key to the right."

Helen looked from face-to-face and said, "This is too weird!"

Naomi's mind hit a brick wall for a second and then she said, "Of course! A trick mechanism – maybe to fool youngsters. Turning the key to the left does nothing, it has to be turned to the right!"

She ran back to the divers and said, "You've got to get back into the water guys."

Two hours later, the police launches crunched up the bank and the divers got out.

"Well?" said Naomi, "Did it work?"

Kearns looked serious for once and pointed to several plastic containers in the bottom of both boats. He said, "There were seven skeletons in there, four fully grown adults, and three younger people."

Naomi said, "Oh my God!" She froze for a second and then said, "Oh my God – you don't think that…"

"They were alive when the wall was sealed up?" said Brooks.

Naomi nodded.

"Impossible to say."

Naomi said, "That would be horrific." She looked over Kearns' shoulder, pointed to the containers and said, "You haven't brought them all up have you?"

"No," said Kearns, "Professor Brooks has taken a small bone from each of the skeletons so that it can be sent away for analysis."

Crowthorne looked at Kearns and said, "Seven, eh? That could be a problem."

"Just what I was thinking," said Brooks, "it could end up being declared a historic grave."

"But we will be able to research the samples?" said Carlton.

"Yes sir," said Brooks, "though it wouldn't surprise me if we weren't instructed to reseal that room permanently."

"And were there any other doors, as Bob had suggested?" said Helen.

"No miss. The room was only small too, so I hope that those poor devils were already dead when they were sealed up in there."

"Will we be able to establish that with the samples that we have?" said Carlton.

"No sir," said Brooks, "we'd need to examine the full skeletal remains to look for evidence of wounding and such, but I believe, given the potential age of the bones, that finding out the cause of death wouldn't serve any good purpose, because whoever killed them, if indeed they were killed, would have died a long time ago anyway."

Naomi looked at Crowthorne and said, "And will you order a DNA sample?"

"Yes," said Crowthorne, "I'll do that at least."

Naomi looked at Stephen, she saw him look back at her, and inside her head she heard him say, "And then, at last – we'll have the truth."

Chapter 44

'Down to Gehenna or up to the Throne,
He travels the fastest who travels alone.'

- Rudyard Kipling.

11:00am Tuesday 22nd September 1868. The Malaterre Estate

Nicolas instructed the driver of the Hansom cab to stop at the gate, and to wait for them there.

The driver acknowledged and said, "Very good sir."

Charles was puzzled by the action but went along with it, and stepped out onto the drive. Seconds later he saw Nicolas step down, and they commenced the walk towards the front door.

The first thing that Nicolas noticed was the silence. No sounds came from workers going about their daily tasks, and worse, not a single bark from one of the several dogs usually in attendance. He slowed his pace.

"I know that I'm being over-protective, Capitaine," said Charles, "and I know that you should have been on your way to your family in France by now, but I do appreciate you accompanying me like this."

"It's nothing Charles, and if it is any consolation, I do not have any family in France."

"I'm sorry to hear that. Did some fate overcome them?"

"No..." he hesitated, and then said, "...maybe – I was an orphan and never knew them."

"And you have no idea about your ancestry?"

"No, none."

"That must be very..."

Nicolas took hold of Charles's right elbow in his left hand and said, "Charles, I don't mean to be rude, but please stop talking."

Charles was shocked and opened his mouth to respond, but something about Nicolas's countenance stopped him. He saw how Nicolas appeared to be looking everywhere all at once, and then the feeling overtook him. He looked from left to right, saw nobody, saw no movement, and he heard nothing too. He became aware that they'd slowed their pace, and when Nicolas slowed even more, he started to feel nervous.

Up on the roof of the north wing, one of the two remaining masked men watched the approach of two men. He'd been under orders to wait until nightfall before departing Malaterre, and to eliminate any visitors, man, woman, or child, who arrived there during the day.

He waited until both men drew closer, and then lifted his rifle, fitted with a new telescopic sight, and aimed it at the man on the left.

Nicolas caught sight of a reflection at roof level on the north wing and instantly gathered what it could be. He pushed Charles hard to the left, and then threw himself to the right.

A second later, a shot rang out and a bullet thudded into the drive between them.

Nicolas pointed towards the south wing, and shouted to Charles, "Run round to the back, zigzag, and keep as close to the wall as you can. – Find shelter and hide." He then ran, zigzagging, in the opposite direction.

The man on the roof of the north wing reloaded, and then cursed having a telescopic sight on his rifle because he couldn't hold either running man in his limited view-finder long enough to be able to take aim. Within seconds, both had disappeared from view.

The second masked man had heard the shot from within the building. He ran into the reception hall, cocked his rifle, and laid it on a small table just inside the front door. He then un-holstered two pistols, and waited for somebody to attempt to enter.

On the south side of the building Charles ran, intermittently zigzagging against the south-eastern wall until he rounded the back. He looked along the rear of the building, and then at the orangery across the garden. He took a deep breath and ran towards it for all he was worth.

As he ran past the corner of the rear terrace he saw two curious things, a dead man lying on his back adjacent to the balustrade, and that part of the low-level stonework below the balusters near the back door had been removed. He had no idea why that had happened, but kept on running until he made the safety of the orangery.

Once inside, he positioned himself between two small windows, and then randomly shot a glance out of both, in an attempt to see if anybody was approaching.

On the north side of the building Nicolas ran along the north-western elevation until he saw a dead man lying below a broken window near the rear. He stopped and kept out of sight in case somebody had concealed himself inside the room. He looked at the dead man and saw that the blood from his multiple chest wounds had dried, and calculated that he must have been dead for several hours.

He yanked the jacket off the dead man and threw it over the broken glass at the bottom of the window frame. He heard nothing from within the room, and figured that if anybody had been in there, they would have reacted upon seeing something come through the window.

In a decisive action, he launched himself through the window and rolled across the floor whilst pulling a pistol from his belt.

Nobody was there.

Up on the roof of the north wing, the masked man had seen somebody run across to the orangery, and he watched as a face appeared at random from one of two small windows. He lifted up his Chassepot rifle, adjusted the telescopic sight, and aimed at the left-hand one.

Nicolas opened the door to the room, looked left, and saw the corridor leading up the north wing. In front of him was the longer corridor that led to the south wing, bypassing the main entrance. He decided upon that. He noted the recessed doorways at regular intervals down its full length, and as deftly as a cat, he ran from doorway to doorway, stopping and listening at each before proceeding. He heard nothing from any room.

Half-way along, an adjoining corridor turned left towards the main reception hall. He knew from his previous visits that the central staircase ran up from there. He listened for a few seconds and then headed that way.

A few minutes later, he opened the door to the reception hall and saw a masked man opposite, looking out of one of the front windows. He stepped into the room, and removed a throwing knife from a concealed cross-belt under his jacket. He said, "Hey!" saw the man turn, and threw the knife.

It buried hilt deep into his chest.

The masked man dropped his pistols, clutched at the knife, and as he fell to his knees, he knocked the cocked rifle off the table.

It hit the floor and fired.

Up on the roof of the north wing, the first masked man heard the shot come from within the building. He guessed that the man in the orangery would stay in hiding, and then went back through the roof door and started to run down the stairs towards the reception hall. Seconds later, he opened the door to the landing above the central staircase, and stepped through.

Nicolas was waiting for him with his back to the wall on the left-hand side of the door. Before the masked man could react, Nicolas whirled around to the left, stabbed a knife into the left side of his neck, and then yanked it towards him, slicing through his windpipe, and severing his carotid artery.

As the man fell dead to the floor, Nicolas wheeled back to where he'd been and listened for any further sign of movement. He remained stock-still for at least two minutes, and heard nothing. He then dropped to his knees, and searched the masked man's clothing for anything that could identify him – but found nothing. He was about to stand up to go and find Charles when he saw a distinctive blue mark on the back of the dead man's right wrist. He pushed up the man's shirt cuff and saw a small tattoo.

Unable to believe what he'd seen, he raced down to the dead man in the reception hall, raised his right cuff, and saw a similar tattoo. He muttered, *"Sainte mère de Dieu,"* and then ran out of the front door in search of Charles.

Following in Charles's footsteps, he raced to the south corner of the building and looked along the rear. He saw the orangery at the far end of the garden and then saw Charles looking out of one of the windows. Although he knew better, he ran across the ground, zigzagging in case there was another man on the roof, and burst through the door. He caught his breath, looked at Charles, and said, "We have to get out of here – now!"

"But what about Saba and the others?"

Nicolas looked straight into Charles eyes and said, "I'm sorry, they're all dead. Now – please get a move on, we *have* to leave."

Before Charles could respond, Nicolas said, "I'll explain later, let's get back to the cab."

The two men ran across the back garden, along the south-eastern wall of the south wing, and down the drive to the gates, but when they got there, the cab had gone.

"He must have left when he heard the shooting," said Nicolas, "so now we walk, and we keep off the path."

Half an hour later, and within the cover of the trees on the side of the cartway, Charles said, "Is it safe to talk now?"

"If we keep our voices low."

"Did you see Saba and the others?" said Charles.

"No, I didn't need to."

Charles stopped walking and said, "What? Then they could still be alive, and we've left them to their fate?"

Nicolas grabbed Charles's arm and said, "Keep on walking. They are all dead, believe me."

"How can you possibly know that?"

"Because the men that attempted to shoot us were men like me. But unlike Philipe and me, they work in units of six. I know, because I was in one." He pulled up the cuff of his right sleeve and showed Charles a scar.

"This is where I used to have a tattoo upon my wrist, the same as the men in Malaterre."

"And what does it represent?"

"Men loyal to Doña María Eugenia Ignacia Augustina de Palafox-Portocarrero de Guzmán y Kirkpatrick, 16th Comtesse de Teba, and 15th Marquise de Ardales."

"What?" said Charles, "Who?"

Nicolas turned to Charles and said, "She is otherwise known as Eugénie de Montijo, the wife of Napoléon III – Empress of France."

Charles's mouth fell open. He said, "Why would Empress Eugenie want to kill us?"

"Because of whom you are."

"I'm sorry," said Charles, "I don't understand."

Nicolas said, "It is protracted, but let me try to explain. Our Emperor is the nephew of Napoléon Bonaparte, not his son. Empress Josephine, your ancestor, was infertile when she was married to Bonaparte, so she proposed a marriage between her daughter Hortense and Napoleon's brother Louis, to produce an heir for Napoléon."

"Didn't Napoléon have any legitimate heirs to succeed him?"

"It is common knowledge that he had illegitimate children, but his only legitimate son died of consumption in 1821."

Charles frowned and said, "But why should any of this historical stuff be affecting us now?"

"Because," said Nicolas, "our current Emperor has always doubted the legitimacy of his title – and whenever any other member of the Tascher de la Pagerie family has come to light with a possible claim to the Empirical title, Empress Eugenie has, how shall we say, always fiercely protected her own, and her husband's, position."

"By sending assassins to wipe them out?" said a shocked Charles.

"It is a cruel world that we live in M'sieu."

The two companions walked in silence as Charles digested the information, and then something struck him. He said, "How did Empress Eugenie know where to send her agents?"

"That," said Nicolas, "is what worries me the most. I dissociated myself from the Empress's inner circle and gave my allegiance to Brigadier Niel, our Minister of War. He was a close friend of Sabine, and he was the one who sent Philipe and me to protect you. But, if Empress Eugenie's men were sent to England, it is possible that the Brigadier never received my message, and that it may have been intercepted." He paused, and then added, "Which of course makes me wonder who will be meeting the rest of the family in Boulogne."

"Holy Mother," said Charles, "their lives could be in danger!"

"That is why I shall be returning to France as soon as I can."

"And I'll come with you…"

"No," said Nicolas, "you must stay in England. But you must move away from Malaterre and maybe even change your name, because when Eugenie's four other men return there and find their companions dead, they will be looking for whoever did it. They will assume that a member of the Page family has survived, and they will be desperate to kill you, to conceal any links to the Empress."

Charles was aghast. He looked down and knew that Nicolas was right. He cast a sideways glance at the man who had been his saviour and realised that from that day on, his life would change forever.

Chapter 45

Tuesday 15th August 2006. Rochdale Police Headquarters

The day had arrived and nearly three weeks had passed since the bones had been recovered from Malaterre.

The meeting had been set up in the conference room on the top floor of the H. Q. building, and present were Crowthorne, Naomi, Helen, Carlton, Stephen Page, Inspector Hugh Kearns, and Professor Benedict Brooks.

Crowthorne passed information packs to each of the attendees, but before anybody could open them, said, "Before you look at the folders, I'd like to pass you to Professor Brooks."

All eyes turned to the Professor.

Brooks looked from face to face and appeared uncertain about how to start. He glanced down at his information pack, and then squared it in line with the edge of the conference table. Seconds later he said, "Thank you, Superintendent Crowthorne." Once again he glanced at everybody present and said, "What we appear to have here is a case of mass murder." He looked around and saw the look of horror on some faces, and the look of resignation on others.

"I say *'appear to have a case of mass murder'* because we can't prove it without more detailed examination. We do know, however, that none of the bone samples showed any evidence of illness, poisoning, wear, or scarring that could have indicated a cause of death, and the only thing that we can be sure of is that they were all found in the same room, and that they all died at roughly the same time."

"And that somebody had walled them in – dead or alive," added Kearns.

Brooks turned to Kearns and said, "Yes – quite." He hesitated and then added, "But even that may not be as straightforward as we first thought."

Kearns frowned and said, "Come again?"

"It's true I'm afraid. Two days after we recovered the bones, a team of marine surveyors found something unusual." He looked around the faces but nobody spoke.

"They were dispatched to survey the entire Malaterre Estate with amongst other things, an instruction to see if there were any more hidden locations, and though they didn't find any of those, they did find that a number of limestone ashlars had been removed from a section of balustrading adjacent to the rear terrace. The first assumption was that they were the stones used to seal up the basement room, but when they measured them, and checked the marks left by the pointing, they found that the stones from the balustrade didn't fit."

"Would they have fitted if they'd been turned end-on?" said Helen.

"No they wouldn't – and before anybody asks, we did try all the possible permutations."

"That is curious," said Naomi.

"And did any of the chaps find where the stones that blocked up the door came from?" asked Kearns.

"No, they didn't, but that wasn't a surprise because of the extensive damage to the southern wing."

"And is the building stable now?" said Stephen.

Brooks turned to Stephen, hesitated, and then said, "That's a difficult one. We have done everything required of us by instruction, and we have done more beside. We can say that it would be safe for qualified personnel to dive there, but what we have in Dunsteth Reservoir is a volatile situation."

"Because of the explosion?" said Helen.

"Not only that," said Brooks, "it's because of all the other factors too. That structure has remained stable, below water, since 1869, and then within less than three months it has undergone major trauma on no less than three occasions and possibly a lot more."

"Are you hinting that somebody else may have undermined another part of the structure?" said Crowthorne.

"No sir," said Brooks, "I am referring to stress-fracturing. It is common knowledge that the building has recently undergone two explosions, one below the waterline, and one above. Each of those events caused major structural damage, and we know that more occurred when two collapses took place on..." he opened his notes, leafed through a few pages, and then said, "...the eighth of July this year, but what we cannot predict is what will happen in the future. We don't know how badly the substrate was affected below the south wing – we don't know what pressures will be exerted on the structure by the flooding, draining and then re-flooding, and because of direct orders not to enter the building, we don't know if stress cracks are present on the interior."

"So what now Professor?" said Stephen.

Brooks turned and said, "Following discussions with English Heritage, it would appear that we will be receiving confirmation that Malaterre will be recognised as a scheduled burial site with a statutory designation, and that the basement room will be permanently resealed."

"And what about the rest of the building?" said Stephen.

"I will be recommending that it is declared unsafe."

"With no chance of being able to dive the site at a future date?"

"I'm not saying that categorically," said Brooks, "but I'll be recommending that special permission will need to be obtained before anybody is allowed near the structure, and only then following a pre-dive structural survey."

"So we may never know the mystery of the missing stones?" said Naomi.

"No, I'm sorry," said Brooks, "but safety comes first."

Kearns nodded his head in agreement.

Silence fell on the room as Brooks looked from face-to-face. He then reached for his notes and said, "Now – the lab results." He caught sight of Stephen and said, "For the benefit of those present who are unaware of the finer details of carbon dating, I would point out that it is necessary to extract two samples of material from each bone to get the best results, but because of the relative urgency of these investigations, and a requirement to get only an approximation of the date of death, we opted to extract one sample only. I should add too, that we have been put under pressure by Superintendent Middleton who is anxious to re-stock Dunsteth Reservoir." He looked down at his notes, turned a page, and said, "The results have confirmed that all of the bodies found in that room died in the thirty year period between 1855 and 1885, which of course, fits in perfectly with the 1869 flooding of the Dunsteth valley."

The horror of the statement rendered everybody speechless.

"The causes of death could not be established, and remain a moot point." He looked around the assemblage, saw that nobody wanted to speak, and then turned to the next page of his notes.

"Now we turn to the DNA samples. As per the request of Superintendent Crowthorne, samples were taken from each of the recovered bones, from those found prior to draining the reservoir, and from Mr. Page – but no matches were found."

Stephen was shocked and disappointed. He said, "Could you please clarify that Professor; are you saying that no matches were found between any of the recovered bones alone, or that no matches were found between me and any of the recovered bones?"

"Both sir," said Brooks.

Unable to believe his ears, Stephen said, "What? No matches were found between my sample and *any* of the other samples?"

"Correct sir."

"And is it possible that an error could have occurred?" said Stephen.

"It is possible – but when the results are sent to us, they come with a ninety-eight percent accuracy, so you can rest assured that the findings are as close to definite as we can get."

Stephen sat back in his seat, and realised that all chances of establishing a link to the Tascher de la Pageries, and claiming the ducal title, had been vanquished.

Naomi and Helen saw the look of disappointment on Stephen's face, but weren't able to offer any words of comfort.

Kearns said, "Am I missing something here chaps? Why were we trying to establish a link between any of the unfortunates in that room and Mr. Page?"

"Family history Inspector," said Stephen. "My ancestors have always believed that they were descended from members of the French aristocracy and a DNA match could have helped us to prove that."

"And members of the French aristocracy were living at Malaterre were they?"

""Up until 1868 or 1869 – yes."

Kearns digested the information for a second and then said, "I see – but matching your DNA to any of those old bones wouldn't have proven a link to the aristocracy – not unless they could have been matched with a known member of the aristocratic family too."

"We are aware of that," said Stephen, "but if the connection had been made, it would have prompted us to try to establish the next link." He paused and then added, "Though now – having listened to Professor Brooks' results, it would appear that our quest is at an end."

Naomi felt the thumb press down onto her shoulder, but heard nothing. She glanced across to Stephen, and wondered if he'd felt it too.

Brooks looked around the room and said, "Does anybody have any questions?"

"I do," said Carlton turning to Crowthorne. "Bob – are you any closer to catching the morons who attempted to kill my wife?"

Crowthorne said, "I have my suspicions, but the official answer is no."

"That seems impossible," said Carlton. "How can some homicidal lunatic fire a rocket-propelled grenade into Malaterre, with a huge police presence, the press, and the public, all armed with a plethora of recording devices, and not have been captured on film?"

"It does sound impossible, I agree – but our men have been fastidious in their investigation, and so far have found nothing."

"And who do you suspect is behind it Bob?" said Helen.

"I'm sorry, I know that we're all involved in this affair, and I trust each and every one of you, but I really can't air my personal suspicions here."

Naomi looked at Crowthorne, ignored his statement, and said, "It has to be the same idiots who've been harassing me and sending me the weird notes."

Kearns and Brooks frowned and looked at Crowthorne.

"Please – Naomi," said Crowthorne, "you know that I can't do this."

Naomi hesitated and then said, "Okay – but you know that it isn't over, don't you?"

Brooks frowned again, turned to Crowthorne, and said, "You do know that if it involves this investigation, I should be made aware of *all* the facts?"

"Yes, of course," said a flustered Crowthorne, "but I promise you Professor, that what Naomi is referring to is a different and unrelated matter."

Brooks looked at Naomi and said, "Naomi?"

Naomi nodded and said, "Yes, Bob's right." She turned to Crowthorne and added, "But, I will want answers."

"And in good time – you'll have them," said Crowthorne.

"And what about the other matter," said Carlton. "The missing man?"

Crowthorne looked at Brooks and nodded.

"I have spoken at length with the Superintendent Crowthorne," said Brooks, "and decisions have yet to be finalised about that. Under normal circumstances we would make every effort to remove the body but because it could be under tons of rubble, and its removal could increase the risk of destabilisation, it may not happen."

"Another aspect," said Crowthorne, "is that we have the written confession of John Hess describing where he deposited the body, and its removal would serve no real purpose as far as an investigation is concerned, especially as John Hess is already deceased. Therefore we are of the opinion that it should be left where it is as part of the scheduled burial site."

Silence descended upon the room until Kearns said, "Does this mean that our involvement in the proceedings is now over Professor?"

"Yes, it is. Specialised personnel appointed by English Heritage will seal up that basement room, and thereafter, re-flooding will commence. The reservoir will be back to normal within a couple of months, and all of this will be over."

"With nothing proven," said Helen.

Brooks turned and said, "Hmm – a bit harsh that – but I do take your drift."

A pregnant silence fell on the room and everybody felt a mixture of frustration and disappointment – so much had happened at Malaterre, and so little had been resolved.

"Bummer," said Helen.

Chapter 46

Wednesday 16th August 2006. The Historic Research Department, Walmsfield Borough Council

Naomi and Helen sat in contemplative silence in their office and although both had sporadic ideas about how to progress matters, each time they opened their mouths to speak, each of them dismissed their own ideas as 'clutching at straws'.

Following a prolonged silence Naomi said, "This is ridiculous H; it's like having sex without an orgasm, the build up's great, but you want a good payoff!"

Helen raised her eyebrows and said "Interesting analogy." She sat back in her chair, looked at Naomi and said, "But what can we do? Our hands are well and truly tied."

Naomi leaned back in her chair, picked up a pencil, and started tapping it on her desk. Her mind was blank and she half-hoped that she would pick up something psychically, but nothing happened. For once in her life she felt anaesthetised – her brain felt like her mouth prior to a tricky filling – numb.

"I mean," continued Helen, "it's not even as though we can sit here and think of an approach that we hadn't considered before. The bones found in the basement room have been put to bed, Max Probus's body will remain where it is, and the original bones found in June are as big a mystery now as they ever were."

"We know that they died at the same time as the folk found in the basement," said Naomi.

"Yes, or at least within that same thirty year period."

Naomi lapsed into silence again and resumed tapping her desk with the pencil.

"And where did those original bones come from?" said Helen, "Another exposed room, a grave – a mausoleum?"

Naomi shrugged her shoulders and said, "No idea." She paused for a second and then said, "Wait a minute, we…"

There was a knock on the door.

Helen looked at Naomi and said, "You expecting anybody?"

"No."

Helen turned towards the door and called, "Come in."

The door opened and Ballseye stepped in.

"Hello Marcus," said Naomi, "what brings you here?"

Marcus frowned and said, "The bus."

Naomi and Helen exchanged glances, and then noticed that Ballseye's long, straggly, grey hair had a plait at the back. The rest of it had been scraped back either side of his bald patch, giving his head the appearance of blowing a pink bubble.

"Interesting coiffure," said Helen.

"Yes," said Ballseye, "It was done by my cousin Walks-Like-Bull."

Helen nearly choked.

Naomi wanted to mask Helen's outburst and said, "Walks-Like-Bull? Is he an American Indian or something?"

"No, he's from Lytham St. Annes."

Helen started to lose control and tried to stop herself from giggling.

Naomi shot her a glance and then said, "So how did he get a name like Walks-Like-Bull?"

"Durr…" said Ballseye, "how do you think – from his mother and father…"

Helen was on the verge of losing it altogether. She got up and said, "Please, no more – anybody want a coffee?"

Ballseye glared at Helen and said, "I'll have a hot chocolate and a Mars bar."

Helen nodded and made for the door, but curiosity got a grip. She stopped, turned around, and started to giggle again. "But why…" she said, "…would anybody name a boy from Lytham St Annes, Walks-Like-Bull?"

"'Cos his mum – my auntie, wanted him to have a name like his dad – Talks-Like-Bull."

Helen burst into unrestrained laughter and found it difficult to stop.

Ballseye looked at Helen with puzzlement on his face, turned to Naomi, and said, "What's got into her?"

"I suppose it's the unusual name of your uncle – was *he* an American Indian?"

"No, he's from Liverpool."

Helen's uncontrolled laughter accelerated some more, and she gasped, "I can't believe I'm hearing this – it's the best laugh I've had in ages…"

Naomi felt the laughter start to rise in her chest and said, "You have to admit that it's a strange name for a Liverpudlian lad?"

Ballseye looked at Naomi with a curious look on his face and said, "Hadn't really thought about it before. I just grew up with it."

"And what does he do for a living?" said Naomi.

"He's a second-hand car salesman."

Helen's face went red with laughter. She said, "Second-hand car salesman? – Are you sure that his name isn't Talks-Bull-Shit?"

Naomi lost it then, and the two friends went into uncontrolled laughter.

Helen managed to control her mirth for a second and then said, "So when you went to visit Auntie…?"

"Gwennie," said Ballseye.

Helen burst out laughing again and stuttered, "So when you went to see Auntie Gwennie and Uncle Talks-Like-Bull is that what you called him?"

"No, just Uncle Talks."

"And your cousin?"

"Walks."

Helen clutched her ribs and said, "*Walks?!* – When he was a boy and his mother called him in, did he mistake it for a crow?"

"I dunno," said Ballseye, "I didn't have much to do with him."

Helen said, "I can't stand this, I'm going for the drinks." She staggered out of the door and headed for the drinks dispenser.

Naomi removed a tissue from her handbag and wiped her streaming eyes. She calmed and said, "I'm sorry Marcus, I hope that you don't think we're rude."

"Makes no odds to me, it's their names not mine."

Naomi recalled Marcus's nickname and wondered whether he was aware of it. She said, "Yes, perish the thought…"

A few seconds later Helen entered with the drinks and Mars bar and put them on her desk.

Naomi glanced up and saw that Helen's mascara had smudged below both eyes making it look as though she was wearing war paint, but before she could say anything, she heard Marcus speak.

"I've got some news for you about the Page family."

The merriment subsided and Naomi said, "Oh yes – sounds interesting…"

Marcus took a sip of the hot chocolate, and sat down. He said, "Charles Page was the only survivor."

Naomi frowned and said, "How do you know that?"

"Because I can't find any record of any other Page living in the UK or in France after 1869."

"But that doesn't follow," said Helen. "They may have changed their names."

"Why?"

"I don't know, to avoid capture, to evade Revenue collectors – there may have been any number of reasons…"

Naomi said, "Stephen Page told me that Charles had had to change his name to Preston to avoid capture by French assassins, and that the rest of the family had disappeared into thin air…"

"There you are then," said Ballseye.

"Yes," said Helen, "but that isn't proof that they weren't still alive and living under a different name."

"Did you know that they were true descendants of the Tascher de La Pagerie family?" said Ballseye.

"Yes," said Naomi, "but…"

"So if there were any direct descendants of the Pageries, how come we had the anomaly after 1901?"

Naomi and Helen looked at one another.

Naomi said, "What anomaly?"

"The title of Duke de La Tascher Pagerie was created by devolution of the Duke of Dalberg who died in 1833. All of the Dukes who followed were related to Emmerich Joseph Dalberg who was a cousin of Philipp von der Leyen, the father of Amelie – the mother of the first Duke."

As per his previous visit, Naomi and Helen were astonished by Ballseye's effortless recollection of minute facts.

Unaware of the colleague's fascination, Ballseye continued, "Everything proceeded as it should until the second Duke, Maximilian died in 1901 – and then the elder branch of the family, which were not related to the first Duke of Dalberg, took the ducal title illegally."

"Illegally?" said Helen.

Ballseye stopped talking and took a bite of his Mars bar. He said, "Yes – after that, Eugene Charles Louis Napoléon Tascher de La Pagerie took the title of third Duke until 1935. Then Robert, the fourth Duke followed him until 1959, and finally, Renaud, the fifth and last Duke, took the title until he died in 1993."

Silence descended upon the office until Helen said, "So what are you getting at?"

Ballseye said, "In 1868, the French Empress was Eugenie and the Emperor was Louis-Napoléon. Don't you think that it's odd that the first Duke to have taken the illegal title was named *Eugene* Charles *Louis Napoléon*? The name suggests that he was related more to the Bonapartes, than the Tascher de La Pageries, and that he was confident that there were would be no claims to the legal title."

"Ooh, that's quite an assumption," said Naomi.

"But one that makes sense, and one that explains why there were no surviving relatives of the English Page family, who *were* direct descendants of the legal Tascher de La Pageries, living in France after 1868."

"Another assumption," said Helen.

"And are there any historical records refuting the claim that the ducal title was taken illegally by the third Duke?" said Ballseye.

"None that I know of," said Naomi.

"Nor me," said Ballseye. He reached for the Mars bar and took another bite.

"So basically," said Naomi, "what you're saying is – that in the absence of any known, living, Pagerie descendants, Stephen Page won't ever be able to verify his family link via his DNA?"

Ballseye screwed up the Mars bar wrapper, threw it in a nearby bin, and said, "Not unless he can get access to the severed hand?"

"What severed hand?" said Helen.

"The one on display in Martinique."

Naomi said, "What are you talking about?"

Ballseye said, "In 1793 there was a slave rebellion on the Island of Martinique. Empress Josephine's father was the Governor there at the time, and during the uprising his hand was severed. It's now on display at the Tascher de La Pagerie museum on Martinique, near the house that the family used to own."

"My God Marcus," said Naomi, "I've said this before, but I'll say it again. You are amazing!"

Ballseye said, "The slave rebellion is why Josephine was despatched to France by her father in the first place."

Naomi was beside herself, she couldn't wait to tell Stephen the electrifying news. She said, "Thanks Marcus, you've made my day, and the next time that you come here, the drinks and Mars bar are on me!"

Ballseye nodded and then caught sight of Helen's mascara. He said, "Or Looks-Like-Pocahontas…"

Chapter 47

Turner opened his office door and looked around the general office. He watched his staff for a few seconds and then clapped his hands.

One by one he caught everybody's attention. Once he was satisfied that they were all listening he said, "Joseph, step up here please."

Pickles got up from his office chair and walked over to his departmental head.

Turner turned Pickles to face the general office and placed an arm around his shoulder.

"Gentlemen," he said, and then he remembered that the Council had started to employ the odd woman clerk, and added, "and of course, ladies – I'd like you to put your hands together for our very own Joseph Pickles."

The hesitant silence was broken as loud clapping began to overtake the usual office sounds.

Turner waited until the clapping had subsided and said, "In recognition of Joseph's superb handling of our civic reservoir project, I am happy to announce that he has been promoted to Office Manager, with an increase in remuneration commensurate with his new position."

Once more clapping broke out.

"His exemplary work in securing the Dunsteth Valley for people of Rochdale, and indeed many more besides, will mean that from next year onwards, we will be able to store enough water in our new reservoir, to meet the demands of our ever-growing population, for generations to come." He paused as more clapping ensued.

He turned to face Pickles, extended his hand, and said, "Well done Joseph!"

Pickles shook the offered hand and said, "Thank you sir, I am very grateful." He smiled with an awkwardness borne out of a complete lack of understanding about how he had succeeded in securing the Dunsteth and Malaterre Estates. That, and a distinct possibility that one day, somebody might ask him.

He recalled the day that he'd returned to Whitewall one week after learning that Malaterre had become deserted, with no trace of the family being found.

He'd been convinced that the Johnsons had been involved, but was shocked to hear their denial in any of the proceedings. And paradoxically, as he stood listening to what he considered to be their fabricated refutation, he got the distinct feeling that they were looking at him with a misguided respect, thinking that he'd been responsible.

Regardless, he'd been treated like royalty by the Johnsons, and true to Abraham's word, he'd received a very generous cash 'thank you' once the purchase of their Dunsteth Estate had concluded. Furthermore, he was now considered to be one of the Johnson's 'inner circle' wherever he went, and was treated with a level of respect and courtesy that he'd never experienced before.

On top of that, he'd received a substantial bonus from Hundersfield District Council once the land had been 'compulsorily purchased' following the desertion of Malaterre, and the inability of the Land Acquisition Department to be able to find the owners in the requisite time.

Now here he was, at work, with no questions asked about how he had succeeded, receiving kudos, a promotion, and a pay rise from his General Manager.

All very surreal.

He smiled and nodded.

Turner turned to face the open office and said in a loud voice, "This calls for a bit of a celebration gentlemen!" The ladies weren't included. "We shall all retire to the local public house after work today, and I shall buy us all a meat and potato pie, and a pint of ale." He stood with a conciliatory smile on his face waiting for a reaction.

One or two "thank you sirs'" were directed at him and then more clapping ensued.

It was of no concern to Turner that most of them would have preferred to go straight home at the end of the working week, but when he extended such a generous invitation, it didn't do to refuse.

He looked down at Pickles and waited for an individual acknowledgment from him.

Pickles looked up and said, "Thank you sir, very generous of you."

Chapter 48

"It is a meeting wrought with joy and sorrow," said Tineke Page.

Naomi put her cup of coffee onto the occasional table situated between her and Helen and said, "Joy and sorrow – why?"

"Since we last met we have received confirmation from the Swiss authorities that a body found in recently melted pack ice was that of my missing husband."

"I'm sorry to hear that," said Naomi, "you must be distraught."

"No, not after all this time; he's been missing since May last year and we have all come to terms with the thought that we would not see him again." She paused and then added, "But now, at least, when his body is returned to the UK, we'll be able to give him a respectable send off."

Helen shot a glance towards Stephen who gave a slight shrug of his shoulders and nodded.

In the weeks following the re-flooding of the Dunsteth reservoir Helen had been on several dates with Stephen, and although he had been a perfect gentleman on each occasion, she had felt that something was missing. At first it hadn't been noticeable, but as the weeks had progressed, a longer period of time had passed between dates, and the enjoyment of their time together felt more like friends enjoying each other's company, rather than a growing relationship. In the end she'd accepted that nothing would happen on the romance front, but on the occasions that they did meet, it would be an enjoyable experience.

And for some inexplicable reason, she got the distinct impression from Naomi that she didn't approve of their liaison.

"And the joy?" said Naomi.

"We have received confirmation that Stephen's DNA matches the severed hand of Empress Josephine's father from Martinique."

Naomi and Helen's mouths fell open in unison.

Naomi whirled around to Stephen and said, "Wow, congratulations – does that mean that you are now the sixth Duke?"

Stephen smiled and said, "Thank you, but no. It means that the door is open to be able to claim the ducal title, but whether we proceed with that will take a lot of thinking about. The important thing for us was to establish the familial link with the Tascher de La Pageries from Martinique. And now we have it."

Helen smiled and said, "Good old Ballseye!"

"And my sister, Kerry," said Stephen.

Naomi looked at Stephen and said, "Kerry?"

"Yes, strangely enough, she'd tried to inform me on several occasions about what she named 'a gruesome artefact' at the family museum on Martinique – which was the hand of course – but for whatever reason, she didn't finally convey it to me until after Ballseye had informed us of its existence too."

"Bull's Eye," said Tineke, "who is bull's eye?"

Helen blushed and said, "I'm sorry, we were using an acquaintance's nickname. His real name is Marcus; he's the guy who told us about the hand."

"And how did he come by the unusual nickname of Bull's Eye?"

Naomi looked at Helen and smiled a wicked smile. She knew that she was in a hole, and she wondered how long and how far Helen would keep digging herself in.

"I'm not sure," said Helen, "maybe it's something to do with…"

Naomi relented and shot out a rescue line. She said, "...his dart playing prowess. We believe that he was something of a minor darts celebrity in his youth, and the name's stuck."

"Ah," said Tineke, "I understand now."

Helen looked at Naomi and mouthed, *"Thank you..."*

Naomi nodded and then could have sworn that she heard Stephen's voice in her head making a 'Hmming' sound. She looked round at him and saw him raise an eyebrow.

"And what is he like this, 'Bull's Eye'?" said Tineke.

"He's an odd character..." Naomi recalled all of Percy's acquaintances and thought, *'along with all the rest'.* She continued, "...if you saw him on the street you would think that he was a scruffy, surly type of man with a permanent frown upon his face, but when you get him talking about a given subject in history, he has a mind for detail that's almost unsurpassable."

"Well, we have a lot to thank him for," said Tineke, "and I would like you to convey our gratitude by giving him this." She held out an envelope. "It is a token from the shop to the value of one-hundred pounds. I hope that Bull's Eye will be able to find more subject matter to suit his taste."

Naomi took the envelope and said, "That's very generous of you Tineke, I'm sure that he'll be delighted to receive it."

"Along with a Mars bar," added Helen.

Tineke raised her eyebrows at Helen.

"Sorry," said Helen, "it's another of Balls...Marcus's eccentricities."

Tineke reached across to a small table, picked up another two envelopes, and gave one to Helen and one to Naomi. "And these are for you," she said. "They are also one-hundred pound tokens as a gesture of our gratitude for all your help."

"This is very kind of you," said Naomi, "but it isn't necessary. We were happy to help."

"Yes, thank you very much," said Helen.

"And you almost lost your life because of our business," said Tineke.

Naomi looked down and then said, "I don't think that that was because of your business. I think that it might have been an old adversary of mine named Adrian Darke."

"What, *the* Adrian Darke? I thought that he was in prison."

"He is, but he goes on trial on the 20th of November this year, after which, I hope that he's sent to Broadmoor or maybe Parkhurst prison on the Isle of Wight. Somewhere far away."

Stephen looked down and said, "He's a slippery character, I hope that the case against him is watertight."

"And security too," said Helen.

Tineke looked at Naomi and said, "In the meantime, do you think that your adversary has been quelled?"

"Not if I know him. I haven't had any unusual or disturbing incidents since the episode at Malaterre, but I think that he's just letting the dust settle."

"And why does he consider you to be an adversary?" said Tineke.

"Because he considers me to be the main reason for exposing his underground drugs facility on Rushworth Moor – and because he'd paid out thousands of pounds to an old Town Clerk of Walmsfield to cover up a secret. A secret that I ultimately exposed, which, once exposed, made him realise that he'd never needed to pay out the blackmail money, because the case against him could never have been proved."

Tineke digested the information and said, "Well I hope that they do put him where he deserves. I find it abhorrent that men of power use their considerable resources to produce drugs that will ruin the lives of thousands of people."

"I agree," said Helen.

"And will you attend his trial?" said Tineke.

Naomi smiled as she thought about the forthcoming weeks. She said, "No, I'll be in Florida." The painful memory of losing the baby flashed into her mind. She said, "My husband and I have been invited to stay with some distant relatives in Dunnellon, and though we hadn't thought that we'd be able to, now we can. We're flying out next Monday and we'll be there until after the Thanksgiving Day celebrations. We're really looking forward to it."

"And will you visit the old church in Charleston that Helen told me about?" said Stephen.

Naomi recalled the strange episode that she'd had when she heard the lines of the country and western song by Don Oja-Dunaway, and had seen the tree-lined route through the windscreen of a grey car. She looked at Stephen and said, "Oh yes – wild horses couldn't keep me away from there. We have a date in history."

"Do you mean a date in the future?" said Tineke.

"No," said Naomi, "I mean a date in history."

Epilogue

*November 2006. St. Andrew's Episcopal Church,
Charleston, South Carolina*

Deacon Del Morrison stepped back from the people crowded around the grave with a smug expression on his face. He knew that he'd been successful in luring everybody away from the real 'Matthews P. F.' gravesite and he waited for the first exasperated comment.

Naomi turned to Carlton and said, "This is exciting isn't it?"

"It is, pet."

"No more than another six inches!" called Spencer to the mechanical digger driver.

The digger driver lowered the mechanical arm and removed another six inches of soil.

Spencer held up his hand and "Okay, hold it!" He stepped down into the grave and looked around. Everything looked natural. He scrutinised the whole area, picked up one or two stones, and then climbed out of the grave. He looked at the waiting digger driver and said, "Okay – another three… "

The arm of the mechanical digger lowered, and scraped away another three inches of soil.

Once again Spencer stepped down and had a look around.

Standing at the edge of the grave Reverend Hughes looked at his watch and noted that it was 10.30am. He had to attend a meeting of the church elders in the parish house at 11am, and he knew that he'd have to fend off more than a few searching questions about allowing the disinterment in the first place.

"Nothing," said Spencer, as he climbed out again. He turned to the digger driver and called, "All right Jake, another three …"

The mechanical arm lowered again and removed another three inches of soil.

Spencer stepped towards the grave, heard Reverend Hughes say something, and turned to look at him. As he did so, he misjudged his footing and slipped over the edge. He fell in, landed on his side, and felt something hard bang his ribcage.

Once the mayhem had settled and all the offers of help had been dismissed, he turned and looked at the soil where he'd fallen. He frowned, retrieved a small trowel from a leather pouch on his belt, and started to clear away the soil.

Seconds later Naomi said, "What's that?"

Spencer looked up and said, "Not sure ma'am." He continued clearing dirt from around the protruding object until he scraped something hard. He stopped, frowned, and then tapped down with the point of the trowel.

Everybody heard a dull metallic sound.

The self-satisfied smugness evaporated from the Deacon's face. He stepped forwards, and looked into the hole.

Spencer looked up at Naomi and said, "This ain't no coffin, ma'am."

Naomi looked at the metal object sticking up from the ground and said, "So what is it?"

Spencer looked down into the hole, and then up at the Sheriff. He said, "It looks like some kind of door handle… "

**If you enjoyed this novel,
look out for the next in the series,
*The Fire of Mars***

Other titles by Stephen F Clegg;

*Maria's Papers
The Matthew Chance Legacy*

www.stephenfclegg.com